By the same author:

The Whore and her Mother:
9/11, Babylon and the Return of the King

Oh What Rapture!

Is a 'secret rapture' going to spare believers from tribulation to come?

Ireland – now the good news!

The best of 'Bread' – personal testimonies and church/ fellowship profiles from around Ireland
Edited by Raymond & Gerry McCullough

A Wee Taste a' Craic!

All the Irish craic from the popular Celtic Roots Radio shows, 2-25

Cover design: Raymond McCullough

Israeli tank and aircraft photos: courtesy of *Dreamstime.com*

***Red Sea at Aqaba photo:* Raymond McCullough**

In Six Hours

... the world changed

Raymond McCullough

Comments on **The Whore and her Mother**:

"... AMAZED when I read this book ... in awe of your extensive knowledge on so many levels: Christian, Jewish, and Muslim culture; the Jewish diaspora ... Greek & Hebrew; and your panoramic view of history through a biblical world view ... thought-provoking and trouble-some ... many will be offended, but you consistently build your case instead of being sensationalistic."

James Revoir, author of *Priceless Stones*

"... thoughtful, insightful ... and you have a knack for putting complicated topics in an easily accessible way."

Jim Darcy, author of *The Firelord's Crown*

".. has the makings of a best seller in its field ... you open up real ideas some of which are somewhat scary to say the least ... difficult to leave down because you have created the 'Must turn the page' feeling threaded right through every line"

Colin T Mercer, UK, author & poet

"Love this kind of stuff ... grounded in research and common sense"

Francis Albert McGrath, Dublin, Ireland, author

"... most thought provoking ... meticulously researched and written with style and passion"

Sheila Belshaw, UK, author of *Pinpoint*

"It's very thought-provoking and solidly presented."

Katherine Holmes, author of *The Swan Bonnet*

"I did not feel you were preaching at all, more laying your cards on the table ... An evocative read, which left me 'thoughtful'"

Molly Hopkins, author of *It Happened in Paris*

"I was so impressed with the level of detail you give and your breadth of knowledge ... well-researched and thorough"

Kevin Alex Baker, author of *Head Games*

In Six Hours

... the **world changed**

*A friendship forged in war takes four young
men on separate journeys to a final destiny
in a Middle East heading for meltdown*

Raymond McCullough

Published by

Precious Oil
P U B L I C A T I O N S
www.preciousoil.com/publications

ISBN 13: 978-0-9929432 2 6

ISBN 10: 0-9929432 2 1

First published **2015**

All characters in this novel are fictional, and any resemblance to anyone living or dead is accidental.

10a Listooder Road, Crossgar,

Downpatrick, Northern Ireland BT30 9JE

Contents

Thanks to my wife, Gerry, for editing and general encouragement, and to Pádraic Fitzpatrick for proof-reading the manuscript and for correcting my Arabic and Hebrew.

Introduction

This thriller series is fiction – i.e. the characters that are referred to are straight out of my own imagination. However, the events they are involved in are based directly upon the predictions of the Hebrew prophets and, of course, my interpretation of them.

This is my attempt to imagine things that have been prophesied for many hundreds of years – many of which are now coming to pass. Just seventy years ago the State of Israel was only a faint hope in the hearts of a few pioneers, scoffed at even by their fellow Jews. Today, Israel is the most advanced and powerful nation in the Middle East, though continually under threat.

Today, the Middle East, and much of the world, are dominated by Islamic fundamentalism. Will that continue? Today, America is the world's only super-power. Could the day come when that is no longer the case? Could the world change fundamentally in just six hours?

My 2011 non-fiction book, *The Whore and Her Mother: 9/11, Babylon and the Return of the King*, investigated some of the unfulfilled Hebrew prophecies concerning the last days – particularly those concerning the modern day city and nation referred to as *Mega-Babylon* and God's plan for the Middle East and other nations of the world.

That book was based on the logical argument that, if we can see one of the most significant of these prophecies being fulfilled today, then we surely ought to pay attention to ALL of those unfulfilled prophecies and perhaps start to live our lives accordingly. Since that book was published, week by week there have been more fulfillments of those biblical prophecies. My online newspaper, *Bread NEWS International*, includes stories of Israelite tribes returning to Israel, archaeological discoveries that confirm the Bible, etc. Find it at:

http://paper.li/f-1316877991

The problem with a non-fiction book on prophecy is that there is a limited market for such a thing. This thriller, and its sequels, are an attempt to bring to life some of the events foretold by the Hebrew prophets and covered in *The Whore and Her Mother*.

Although the book has been researched as carefully as possible, I have never been a member of the US Military, the Afghan National Army, or the Israeli Defence Forces, nor have I ever been in any combat situation – so I apologise in advance for what I'm sure are many mistakes in my description of the technique and operation of these forces. I'm sure members of either military could list many technical errors I have made. This is simply a work of fiction – telling a story – it is not intended to be accurate in every military detail.

I have, though, tried to be as close to reality as possible – for instance with descriptions of vehicles and weapons, such as the *Bright Arrow* Active Protection System and the *CombatGuard* APC – all of which are available at this moment and are at least planned to be deployed in greater numbers in future.

Israel certainly had a major role in the development of the *Stuxnet* software, but beyond that I have no special knowledge. The special unit at *Haifa Technion* is my invention – it does not exist (as far as I am aware), but I'm quite sure Israel has a special cyber-warfare unit somewhere, working on similar software.

1 – Eastern Mediterranean, Near Future

*"At evening time, terror … (**Yeshayahu**/Isaiah 17:14)*

The missile struck shortly after the *ElAl* New York-Tel Aviv flight had passed over the island of Rhodes. There was a blinding double white flash of light, which lit the evening sky from horizon to horizon – and kept on glowing, eerily. There were gasps and shrieks from different parts of the Boeing 757 aircraft.

Then the blast turbulence hit the airplane. It had been a smooth flight so far, with a cloudless sky slowly darkening as they approached their destination in Tel Aviv. Now it felt as though they were flying through a very severe thun-derstorm. The plane bucked and rocked violently and the gasps turned to screams. Immediately, the seat belt signs were illuminated.

Presently the motion quietened and a murmur of conversation broke out throughout the plane.

'That was a bomb, for sure!' an American accent said confidently.

'What on earth kind of bomb was it?' another voice queried, 'Was it a nuclear strike?'

The intercom buzzed and the calm voice of the Israeli captain came on. *'Ladies and gentlemen, sorry for the unexpected turbulence. We will be beginning our descent to Ben Gurion Airport in a few minutes. Meanwhile, we are trying to find out what exactly that was we just witnessed, there. As soon as we know for sure, I'll inform you. Please remain calm and stay in your seats for now. Thank you.'*

The passenger on Shaul's left turned to him, 'What the hell do you think that was, then?' His voice had a slight wobble of fear in it. 'Must have been one almighty explosion,' said Shaul, 'to light up the whole sky like this. I don't know, possibly a nuclear missile?'

Just as he spoke they heard a passenger on the starboard side of the plane say something about a 'mushroom cloud', then, 'Oh my God!' and similar exclamations as more passengers witnessed the bright cloud ascending higher and higher into the night sky on the right hand side of the plane.

A man's voice could be heard reciting, *'Sh'ma, Israel, Adonoi elohaynu ...'* – the Shema prayer. Many others joined in.

'They've finally done it,' one lady said, as another woman began weeping quietly. 'It's the end of Israel. We're gonna be blown out of the sky! We're all gonna ...' Her voice was rising on an increasing note of panic.

Thankfully, right then the captain's calm voice came back on the intercom. *'We've just heard back from the control tower. What we just witnessed a few minutes ago apparently was indeed a nuclear strike against Israel. The missile appears to have hit somewhere south of Tel Aviv, thankfully missing the main populated areas of the city, though nobody has any idea yet of exactly where, or how many casualties there might be.*

'Meanwhile, as we're so close to our destination, we've been cleared to land at Ben Gurion Airport, though all later flights are being diverted to European airports. I don't know if we're the lucky ones, or not!

'A state of emergency now exists throughout Israel, so please expect delays when we do get on the ground. I would ask you all to remain calm, fasten your seat belts and return your seats to the upright position. We'll be landing in a few moments. We'll find out what's happening to our dear country, then.'

Shaul found himself releasing his seatbelt, standing up and moving to the front of the plane. 'My friends', he spoke loudly enough to bring a relative quiet to the passengers, 'I would like to read a Psalm, if I may?' Several of the passengers nodded. One man shouted out, 'Amen! Please do.' Encouraged, Shaul continued, 'I think this is very appropriate to this new situation:

> *'Tehillim/Psalms* **83:2** O God, do not be silent; do not hold aloof; do not be quiet, O God! **3** For Your enemies rage, Your foes assert themselves. **4** They plot craftily against Your people, take counsel against Your treasured ones. **5** They say, "Let us wipe them out as a nation; Israel's name will be mentioned no more."
>
> **6** Unanimous in their counsel, they have made an alliance against You— **7** the clans of Edom and the Ishmaelites, Moab and the Hagrites, **8** Gebal, Ammon, and Amalek, Philistia with the inhabitants of Tyre; **9** Assyria too joins forces with them; they give support to the sons of Lot. Selah. **10** Deal with them as You did with Midian ...
>
> "**14** O my God, make them like thistledown, like stubble driven by the wind. **15** As a fire burns a forest, as flames scorch the hills, **16** pursue them with Your tempest, terrify them with Your storm. **17** Cover their faces with shame so that they seek Your name, O Adonai. **18** May they be frustrated and terrified, dis-

graced and doomed forever. **19** May they know that Your name, Yours alone, is Adonai, supreme over all the earth.'

There was complete silence on the plane as Shaul turned the pages to another text. 'And also from the prophet, *Yeshayahu:*' he continued:

'**Yeshayahu/Isaiah 17:12** Ah, the roar of many peoples
That roar as the sea roars,
The rage of nations that rage
As the mighty waters rage—
13 Nations raging like massive waters!
But He shouts at them, and they flee far away,
Driven like chaff before winds in the hills,
And like tumbleweed before a gale.
14 *At eventide, lo, terror!*
By morning, it is no more.
Such is the lot of our despoilers,
The portion of them that plunder us.'

'My fellow Israelites, this evening we do indeed have terror, but perhaps, HaShem willing, by tomorrow morning things will look completely different? *Toda raba.*"

"Amen, amen!" several of the passengers responded.

One elderly man began to recite a prayer,

'Baruch ata Adonai, Yisrael go'eil. Blessed are you, O Lord, the redeemer of Israel. Look upon our affliction and plead our cause, and redeem us speedily for your Name's sake, for you are a mighty redeemer. Blessed are you, O Lord, the redeemer of Israel.'

Again many passengers responded with *'Amen.'*

At that moment, two fighter jets with Israeli markings appeared either side of the airliner, raising a cheer from the shocked, but now slightly reassured, passengers.

The fighters veered off shortly after as the airliner flew over the beaches and tower blocks of Tel Aviv, landing normally at Ben Gurion Airport, to a more enthusiastic burst of applause than usual, as the wheels touched Israeli soil and a certain amount of the built-up tension was relieved, however temporarily.

The captain's voice came back on, *'Ladies and gentlemen, we are officially at war. Missiles, rockets and mortars are being fired at Israel from several directions – including Gaza, Lebanon and Sinai. The nuclear missile appears to have been fired from Syrian territory. IDF drones and jets are already responding to these attacks.*

'We would ask all passengers to remain in your seats with your seat belts securely fastened. When we are ready to disembark, please allow any IDF or reserve personnel to de-plane first. More missiles may be on their way – it's a strong possibility. Ladies and gentlemen, it seems that our dear country is once again at war!'

As usual the passengers – with the exception only of a few bemused and terrified tourists – completely disregarded these instructions, immediately beginning a mad scramble for their belongings.

'Do you see my bag. Get my bag, Irving?' cried an elderly Jewish woman in a plaintive New York accent. 'Why are they allowing all these young people to leave first? It's not right. The airport isn't a safe place. Surely, *we* should be allowed to leave first.'

'They're gonna be fighting for Israel, my dear. And mebbe they're gonna die a lot sooner than we will, who knows,' the soothing voice of her elderly husband said.

Shaul left the plane with other military personnel and as he entered the bus laid on especially for them a young man approached him, *'Segen* (Lieutenant) Shaul Levine?'

'*Ken*, (Yes)' replied Shaul.

'We have a vehicle waiting for you outside the terminal.' The young man added, 'Please stay close behind me.'

2012

In Six Hours ... the world changed – *Raymond McCullough*

2 – Conversation in Kabul

The evening sun beat down on the dry and baked cityscape below. A cloud of dust appeared far down the road and gradually, the over-powering silence was broken as – at first almost imperceptible – the distant whining and groaning sound of approaching vehicles grew louder and louder. As the vehicles drew close to the base the sentry spoke into his handset and the gates of the compound began slowly to swing apart.

As they opened, four Humvees in desert camouflage charged through the widening gap between the gates in a cloud of swirling dust, turning left as they entered the compound and coming to a halt in front of a nondescript single storey building.

The men who piled out were almost identical in their dust-covered faces and military fatigues – racially indistinguishable, except that the ANA members (Afghan National Army) mainly refused to conform to US military standards, most of them wearing scarves and other evidences of non-conformity. The men looked exhausted and yet hyped up as they staggered out of the vehicles and into the relative cool of the shade of the building.

Twenty minutes later – freshly showered and changed into off duty gear – Shaul Levine headed into the mess hall, where a couple of his team where already sitting. Nodding to them briefly, he headed straight to the drinks machine and watched longingly as a cool can of Coke was delivered, silently draining half of it before placing the cool can against his perspiring forehead.

'Phew, I really needed that!' he reported, looking over to his comrades Micky Devlin and Brandon Thomas, 'Mind you a beer would've been even more welcome!' He dragged a chair over to their table and joining them. *'Dev,'* he muttered to the tall, well built, black haired man.

'Wha's that yer readin', Doubtin'?' he asked the other occupant at the table – a slim black man with a shaved head, currently concentrating on the book he was reading. They often called him *'Doubtin' Thomas'* just because he didn't seem to be afraid to live his faith out in front of them.

'Just the usual,' he mumbled with a distinct southern drawl.

'That'll be the Bible then, eh?' Shaul asked.

Brandon refrained from responding.

As Levine sat down, a swarthy man entered the mess and retrieved another coke from the machine. He headed over to join them at their table. 'Salaam alekum,' he greeted them politely.

'Alekum salaam, Ali.' they chorused in reply.

'Oh, hi there, Zai,' Brandon looked up and muttered a moment later.

'Don't mind him, Ali,' said Dev, 'When he gets into his Bible study he doesn't notice anyone, or anything.'

'Yeah, the Taliban could be firing right over his shoulder and he wouldn't even notice it!' said Levine, his accent distinctly New York.

'I think I might just notice that,' Brandon grinned, looking up again.

'So what's so interesting about what yer readin' today?' asked Shaul.

'Actually, it's pretty relevant to all of us right here,' Brandon replied. 'I'm reading the book of Ezekiel – one of your Hebrew prophets, Shaul – and he's just been to visit the Khyber Pass right here in Afghanistan.' (He pronounced it *Afanistan*, he and the other Americans having been told enough times now by Ali and his friends how it ought to be pronounced.)

'OK, I'll bite,' said Shaul, 'How did a Jewish prophet manage to get from Israel to Afghanistan? Oh I get it, he just took the next *El Al* flight from Ben Gurion, right?'

'Well,' said Brandon, 'You're not too far out. For a start he wasn't *in* Israel, he lived among the Jews who were carried off to captivity in Babylon by King Nebuchadnezzar – so he was actually in what is now Iraq. Secondly, he was supernaturally transported by the Holy Spirit to sit among the Israelite exiles at the Khebar – or Khyber – River. Later he was transported back to Jerusalem as well, to witness things that were going on there.'

'Boy, these prophets sure got about a bit in them days,' Mickey laughed, 'Just kiddin' – I'm listenin', I'm listenin'.'

'Okay,' said Brandon, 'if you're sure you want to hear it. I don't wanna bore you guys, or nuthin'.'

'Carry on,' said Shaul, breaking off his gruff rendering of the *Bony M* song, *'By the rivers of Babylon',* 'We'll let you know when we're gettin' bored.'

'Right then,' Brandon continued, 'The very first thing God told Ezekiel was that he was to be a watchman. If he didn't speak out to warn the people, their blood would be upon his hands. If he spoke, and they refused to listen, their blood would be on their own heads, but he'd be OK.'

'OK, I think we get the message, Brandon,' said Mickey.

'The next point we need to bear in mind,' said Brandon, getting into the swing of his explanation, 'is that Ezekiel was a Jew – and so were all the people who'd been taken off captive to Babylon with him. By 'Jew' I mean they were nearly all from the tribe of Judah, with a few from the tribe of Benjamin and some priests and Levites, who were all from the tribe of Levi. With me so far?'

'Yep,' the others muttered.

'OK, the people he was carried off in the Spirit to meet at the Khyber River were *not* Jews. They were Israelites who had also been carried off nearly two hundred years earlier by a different king – the king of Assyria. They were from the other ten tribes who used to live to the north of Judah, but who were carried off into captivity, while Judah survived for a while longer.'

Mickey asked, 'Does the Bible actually refer to the Khyber Pass, then?'

'Well, the Khyber river – yes!' Brandon answered.

'OK,' said Shaul, 'two questions. First, it might be a small point, but by my reckonin' three plus ten makes thirteen. There are only twelve tribes of Israel, surely?'

'Good point, Shaul,' Brandon answered. 'There *are* thirteen tribes, in a way. The tribe of Levi – the tribe you belong to – were a special case, called by God to serve as priests in the temple, singers and so forth. So they didn't receive any share in the land of Israel. Instead, the tribe of Joseph got a double portion, divided between his two sons, Ephraim and Manasseh. Strictly speaking they're half-tribes. Ephraim was probably the biggest of the ten tribes, so often the prophets just referred to Ephraim for short, when they meant the whole of the ten tribes.

'What was your other question, then?'

'Where the hell did those ten tribes disappear off to?' said Shaul. 'Every-body knows who we Jews are – although I suppose a few more have appeared out of the woodwork, in Russia, Brazil and so forth – but where are these other guys you say were *not* Jews?'

'Another excellent question, Shaul. Go to the top of the class!' Brandon chuckled. 'But maybe I'm not the best person to answer this one. Maybe Zai can help us out here? You got any thoughts on this, Ali?'

The three men turned as one to look at the swarthy man they called Ali. 'Er, I think you might be referring to the Pashtuns, Brandon, yeah?'

'Yeah. You're a Pashtun yourself, Ali, aren't you?' Brandon asked.

"Yes, indeed, Brandon. My full name is Khan Ali Yusufzai. I am proud to be a Pashtun of the tribe of Yusufzai, which actually means 'Sons of Joseph'.

Many Pashtuns believe that we are descended from the ten tribes of Israel. Even the British believed this when they ruled India. They said we looked 'more Jewish than the Jews' – but we are *not Yahoodi*. We are not Jews!'

'Exactly!' said Brandon. 'What about the Star of David? Does that mean anything special to Pashtuns?'

'Actually,' Ali answered, 'back home in my village, there are many Stars of David. We put them on our schools and often in our homes, too. But we are proud Moslems. We are not Jews. We have our own Pashtunwali code.'

'What's Pashtun wally, then?' asked Mickey.

'It's the moral/legal code of all Pashtuns,' said Ali. 'Maybe 3,000 years old, but it's never been written down.'

'And just how many Pashtuns are there?' asked Mickey.

'In Afghanistan?' asked Ali, 'About ten, twelve, maybe thirteen million – probably more than that again in Pakistan.'

'So, we're talkin' mebbe 30 million of you guys?' said Shaul. 'Does that include the Taliban, too?'

'Yes, the Taliban are Pashtun, also,' said Ali.

'Jesus!' exclaimed Micky. 'I can't see any of those guys headin' over to the promised land to give Israel a hand anytime soon. Can you, Solly?'

'Right now, they're the enemy, sure enough,' Brandon answered. 'But one day – not so far away – Isaiah says there will be a highway from Egypt to Assyria, connecting them both to Israel. That the Euphrates River will dry up into seven streams 'so that my people can cross over dry shod.' Course that'll be after the big war in the Middle East.'

'And the Bible talks about this, too?' asked Mickey, intrigued. 'How big a war is that gonna be? There's already been one in Iraq! Remember?'

'Yeah, well the President pulled us outta there, didn't he?' said Brandon.

'Yeah, great decision that was,' Mickey retorted.

'So what's this war in the Middle East, Brandon?' asked Shaul. 'Are we likely to be fightin' there, next?'

'Well, it certainly involves Israel,' said Brandon. 'Most things the prophets talk about concern Israel. And God deals with nations according to how they treat Israel.'

'So, you're what – a black Christian Zionist, then?' asked Shaul.

'I am in a way," Brandon replied, 'But it doesn't mean I automatically go along with everything Israel does. I mean, Israel has abortion as a means of birth control – nobody even opposes it there. Back in the US, as we know, it's a big controversy, but not in Israel. Then there's the way they treat fellow Jews who believe in Yeshua.'

'Believe in who?' asked Mickey.

'It's the Hebrew name for Jesus,' Brandon answered.

'Ah, you mean like those '*Jews for Jesus*' guys?' Mickey responded.

'Yep.'

'Seems like a contradiction in terms,' said Shaul sarcastically. 'How can you still be a Jew if you believe in Jesus. You'd be a Christian, then, wouldn't you? You'd have abandoned Judaism?'

'They don't see it that way, Shaul. They see faith in Yeshua as fulfilling everything that their Judaism is about.'

'Mebbe,' Shaul muttered, unconvinced, and wondering slightly why his reaction was so aggressive all of a sudden. He changed his voice to a brighter note, 'Anyway, you were gonna tell us about this war?'

'Yeah. I call it 'The Six hour War',' Brandon continued. 'Cause it will start one evening and be over before morning – at least from Israel's point of view. The action will probably continue for a while after that.'

'Like the Six Day War, only shorter?' asked Micky.

'Exactly!' answered Brandon, 'though some people refer to it as the Psalm 83 war.'

'So, who's gonna start it?' asked Shaul. 'We pre-empted the Arabs in the Six Day War and we're already threatening to attack Iran, if they keep on developing nuclear weapons.'

'This one's gonna be different," said Brandon. 'More like the Yom Kippur War of 1973. It will take Israel by surprise and it will probably involve a nuclear missile attack against Israel – probably from Iran, though it could just as easily come from Syria.

'Isaiah 17 begins by prophesying the complete destruction of Damascus, but it ends by describing *all* of Israel's enemies becoming like dust, or chaff, in the wind. Like tumbleweed in a gale.'

'But how do you know that didn't already happen way back when?' asked Mickey. 'What makes you think it means today?'

'Well, one good reason is because Damascus' claim to fame is that is has *never* ever been destroyed, throughout history. It is the world's longest continually inhabited city.'

'You said nuclear missile attack?' Mickey queried. 'Don't tell me the Bible talks about nuclear missiles? Come on!'

'Well, it doesn't specifically say 'nuclear missile',' Brandon agreed, 'but, in Zechariah, it describes a container that's like a flying scroll – thirty feet long and fifteen feet in circumference – with wings like a stork, lifting it up between heaven and earth. It has a cover of lead and inside it contains wickedness, fire, a curse, which will be able to destroy both timber and stones. Sounds like a nuclear warhead doesn't it?"

'OK, so it's a nuclear attack on Israel, then? A lot of people are gonna die, if that's the case?' said Shaul, intrigued. 'But Israel still comes out OK? How can that be?'

'Yes, a lot of people are gonna die in Israel,' said Brandon, 'because of the policies the US, Russia, the EU and the UN are trying to force on them. But Israel will react quickly and the outcome will be totally miraculous – just like it was in 1948, '67 and '73!

'All the Arab and Muslim nations around them are gonna gang up and attempt to wipe out Israel once and for all. But their enemies are gonna be overcome by fear instead and flee before them – even Iran! Israel will end up controlling the whole Middle East – with no enemies in sight!

'That's when the highway will be open for the ten tribes to return to Israel. There will be no nation of Iran in the way. And Egypt and Sudan will no longer be a barrier to the tribes coming from Africa.'

'Africa?' exclaimed Mickey. 'Look, I can see that Pashtuns might look like Jews, but where the hell are you gonna find any Jews in Africa?'

'There are already more than 100,000 black Jews in Israel,' said Brandon.

'Yeah, those *Falasha* guys – I think that's what they call them – from Ethiopia, aren't they?' Shaul asked.

'Yeah, they prefer to be called *'Beta Israel'*. But like I said, we're talkin' about Israelites here – not Jews, but from the other ten tribes. They were exiled 200 years earlier and travelled further away and were much more distant from temple worship and stuff. So, they don't appear too 'Jewish' any more,' said Brandon. 'There are many more 'Black Jews' in Nigeria, South Africa and Zimbabwe – and possibly a few other places.'

Just then a whole bunch of soldiers arrived in the mess. The noise level rose sharply and some of them came over to challenge Shaul and Mickey to a game of pool.

Ali got up to join a group of fellow ANA soldiers who called him over. Brandon went back to his reading, until he in turn was drawn into a pool game.

3 – Word from Afghan

In New York, Reuben Levine clicked on the email that had just arrived from his younger brother in Afghanistan:

Hi bro,

Hows the financial world doin these days?

We're still doing the usual – patrols n stuff. Things seem a little bit quieter here than they've been for a while. We're not getting shot at quite as often!

Got into an interesting conversation the other evening after we came back from patrol. Brandon Thomas – we call him Doubtin', cause hes always reading his Bible and prayin n stuff.

Anyway, Devlin asked him what was so interesting about what he was reading and he started talkin about the lost tribes of Israel being in Afghanistan and Pakistan and Africa and places – and them gonna be comin back to Israel after what he calls the Six Hour War in the Middle East!

How come weve never heard about any of this stuff back home? I mean, we're supposed to be the chosen people n all, so why do we never hear anyone talking about these things, eh?

Anyway, I actually managed to get hold of a Jewish Bible from the chaplain (in English, of course – you know how little Hebrew I can understand!) and started reading some of these prophets, like Isaiah and Jeremiah.

This is crazy stuff – I never knew the Tanakh talked about all this stuff. Why do the rabbis never mention this kinda thing, eh? We might have paid a bit more attention to them, if they had, don't you think?

Anyway, another two months and this tours finished and I'll be back in the Big Apple again.

Dunno what I'm gonna do with myself after the army, tho.

Hope your all well.

Your little brother,

Solly

* * *

Brandon Thomas switched on the PC and connected to the internet, laying his hand on the screen as he prayed for a good connection. The local time was 11:30 pm – nine and a half hours ahead of North Carolina time – early afternoon there.

Once he had *Skype* up and running he clicked the icon with the picture of his wife and two kids smiling back at him. After an anguished few seconds waiting the connection was made and he could hear his wife saying his name, while the two kids almost screamed, 'Daddy, daddy!' Then his wife and children appeared on the screen.

'Hiya, love. Hi kids.' he said, struggling to keep his voice steady. 'I love you guys.'

'Daddy, daddy, daddy,' the youngest, two year old Caleb, cried – hardly able to contain his excitement.

'I'm not a guy, I'm a girl, Daddy,' said Hannah – two years older than Caleb, and already inclined to be pedantic.

'Yes, I know that Hannah,' said Brandon. 'Have you gu – you kids been good for your mom, then?'

'Yes, we have,' the children chorused.

'They've been so excited about going to see you on *Skype*,' said Alyssa, Brandon's wife of six years. 'I haven't been able to get them to settle to anything, they've been so wound up. I'm hoping they're gonna sleep tonight after this, but I'm gonna take them out to the park for a while and then for a burger before bedtime – just to make sure.'

'You're looking good, darling,' Brandon told his wife. 'Hope these trouble-makers aren't wearing you out?'

'You're looking well yourself,' Alyssa smiled. 'How are things going over there?'

'Well, you know I can't say much, but things are getting better. I'm keeping pretty fit with all the patrolling we do.'

'Daddy, daddy ...' Caleb cried impatiently.

'Yes, son?' Brandon answered.

'When are you coming home to see us? Are you coming home soon?'

'Yes, fairly soon now, little buddy. Daddy has a few more jobs to do for Uncle Sam and then he'll be coming home to look after you.'

'I miss you daddy. You haven't even seen my new bike, have you?'

'I miss you too, son. No, I haven't seen your bike. Can you ride it all by yourself, then?'

'Of course, I can, Daddy. You just sit on it and push. I can ride it all around the yard. I ride it every day.'

'Yeah,' said Hannah, 'He's a danger to everyone near him on that bike!'

'That's great, Caleb. I tell you what, son, you keep practicing on your bike and when I get home we'll buy you a new bike that has pedals on it – OK?'

'Sure, Daddy. Great!' Caleb answered, his face beaming.

'How are you getting on with the other guys, Brandon?' his wife asked.

'Actually, I had a really interesting conversation earlier today with three of my crew – Levine, Devlin and Yusufzai. I was reading the Word after we came in from patrol and they asked me what I was reading and I just happened to be reading from Ezekiel – you know, the bit about the Kebar River and all?

'Well, I related it to where we are, here – not too far from the Kyber River – and I told them a bit about the ten tribes and stuff. You know, it was really weird, we had a Jew from New York, myself, an Igbo from North Carolina, and a Afghan Pashtun from the tribe of Joseph – all of us from the tribes of Israel – plus Dev, of course, who's Irish American. They seemed pretty interested, especially Solly. He wondered why he'd never heard any of this from the rabbi. So, keep praying for these guys.'

'We sure will,' said Alyssa, 'that's great.'

'Daddy, Mom and Caleb and I pray for you and your friends every night – and we all pray for y'all at church, too.'

'That's great, Hannah. I'm glad to hear that. Do you like church?'

'Oh, yes,' she answered, 'Caleb just plays with toys with the other little kids, but we learn stories from the Bible and we learn how to pray and sing songs 'n' stuff.'

'What's your favourite story from the Bible, then, Hannah?' he asked.

'I love all the stories about Jesus helping people and healing them – and the one about David and Goliath, the giant warrior. David killed this big giant with just a little stone – and then he cut off his head! That was a great story.'

'Yes, it is, Hannah. And one day we're gonna go to that place where David used to live – and where Jesus used to teach his disciples and do all those miracles. Would you like that, Hannah?'

'Can we, Daddy? That would be incredible!'

'Daddy, did you know that Jesus disciples didn't call him Jesus?'

'What did they call him, then, sweetie?'

'His real name is Yeshua. They called him Yeshua, but we call him Jesus in our language – but he doesn't really mind as long as we talk to him.'

'That's right, sweetie. He just wants you to bring all your troubles and worries to him and tell him about them. Well, I've got to go and get myself to bed, now, kids. We're out on patrol again early tomorrow. Do you know it's nearly midnight here?'

'Midnight? Caleb asked, 'but the sun is still shining outside – and we haven't had our dinner yet, even.'

'It is where you are, son, but I'm nearly halfway around the world from you. The sun has already gone around to your side of the world, but very soon it'll be back here – while you're in your bed, dreaming – and I'll have to get up and go out on patrol with my buddies.

'Only another couple of months, love, and my tour will be over. then I'm looking forward to being with you all again, for good,' he told Alyssa.

'That reminds me,' she replied, 'Josh down at the garage was asking about you. Apparently he's been pretty busy recently and he was wondering if you'd be interested in working with him when you leave the Army?'

'Hmm, interesting,' said Brandon, 'It depends on what terms, but you can tell him I just might be interested.'

'OK, I will. Be careful over there, won't you love? I'm always praying that God will watch over you.'

'I always am, Alyssa darling. And He sure does!'

'Night, night, kids. Be good for your Mom, now. And keep saying your prayers. God bless y'all.'

'Bye bye, Daddy. Bye bye. Love you, Daddy,' they shouted.

'And I love you, too, Brandon. God bless you,' Alyssa added softly.

'Bye darling. I love you. Bye.'

Brandon cut the connection, sat back in the chair and sighed. He already missed his family, though it seemed like there might be something for him after the Army, after all. He hoped he could work something out with Josh Williams and his auto repair business. It would give him an income while he worked out some of the other plans that were growing in his mind.

2013

In Six Hours ... the world changed – *Raymond McCullough*

4 – The 'Daughter of Babylon'

It had been a difficult day for the team. The morning had started well. They passed Abdul Haq Square and the former Soviet-era communities of 1st, 2nd and 3rd Mikrorayon – relatively modern Russian-built 'micro-communities' of apartment buildings, with their own shops, schools and even parks. Their convoy began patrolling Deh Sabz, a residential area in the north east of the city, between Great Massoud Road, leading to Kabul Airport, and the Nangarhar Highway heading out of the city to the east.

They stopped periodically and conversed with residents, shop-keepers and other citizens – following the 'hearts and minds' policy of the US government to build relationships with the Afghanis. They had crossed Massoud Road and travelled through the Wazir Akbar Khan residential area to Malik Azghar Square, where they headed south west, parallel to the Kabul River.

Everything had been quiet until about two hours into the patrol, when their vehicles began to come under intensive fire from surrounding rooftops on their left. Shaul directed them to swerve into a courtyard between some industrial buildings, parking the Humvees close to the buildings to make themselves less of a target. He also radioed that they were under intense fire and requested helicopter backup.

'Brandon, you and the other drivers get these vehicles turned around, ready to get out of here again. Keep your guns trained upwards towards the roofs. The rest of you with me. Let's clear this building and get up to roof level.'

Leaving Brandon Thomas, the other drivers, and some extra men manning the machine guns on the vehicles, Shaul led a team of US soldiers and ANA trainees up the stairway of the building on their left. They were forced to fight their way slowly to the top, leaving several dead Taliban on the stairway and one American, Marquez, wounded in the right shoulder and being tended to just below the rooftop.

Levine, Devlin and Yusufzai emerged from the stairwell and led their team across the rooftop to the parapet, where they trained their weapons on the surrounding rooftops, from which the onslaught was still continuing. Ali was carrying the grenade launcher and Shaul signalled him to set it up,

21

directing his fire as Yusufzai crouched behind the protection of a water tank. Dev and the ANA soldiers continued to fire their M4 assault rifles and Shaul his MP5 submachine gun towards the enemy forces.

Suddenly, one of the ANA soldiers was flung back and slumped behind the parapet. Dev crawled across to him, but it was too late to do anything for the soldier, Yousef Rabani, who had been shot in the head and killed instantly. Typical of his ANA comrades, he had refused to wear the US issue battle helmet, instead wearing a scarf wound on his head like a turban – colourful, but no protection against a bullet.

Zai's first grenade exploded on the rooftop to their right with little effect, but the second, with further direction from Shaul, took out several of the Taliban fighters. Incoming fire, however, was still coming from the roof immediately ahead of them. While Dev and his ANA comrades continued to return fire, hoping to keep the enemy pinned down, Shaul signalled Ali to move around the protecting water tank to his right, again directing his grenade fire towards the new target.

Two more grenades and most of the opposing guns had fallen silent. Dev spotted one of the rebels changing position and fired, scoring a direct hit. Suddenly there was no more opposition. The remaining Taliban had cut their losses and fled. Dev directed his attention to another ANA soldier – Shinwari – who had also been lightly wounded in the skirmish.

Now Shaul could hear the sound of a helicopter as his radio crackled to life. He directed the aircraft to their rooftop and Dev and some the others quickly loaded up the two wounded men, plus the body of Rabani, into the helicopter, which quickly departed for the base.

Shaul, meanwhile, took a long slow look around the surrounding roofs before directing his men to retrace their steps down the stairwell to the waiting Humvees. Thomas and the other drivers had meanwhile manoeuvred the vehicles ready for a quick departure. 'All quiet here now, Lieutenant,' Brandon reported.

'Let's get out of here,' Shaul growled impatiently – he hated losing a man, and they had also lost two wounded from the patrol.

'Back on patrol – and keep your eyes peeled on those rooftops,' he barked.

The convoy returned to the main street and resumed their patrol – seeking to release the built-up tension and sharply vigilant in case of any further attack. The rest of the day was uneventful – apart from a crowd of men arguing around a traffic accident, which broke into a fistfight as their vehicles were squeezing past.

As the sun shone lower in the sky, the patrol continued back along the main road, with the Kabul River on their right. Shortly after they entered the base compound and, after parking their Humvees, entered the building they'd been calling home for several months now.

* * *

Once they'd showered and changed the boys gathered in the recreation room to wind down from the hectic events of the day.

Shaul came in shortly after them and reported, 'Seems like Marquez and Shinwari are gonna be OK. They're both comfortable and resting up. Marquez will be heading home Stateside soon, but Shinwari should be back with us in a few days.'

The men nodded sombrely and Devlin commented, 'More than can be said for Rabani!' There was a solemn mood in the room.

Brandon once again had his Bible with him. Shaul, nodding towards it, remarked, 'One of these days, Doubtin', you're gonna find yourself out on patrol with no weapon on you – only that book there in your hand!'

'Well, that might be no bad thing,' Brandon replied. 'It's referred to as the 'sword of the Spirit', you know. No better protection.'

'Yeah, like it'll drive back the Taliban and stop bullets,' Shaul retorted.

'King Yehoshaphat went out to battle Moab and Ammon and sent the singers out in front of the army to sing to the Lord and y'know what happened?'

'They all got killed?' answered Dev with a grin, somehow guessing this was probably not the right response.

'Far from it,' Brandon replied. 'As they began to sing to Yahowah, their enemies turned on each other – the Moabites and Ammonites first killed all of the Edomites, then they killed each another. When the men of Judah got there all they found were dead bodies – no one left alive! All they had to do was carry off the plunder. And even that took them three days!'

'Pity we couldn't use that strategy against the Taliban,' mused Shaul.

'I'm totally convinced that that will happen again,' said Brandon. 'Probably when the people of Israel are in dire straits, at their most needy. Then they will call upon Yahowah for help – because America will have deserted them! And HE will defeat their enemies– put the fear of Israel upon them and cause them to fight against one another. It happened before in 1948, during Israel's War of Independence.'

'OK. What happened then?' Micky asked.

'It was during the battle for the town of Safad, or Zefat, in the north of Galilee – one of the towns where there was an ancient Jewish population, but made up of Torah scholars, not fighters. The majority of the town was Arab. The Israeli Palmach were sent in and had to fight from house to house, losing many of their men in the process. They were also supplied with a couple of homemade *Davidkas* – very inaccurate, but also very noisy, mortars. The mortar made a strange whistling sound when fired.

'One morning they moved out, expecting the usual barrage of enemy fire, but found house after house empty. The whole Arab population had fled, based on a rumour that the Israelis had acquired a nuclear weapon. The rumour had started because of the strange sound made by the mortar shells. Safad has been a completely Jewish town ever since.'

'So, you think America will turn their backs on Israel in the future,' asked Ali.

'Yes, the Bible says that *all* nations will be against Israel – that will include the United States, unfortunately.'

'Why unfortunately?' Devlin asked.

'Because every time that America has broken a promise to Israel, or acted against their interests, they have opened the door to natural disasters and other judgements.'

'So, you believe that God judges America if they act against Israel?' asked Ali.

'In Genesis 12, Yahowah promises Abraham, "I will bless those who bless you, and whoever curses you I will curse; and all peoples on earth will be blessed through you."'

'What about if they help Israel?' Ali asked.

'Then they will be blessed. There is a book called, *As America Has Done To Israel*, by a guy called McTernan, that spells out the correlation between decisions US presidents and other leaders have made against Israel and a corresponding natural disaster in the USA within twenty four hours.'

'Wow! That's interesting!' said Dev.

'The same rule applies to every nation. Great Britain were blessed when they supported the creation of the State of Israel, but when they reneged on their promise and gave away more than 78% of the promised land, they declined rapidly and lost their empire and world dominance.' Brandon added.

'So, you think America will follow in the footsteps of Britain?' asked Shaul.

'There is a nation spoken of in prophecy many times – codenamed Babylon, or Mega-Babylon, or the 'daughter of Babylon.' Those prophecies have yet to be fulfilled. So, how many 'daughter' nations are there – nations referred to as having a mother?'

Chapter 4 – The 'Daughter of Babylon'

'Hmm, well, The UK is regarded as the mother of several nations – Australia, New Zealand – South Africa, even. And, I suppose, of the United States, as well?' Micky answered.

Well done,' Brandon congratulated him. 'And we could add Jamaica and a few others, but they're not really of any importance. And which of those countries contain mega-cities, then?'

'Well, there's London, I suppose – and New York, Los Angeles ...' said Shaul.

'Mega-cities? There's Tokyo and Osaka, Delhi, Mumbai, Kolkata – lots of huge cities in China and India,' said Michael.

'Paris,' answered Ali.

'Yes, all mega-cities, but most of them not in 'daughter' nations,' said Brandon.

'So that leaves ...'

'New York and LA,' Devlin exclaimed.

'Correct!' Brandon said. 'But there are many more clues as to this city and nation. She dominates the nations of the world – militarily and economically. She controls trade in gold, silver, precious stones ... For instance, where are the centres of the world's gold trade?'

'London and New York,' said Solly, thinking of his brother, Reuben, and his father, who both talked a lot about such things.

'Right. What about world trade in diamonds, then?'

'Er, Tel Aviv,' said Shaul.

'And New York,' added Dev.

'And also Antwerp, in Belgium,' said Brandon. 'But only two of those are mega cities, and only one is in a daughter nation.'

'So, you're really saying that this mega-Babylon is New York City?' said Ali.

'Yes, but there are lots more clues to confirm this. "To whom the nations stream," is another – think of the UN headquarters in Manhattan,' said Thomas.

'Well, what else does it say about this 'daughter of Babylon', then?' asked Shaul, genuinely intrigued by now.

'Quite a lot. The two longest chapters of the book of Jeremiah are all about Babylon – chapters 50 and 51 – what she will do and what will happen to her. Isaiah also has four chapters about Babylon. Habbakuk is mostly about Babylon and there are two full chapters and two part chapters in the New

Testament Book of Revelation which are also about Babylon. If you put them all together into one document – as I have done – you begin to see the same things being said by different prophets, the same points being emphasised over and over.

'For instance,' Brandon continued, now with a captive audience, 'There are several similar prophecies saying that God's people should flee from Babylon, get out and not suffer her judgements.'

'Does that refer to the Jews, then?' asked Shaul.

'Well, that's another of the clues, actually. Babylon has to have a significant Jewish – and also Israelite – population. Jeremiah refers to both the "sons of Israel and the sons of Judah" weeping and saying, "Show us the way to Zion."'

'Well, being from New York myself I know that it's the largest Jewish population of any city in the world. But who would the 'sons of Israel' be, then? Are they Jewish, too?'

'Not Jewish, but Israelite, though – part of the Ten Tribes.'

'So, who would they be in the US?' asked Devlin.

'I don't know for sure. But I *do* know that, like myself, a significant number of black Americans have Igbo roots – remember I said before that Igbo was a corruption of 'Hebrew', and that Igbos are of Israelite descent? Of course, there are many Pashtuns and other Israelites living in America – but there would need to be a few million to balance the six million 'sons of Judah' who live there.'

'OK, so these guys are warned to flee from Babylon/America,' said Shaul. 'Why? What will happen to America?'

'Eventually, it will be destroyed – "in one hour",' said Brandon. 'Probably by nuclear missiles and other devices. The destruction will be carried out by a conspiracy of ten different powerful nations – nations upon whose backs America/Babylon rides at present, and to whom she is also in debt. One of the prophecies refers to her debts being called in.'

'Wow! That means China, for sure, said Devlin. 'Probably Russia, too.'

'Yes, and Japan and perhaps others of the G8 nations, who are the strongest nations in the world, economically,' said Brandon.

'And these ten nations will then be the strongest economies in the world,' said Dev.

'Yes, the whole world will be devastated economically by the fall of America. Almost every nation in the world depends greatly on trade with the USA, which won't be there to trade with any more. Nor will there be a dollar reserve currency any longer. We can already see that coming with the *BRICSA* thing.'

'BRICSA?' asked Ali.

'Acronym for Brazil, Russia, India, China and South Africa,' Brandon answered, 'who are all considering setting up a new reserve currency based on what they call a 'basket of currencies'.'

'So, Jews and Israelites – whoever they may be – are told to flee from America. Where to?' asked Shaul.

'Well, not only Israelites and Jews, but also many Christians, will hope-fully heed the warnings to flee America. The Babylon prophecies speak several times of the survivors of the fall of Babylon returning to their own countries. Dev here, for instance, would presumably go to Ireland, where he probably still has family. Germans would go to Germany, Swedes to Sweden, Hispanics to the Latin American countries, Chinese to China, etc.'

'That's right. I still have an uncle and aunt in Ireland – cousins, too. They live somewhere near Kilkenny.' said Devlin. 'I've never been there, but I'd love to see the place.'

'So ...,' pondered Shaul, 'you were telling us before about this huge war in the Middle East. Does that come before or after this Babylon thing?'

'Oh, I think before,' said Brandon. 'One of the reasons for God's judge-ment upon the 'daughter of Babylon' is her being the cause of so much death and destruction in Israel. The prophecies also say that things will get better – for Jews and Israelites – in Israel, but will get much worse in Babylon.'

'You mean like this peace process that the US is so concerned to bring about – though no president yet has managed to make it happen!' said Sol.

'Nor do I think they ever will,' said Brandon, 'for the simple reason that the so-called 'Palestinians', and all the Arab Muslims surrounding Israel, will never accept a Jewish controlled state on what they regard as sacred Muslim territory – territory once ruled by Muslims in the past.

'Yes, I do believe that the policies of the US concerning Israel will cause more and more bloodshed there – and more and more judgement upon America. And when the *Six Hour War* happens and, miraculously, Israel come out the victors, taking control of the Middle East, the USA will *not* be cheering them on. Nor will China, or Russia, for that matter.

'In fact, I think things will become more and more difficult for Jews, Israelites and for Bible-believing Christians in the US – much like they did in Germany in the nineteen thirties. Then it will be time to flee. Jeremiah says to be like *"the goats who lead the flock."*'

'In other words, get out out while you still can!' said Shaul.

'Yes. But there will be Jews, and Christians, who won't listen to the warnings, who will refuse to believe it could get that bad – just like in Nazi Germany. Many of them will die in the destruction, some will survive, but with nothing – needing help even to get out of the ruins of America.

'Don't forget, there won't be any airports, no internet or phone system, probably no ports for ships to dock, either. Survivors from New York, for instance, will have to walk into Canada and, hopefully, get help there to send them on to Israel. Survivors in LA will have to walk into Mexico, and move on from there. The prophecies say the land will be desolate – unfit for anything, even ordinary wildlife, to survive there!

'All those Preppers you hear about, living in cabins in the woods and stockpiling canned food and weapons are just wasting their time – they won't be able to live off the land, as many hope to. The land won't produce anything any more and the water supply will probably be polluted, among other things.'

'Wow! That sure is a sobering thought,' Devlin mused. 'You really reckon we're gonna have to abandon the good ol' United States some day?'

'I'm certain of it,' said Brandon. 'And I'm also planning where to go before it happens. It's a good idea to be prepared in advance, so we know what to do as things start to get really bad.'

'So, what you're saying is, Jews will need to make aliyah to Israel, the Irish – like me – will have to go back to Ireland. Where are you gonna go to, Brandon? Where are your ancestors from? Oh yeah, I think you said Nigeria, isn't that right?'

'Like I said earlier, my ancestors were the Igbo people, about twenty eight to forty million of whom live in southern Nigeria. When I get out of the army and get settled a bit I want to go there and get to know some people in that country. My people are Israelites, and I want to be there to lend a hand when they begin to return to the land of Israel!'

'Looks like I'm the odd-one-out,' said Dev, 'I'll be heading to Ireland, while you three guys will ultimately be heading to Israel.'

'Well, you'll be more than welcome to come visit the new Israel, Dev. Whaddy'all say we agree to meet up in Jerusalem when the *Six Day War* is over and the ingathering begins?' Brandon proposed.

'OK, it's a date,' said Shaul, coming under the spell of Brandon's words, 'just supposing it all happens that way.'

'Devlin?' Brandon asked, looking Dev in the eye.

'Sure! I mean I'd love to see the place when all this has happened. As Sol said, supposing it turns out the way you've said.'

'What about you, Zai? You've been very quiet?' he gazed intently at his Afghan comrade.

'Well, my friend, what you say has been very interesting to me. My people – the Pashtuns – have always believed that we were descended from the ancient Israelites. So, the land of Israel is really our ancient homeland. If there is a Pashtun movement to return to that land, and if we truly would be welcomed there, I would be very willing to be involved.'

'I'm serious about this,' Brandon added. 'When we leave the army we'll be able to keep in touch through the internet. But one day I want to see you three guys in Jerusalem, when this all comes to pass. OK?' He took Shaul's hand in both of his. Dev clasped their hands, too, and, finally, Ali also joined his hands with the others.

'OK, Brandon,' they answered in chorus. The pact was sealed.

In Six Hours ... the world changed – *Raymond McCullough*

2014

In Six Hours ... the world changed – *Raymond McCullough*

5 – Manhattan, New York City

Aaron Levine – Shaul's father – accelerated slightly as the red light ahead changed to green. Beside him his wife of forty five years, Miriam, was chatting excitedly about their coming holiday in Florida. They preferred to drive there these days – air travel had become much too difficult and uncomfortable.

They never even saw the truck that hit their car full tilt from the right, running the red light. Miriam died instantly. Aaron, already in a deep coma by the time the emergency crew extricated him from the vehicle, died a few hours later in the hospital.

* * *

Shaul meditated on that sad event as he turned the key in the complicated security lock of his parent's former apartment in the old brownstone building they had owned in Manhattan's Upper West Side. The Army had flown him back in time for the funeral and then given him some leave to recover from the trauma of losing both parents at once. It meant that essentially, his tour of duty in Afghanistan was over.

He, his brother and other members of their family and friends, had paid their last respects to his parents at the *Riverside Memorial Chapel*, on West 76th Street, not far from their Manhattan apartment. Shaul now had custody of both their ashes which, he and his brother had agreed, he would soon arrange to have buried in Israel.

Four weeks later, Brandon and Micky had also returned, having finished their tour in Afghanistan and had arranged to meet up with Shaul in New York. They had drunk a few pints and commiserated with him on the loss of his parents, but eventually Brandon had to go back to his family in Raleigh, North Carolina, and the possibility of a job with his friend there.

Mickey Devlin had stayed on for a few more days, but he also had now returned to Boston and his family there. Apparently, he was heading over to Ireland for his cousin's wedding very soon. Mickey was unsure about his future – thinking maybe of doing a university degree. But as his family owned a large pub in Boston he always had the option of working there in the meantime.

Having now left the Army, Shaul had not yet decided what he was going to do next. The apartment was dust-free and tidy – courtesy of the cleaning service hired by his brother, Reuben. But there was still a lingering scent of leather, his father's pipe tobacco and furniture polish.

On the lounge wall hung a photograph of his parents in their forties, looking fresh and suntanned, while on holiday in Florida. He remembered how his father regularly talked of *'next year in Jerusalem'* – they had always intended to visit Israel – but somehow it had never happened. And now, of course, it was too late.

Shaul suspected that his parents, like many American Jews, had thought of Israel as some kind of special Jewish museum, an experiment, to prove that such a thing was possible. They certainly had little idea of what day to day life in Israel was like and the idea of making aliyah was totally beyond their understanding. After all, life was too good, too comfortable, in America.

Shaul, brought up in this atmosphere, wondered, *Why have I never con-sidered these things before?* His brother was focussed on *'making a living'* – the business of making money. He himself had joined the military as a means of breaking out of the Jewish stereotype and seeing the world.

Well, he had seen one bit of it, Afghanistan. And what had he learned from it? His mind drifted back to the conversations they'd had with Brandon Thomas. Brandon, a black southerner, seemed to know more about Israel and the Jews than he, a New York Jew, did. Well, his interest had certainly now been awakened.

Shaul opened up his dad's Mac laptop and went to *Google Maps*, looking first at Afghanistan and Pakistan, then Kashmir, then he searched for the Mizoram and Manipur provinces of India. Finally, he scanned across Africa, from Nigeria, to Zimbabwe and South Africa. Could all these disparate peoples really be fellow Israelites?

It seemed too fantastic a story – and yet Brandon had insisted that this was simply the promise of the God of Abraham through His prophets. I gotta get myself a Bible, thought Shaul. One of those modern translations, but a Jewish Bible. The idea of using a Christian Bible just didn't seem right to Shaul.

He decided to search for a modern translation online and eventually he found himself reading from the fifth Book of Moses:

> **Deuteronomy 4:23**. Beware, lest you forget the covenant of the Lord your God, which He made with you, and make for

yourselves a graven image, the likeness of anything, which the Lord your God has forbidden you.

24. For the Lord your God is a consuming fire, a zealous God.

25. When you beget children and children's children, and you will be long established in the land, and you become corrupt and make a graven image, the likeness of anything, and do evil in the eyes of the Lord your God, to provoke Him to anger,

26. I call as witness against you this very day the heaven and the earth, <u>that you will speedily and utterly perish from the land to which you cross the Jordan, to possess; you will not prolong your days upon it, but will be utterly destroyed.</u>

27. <u>And the Lord will scatter you among the peoples, and you will remain few in number among the nations to where the Lord will lead you</u>.

28. And there you will worship gods, man's handiwork, wood and stone, which neither see, hear, eat, nor smell.

29. And from there you will seek the Lord your God, and you will find Him, if you seek Him with all your heart and with all your soul.

30. When you are distressed, and all these things happen upon you <u>in the end of days</u>, then you will return to the Lord your God and obey Him.

Well, thought Shaul, that prophecy has certainly come to pass. I wonder are we *'in the end of days'* now? Brandon had certainly seemed to think so. But what about these widely scattered Israelites returning to the land? Where did it mention that?

He continued to browse and search this newly discovered resource, until he came across these words in Isaiah 43:

Isaiah 43:1 But now this is what Adonai says,
he who created you, Ya'akov, he who formed you, Isra'el:
<u>"Don't be afraid, for I have redeemed you;</u>
I am calling you by your name; you are mine.
2 When you pass through water, I will be with you;
when you pass through rivers, they will not overwhelm you;
when you walk through fire, you will not be scorched — the flame will not burn you.
3 For I am Adonai, your God, the Holy One of Isra'el, your Savior — I have given Egypt as your ransom, Ethiopia and S'va for you.
4 Because I regard you as valued and honored, and because

I love you.
For you I will give people, nations in exchange for your life.
5 Don't be afraid, for I am with you.
I will bring your descendants from the east,
and I will gather you from the west;
6 I will say to the north, 'Give them up!'
and to the south, 'Don't hold them back!
Bring my sons from far away,
and my daughters from the ends of the earth,
7 everyone who bears my name,
whom I created for my glory —
I formed him, yes, I made him.'"

8 Bring forward the people who are blind but have eyes,
also the deaf who have ears.
9 All the nations are gathered together,
and the peoples are assembled.
Who among them can proclaim this
and reveal what happened in the past?
Let them bring their witnesses to justify themselves,
so that others, on hearing, can say, "That's true."

10 "You are my witnesses," says Adonai,
"and my servant whom I have chosen,
so that you can know and trust me
and understand that I am he —
no god was produced before me,
nor will any be after me.

'Wow', thought Shaul, *'That says it all in one passage. God will give nations in exchange for Israel. He will bring us from east, west, north and south – because we are His witnesses, his chosen people. Israel is so important to him that he will exchange other nations for our sake.'*

Shaul meditated on these words. For all of their nearly 2,000 year estrangement from their own land the Jews had many times wondered just what was so special about being the *'Chosen People?'* Often it seemed they'd been chosen only for destruction, persecution, pogroms, wars and near extermination. That sure didn't sound like such a great inheritance, really!

But according to what he'd just read, Israel, (not just the Jews), were chosen to be witnesses that God is who he says he is – God. It actually said, *'Adonai'*, which Shaul remembered was a substitution for the sacred name of God – *'YHVH'* – whose name he knew religious Jews were no longer allowed to pronounce.

As he meditated on all these things he finally made up his mind. He had the perfect excuse – taking his parents ashes to be buried on Har Ha-Zetim

– the Mount of Olives. His parents had never made it to Israel – not even for a visit – despite their wealth. Shaul decided that not only would he visit Israel, but he planned now to remain there for a time, learn Hebrew, explore the land and, possibly – if he found it seemed the right thing to do – even to make aliyah to Israel. After Afghanistan, life in the United States had lost its allure for him.

The lure of the land – Eretz Israel they called it – had now gripped him. He wanted to see if this would become his land, too. This was the perfect time to make this move. He was free from military service, having served his four years in Afghanistan. He was physically fit and unattached. There was nothing to tie him to the USA anymore.

He had resisted his brother's efforts to draw him into 'managing his father's affairs.' His brother, Reuben, loved business and could take all that in his stride. Shaul was more the adventuring type and now, with the experience of Afghanistan behind him, he was ready for something new and different and challenging. What better than a new land, a new language, the birthplace of his own people?

He went back to his father's computer, to the Jewish Agency website and looked up the Aliyah Office in New York City – on Third Avenue, as it happened. He rang their toll free number and made an appointment for the next day.

After talking with the Jewish Agency and filling in all the necessary forms, Shaul needed to gather up some paperwork to have with him when he arrived in Israel – birth certificate, letter from his rabbi, etc. He realised his biggest hurdle would be the Hebrew language – he understood only a very few words at the moment and knew he would be unable to carry on even a simple conversation in Hebrew.

He rang his brother Reuben to tell him he would now be delivering their parents ashes to Jerusalem in person and to tell him to go ahead with organising the sale of their parent's apartment. Then he contacted Brandon, explaining his plan – such as it was! – and asking him for any suggestions he might have about visiting Israel.

He also booked an apartment in Tel Aviv for two months – the *Ulpan* (Hebrew language school) he would be attending was also in Tel Aviv. A few days later, after organising the necessary paperwork to take with him, Shaul was on an *ElAl* plane on his way to Israel.

In Six Hours ... the world changed – *Raymond McCullough*

6 – Shannon Airport, Ireland

The *Aer Lingus* 757 arrived pretty much on time at Shannon Airport, near Limerick, in Ireland – helped on its way by the jet stream. The flight had been uneventful and Devlin had spent most of it reading an action thriller on his newly purchased *Kindle*, after giving up on the in-flight movie – a romantic comedy which he'd found he wasn't in the mood for.

Dev made his way slowly through customs and waited at the carousel for his case to appear. When he entered the *Arrivals* hall he quickly spotted the sign saying, *Michael Devlin*, held up by a very attractive raven-haired young lady in her early twenties.

'Hi, I'm Micky Devlin. Who're you, then?' he asked with a smile.

'Niamh O'Leary. I'm a good friend of your cousin, Kathleen,' the girl replied. 'She's tied up with wedding stuff at the moment, so she asked me if I'd collect you from the airport and bring you back to Kilkenny.'

'Nice to meet you, Niamh,' said Micky.

'Likewise, I'm sure,' Niamh answered.

Devlin trailed his single suitcase behind him out to the car park, while Niamh insisted she carry his laptop for him. They got into her 2008 silver/grey Audi A4 and headed for the motorway into Limerick, the Shannon Estuary appearing from time to time on their right. Soon the motorway dived into a tunnel under the still tidal Shannon River and subsequently became the M7 heading towards Dublin, bypassing the city of Limerick to their north.

'I wasn't expecting such good roads, here,' said Dev.

'Thought we all lived in little thatched cottages, too, no doubt – wi' the pigs sharing the front parlour, eh? God, *The Quiet Man* has a lot to answer for!' said Niamh spiritedly.

'No ...' Michael began.

'This yer first time in 'the aul' country', is it?' she interrupted him.

'Yes,' said Michael, 'First I was at college, then in the military for four years, so this is the first chance I've had to visit the 'aul' country', as you call it.'

'"*Visit exotic, interesting places, meet exotic, interesting people – and then kill them*", eh?' Niamh quoted.

'Not exactly,' said Michael, 'but I did do several years in Afghanistan. Not the safest place in the world. Plenty of Taliban shooting at you. That sorta thing.'

'I bet *you* did yer share of the shooting, too, didn't ye?' Niamh said. 'And yez wonder why on earth people around the world don't just love all yez Americans to bits!'

There was silence for a minute, though neither of them felt any compulsion to fill it. Michael already felt quite at home in the company of this outspoken young woman.

Eventually, he commented, 'Its very green, isn't it? Even Boston, where I come from, isn't as green as this.'

'That'd be all the rain, so it would. D'ye know how we forecast the weather here in Ireland?'

'No,' said Michael, wondering what was coming.

'If ye can see the mountains, it's gonna rain. And if ye can't see them, that'd be because it's already raining!'

'Right! I'll keep that in mind,' Michael chuckled.

'Yep, its pretty accurate, ye'll find.'

'Do you live in the same place as Kathleen?' he asked.

'Not too far away, near Carlow. But I work in Dublin, now,' she said. 'I share a flat with a coupla girls, there. Takes me about an hour to get home, traffic permitting.'

'What do you work at, then?' he asked.

'I work in an estate agents – what you would probably call *real* estate, right?'

'OK, a realtor. How's that business these days?' he asked.

'Completely shit this last few years, if ye want to know. But it's started showing a few signs of life again, recently. To be honest I'm just lucky to still be in a job at all. Haven't had a pay rise in the past two years, though.

'You don't know anyone looking for a four bed-roomed luxury house in a brand new 'development', do ye?' she asked.

'Why, are you trying to sell one at the moment?'

'One! We've got several hundred of them on the books. Whole estates of them just sitting there with nobody living in them. '*Ghost Estates*' they call them, now. There must be at least a coupla hundred thousand empty homes around the country at the moment. Some people reckon maybe even up to four hundred thousand homes, altogether.'

'That's an awful lot of empty space,' said Michael, 'Enough for one and a half, maybe 2 million people, eh? But there's only about five million people in Ireland, so how come they built so many, if there was no market for them?'

'There's certainly no market for them NOW,' said Niamh, 'The government are talking about buying up a lot of them and putting poor people into them. Trouble is, the government don't have any money to spare, either – it would take tens of billions of Euros.

'When they were built the economy here was really booming – the *Celtic Tiger*, they called it – and house prices were just going up and up. Everybody wanted in on the act, so a lotta people invested their money in the housing market. It seemed like they just couldn't lose.

'Ha! Then came September of 2008 and you guys over in America selling bad debt from one bank to another. Suddenly, the bottom dropped out of the housing market and everybody got caught out – here, England, Europe ... all in the same boat. But probably we got the worst of it here in Ireland. Even up in the North things aren't half as bad as the economy down here. And all the politicians can do is blame each other, while the banks are still paying out huge salaries and bonuses to their top executives – the guys responsible for the crash in the first place!'

'Yeah, it's pretty much the same back home in Boston,' Dev agreed.

'What are you for doing, now ye've finished with the Army?' she asked.

'I'm not sure. I've obviously been thinking about it while I was out there,' said Dev. 'Probably some kind of business. My dad owns a pub outside Boston, so I work there for him at the moment. I've worked there part time since I was a wee lad.

'The trouble with having been in the Military for four years is it saps your initiative a bit – everything's been organised and planned by someone else all that time. Takes a wee while to get used to civvy street again and making decisions for yourself. I'll probably stay with the pub for a while, until I can decide what I really want to do.'

'I suppose you're looking forward to Kathleen's wedding – and Damien's too, of course?' he asked. 'Women love weddings, don't they?'

'Well, it'll be a bit of an event, all right, but its no big surprise, or anything. We could all see it coming, like.'

'According to the invitation I got, the ceremony tomorrow's not going to be in a Catholic Church. That was a bit strange, I thought?' said Micky.'

'Not really, said Niamh, 'You gotta realise this is a post-Catholic country these days. Has been for years. Hardly anyone goes to mass anymore. And can ye blame them, with all the abuse scandals about priests and the church trying to cover them up and letting them carry on their acts somewhere else. Ruining the lives of innocent children.'

'I take you don't go yerself, then?' said Michael.

'No, I don't. I've been to the 'born-agains' once or twice, though. Kathleen invited me. They seem like a nice bunch – just very ordinary people. They go out on the streets and feed the homeless and stuff like that. Their music is pretty catchy, too. And it does no harm that the pastor guy is quite young and a bit of a dish,' she smiled.

'Right, so Kathy belongs to this group, then? What are 'born agains', anyway?' he asked, puzzled.

'They're called, '*New Life Church*,' she said. They're not Presbyterians, or Protestants, or whatever – just 'born agains'.'

'I see,' said Micky, not much the wiser. 'If they're not Catholic, surely they must be Protestant?'

'I don't know,' she replied, 'We usually think of the Church of Ireland as the Protestants and the Presbyterians as separate. Actually, I went there once as well. It wasn't quite as lively as *New Life* – toned down a bit – but they seemed a nice enough bunch, too.'

'Ireland has certainly changed a lot', said Dev, 'I had assumed it was still pretty much a Roman Catholic stronghold.'

'Well, we still don't do nuclear, or abortion – nor likely to,' she replied, 'So I guess we're still a bit different.'

'What does Kathleen's fiancé think of all this 'born again' stuff, then?' Dev asked.

'Oh he's one as well,' said Niamh, 'Has been for ages. That's where they met. They're both very involved with *New Life*.'

'So I guess there won't be too many pints being sunk at the reception, then,' said Dev, 'I was kinda looking forward to a good old Irish hooley. Bit of 'drink taken.' Wrong again, Devlin, eh?'

'Ach, I wouldn't think so,' Niamh answered, 'They're not at all straight laced. I doubt if they'll be getting paralytic, like, but they've a great band organised, so I think ye'll have yer jigs 'n' reels all right. Maybe not so much of the '*Take me home again, Kathleen*', though!'

'Don't worry,' said Dev, 'I'll not miss that one little bit. We get enough of that in the pubs back home in Boston.'

'Ye like the aul' Celtic stuff, then? *Dropkick Murphys* 'n' all that?' she asked.

'Maybe not them, specifically, but yes,' said Devlin, 'We have some great Celtic bands over at home.'

'I've heard yez have,' said Niamh, 'But we've some great wee bands and singers here, too, ye know?'

'I don't doubt it,' said Devlin, 'Mebbe ye'll take me to hear some of them, if yer free, that is?'

'Aye, mebbe I will,' said Niamh.

Just over an hour from the airport – before the M7 became the M8 – they turned off onto a smaller road which led to Durrow and the main N77 Portlaoise/Kilkenny road. Thirty minutes later they were circling the outer ring of the mediaeval town of Kilkenny, crossing the River Nore before branching off to the south for Thomastown, a small town also on the River Nore.

'Ye don't play golf at all do ye?' asked Niamh suddenly.

'No,' Micky hesitated, 'Can't say I've ever played it. I'm more the American football type, myself, to be honest – but I haven't even played that since college.'

'That's OK,' said Niamh, 'Just 'cause if ye did we've got one of the world's best golf courses just down the road at Mount Juliet, so we have. Held the *Irish Open* there a few times, and a good few other championships. Quite a few times I've given people lifts who were on there way to watch some big championship.'

Michael smiled, 'You often give lifts to strangers, then, do you?'

'Ach, sure ye couldn't just leave the poor craythurs standing there, could ye?' she answered, 'Mind you, I don't just give lifts to any old Tom, Dick or Harry, ye know.'

'I'm sure you don't,' said Mick.

'Quite often they're tourists – Germans, or Americans like yerself, or Spanish, or whatever. Mind you, we're not getting so many tourists these days. They're a bit thin on the ground, this weather.'

'Right.' Michael speculated to himself as to whether the Irish weather was maybe *the* reason that there were fewer tourists these days.

It was quiet in the car for a while, but as they drove through the small but picturesque town of Thomastown, Niamh said loudly, 'Nearly there, now. '

Micky started awake, 'Wha ...?'

'I think we lost you there for a few minutes! We'll get you settled in and ye can maybe have a nap, if ye want, and then they've a big meal planned at the house. If yer up for it at all, we can go for a pint or two in Kilkenny later on?'

'Sounds great to me,' said a very sleepy-voiced Devlin. 'Sorry, I guess the jet-lag is kicking in now. I hope a coupla hours sleep will bring me back to life again. It always worked back in Afghanistan. So, I'll look forward to a bit more *'craic'* later on. Will anybody else be joining us? he asked.

'I'll see if I can rustle a few of them up. Give ye a proper Irish welcome. Here we are. This is it.' she announced.

'Great,' Dev mumbled drowsily.

Micky managed to stay alert long enough to greet his cousin, Kathleen, and her family but, thankfully, after a few minutes of introduction and comment about his obvious 'Devlin looks' – and where he favoured his mother or his father – they allowed Niamh to show him up to his room, where he pulled off his shoes and trousers, crawled under the quilt and sank mercifully into oblivion.

7 – The Holy Land

Shaul had been in Israel for two months now and had seen a little bit of the country. Based in Tel Aviv, he was renting an apartment in Dizengoff Street – right on the corner of Dizengoff Square, actually – for his first two months, with an option to extend his stay. The apartment wasn't cheap, but his father's death would leave him quite well off and, in the meantime, his accumulated US Army salary would keep him going for quite a while.

Each day he had five hours of learning Hebrew – something he struggled with at first, but now seemed to be getting more comfortable with. After *Ulpan*, each afternoon and evening he had spent a lot of time wandering around the city, getting used to the transport system, but most of the time just walking the streets, having meals in the coffee shops, restaurants and pubs that Tel Aviv was plentifully supplied with.

He'd discovered an Irish pub – *Molly Bloom's*, on Mendele Street, one block east of Tel Aviv beach – that he knew Devlin would enjoy. They had great food, plenty of lively Irish music and even professional Irish dancers. To his great surprise, when he enquired, he discovered that there wasn't a single Irish person among them; they were all native Israelis – or *sabras*, as those born in Israel were known.

These were also great places to meet Israelis and talk – for most were only too willing to talk – especially about Israel. Everyone he met had an opinion on Israel, the government, American policy. He was often reminded of the old saying, 'Where you have two Jews, you'll get three opinions.' He heard every shade of political attitude from *Peace Now* advocates – 'two states for two peoples' – to one right wing settler supporter who insisted, 'the only good Palestinian is a dead one!'

Nevertheless, he was surprised at the general lack of hatred towards Arabs and at the total admixture of the two peoples in their daily life. On the beaches – especially in Jaffa – he discovered Israeli girls, scantily clad in bikinis, mixing with Muslim Arab women, covered in black, or dark blue, from head to foot – all happily splashing in the sea, or lying or sitting in the hot sun.

The choice of food was unbelievable – all the typical foods from the Middle East; falafel, shawarma, tabouleh, bourekas, shaksouka, etc., plus food from all the nations the Jews had made aliyah from – Yemenite, Greek, Italian, eastern European, Indian, Chinese, south American, Turkish – the list was endless. It would have been possible to eat in a different type of restaurant every night for weeks on end!

Eventually, Shaul decided he needed to limit his food consumption or he was seriously going to put on weight. His favourite was the Israeli break-fast, which would keep you going for most of the day – with an omelette, or other kinds of egg, plus salad with feta cheese, assorted dips and spices and freshly made bread – different in every restaurant or coffee shop. The sweet iced coffee that was sold on every street was a great thirst quencher, too.

Most days he would head to the beach immediately *Ulpan* finished – either in Tel Aviv, or further south in Jaffa, or Holon. He was invited to join in handball games, soccer, tennis, and made several acquaintances among the locals. The women were unbelievable – both Jews and Arabs – though it was obvious that the Jewish girls dressed leaving much less to the imagination. So far, though, he had not embarked on any relationship.

Many of the young people – both male and female – were wearing Army uniform, and these he often cultivated, asking them about their experience in the IDF. Most were only too willing to talk to him, and when he revealed his own background in the US Forces in Afghanistan, the conversations lengthened. Most encouraged him to push for military service sooner, rather than later – he didn't need to start with the IDF for a year at least. They emphasised the unique bond that IDF service gave all Israelis. The quickest way to integrate into Israeli society, they said, was service in the Army.

When these young men – and women – described their training he could tell that it was pretty thorough – though it seemed much more informal than the US Army. They often called their officers by their first names, for instance, and from their descriptions there appeared to be much less verbal abuse by officers – as often depicted in movies about US Forces and also about the British Army – instead more of an 'all in this together' attitude. He also began to realise that at twenty three he was already regarded as an 'old man' in IDF terms.

After three weeks of sampling Tel Aviv/Jaffa, Shaul decided he wanted to see more of the rest of the country – starting with the north. He packed a kit bag and, armed with a spiral bound map of Israel, on Friday morning he hopped on a train to Netanya, spending a day on the beach and eating at one of the restaurants in Ha'Atzmaut (Independence) Square before retiring to the room he had booked nearby. Saturday morning he moved on to Haifa by *Sherut* taxi – there were no trains or buses on Shabbat. The *Sherut*, though, was relatively inexpensive.

From Haifa Central Station he walked towards Mount Carmel and a few blocks west to Ben Gurion Boulevard, where he had booked a room. This turned out to be at the upper end of the street, right beneath the Bahai Gardens, which loomed above the city – bright green during daylight and a vertical strip of glittering lights by night. In Haifa he found there were many more Arabs than in Tel Aviv, or even Jaffa. Many of the restaurants were Arab-owned, side by side with Jewish ones.

After breakfast in Ben Gurion Boulevard he wandered down through the centre to the huge Port of Haifa and then walked west to Bat Galim beach, where he found the Carmel cable car which travels up to Mount Carmel – even on Shabbat. When the three spherical cabins arrived he joined a small group of tourists – who turned out to be from Brazil – as they crossed above the freeway below and ascended about halfway up the mountain.

At the upper station there were some restaurants and a viewing point over Bat Galim beach and the *Maritime Museum*, with its ships and submarine, immediately below. A sign directed the Christian tourists to the *Stella Maris Carmelite Monastery* 100 metres further south, leaving Shaul alone to savour the view over the western part of the city, Haifa Bay and the Mediterranean. After a while he walked south past Stella Maris to visit *Elijah's Cave* – a dark rectangular cavern cut into the solid rock of Mount Carmel, which was being used as a synagogue.

After climbing back up the steps to Stella Maris he followed Tchernikovsky Street and admired the view over Haifa Bay as he walked east along it and Sderot Hatsiyonut until he reached the spectacular *Bahai Temple Gardens*, which bisected Mount Carmel from top to bottom – lighting up the whole mountain spectacularly at night.

From this point downward, steps led all the way to the foot of the mountain, while above the roadway, more steps led even higher up, while a path zig-zagged back and forth across them, leading to Yefe Nof Street and Yefe Nof Garden just beyond it. On another day he could have travelled on the Carmelit – an underground funicular railway – but today it would not be open until Shabbat ended. Instead, Shaul climbed the winding path through the upper part of the gardens and sat for a while in the shade of the mountain, watching life carry on in the busy city and port below.

From this vantage point he could see all the ships outside the bay, waiting at anchor to enter the port. Across the bay to the north were the white buildings of the ancient Crusader port and modern city of Akko, with the city of Nahariya beyond and then the ridge of the mountains of Lebanon in the far distance. To the north east the hills of Ha Galil – the Galilee – spread east-wards: forests, kibbutzim and Arab villages inter-mingled.

Immediately north of the city below him were the localities known as *Ha Kiryot* (literally 'the villages') – comprising Kiryat Yam, to the west, along-side the sea; with Kiryat Motskin and Kiryat Bialik inland of this to the east, separated by the older Highway 4 and encompassed on the east by the new

Highway 22. This, at its southern end, joined Highway 23 to the right of where he sat, then disappeared into the new tunnels underneath Mount Carmel, rejoining Highway 4 again south of the city.

Immediately below his vantage point, apartment buildings spread along the side of the hill, many of them entered by a bridge from the rear several floors up, so that tenants often took an elevator down to their apartment and up again to leave it. Shaul had never been to San Francisco, but he imagined from what he had seen so far of Haifa, that there were great similarities between the two cities.

So far today he had passed a place of Christian pilgrimage (also purported to contain an *'Elijah's Cave'* in its crypt); the Jewish cave site, complete with trappings of a synagogue, and below him the temple and world headquarters of the Bahai religion. Somewhere, no doubt, there was also a Moslem or Druze holy site also. Above, on top of the mountain, he knew there were Druze villages. It reminded him that Israel had indeed become a 'Holy Land' to several faiths.

After a short while Shaul walked east again along Yefe Nof Promenade, which eventually brought him over the crest of the mountain to Haifa's Carmel Centre, located right on the top of Mount Carmel. He found a wide choice of restaurants and takeaways here – though the Jewish ones were closed for Shabbat. He chose one that was open in a shaded side street off Sderot HaNassi, where he could sit outside and eat shawarma and fries accompanied by an iced coffee.

When he finished his meal he asked for, *'Ha kheshbon, va ka sha?'* (the bill, please?), trying out one of his new Hebrew phrases. As he paid he enquired if the waiter spoke *Anglit* – English, which he did – and so he enquired where to get a *Sherut* that would take him further west towards Haifa's celebrated Ha Technion Institute – Israel's oldest university. Then he crossed the main road and waited for one which took him most of the way – walking to complete his journey.

By the time he reached *Technion City* – as it was known – the sun had moved around Mount Carmel to the west, lighting the city below with a golden glow and illuminating the Eshkol Tower of the *University of Haifa* high above him to the south. He'd read that the city proposed to build a cable car from the bus terminal far below, to *HaTechnion* and finishing at *Haifa University* above – a distance of more than four kilometres. The project had been launched several years ago, but lack of finances had held it up for several years. Apparently, work on the $200M project was now beginning.

Inland to his right he could make out among the forested hills a number of towns, kibbutzim and Arab villages. South of the hills was spread out the wide plain of the Valley of Jezreel, with the distinct circular shape of Kibbutz Nahalal in the distance – once home to the famous one-eyed general,

Moshe Dayan – with the criss-crossed runways of the Ramat David military airbase just south of it resulting in an almost 'skull and crossbones' effect.

At length he found another *Sherut* which took him back to Carmel Centre. He then entered the Carmelit Gan Ha'em station – now open again after Shabbat – and took the short underground funicular trip down to Paris Square, close to the Central Railway Station. He still had his kitbag with him so all he needed was a good meal and then he could take the train back to Tel Aviv. He found a suitable Italian restaurant between Paris Square and the station and spent a leisurely hour there filling up with pasta and Italian ice cream.

When he entered the station and purchased a ticket he had a twenty minute wait, so he wandered around the station, reading with interest a sign describing the new railway line to Bet Shean, which was already under construction. Eventually, the new railway was intended to cross the Jordan River border on a new bridge and connect – via a proposed new Jordanian built line – to the city of Irbil, which would give the nation of Jordan access to the Mediterranean Sea for the first time in many decades.

On the train journey back to Tel Aviv Shaul reflected that Israel could indeed be the light of the Middle East – bringing modern prosperity for all – if only they wanted that more for their children than they did the destruction of Israel. The blind hatred of Hamas, Fatah, Hezbollah, ISIS, the Muslim Brotherhood, and all the others, meant that they spent most of their energies in destruction, with very little left for building a future.

Israel, on the other hand, seemed to be obsessed with building – new multi-storey office and apartment buildings, widening freeways, new railway lines – including one to Eilat, already under construction, which would join the Mediterranean to the Red Sea – a new underground light rail system in Tel Aviv, new high speed link to Jerusalem ... tower cranes and bulldozers were evident everywhere. If only the Arabs were willing to throw themselves into this building for the future, surely they could also share in the prosperity?

He had learned a lot from his many conversations with Israelis. Everyone had a different angle on 'the situation', but the consensus was always that the Israelis were quite willing to live in peace with their Arab neighbours, if only they would give up their age-old hatred.

On the subject of 'land for peace' and a 'Palestinian state' he found that the majority of Israelis no longer believed that those policies had any future. One young man described it this way, 'We keep giving and giving, making concessions, and they keep on inciting their people to murder us.

'How can we have peace negotiations with people who believe Israel has no right to exist – who have convinced themselves that we do not belong here, that we are really Europeans? Do you realise that over fifty per cent of Israelis – even today – are of Middle Eastern and North African origin. Of course we belong here!'

For his next trip Shaul took a day off from *Ulpan* and on Thursday morning boarded a coach to the city of Tiberias, on the shore of the Sea of Galilee, with its distinctive black basalt rock buildings, Crusader walls, forts and towers, old mosques and Christian pilgrimage hostels and monasteries. During the day he swam in the Sea of Galilee, then took a boat trip out into the sea. Across the sea he could see the brown hills of the Golan Heights – the biblical territory of Bashan – in Joshua's day the home of the tribe of Manasseh.

At night Tiberias came alive, with constantly flowing traffic, many brightly lit and busy restaurants, and young people everywhere. Across the now darkened sea – lit here and there by noisy disco boats – strings of lights twinkled both along the bottom of the Golan at the opposite edge of the sea, and along the top – the Druze villages.

In the morning Shaul took another bus – this time along the length of the Jordan Valley as far as the Dead Sea, then up the steep mountain road to Jerusalem. Along the valley he only caught a brief glimpse of water as the Jordan wandered back and forth, usually only obvious by the trees growing on its banks. On the other side was the Hashemite Kingdom of Jordan.

Why 'Hashem-ite', he wondered. *HaShem* was a distinctive Jewish word, meaning 'The Name' – a reverent way of referring to the God of Israel, YHVH. He knew Hashem was often found as an Arab surname, in fact he had passed a shop in Haifa belonging to a Khalil Hashem. Were those Arabs really lost Jews, not understanding they actually had a Jewish name?

The bus passed through an IDF checkpoint and entered the territory the Palestinian Authority wanted as part of their state – although, for obvious security regions, the Jordan Valley was still controlled by Israel – except for the town of Jericho, which existed in an island world of its own at the lowest point on earth. Jericho seemed to have no riots, no suicide bombers – maybe because geography cut them off from the rest of the 'West Bank'.

On the way to Jericho the bus passed quite a few kibbutzim – islands of green, usually the dark green of date palms, with their huge bunches of ripening fruit, other times with a sea of light green banana trees, with their large fronds waving in any breeze – again with huge bunches of fruit ripening.

At last the shimmering gleam of the Dead Sea appeared, and the road swung towards the Jordan border as it circumnavigated Jericho. They left Highway 90 – which continued along the western shore of the Dead Sea to Ein Gedi, Arad and, eventually, Eilat and the Red Sea. The road passed a number of Arab establishments selling – among other things – huge Ali Baba-type terracotta jars. Outside one of these a very bored-looking camel, with worn through knees, was tethered closely to a steel spike.

The road now entered the wilderness of Judaea and ascended via a number of bends the 4,000 feet to bring it to Jerusalem. The hills on either side were either a blinding white, or cream colour. There was little sign of life or cultivation – except for the occasional huddled group of Bedouin tents, surrounded by sheep and goats, sometimes camels, and piles of scrap cars, etc.

As the bus ground its way up the hills they passed a large sign which announced that they had now reached Sea Level. It really brought home to Shaul just how low down Jericho and the Dead Sea were – something like 1,300 feet below sea level.

As they drew nearer to the city every now and then a sign appeared directing traffic to a settlement, where modern apartments overlooked the bare white of the wilderness. They came to a huge one – Maale Adumim – and then the road became a highway and Jerusalem appeared ahead – the Mount of Olives on the left and Mount Scopus further north.

The road swung north around these hills and then entered the city, which consisted of even more hills, now congested with narrow streets full of bustling people of every type of dress. Many of the Jews were just as sun-scorched as the Arabs – the only difference being the amount of bare skin exposed to view.

In the case of the Arabs it was only the face of the older men beneath a *kaffiyeh*, the bare arms beneath a T-shirt of younger men. With the Jews it was often just a tank top, though the Orthodox were also distinct in their hats and long black coats, with pale white faces.

The Arab women were fully covered, usually with the niqab scarf covering their hair – now and again a full black or dark blue burka. Orthodox Jewish women would also wear a scarf, with formal dress, but most ordinary Israeli women wore jeans or in the case of the younger ones, short skirts, with skimpy tops, showing off their olive skin.

The traffic was often at a standstill – especially as they passed the Mahane Yehuda market, where throngs of people crossed the street heedlessly, despite the traffic. At last the bus arrived at Jerusalem Central Bus Station – which appeared to be anything but central, being a mile or two from the modern city centre and even further from the Old City.

Next to it work was going on rapidly on building the new *HaUma Railway Station*, eighty metres underground, to which the new high-speed railway line would arrive from Tel Aviv and Ben Gurion Airport. It was now almost ready – awaiting only the completion of the new station.

The new electric line would make its way through 37 kilometres of tunnels – one burrowing underneath the West Bank at Latrun – and over six kilometres of bridges. Eventually, the line would continue on to Mamilla, next to the Old City and from there eventually link up to *Malha Station*, in the south of the city, and currently the only railway station in Jerusalem.

Shaul had already spotted the new *Light Rail* train as they had come past Mahane Yehuda, so outside Central Bus Station he crossed the street, bought a 10-journey ticket and waited for the next train. He hopped on and scanned his ticket in front of the little grey box at the door, for the two mile journey to Zion Square. He would really have to start thinking in terms of kilometres. They didn't have miles in Israel so, three kilometres.

By the time he reached Zion Square it was only an hour or two to sunset and the beginning of Shabbat, so he wandered up Ben Yehuda Street until he found a restaurant still open. There he stopped for a shawarma with fries, eating it at a table out in the street in the sunshine and washing it down with a *Maccabi* beer. Later he would explore what he could of this intriguing ancient city.

8 – Lady in Kabul

Ali had a four day R&R pass, as did the other members of his squad. He arrived at his uncle Yousef's home in the north of Kabul, for once dressed in civilian dress – a clean white shirt with a tie and dark trousers.

Military battledress would NOT be appropriate here, though most of his family were reasonably happy with his employment with the Afghan National Army – the ANA, as their American colleagues referred to it. Jobs were pretty scarce in Kabul these days, so a position in the ANA provided regular, though sometimes dangerous, employment and the salary was not to be sniffed at.

Although Kabul is a huge city of over four million, it is really a collection of neighbourhoods, or villages. As Ali paid off his taxi and entered the small street where his uncle lived, he had to skirt around a crowd of young boys playing football – some of their fathers watching them carefully from nearby doorways. Life in Kabul was as near to normal as it had ever been in Afghanistan, but security was still not something that anyone took for granted.

The gathering at Ali's uncle's home was a typical Afghani social occasion. The house was already full of people – both male and female. His uncle and his family greeted him enthusiastically in the traditional manner. Ali answered their questions about his well-being and he in turn asked how they all were. When they had covered all the usual topics they encouraged him to partake of the tables laden with local food and non-alcoholic drinks. He moved towards the food, carefully observing all the people in the room as he went.

In one corner was a young lady in a green dress, whom he had never seen before – he would certainly have remembered. She appeared to be of average height, a slim figure, with an oval face and beautiful long dark hair like a silken veil. He quickly filled a plate with a selection of food and grabbed a drink of freshly made minted lemonade and looked around for his cousin, Elina, so she could introduce him to this interesting stranger. As he waited for his cousin to finish her conversation he noticed the young lady in question glancing shyly in his direction.

Aha, he thought to himself, *a spark of interest there, too, maybe – and what beautiful eyes!* His interest was quickened.

His cousin finished her sentence to her friend and turned to him with a smile, 'Ali, how are you? How's life in the Army?'

'I'm fine,' he replied, 'and so's the Army. I wondered if you might introduce me to the young lady over there in the corner?' As they both looked in that direction the beautiful eyes focussed on him again enquiringly.

'Why certainly, Ali, it will be my pleasure. Khaista is a friend of mine from work,' she responded, leading him towards the corner of the room.

'Khaista, I'd like you to meet my cousin, Khan Ali Yusufzai, a brave soldier in our Afghan National Army,' she began.

'Salaam alekum. I'm very pleased to meet you,' she said in a deep strong voice.

'Ali, this is Khaista Afridi, who works with me in the local government offices.'

'Alekum salaam,' said Ali, 'and I am also very pleased to meet you.'

Khaista turned her full gaze on him as Elina introduced them. Her eyes were indeed mesmerising, magnified by the kohl she used to enhance their effect. Ali already felt himself coming under their spell. Elina nodded to them both and drifted circumspectly away.

'Elina tells me that you work with her in the government offices. Do you find that interesting?' Ali asked, as he sat down on an empty chair next to her. He could detect her perfume, a sweet sharp fragrance.

'It's not that exciting,' Khaista replied, 'but it does bring in a reasonable salary. I'm also studying part time at *Da Kābul Pohantūn* –the University of Kabul.'

'Oh really?' replied Ali. 'That's interesting. What course are you taking?'

'I'm doing a part-time course in Software Engineering at the *Faculty of Computer Science.* It is connected to my job with the government, so when I graduate I hope to receive a promotion. We have a lot of contact with the *University of Maryland,* in the USA.'

'Very good,' said Ali. 'I can see you are a career-minded woman. How do you find contact with the Americans?'

'Very enjoyable,' she replied. 'We have one class each week where we work together with colleagues in Maryland via the internet. I enjoy talking to them and learning a little bit about their life in America.'

Chapter 8 – Lady in Kabul

'I'm with the ISAF forces – the *International Security Assistance Force* – so I'm with Americans every day on patrol around Kabul,' Ali added. 'Our lives are often in each other's hands, so we benefit from having a good relationship. For the past two years there were three American friends in particular in the squad, that I worked with every day – Levine, Devlin and Thomas. Unfortunately, they finished their tour of duty recently and they've all returned to the United States.

'Actually, ISAF will finish at the end of the year – it's going to be replaced by something called the *Resolute Support Mission*. So now I'm working with a new bunch of Americans and I'm starting all over again.'

'Tell me more about those friends. What were they like?' Khaista asked, her deep brown eyes focussing fully on him again.

'Well, Lieutenant Shaul Levine is Jewish, from New York City. He led our platoon. His family are well off business people in New York. His brother is qualified as a lawyer and handles the family business for his father, who is getting older and leaves things more and more in his son's hands.

'Shaul was a bit of a rebel. He said he wasn't interested in running the family business – that's why he joined the army. He was a pretty good commander – thought of his men first and foremost. He was pretty upset when one day we lost a man – an ANA soldier – and two others injured, in a firefight with the Taliban.'

'Goodness,' she exclaimed, 'you must live a very dangerous life.'

'It has its moments, sometimes,' said Ali, 'but most of it is routine. We often talk to local leaders and hear their complaints. I usually translate for the Americans – although some of the previous squad were picking up a bit of the Dari language.'

'What about your other two friends? What were they like?' she enquired.

'Devlin – Micky – was from Boston. He's Irish American, a big guy, Roman Catholic – dark hair and blue eyes. His family apparently own a bar in the Boston area – I guess it must be an Irish bar. Brandon Thomas was a black American from North Carolina. He was our driver and he knew a lot about vehicles, being a professional mechanic. He was hoping to start work with a friend who has a garage business in North Carolina, when he got back home.

'Brandon is a little bit older than the others. He's been married for a few years and has a young son and daughter, which he talked about quite a lot. He's also a Pentecostal Christian – a sort of Protestant denomination – which I found very interesting. He was really into studying the Bible and he seemed to know a lot about the history of the Jews and Israelite tribes. He already knew a lot of the history about the Pashtuns – he knew I was from the tribe of Yousef, for instance.'

'Yes, and I am also, from the tribe of Ephraim – Afridi,' she replied. 'I also find our Pashtun history very interesting. This Brandon must have been a very exciting comrade to be with every day? And Levine – you actually worked every day with a Jewish guy!'

'Brandon *is* interesting. He seems to know more about Jews and Judaism than Shaul does, although I could see Shaul's interest growing as he listened to Brandon's talks about Bible prophecy and coming war in the Middle East.'

'Bible prophecy? I find that a fascinating subject. The *Tawrat* is meant to be one of the holy books of Islam, but most Muslims have never read it. Or the prophets, either. Have you ever read it, Ali?'

'No, but I did find it interesting listening to Brandon. The guys made fun of him, called him 'Doubtin'' – you know, like doubting Thomas in the Gospel – the *Injil*? But he never seemed to mind all our stupid questions. He seemed to come more alive when he talked about the Bible, which made what he had to say all the more fascinating.

'The last conversation we had – the same day we lost Shinwari and had two guys wounded – he was talking about the future destruction of America – or Babylon, as he referred to it. He also referred to a coming nuclear war between Israel and the surrounding nations, including Iran – he calls it the Six Hour War.

'He believes that when that war is over Israel will miraculously be the victor and their enemies will be scattered over the whole world. That is when he believes the *Bani Israel* – the so-called 'lost' ten tribes – will be gathered in to the holy land of Israel.

'Pashtuns from here and from Pakistan, Kashmiris, the Menashe tribe from eastern India and Myanmar, Igbo from Nigeria, in Africa – and other African tribes. Brandon is of Igbo background himself – apparently it's pronounced 'Eeboo', a corruption of the word, 'Hebrew'. A lot of black Americans have Igbo roots – their ancestors were enslaved by Muslim tribes who hated them. I guess that's where Brandon first developed the interest in Bible prophecy.'

'Wow! That was a fascinating guy to be working with. What do you think of all these ideas of his, then?'

'Well, actually, I'm quite intrigued by them. Like yourself – and many other Pashtuns, I'm sure – I've always been aware of our background, of being from the tribes of Israel. There is apparently a Pashtun guy, another Aafreedi – from Malahabad, India, of all places, with a doctorate in Jewish Studies – who has been studying our history in an Indian university and has also studied in Israel. And apparently another Indian doctor is testing DNA samples from Indian Pashtuns at Haifa Technion, in Israel.'

'Is this guy a Muslim, or what?' asked Khaista.

'Not sure,' said Ali, 'I looked up his website and, though he is of Muslim background, he doesn't appear to practice any religion, though he does believe in God.'

'It must have been really intriguing, working with a Jew, a Catholic and a Pentecostal Christian who studies the Bible – and yourself, a Muslim! Was it a bit confusing, or what?' she said.

'Well, the other two guys didn't seem to know much about their respective religions – compared to Brandon, anyway. He really seemed to take the Bible literally. I guess Dev and Sol believe in God – as do I, of course – but we don't really centre our lives around it, as Thomas seemed to.'

Khaista sighed, 'It would be nice to have that amount of conviction. I suppose it's that kind of certainty that motivates the Taliban and others.'

'Yes,' said Ali, 'they are certainly motivated to keep on fighting us, that's for sure! Anyway, if you are interested, give me your email address and I will send you the links to the Aafreedi guy's website.'

'OK,' said Khaista, raising her beautiful eyes to look at him, 'that will also mean you can easily get in touch with *me* again, won't it?' as she wrote out her email address on a slip of paper, handing it to him.

'Would you like me to keep in touch with you, then?' asked Ali.

'Yes,' she said, 'I think so – if you want to, that is?' her eyes were again pulling him under her spell.

'I certainly want to,' said Ali, 'You are a very beautiful woman, Khaista – with a beautiful name, also. You also seem very perceptive. Perhaps we could meet up for a meal when I'm next off duty – maybe at the University? That should be safe enough, don't you think?'

'Yes,' said Khaista, remembering the recent suicide bombing at a local restaurant that had been very popular with foreigners. 'See, I've also given you my mobile number, so we can work out a time when we are both free. I see your cousin, Elina, heading in our direction. It has been very nice talking to you, Ali.'

'I've enjoyed it very much, too, Khaista. I hope to see you soon.'

As Ali travelled home in a taxi later, he reflected on the girl he had just met. She was certainly intriguing – beautiful to look at, intelligent, animated and able to hold her own in a conversation. *And those eyes! Bismillah! Those eyes could hypnotise a man.* The more he thought about Khaista the more he looked forward to their meeting again and to getting to know more about her.

He was still on leave the next day and had emailed Khaista the link to the Pashtun website that he had promised her. He also added that he very much wanted to meet her again and to continue their interesting discussion.

While still on his PC his mobile rang and he was surprised to see it was his cousin, Elina, calling, 'Well,' she jumped in immediately, '*You* have certainly made an impression. All I've heard from Khaista all morning is questions about you. How well do I know you? What do I think of you? How long have you been in the army? What did you have for breakfast? Honestly, she has exhausted me already and it's barely lunchtime.

'You've obviously scored a big hit there, Ali. I've never seen Khaista so captivated by a man. So, if you're as interested in her as she seems to be in you, I wouldn't hang around. I'd get in touch with her ASAP – as the Americans are fond of saying – and arrange to meet her again. I don't think I'll be able to stand the suspense, otherwise.'

'OK, Elina,' Ali responded, amused by her excitement. 'Actually, I've just been emailing her – so, if she replies, I'll send her another one and see if we can arrange to meet when she's next at the University. Thanks for the call, Elina. I'm sure Khaista will keep you up to date with the news!'

'OK, Ali. *Salaam alekum!*'

'*Alekum salaam,*' Ali replied.

Hmmm, he pondered. *Seems like Khaista is interested in me, too. This could be the start of a great friendship,* he thought. He liked to repeat her name over and over, visualising her appearance. He couldn't find fault with anything about her.

If this continues, he thought, *I'm certainly gonna get a lot of heckling from the boys on the squad.* He smiled to himself, not minding that one bit.

9 – Thomastown, Ireland

After two hours of restful sleep Micky felt himself being shaken awake by Niamh. 'Wakey, wakey, there sleepy head. We're gonna eat in about twenty minutes. Thought you might want to take a shower, or whatever, before taking on the full force of the Devlins of Ireland.'

Micky rubbed his eyes and thanked her, saying, 'I'll be down shortly. I'll feel a lot better after a shower, right enough. See y'all in a few minutes.'

When she'd closed the door again he roused himself and stumbled into the shower for the next ten minutes. He dried off and dressed quickly, not wanting to keep his new-found family waiting.

When he arrived downstairs he found that he needn't have hurried. The family were sitting around in a very relaxed manner and dinner did not appear to be immediately forthcoming. 'Guess we're on Irish time, now,' he thought to himself.

The meal was eventually served and they all gathered around the table to large helpings of roast beef, with gravy and roast vegetables. 'Help yerself to the spuds, there, Michael – stretch, or starve.' Kathleen's father, Sean, told him. Michael didn't need to be told a second time.

The conversation during the meal was relaxed, with plenty of enquiries about his family back home in Boston and how they were all getting on.

'And how are ye findin' old Ireland now? This is yer first time over here, isn't it?' asked Kathleen.

'Well, I haven't seen that much of it yet, but it's a lot more modern and sophisticated than I'd expected – and very green!' he said. 'I wasn't expecting the freeways all the way from the airport. I guess I kind of expected country lanes and thatched cottages – we Americans probably have a very idealised picture of 'old Ireland'. But I'm looking forward to seeing more of the country now that I'm here,' he said. 'Niamh offered to take me into Kilkenny later on, if anyone would care to join us?'

Kathleen replied, 'I'm gonna be too busy getting last minute things organised, but I'm sure some of these guys will go with you and show you around.'

In the end, Kathleen's two brothers, his cousins James and Paul, joined him and Niamh for the trip to Kilkenny. They parked in The Parade, right in the centre of the town, beside the huge bulk of Kilkenny Castle, with an imposing Bank of Ireland on the other corner.

'Very impressive,' Micky remarked. 'How old is it, then?'

'It was built around the early 1200s,' said Paul. 'The Butler family lived there for nearly six hundred years. Then back in the sixties they decided to give it to the people – for a payment of fifty quid!'

'Seems reasonable,' Micky quipped.

'Yea, property values have certainly gone up a bit since then,' Niamh commented. 'Do you want to see the castle, then?'

'Sure,' Devlin replied with enthusiasm.

They walked up the Parade and turned left through a large arch into the grounds of the castle. Inside Micky found himself standing on a grassed court-yard, surrounded by the imposing walls of the castle on three sides, the fourth comprising a large park, which sloped away into the distance. As they wandered across the courtyard to the north wing of the castle the River Nore became visible far below.

They drifted along the river walk beside the castle until they came to John's Bridge, then turned back up Rose Inn Street towards The Parade again. Across the road there were several ancient buildings with crooked roofs, prominent among them being a pub called *Caishlean Ui Cuain*. Devlin tried haltingly to pronounce the Irish name.

'Do ye fancy a pint, then, Micky?' asked James. 'I think we've worked up a thirst by now, eh?'

'I'm in your hands, lads,' Micky replied.

Soon they were settled at the bar inside *Caishlean Ui Cuain,* with classic rock music playing through the speakers, and Dev had to decide whether he wanted a pint of *Guinness* – which he was familiar with from his father's Boston pub, of course – or to experiment with the reddish coloured Kilkenny beer. He opted for a *Guinness* this time around and the others said they'd join him.

'I've been told that the *Guinness* tastes different when brewed here in Ireland,' he said. 'I'll maybe try your Kilkenny beer another time.'

'Aye, ye'll find its creamier here – it's the Liffey water that gives it its flavour,' said Paul, turning to the approaching barman, *'A ceathair pinta beor dhu, le da thoil* (four pints of black beer, please),' he said.

'That'll be the dead rats and rubbish that does it,' Niamh suggested.

Chapter 9 – Thomastown, Ireland

Micky decided she was winding him up and said nothing. When, after a lengthy wait – *Guinness* taking longer to pour than normal beer – the four black and cream pints arrived, he supped at his appreciatively. 'Mmm, it does taste different. Much creamier, softer flavour than back home.'

'Well, ye see, we don't want to send the good stuff outside of Ireland, so we sell the 'export' variety to yous Yanks, and keep the best for ourselves.' James explained.

'Right,' Micky smiled. 'Cheers, lads.'

'Slainte! (health)' James, Paul and Niamh replied in chorus.

They chatted amiably about Ireland and Boston for a while and Dev offered to buy another round, but James held his hand up to him, 'Yer money's no good, here,' he said. 'We're buyin' – but mebbe we should wander up to Kyteler's, eh?' he turned to his brother and Niamh enquiringly.

'Aye, why not? See a bit more of the town,' said Niamh.

They drank up and headed out of the bar, turning left into High Street and crossing to the other side. As they wandered up the hill they passed under a series of arches of a large old building which jutted out over most of the width of the footpath.

'This is *The Tholsel,*' Niamh announced. 'It's the Town Hall these days, but it used to be a Customs House, a courthouse, a guild hall and a place for collecting tolls. It dates back to the 1580s, or so.'

'That's pretty old,' Micky replied, impressed.

'Well, Kilkenny is a medieval town, so all these buildings are pretty old,' Paul explained. 'Kyteler's Inn – where we're heading – dates back to the thirteenth century.

'The lady who first owned it, Alice de Kyteler, had a bit of a reputation. She married four times and ended up with quite a fortune, but then people got jealous of her and accused her of witchcraft. I think they suspected her of doing away with some of her husbands. Anyway, she was sentenced to be burned as a witch.'

By this time they were at the arched entrance of a large grey stone building, which turned out to be the Kyteler's in question.

'Sentenced?' Devlin queried.

'Yep, she had plenty of good connections, who slipped her out of the country before they could actually carry out the execution, Paul replied. 'Although her maid was not so lucky – she was tortured and burned as a witch.'

'Whew,' Micky said, 'Quite a story.'

'Well, thank God times have changed,' Niamh remarked as they entered the archway. 'C'mon, I see a table free.' She skipped across the crowded bar and secured a table that had just become vacant as a group of Japanese tourists left the building. In the corner a group of traditional musicians were just getting ready to play.

As they sat down at the table, James remarked, 'I see we're gonna have a bit a' traditional music. More culture for ye, Michael.'

'Sounds good to me,' Devlin replied.

The musicians – two fiddlers, a guitarist, tin whistle and a bodhran player – began a set of jigs, while James struggled to the bar for another round. When he had received his order, Paul joined him and helped him carry the glasses back through the growing crowd. They sipped their pints and began to enjoy the music.

The music and the *Guinness* seemed to send Devlin into a very relaxed state of mind – aided by his jet lag, no doubt. His mind drifted with the music to an Ireland long ago of green hills, brown bogs and purple mountains.

The set of several jigs came to an end and the audience clapped their appreciation. There was a sound of shushing around the bar and then a girl with beautiful clear voice began to sing a 'slow air' – a haunting, melancholy lament for her lost love. Devlin mused, *I could easily get used to this kind of an evening.* He glanced across the table and caught Niamh's eye, watching him with interest. Something stirred in him as their eyes locked.

The beautiful song came to an end and the audience clapped and cheered their enthusiasm for the singer.

Niamh's face took on an amused look, 'Enjoying the session, then, are ye?' she asked.

'Yes, indeed,' he nodded, holding her gaze and having almost to shout to be heard. 'I like Irish music and these guys are really good, aren't they?'

'They are,' she agreed. 'I think they play here regularly.' The conversation was ordinary, but Micky felt an extraordinary effect from Niamh's eyes focussed on him. He wondered if she was experiencing the same thing. She certainly seemed to be giving him all of her attention.

It was 1 a.m. when the music stopped. 'I reckon we'd better get back to Thomastown, now. We've a wedding tomorrow,' said Niamh.

The boys nodded and Micky remained silent, in a contemplative mood, as they left the bar and headed down the street to Niamh's car. Paul stumbled as they crossed the street.

'Just as well I've only had the one pint, isn't it, or we might never make it to this wedding,' Niamh commented.

Chapter 9 – Thomastown, Ireland

'Aye, you're the designated driver tonight,' Niamh, said James.

As she drove out of Kilkenny towards Thomastown Michael looked back at the two brothers in the back seat.

'Dead to the world,' he said to Niamh, nodding over his shoulder.

She smiled meaningfully at him, then fixed her eyes on the road again.

Michael wondered how he should respond to this girl who was beginning to intrigue him. He wished she weren't the one driving tonight.

Niamh rested her hand briefly on the gear lever. Instinctively, Micky reached over and rested his hand upon hers, looking into her face at the same time. He felt something like an electric shock at the contact and gripped her hand gently. She smiled at him again, before returning her eyes to the road, leaving her hand in his.

They continued in a charged silence for several miles. Then, as they entered Thomastown, she had to change gear to negotiate the town centre and the contact was broken. Soon Niamh pulled the car up in front of Kathleen's house. It took a few minutes to waken the sleeping beauties in the rear, who eventually stumbled out of the car and into the house, making loud shushing sounds to each other as they went.

Niamh locked the car in the drive and came around the front of it towards Michael.

'Thank you for a lovely evening,' he said quietly. 'I really enjoyed that.'

Niamh smiled gently at him then turned towards the doorway. Michael followed her through the door and she closed it quietly behind him. They were only inches from one another. Michael reached for her hand and held it as she turned towards him, 'Welcome to Ireland, Michael Devlin,' she whispered.

He pulled her firmly towards him, placing his other hand behind her head, and kissed her gently. She gave a little moan and, letting go of his hand, reached both arms around his neck. He placed his now free hand around her back in a strong embrace, while kissing her more seriously now.

They continued in this clinch for several minutes. Eventually they separated a little and she gazed up into his eyes, 'Well, Mr. Devlin. That was interesting!'

'You're a beautiful girl, Niamh O'Leary. I could really get used to this!'

'Me too,' she murmured, pulling him into another long kiss.

As they separated slightly again for air, he held her close, holding her gaze.

'I'm sorry, but I'll have to get some sleep before this wedding gets going in a few hours,' she whispered.

'Of course,' he said, releasing her slightly. She took his hand and moved towards the stairs. Outside his room they embraced and kissed again, hungry for more of one another. Then she looked into his eyes and said, 'Goodnight, Michael. See you tomorrow,' and slipped down the hallway to her own room.

Micky soon fell into a deep dream-filled sleep, dominated by tantalising visions of the beautiful Niamh O'Leary.

10 – Jerusalem

Shaul had finally arrived in the capital of Israel, Jerusalem – a city dating back thousands of years into history, and a capital not recognised as such by nearly all of the other countries of the world – including, in practice, the United States, who still refused to move their embassy from Tel Aviv.

Shaul could sense a different atmosphere here from his travels so far in Tel Aviv and the Galilee. Maybe it was because of the publicity about recent events in the city, where Jews – some of them American citizens – had been driven over, stabbed and attacked in other ways – at *Light Rail* stops, in synagogues, at bus stops, etc.

He had found a reasonably cheap hotel a little west of Zion Square and wandered out to take a look at the city. Zion Square, he discovered, bordered the southern side of Jaffa Road – once the busiest road in Jerusalem, but now an entirely pedestrian zone as far as the eye could see in either direction.

The *Light Rail* trains were normally the only vehicle to be seen among all the pedestrians, but even they were absent now that the sun had set and Shabbat had begun. The *Light Rail*, he now knew, travelled from the extreme south west of the city – entirely Jewish – through the centre and along the north side of the Old City walls, ending up in the north east of the city, which contained both Jewish and Arab residential areas.

Shaul wandered from Zion Square down Yo'el Moshe Salomon Street, then wandered back up the parallel street, taking in all the little bistros, pubs, book and art shops, all closed now – until he found himself back at Zion Square.

He continued to wander uphill, eventually meeting King George V Street, where he turned left as far as the Great Synagogue, then walked back north as far as Jaffa Road again. He walked on down Jaffa Road, past City Hall Square – fronted by a virtual forest of palm trees – then turned left around the impressive structure of the Notre Dame Hospice, opposite the north west corner of the *Old City*.

He remembered reading that this had been the front line with Jordan during the nineteen years of their occupation and annexation of what Jordan began to call the 'West Bank' – an annexation recognised only by the United Kingdom and Pakistan. In 1967, during the Six Day War, many Israeli soldiers died here in their attempt to reach the besieged Hadassah Hospital and the Hebrew University on Mount Scopus.

Eventually, of course, they had succeeded in reaching Lion's Gate, on the east side of the Old City – the Jordanian troops having disappeared during the night. Every Israeli now had a mental picture of the three young paratroopers on the Temple Mount and Motta Gur's now famous announcement, 'The Temple Mount is in our hands.'

Thus began the whole dispute over Israel's control of Judaea and Samaria – the 'West Bank' as Jordan had christened it and as the whole world now knew it – conveniently forgetting that this had been the Israelite homeland for thousands of years. Apparently, as Prime Minister Netanyahu had recently commented, the horrible Jews were now 'occupying' Judaea – how despicable!

He could see the western ramparts of the *Old City* now lit up by the afternoon sun, before he walked on downhill past New Gate, along the city walls towards Damascus Gate – the main entrance to the *Old City*. He looked around the area, which seemed to be filled with what he took to be Arabs – certainly many were wearing kaffiyehs – before strolling down the steps towards the ancient portal that was Damascus Gate.

The steps were thronged with Arab sellers of all kinds of merchandise – an impromptu market. As he squeezed his way through the throng of people coming and going through the towering zigzag gate, he entered the *Old City*, with the aroma of sweets, spices and fresh bread filling his senses.

Here you could buy almost anything – from clothes, to leather goods, to T-shirts, to tourist souvenirs. As he meandered slowly through the thronged and shady narrow streets he passed mosques, churches, yeshivas and synagogues.

Flowing towards him as he ascended a street to the right came a motley crowd of tourists – American, European, Asian, African, South American; swarthy Arabs in Moslem dress; pale-faced Orthodox Jews in long black coats and black hats, or *kippot*, their faces framed by ringlets, groups of Christian pilgrims of different nationalities, carrying crosses and singing hymns; IDF soldiers in uniform. It seemed as if the whole world was represented in this small space.

Every now and then he, and the other pedestrians, had to move quickly aside to avoid being run over by the regular traffic of miniature tractors, pulling trailers loaded with anything from fruit, to sacks of grain, loaves of bread, or empty cardboard boxes. Every few feet the limestone-paved street stepped up or down, with a series of pairs of ramps – one stone sloping from step to step at each side, to facilitate the exact wheel span of these small tractors.

Many of the stall holders tried to entice him to stop and look at their merchandise, offering cups of tea, bargain prices or having 'something very important' to tell him. After a bit of this he kept his eyes focussed always ahead, appearing not to hear their calls, or those of small boys who continually tagged along offering to 'be your guide'.

Shaul did not need a guide – he simply wanted to breathe in the whole atmosphere of this incredible place. At one point he had turned left and then downhill again and now found himself crossing a narrow main street and entering a wide covered street, with a roof towering above – the Khan. Here were yet more shops – selling spices, fruit, shoes, watches, jewellery ... To the right he spied the entrance to a Turkish bath.

At the end of this street steep steps led up to a large gateway, with only one half of the large wooden doors open, through which he could see bright daylight. As he climbed the steps he was confronted by an Israeli policeman, who held his hand up to Shaul, explaining that only Muslims were allowed through the gate at this time.

'*Beseder*', Shaul nodded, but continued to look through the gateway.

Ahead he could see broad steps, leading up to the huge plaza of the Temple Mount. To the left he could see the magnificent golden dome and the light blue ceramic tiled walls of the *Dome of the Rock* mosque, while to the right he could see an area where Arabs queued up to wash their hands and feet at a series of basins and water taps.

He thanked the policeman and turned back through the Khan to the main street where this time he turned left, following a sign which said, 'Western Wall Tunnel'. As he approached the tunnel he had to queue to be thoroughly searched by more police personnel, before being allowed to pass down the tunnel.

On the right was a stairway which seemed to lead into the bowels of the earth. As he leaned on the wall to look down he could see ancient columns descending into the darkness. A sign said, '3,500 years of Jewish history'. He read a little about the ancient Hasmoneans and other civilisations, which apparently dated back to 3,500 BCE. For the past 3,000 years, apparently, this city had been the capital – actual, or spiritual – of the Jewish people. It really brought home to Shaul the real antiquity of the Jewish presence in this land.

According to his army buddy, Brandon Thomas, the Arabs had only begun to call themselves 'Palestinians' after Israel conquered this *Old City* and the so-called 'West Bank' in the *Six Day War* of 1967. For nineteen years before that they'd had the opportunity to claim a separate state, but instead were quite happy to simply call themselves Arabs, south Syrians, Jordanians, etc. As Shaul gazed down into the depths of history represented by this archaeological excavation, he realised how false was the comparison between the claims of Israel and the Arabs.

King David lived here more than 3,000 years ago! Joshua ruled here more than 350 years before that!

Shaul continued past another security check and entered the huge plaza of the *Kotel*, the Western Wall. It sloped to his left down to the wall itself, where many Orthodox Jews were bobbing – davening – as they prayed. Many of those praying, he noticed, were not in any religious garb – apart maybe from wearing a kippa. Further along, beyond a low barrier, was the women's area.

He turned to the left and approached the wall – subject of the prayers of Jews the world over for centuries, his father included. Leaning his right hand against these ancient stones, he prayed briefly for peace in this land and for direction for himself.

The plaza was partly filled with groups of yeshiva students, the usual tourists with cameras, groups of young soldiers ... To the right the modern apartment buildings of the re-built Jewish Quarter towered over the plaza. Ahead, on the south side, was the main entrance, with heavy security and, beyond the gates, many tourist coaches.

As he wandered into the centre of the plaza he could see the black dome of the *Al Aqsa Mosque* above the wall to his right, with the golden *Dome of the Rock* visible again on his left. He began the climb up towards the Jewish Quarter, passing modern apartments and a beautiful, secluded garden tucked in between the buildings.

As he wandered the narrow modern streets he noticed a sign and followed it. It brought him to a stepped square, at the upper side of which was a large cylindrical clear glass enclosure, with a domed glass roof, which contained the huge Golden Menorah. Made of solid gold, and constructed by the *Temple Institute* ready to install in the new Third Temple, it was more than six feet high – two metres, Shaul corrected himself – and an accompanying sign said that it contained 43 kg (95lbs) of 24 carat gold.

Wonder how much that's worth? Shaul pondered. *At $2,000 an ounce, that's ... wow! $3 million!* Not that anyone was going to be able to steal it – *How could they carry it away?*

The Jewish quarter was relatively quiet and secluded, but as he reached the Cardo area it became quite busy again. He entered a kind of square, with a small pizza restaurant across the street – closed for Shabbat, of course. Ahead were steps leading down into the old Roman ruins of the original Cardo – the Roman version of a shopping mall.

Chapter 10 – Jerusalem

He could see that the original Roman shops – some carved out of the bedrock at their rear – had led off either side of a wide main thoroughfare, supported by stone columns and paved in well polished stone slabs, from the centuries of feet treading on them. To the right, the Cardo continued underground, with the three narrow souks of small shops – selling, meat, fish, bread, spices and many other goods – running parallel above.

The Cardo contained many upmarket art shops, Judaica stores, boutiques, jewellery stores, even a bank. It had also contained the Golden Menorah until a few years ago, when it had been moved to its new location at the edge of the Kotel, closer to the Temple Mount.

From the Jewish Quarter Shaul wandered north, crossing David Street into the Christian Quarter, where he followed the tunnel that was Christian Quarter Street, with many small shops – including a falafel stand – where he decided to try the famous Middle Eastern veggie sandwich.

The proprietor put a couple of the deep fried hummus balls into a newly warmed pita and smiled at him as he pointed to the various options – salad, olives, sauerkraut, tahini, yoghurt and other sauces – for inclusion in his falafel. Shaul made his choices, thanked him – *shukran*, in Arabic – paid what seemed a very modest price and wandered on, munching as he went. *Must remember this is the best place for falafel in Jerusalem.*

He took a left towards the courtyard leading to the Church of the Holy Sepulchre and entered the building. He found it quite an alien place, crowded, dark and smelling of incense, with many different Christian priests – each leading a group of pilgrims, each in the distinctive garb of his own denomination.

He left there and headed towards Jaffa Gate, where traffic entered through the gap in the wall – made more than a century before, for the German Kaiser Wilhelm, when he visited in 1898. Beside the gate was the Citadel of David, a stone fortress on the city wall.

He turned left past the Citadel, a police station and the Bank Leumi, following the traffic. This was apparently the Armenian Quarter and he noticed posters about the Armenian genocide of 1915, during the First World War. Apparently, many of those who survived forced marches into the Syrian desert had made it to Jerusalem and lived there still.

Shaul continued out through the pedestrian part of the gate which, like all the gates of the Old City, did a zigzag – *so no attacking enemy could shoot straight through it*, Shaul supposed.

Outside was a plaza with various stalls, leading across a bridge to the Mamilla Mall – a long straight modern street, with restaurants and high class stores all the way along. It led him back to the centre of the city, back along Jaffa Street to Zion Square.

He retired to his hotel and rested for a while from all the up and down-hill walking. Tomorrow he had an appointment on the Mount of Olives – not the safest part of Jerusalem these days – to bury his parents ashes.

Later on, after dark, he went out into the city again. The square was busy with people heading out to eat, shops open. Shaul found a restaurant with a kind of greenhouse attached to an old stone building – between Ben Yehuda Street and Jaffa Street – and ordered a chicken schnitzel with sweet potato ravioli for his evening meal, washed down with a couple of bottles of *Maccabi* beer.

In Ben Yehuda Street and Zion Square musicians of all ages were playing everything from klezmer to classical music. Most people were dressed up for the after-Shabbat evening. At the table next to him four Orthodox men were talking loudly in distinct New York accents.

Tomorrow his official reason for being here would be accomplished. He needed to decide what his future would be. Sure, he could wander around Israel some more – like a tourist, or a bum – but he really wanted to feel that he belonged in this country – not just a visitor. The best way to do that was to make a commitment to the country – to join the IDF. The only problem was would his Hebrew be good enough yet?

When he had buried his parents ashes tomorrow, he would check out the Aliyah Office and see if he could move things forward a bit.

Next afternoon Shaul took the *Light Rail* to Damascus Gate. That was as close as it went to the Mount of Olives, so he found an Arab *Sherut* and travelled with several other passengers going the same way – it only cost him two shekels, about fifty cents. He met with the Cemetery representative, who showed him to the tomb booked by his father many years ago.

As they made their way across the hillside covered in graves, the man from the Cemetery explained that the site had been divided into Sephardi and Ashkenazi areas, and that the Askenazi area had since been divided again into two separate areas. *Hmm, even in death we want to be separate,* he thought.

They arrived at his parents tomb, where the stone lid had already been moved to one side. Shaul placed the two urns into the tomb and prayed briefly. The official nodded to an Arab workman, who then replaced the heavy stone lid. Shaul waited until he had finished and then placed a small stone on top of the lid – as Jews traditionally did, unlike the Christian tradition of placing flowers.

Then he retraced his steps back to the top of the hill, where a Bedouin man with a very scruffy-looking camel was offering rides to any tourists who might appear. Shaul – still moved by the burial – shook his head without speaking and continued towards the square outside the *Seven Arches Hotel*, ignoring the persistent calls of the Bedouin, who'd been hoping for another customer in Shaul.

A number of *Sheruts* were lined up at the side of the square. Shaul spoke through the window of one – a Volkswagen pickup truck, with a rear seat – asking how much to Damascus Gate. The driver didn't appear to speak English, but a younger man, around eighteen, seated beside him, answered, 'Two shekels,' and opened the door gesturing for Shaul to get in.

Shaul, checking that this man was not going to up the price down the road, asked the driver, 'Two shekels?'

'*Na'am*,' he replied (Yes).

'Two shekels,' Shaul insisted, 'Not three shekels, or more, *beseder*?'

'*Na'am, na'am*,' the driver replied.

The young man assured him there would be no problem and Shaul got into the front bench seat beside him.

A couple of hundred metres from the square the taxi pulled in and another Arab man got into the back seat. The taxi drove north along the hill, then made the steep descent into the Valley of Kidron and up again towards the north east corner of the Old City. When it came level with Herod's Gate it pulled in and the Arab passenger got out.

A few minutes later the vehicle pulled up outside Damascus Gate. The street was already dark and the sparsely placed streetlights did little to illumine the gloom. The driver looked at Shaul and said, 'Twenty shekel!'

'*La, la, la*,' exclaimed Shaul. 'Two shekels.'

'Twenty shekel,' the driver insisted.

The young man intervened, 'You give him twenty shekel, or he scare you,' he added, unhelpfully.

Shaul looked around him. The area seemed to be peopled only with Arab locals. There was no longer a sign of any tourists, and certainly no Israeli police. He didn't like to be made a fool of, like some gullible American tourist. On the other hand he imagined this – a totally Moslem area – was not the ideal place to pick a fight.

The young man called to another Arab, who had been lounging against a wall nearby. It turned out he spoke good English.

Shaul explained to this man that he had agreed to pay the driver only two shekels at the start of the journey. He added that he didn't mind paying four shekels, as there had only been one other passenger, but that he was not going to keep escalating the price.

The stranger spoke to the driver and told Shaul to give him four shekels – only a dollar, in fact, but the amount was not really the point.

'Four shekels?' Shaul checked.

'Four shekel,' the driver agreed.

'Not four shekels, then six, eight, ten, la?' Shaul insisted.

The driver appeared to agree.

Shaul handed him four shekels, whereupon the driver began asking for more once again. At this point Shaul had had enough of this type of negotiation. *I'm probably going to get beaten up by a crowd of these guys*, he thought to himself.

Even so, he opened the passenger door and jumped out of the Volkswagen. The driver opened his door and jumped out also. They faced each other in front of the vehicle where, surprisingly, the driver's face suddenly broke into a grin and he reached out to shake Shaul by the hand. Surprised, Shaul shook his hand, grinning back and then walked off towards the *Light Rail* stop with a great sense of relief.

Obviously, it had been a test and, apparently, Shaul had passed. Something to bear in mind in any future dealings with the Arabs.

11 – Raleigh, North Carolina

Brandon had been home and out of the Army for two months now. The job promised by his friend, Joshua Williams – Josh – had amazingly become a reality. In fact, the garage business was doing so well that Josh was talking about maybe needing to take on an apprentice, though he reckoned that might really stretch the cash flow for a while.

They might also need to invest in some new equipment. He tended to talk business matters over with Brandon these days on a fairly regular basis and to treat him as almost an equal in the business. Eventually, after a long discussion with Alyssa, Brandon brought up the subject that had been on his mind for some time.

'Listen, Josh,' he began, 'Feel free to say no, but please hear me out first. We've got a good little earner here and I agree it might be time to expand, but that is gonna take a hefty injection of cash in extra equipment and wages for an apprentice.

'Now, I've got my Army Separation Pay coming through and I've been discussing this with Alyssa. First, I'm hoping to mebbe travel to Africa in the near future – a visit to Nigeria, and we've also decided to put some money into a retirement plan. But that will still leave me with several thousand dollars left over after I pay all the taxes – around $45,000. The question is, would you be interested in me becoming a full partner in the garage – if I'm prepared to invest that in the business?'

'Wow!' said Josh. 'That's certainly an interesting proposal. It could be a great idea. Listen, let me think about it for a couple of days – talk it over with the wife and play around with the figures a bit. I'll let you know as soon as I've made up my mind. OK?'

'Sure,' said Brandon, 'Take your time, man. We don't want to rush into anything until we're both sure about it. By all means discuss it with Shirelle – she knows the figures best from doing the accounts.'

Brandon went back to work underneath the truck he was repairing.

A couple of days later Josh arrived for work and found Brandon waiting for him to open up. 'Well, Brandon,' he said, 'I think this will work. Shirelle and I have discussed it up and down and we think this is the best way forward. We're gonna accept your offer. We'll get a lawyer to draw up an official agreement and when we sign that we'll be partners. Welcome to the business, Brandon!' He held out his hand and Brandon gripped it, ending up in a hug.

'Thanks, man,' Brandon replied. 'I really appreciate it, Josh.'

'No way, man,' Josh responded, 'your partnership offer means we can really go places. We need to sit down – maybe this evening, if you're free? – and discuss exactly what equipment we need and what money we should spend on this expansion. '

'OK,' said Brandon, 'sounds good to me. Now, we better get some work done. This is gonna mean a lot of hard work for both of us. I've had a few ideas about how we might want to organise things in the future. We can discuss that tonight, too.'

'Sure thing man,' Josh began to whistle as he bent over the engine of the Ford pickup he was servicing.

Later, Brandon swung his car into their driveway with a squeal of brakes. He jumped out and ran into the house, calling Alyssa's name.

'Where's the fire, Brandon?' she called out.

'Listen, woman,' he answered, 'Josh has agreed to our proposal. Whaddya think of that, then?'

'About the partnership? That's great, Brandon. Praise the Lord! That's a real answer to prayer,' she said.

'Yeah, I reckon it is,' Brandon replied.

'Sit down now and tell me all about it from the start,' she ordered.

'OK, OK!' Brandon laughed.

12 – Kabul University

Ali and Khaista had arranged to meet at a restaurant within the campus of Kabul University. Arranging a get together in any public venue in Kabul these days was fraught with difficulty. A Greek restaurant, which had become popular with both locals and ex-pats, had just recently been blown up by a suicide bomber and people were understandably cautious. The University, though obviously less romantic, was a fairly safe option, by comparison.

Khaista, wearing tight faded jeans, brightly coloured green and white trainers and a snug fitting knitted woollen top in white, was already waiting at a table when Ali arrived. 'Hi, there,' they both said at the same time, then laughed nervously.

'I must say, you are looking very cool, Khaista,' said Ali as he sat down opposite her.

'Thank you, sir,' she replied, with a twinkle in her eye. 'You are looking more informal today, I see.'

'Yes,' said Ali. 'Do you think I would fit in as a student, then?'

'Hmmm, possibly,' she said. 'Shall we order some food? I've been working hard all morning and I'm just about starving now.'

'Sure,' said Ali, 'it's my treat, though.'

They walked over to the counter and selected their food, which Ali paid for, then carried it back to their table.

'Are you enjoying your course, Khaista?' Ali asked.

'Yes, I've been working on a project this morning, which involved a lot of research and investigation. Then I managed to get some of that research down into written form. So, a reasonably productive time. What have you been up to?'

'I was looking up that website again that I emailed you the link to, the one by the Indian Pashtun guy – Aafredi? There is some interesting material there. Did you get a chance to look at it yourself, yet?'

'I had a brief look, but I didn't do any in-depth study of it yet. It certainly looks very interesting. I never realised that there was a Pashtun community based in India. You always tend to think of India as a Hindu country, don't you?'

'Yeah, well it is, of course, but India is actually the world's third largest Muslim country, also, with nearly 11% of the world's Muslim population – almost as many as the whole of Pakistan, and about six times the population of Afghanistan.'

'Wow, that really puts it in perspective, doesn't it. I suppose then it's no big deal to have a few thousand Pashtuns living there?'

'A few thousand? There are nearly as many Pashtuns in India as there are here in Afghanistan! More than eleven million in India, and just under thirteen million here, with nearly thirty million in Pakistan.'

'So, if what your friend, Brandon, and others, think – that we are descendants of Israel, that would make over fifty million Israelites in this part of the world.'

'More than that, actually. The Kashmiris also claim Israelite ancestry,. there are about six million of them. And the Tribe of Menashe, in India and Myanmar, would add another four million, or so. So that would make another ten million – about sixty three million Israelites!'

'Sixty three million! – that's nearly ten times the population of the State of Israel. I mean, how many actual Jews are there in the world?'

'I think it's around fifteen million, or so.' said Ali. 'and then there are all the Israelite tribes in Africa, too. There are somewhere between twenty eight and forty million Igbo in Nigeria alone. Then there are Lemba, Tutsi, and other tribes – could be another fifty million, altogether.'

'So, if all these Israelite tribes got together in one place, including the Jews there'd be ...'

'... around 125, or 130 million people,' said Ali.

'That's incredible,' she said. 'But do you think it would ever happen?'

'I don't know,' said Ali, 'but people like Brandon believe that the Bible prophesies that this will happen. He says there are more than two thousand of the Menashe – from the tribe of Manasseh – already living and working in Israel, serving in the Israeli Defence Forces.'

'Well, if we're both from the tribe of Yusuf, maybe we should be looking into these things?'

'I've been thinking that myself, recently. And there must be others who are interested in finding this stuff out – maybe right here in Kabul. We should make some discreet inquiries.'

'What about Christians? Do you know of any, here?'

'You mean Afghani Christians, I suppose? There are probably quite a few Americans and others in the expatriate community.'

'Yes, I wonder if there are any Afghani ones?' she replied.

'If there are, I'll bet they keep a very low profile,' said Ali. 'But we don't need to find Christians to study the prophecies in the Bible. We should be able to find something on the internet.'

'Let's take a look,' said Khaista, taking out her mobile phone. After a few minutes silence while she typed into her phone browser, she looked up again and said, 'Yes, there are several Bible apps – one in Dari, one in Pashto, one in Hasaragi ... the Pashto one, I think.'

'Yes,' said Ali, taking out his own phone.

'The books are listed under *Injil* and *Tawrat*,' she said. 'Oh no!'

'What is it?' said Ali.

'How many books should there be in the *Tawrat*?' she asked.

'I'm not sure,' said Ali, 'quite a few according to what I've heard from Brandon.

'Well, there are only six available in the Pashto version, plus ... twenty seven in the *Injil*.'

'Hmm, well it's the Tawrat that we're interested in as far as prophecy is concerned and I think there should be more to it than six books. Let's check the Dari version.'

'Yes,' she said a minute later, ' a lot more – maybe thirty, or forty.'

'That sounds more like it,' said Ali. 'Looks like we'll have to stick to the Dari version, then. At least it is available. Actually, there is a free download for Android devices. I think I'll download it later.'

'OK, and I will too. But we don't really know where to look among all these books, do we,' she asked.

'No, I suppose not,' said Ali, 'but I could probably email Brandon and ask him for some advice on where to read.'

'Good idea,' she replied. 'Now, what had you planned to do this afternoon? Are you free for an hour or so?'

'Yes, what do you have in mind,' he asked.

'It's a protest, organised by the Hadia organisation, which some of my friends belong to. It's called, *"Light a candle for Mah Gul"* – in Shahr-e Nau Park,' she said. 'It's to support women who have been beaten, raped or murdered in the last year. Mah Gul was a young woman of twenty, from Herat, who refused to be forced into prostitution by her mother in law.

'She was tortured and had her head cut off and the protest is to ask why the government don't do anything about these things. Violence like this has become far too common – something needs to change. You don't have to come with me,' she added.

'No, I'd like to,' said Ali. 'I've heard about Mah Gul and I don't agree with violence against women. I think if you are a real man you will not strike, or in any way abuse, a woman.'

'Great! I'm glad you think that. I hoped you'd be happy to come. But we'd better get a move on. It starts in less than an hour and it's a good walk from here.'

They collected their trays and left them back – Ali musing to himself that he was quite happy to go anywhere as long as Khaista was going with him.

'By the way,' said Khaista, 'Thank you for buying me lunch.'

'My pleasure,' Ali replied. 'Wasn't there a young woman hung quite recently over something quite trivial?'

'Yes,' said Khaista, as they hurried across the University campus. 'That's why they're having this protest – to try to get the government to do something to stop this from happening. If they do nothing, then these sort of men will be encouraged to keep on treating women in this way.'

Khaista produced a *niqab* from her bag and tied it carefully around her hair and they headed towards the rear entrance of the University and along Mazar e Sakhi Road, down a long winding road to Salang Wat Road, through a side street to Ahmad Zaher Road, then right into Zargona Road, on which the park was situated – quite near to where several government buildings were located – including the one where Khaista worked when she wasn't studying.

'We sometimes come up here to have our lunch – your cousin Elina and others from work,' said Khaista, removing the scarf from her head as they entered the park.

'I watched a documentary just recently,' she added, 'about an English woman called Emily Pankhurst, back in 1905. Women in England were fighting for the right to vote, equality and other rights. People thought they were crazy. The media made fun of them, but those women kept on fighting for their rights and they didn't give up. Eventually, the law was changed and women were given the vote. That's why I wanted to be here, today. If we don't give up we can eventually change things here, too.'

They arrived in time to hear a young woman – one of Khaista's friends, apparently – give a short speech about women and men working together to bring about a peaceful country – instead of killing women, encouraging them to get an education and to be able to contribute to Afghan society.

Chapter 12 – Kabul University

After the speech each of the young people participating lit a candle and placed it on a stone slab, while a young man sang a lament. Ali joined the others in lighting and placing a candle. The crowd was small and many present were bemused onlookers who just happened to be visiting the park.

After chatting a little to some of her friends, Khaista returned to Ali. 'I'm sorry,' she said, 'it's been great seeing you again and chatting, but I've got to get back to the University now to do some work. My friend, Haleema, is here in her car and has offered me a lift back.' She raised her eyebrow at Ali.

'No problem,' replied Ali, 'I was wondering if you might be free tomorrow evening?'

'I could be. What have you got in mind?'

'Well, there's a poetry evening on downtown – in the centre. I could pick you up in a taxi, if you'd like to go?'

'I'd love to. I never figured you as a poetry guy. You're a real man of surprises, Ali. I'll text you my address. What time do you want me to be ready for?'

'Say seven o'clock?' replied Ali. 'Meantime, I think I'll head home and download that Bible in Dari. By the way, I've remembered that one of the books that Brandon was reading was the prophet Ezekiel. So that might be a place to start reading. I'll look forward to meeting you again tomorrow evening, Khaista. *Salaam alekum.*'

'Me too, Ali. *Alekum salaam.*'

Ali headed towards the business district at the centre of Kabul, looking out for a taxi to take him home and whistling to himself as he went.

In Six Hours ... the world changed – *Raymond McCullough*

13 – Wedding in Kilkenny, Ireland

Devlin woke in time to hear the rush of feet up and down the stairs and doors opening and closing – last minute wedding preparations, he presumed. He hurriedly showered and dressed in his suit for the occasion. The boys – Paul and James – joined him at the breakfast table and later gave him a lift to the church in Kilkenny. Niamh, apparently, was completely tied up in the preparation of his cousin, Kathleen, for her 'big day'. Anyway, she'd be travelling in the hired car.

He sat halfway down the congregation – which was not in what he thought of as a church building, being used to a traditional Roman Catholic setup. This reminded him more of a restaurant, or a hotel reception room. The room was large, modern and tastefully decorated – with light woods predominating.

For the wedding it had been enhanced with large bunches of flowers strategically placed around the room and on either side of the low platform at the front. The bridegroom – Damien – was seated on the front row and looked around expectantly every now and then, waiting for his fiancée to appear. The music playing in the background was different from what Dev was used to in the Catholic Church back home – it sounded like light rock, with a Christian theme.

As the music faded and then changed to Procul Harem's *'Whiter Shade of Pale'*, Micky looked around and saw the bride appear at the doorway, her hand on his Uncle Sean's arm. As they proceeded slowly towards the front of the room, his eyes were fixed on one of the bridesmaids following behind. Niamh, like her two companions, was dressed in a shimmering emerald green dress, and Dev was transfixed. She truly looked beautiful.

The service progressed and Dev joined in the lively songs, half listened to the couple giving their vows and the pastor – a bearded young man in a light coloured suit and blue shirt – sharing his thoughts on the meaning of marriage. But his attention was mainly diverted to Niamh, sitting in the front row. At one point she turned around and looked at him and a smile filled her countenance. Micky smiled back.

Meanwhile, the pastor was saying something about love not being just a nice feeling, but the realisation that this was the one person that you wanted to spend the rest of your life with. As Dev meditated on that thought he realised that was exactly how he felt about Niamh. Should he blurt that out to her – he thought not. She might run a mile and he couldn't take the risk of losing her now that he had found her.

He would have to try and take it slowly for her sake – after all, they had only met for the first time less than twenty four hours ago. But suddenly Devlin was sure this was the woman for him. *Will I be able to persuade her to come over to Boston to spend a week or two with me?* he wondered.

The young pastor was now talking about love being a sacrifice – all about giving and not about what you could get. As Dev looked around the congregation he realised that many of them were his own age and younger and that the pastor was trying to give them guidance for their own relationships.

He was summing up now, comparing the husband/wife relationship with that of Christ – or, the Messiah, as the pastor referred to Him – and the church, his bride. He added that any marriage would be all the stronger if it was a 'three-fold cord', with the Messiah, Yeshua, included in the relationship.

His reference to Yeshua reminded Dev of his mate from Afghanistan, Brandon Thomas. He wondered if Brandon went to a church something like this. Maybe he should check it out himself, after all it couldn't do him any harm – and Niamh seemed kinda interested in it all, too. He wondered if it might come up in conversation with her.

The congregation stood for the final song – another lively one with a catchy tune. *Maybe the Catholic Church should add in a few songs like this,* he pondered – not realising that many of them already had – *They might keep more of their parishioners if they did.*

The bride and groom began their journey down the centre of the room, followed by Niamh and her fellow bridesmaids. Niamh gave him a cool searching look and a slight smile. He wondered what she was thinking and if, maybe, she might feel the same way about him as he had discovered he was feeling about her.

Dev got a lift to the reception – in the Newpark Hotel, just on the Dublin side of Kilkenny – with James and Paul, and the three of them headed for the bar with several others and soon had a pint each in hand, while the wedding party wandered around the grounds with a photographer giving them orders.

At the reception he was seated with his cousins and other members of the Devlin family, who chatted away to one other, bringing him into their conversation at intervals. When a response was not required he meditated on this new experience – of caring for someone and hoping that they cared for him in the same way. The whole thing seemed kind of unreal, but still a pleasant experience. He wondered if part of it was just being in a different country, a new situation – though it seemed completely different from his first experience of Afghanistan.

After the meal – and a series of serious and not-so-serious speeches – the floor was cleared and dance music began to play. The bride and groom took the floor first and then the others began to join in. Dev made his way over to where Niamh was sitting and asked her to dance. She smiled sweetly up at him and said, 'Of course!' as she rose to take his hand.

Again Dev experienced that electric spark as they touched and, the first dance being a slow one, a sense of fire burning as he held Naimh close to him. She seemed to melt into him and they drifted around the room as one. The spell was broken when the DJ suddenly began to play a lively pop song and, with a look of mutual agreement they drifted away to a seating area away from the other guests.

'I expect I'll be dragged back in in a few minutes,' Niamh said. 'I hope you enjoyed the wedding.'

'Yes,' said Micky, 'It was different from what I'd expected, but I did enjoy it. The pastor seemed very young, but he said some good stuff.'

'You're used to the normal Catholic service?' she asked. 'Took you by surprise that your cousin had become an evangelical, eh?'

'Yeah, the 'born agains', as you called them yesterday.' said Micky. 'I found it very interesting – reminded me of a pal of mine I met in Afghanistan, Brandon Thomas.'

'Oh yeah?' she queried, 'How come?'

'Well, Brandon's a black guy – one of our team out there – from North Carolina. I guess you'd call him a Pentecostal, although I'm not too well up on all the terminology. Anyway, he was always reading his Bible any chance he'd get. We used to call him 'Doubtin'' – y'know, 'doubtin' Thomas?'

'Yeah, I get it. Did he talk to you guys about his faith, then?'

'Oh, yes, he sure did. We had some very interesting conversations out there. Brandon had a way of making the Bible seem like he was reading from tomorrow's newspaper, y'know what I mean?' Dev asked.

'Oh yes, I know what you mean. Darragh – the pastor – he talks like that, too. He makes it really come alive, like.'

'So, you've been to hear him a few times, then, have you?' Micky asked.

'Quite a few, yes. I've been learning a lot from him. He makes complicated things sound simple, which really helps.'

'So, are you planning to join his church, then, Niamh?'

'I'm not sure yet. I've seen a big change in Kathleen and her new husband, Damien, since they became believers – and in several others. They all seem to be contented, y'know? They seem to be able to be happy without having to do anything special to achieve it. Peaceful, y'know? It makes me kinda jealous.'

'So, you believe there is something real there? Is that it?'

'Yes, I guess so. What do you think of it all?'

'Me?' Dev said, 'I don't know. I enjoyed listening to Brandon, y'know? But we were a strange mixture. Brandon has Igbo roots – y'know from black Nigerians, who came originally from Israel, he says? Then there was our team leader, Shaul Levine – Solly. He was a Jew from New York.

'And then there was Ali – Khan Ali Yusufzai. He was a Pashtun ANA soldier – from the Afghanistan National Army? Apparently the Pashtuns are also of Israelite descent. So, out of the four of us, I was the only one who didn't have some Israelite connection.'

'Wow! That was an interesting mix, indeed. Darragh talks about the Jews and Israel and stuff a lot, too – y'know all to do with the 'end times' 'n' all that?'

'Well, it can be pretty fascinating stuff, actually. Here we are talking about it at a wedding, after all,' he laughed. 'I got more and more intrigued by Brandon's talks. He's a really sincere guy, y'know? Someone you would stake your life on when you're out on patrol with him?'

'I guess being in a war zone means you get to have friends you can really trust, eh?'

'Yes, indeed,' Dev replied, 'I trusted all those guys with my life, literally. And here I am to prove it!

'Brandon talked a lot about the 'last days', as he called them. About Israel being surrounded by enemies and those enemies trying to destroy them once and for all. He believes a nuclear war will come in the Middle East, but that Israel will miraculously survive it and that their enemies will flee from them and they will end up with control of a large part of the Middle East – like Lebanon, Syria and most of Jordan? Anyway, we kind of made a pact that when, and if, that happens we will all meet up again in Jerusalem.'

'Hey! That's kind of interesting – exciting, even.' Niamh added. 'It's giving me goosebumps just listening to you say it! You should definitely have a chat with Darragh while you're here. He loves all this prophecy stuff, too. It's intriguing, isn't it?'

'Yes, I think so. I mean, at the moment I'm just a nominal kinda Catholic – I believe in God, but I haven't committed myself to anything more than that.'

'And do you think that you will, sometime?' Niamh asked, looking at him.

'Maybe,' he said, 'What about you? Do you see yourself becoming a 'born again'?'

'Another maybe, I suppose,' she said, 'I'm still mulling it over. It would be nice to have that certainty in your life, I think.'

'I know what you mean,' Dev replied. 'When you're in a life-or-death situation these kind of things really come home to you. I did a lot of thinking over what Brandon was saying out in Afghanistan. I guess I just haven't had the guts yet to make up my mind one way or the other.'

'Yeah,' she sighed.

'Y'know what?' said Micky. 'I've never talked to anyone about this stuff before – not even to Brandon. You're really easy to talk to, you know that?'

'So are you,' Niamh whispered. 'I've not really talked to anyone about it, either. You're really easy to talk to, too.'

For a while they just looked at one another, then Dev said, 'How about we go for a walk outside? Someone is bound to interrupt us here any minute now.'

'OK, just out around the grounds. People will panic if we disappear completely. I can't abandon Kathleen on her wedding day, y'know.'

'Sure, I know. she's my cousin, too,' he said. 'But I do enjoy talking to you. Let's disappear for just a short while.'

Dev took Niamh by the hand and they headed out the rear exit of the hotel into the grounds and soon found themselves under a tree, with a grassy wooded area stretching away from them beyond the fence.

'Y'know, every time I touch you I feel I'm in danger of getting electrocuted from the spark,' he said.

Niamh just looked up at him. He pulled her close and kissed her fervently.

'That's better,' she said softly. 'I felt a bit of a spark, too, y'know.'

'I only met you yesterday, but I feel as if I've known you for ever,' he said huskily.

'I know what you mean,' said Niamh. 'It's kinda weird.'

'I'm really glad now that Kathy sent you to pick me up. Coming to Ireland has been a great idea, so far.'

'It can only get better, then,' said Niamh, looking at him cheekily.

'Too right,' he said and kissed her again, fiercely.

When they parted for breath, he held onto her tightly. 'I was thinking about you all through the ceremony,' he said.

'Oh yeah?' she said softly, 'Well, I was thinking about you, too. You're a bit of a distraction, really, Michael Devlin!'

'Speak for yourself, Niamh O'Leary!' he retorted. 'You're a very attractive woman, y'know!'

Niamh smiled.

'Anyway, we were having a serious conversation a minute ago. Weren't we?' he asked.

'Yes, we were – before you, er, distracted me!' said Niamh mischievously.

'What we were talking about, I'm really glad to be able to share it with you. I don't know but it seems significant that we are able to have a conversation about something as serious. Does that make any sense?' Micky asked.

'Yes, I think so.' said Niamh. 'I've been thinking about these things for a while, but I haven't felt ready to talk to Darragh, or even Kathy, about them – and yet I *can* talk to you, whom I only met yesterday. What does that say, eh?'

'I don't know what it says, but it does say something – something significant, to use your phrase.'

'Niamh! Niamh! There you are! I've been looking all over for you guys. Kathy's wondering where on earth you both are.' It was Niamh's fellow bridesmaid, Siobhan.

Niamh and Dev moved apart a little. 'Hi Siobhan, we just stepped out for some fresh air and a bit of a chat,' Niamh answered.

'I suppose we'd better go back in,' said Dev.

'Definitely,' said Siobhan, 'Unless you want Kathy to have a heart attack, that is! What were you two so eager to talk about then?' she asked.

'Oh, this and that,' Niamh replied vaguely.

'Looked like less of this and a lot more of that to me, Niamh O'Leary!' she exclaimed.

'Aye, well, there you are now,' Niamh replied with a smirk, leaving Dev wondering exactly what she was talking about.

During the rest of the evening Dev danced with Niamh, Siobhan and their friend, Criostal, the third bridesmaid – and chatted with them and with Kathy's two brothers, James and Paul, and his uncle Sean and aunt Mary. There was no further opportunity for Michael and Niamh to be alone together.

When the time came for the newly-weds to depart for their honey–moon – they were spending the night in an hotel in Dublin and flying off to Portugal in the morning – Niamh was ready with the others for the tradition of the bride throwing her bouquet. Niamh leapt high and grasped the bunch of flowers, catching Micky's eye when she had done so, and then blushing.

The evening wound to a close and eventually a fairly inebriated bunch of well-wishers departed from the Newpark Hotel in a series of taxis – Paul and James wisely leaving their car in the car park to be collected the next day. When they arrived back at the house Micky and Niamh managed a quick goodnight kiss and cuddle before yielding to exhaustion – his from ongoing jet-lag, hers from the excitement of the wedding preparations – and retiring to their separate rooms.

In Six Hours ... the world changed – *Raymond McCullough*

14 – Email from an Oleh

Hi bro,

I'm still in Israel and you'll be pleased to know that our parents ashes are now safely buried on the Mount of Olives, as Dad requested.

While I was in Jerusalem I finally decided to make aliyah – I'm now officially an Oleh – a new Israeli citizen – with papers to prove it! I'm beginning to feel really part of this country, now – although learning Hebrew has been quite a struggle.

The other news is I've asked them to speed up my recruitment into the IDF. Officially, at my advanced age (haha) I only need to do six months duty in the Army, but I've asked for placement in a combat regiment, which means I'll automatically do a two year tour of duty.

But I'm quite happy with that. You're not really a full part of this country unless you've done your time in the IDF. It's like people back home asking you what college you went to, y'know?

Anyway, that was a few weeks ago and I still haven't heard anything.

Hope you and the family are all doing well.

L'hitraot (see you)

Your brother,

Sol.

* * *

Hi there, Shaul,

Thanks for letting me know about the ashes. I've had Mom and Dad's apartment on the market for several months now and recently there's been some interest.

Otherwise, there's nothing much of news to tell you. Leah and the kids are doing well and business is business – always something more to deal with.

I'm glad you're enjoying your time in Israel, though I would have thought that maybe by now you would have got that out of your system. I don't know what kind of future you think you can expect in Israel – compared to back here at home in a civilised country, where we have everything we need.

It looks like it's going to take longer than I thought for you to learn that.

Anyway, I wish you all the best.

My G-d continue to look after you.

Your brother,

Reuben

15 – American Igbo Jews

Now that his family had some financial security, Brandon had begun more seriously to research his Igbo origins. He had read several books about the Igbo of Nigeria – especially those who called themselves Igbo Jews. And recently, a New Yorker called Jeff Lieberman had produced a documentary about the Igbo Jews in Nigeria, called *Re-Emerging: The Jews of Nigeria*. Brandon discovered that you could buy the DVD online and had managed to get a copy of it.

He found, also, that there was quite an Igbo organisation in the United States. There was an *Igbo Union, Atlanta* – which was just over four hundred miles from Raleigh – a six hour trip. He talked to Alyssa about maybe taking a trip across to Atlanta.

'Sure, honey,' said Alyssa. 'But I don't see the point in the whole family going. The kids would be a pain on such a long journey. and what am I gonna do while you're at some meeting – babysit? No. You go on your own some weekend and we'll be fine here at home where the kids have plenty of things to do and friends to play with.'

So, a few weeks later Brandon set off after lunch one Friday, heading west on Interstate 40 as far as Hillsborough, then taking Interstate 85 through Greensboro, then Charlotte, into Georgia – *'The Peach State,'* as the sign proclaimed – and then all the way to Atlanta. He arrived just after eight o'clock in the evening, found the cheap motel he had booked and checked in.

The motel also had a dining room, but Brandon preferred to check out Atlanta's restaurants for something to his taste. He didn't fancy sushi, or any-thing particularly exotic, and eventually found what he wanted in a steak house called *Bones*. He had himself a leisurely meal with a soda and then found the venue for tomorrow's meeting of the *Igbo Union, Atlanta*. Then he went back to his motel and phoned Alyssa to say he'd arrived safely and had eaten.

Before retiring he got out his Bible and read for a while. Then he prayed, 'Lord, I really want to meet up with some Igbo people who are interested in this whole tribe of Israel thing. Please direct me to spend my time wisely tomorrow – to meet the right people. Give me a divine appointment or two. Thank you, Jesus.'

He undressed then and went to bed.

Next morning, after dressing casually, but neat, and after a good breakfast in the motel dining room, he packed up, checked out and drove to the *Igbo Union* venue. He was about thirty minutes early for the gathering, but there were already quite a few people milling about.

They all greeted him enthusiastically, asking him, 'Where you from, bro.' and giving him enthusiastic hugs. It reminded him of the welcome at his own church on a Sunday. When he replied that he'd driven over from Raleigh they were suitably impressed.

'And you've never been to an *Igbo Union* gathering before?'

'Nope. First time,' he said.

'So, what brought you all the way over here from Raleigh, North Carolina, bro?' one of them asked him.

'Well,' said Brandon, taking a breath and plunging in, 'I'm an Igbo and a Pentecostal/Messianic believer and I know that, in Nigeria, there are several thousand Igbo Jews. So, I hoped I might come across some Igbo Jews in the USA. I guess I'm probably a little bit crazy to think that, eh?'

'Oh no, you're not "a little bit crazy", you're a big bit crazy ...' began one of the guys who had welcomed him, 'Only kidding you,' he added.

'My name is Leo, by the way – Leo Okembe. We might be able to introduce you to some of those people. I don't think any of them are here right now, but if they turn up later we'll be sure to introduce you to them.'

'Well, that would be right decent of you,' replied Brandon. 'I sure would appreciate that.'

'But in the meantime, the Igbo women have been preparing all this food and then later we're gonna have some speeches and some dancing – all a celebration of the Igbo culture. I take it you have never been to Nigeria, Brandon?'

'No, not yet,' said Brandon, 'but one day – very soon – I'm hoping to go there.'

'That's great,' said his new-found friend, Leo, who then led him over to one side of the hall, where tables full of various kinds of food had been laid out – with Igbo women bringing more food out.

'This here's a friend of mine, Brandon,' Leo introduced him, 'Come all the way over from Raleigh, North Carolina.'

'Well you're right welcome, Brandon,' one of the women replied, 'Just you help yourself, there,' she told him, smiling broadly, 'It's all authentic Igbo food.'

Brandon thanked her and selected several items from the groaning tables. Many of the food items were based on sweet potatoes – or yams, as they called them in Africa – apparently the staple diet in Nigeria. Brandon enjoyed the selection of food and then sat down on a chair as the celebration began in earnest.

There were a number of talks on Nigeria, from Nigerian Igbos – on current affairs there, the government, economy, etc. There were also talks on business methods and ways of promoting Igbo culture and prosperity within the United States. Brandon learned that there were probably around four million Igbo in the Americas.

When the talks finished there were various demonstrations of Igbo culture – some of which Brandon found pagan and rather strange to a Pentecostal. He did enjoy the dancing and the colourful costumes of the various dancers. As the formal events came to an end more food appeared and people began to mingle, eat and talk.

In the process of wandering around, Brandon discovered an organisation known as the *Council of Igbo States in Americas*, and that they were holding a *World Igbo Festival of Arts and Culture* at a place called the *Igbo Farm Village* in Staunton, Virginia, in just a couple of months.

He thought that might be something he could bring Alyssa and the kids to. After all, Staunton, VA, was only about two hundred and twenty miles north of Raleigh – a four-hour drive. He grabbed a couple of the flyers for it to take home with him.

As he did so his friend from earlier, Leo, grabbed his arm, 'There you are, Brandon, my friend. I have been looking for you. This is another friend of mine, Aaron Chidiegwu, from Virginia. He is here with a friend of his, also from Virginia, Yaakov Uzoma. They are both Igbo Jews.'

Brandon turned to see a tall, well built black man, with a full beard. His companion was smaller and slender, with a neat goatee beard. Both were wearing dress trousers and African shirts – one bright green and yellow, the other green and red.

'*Shalom aleichem,*' Brandon greeted both men, shaking their hands firmly, 'It's really great to meet you both.'

'And you, Brandon,' said Aaron, 'Are you also Jewish?'

'Not exactly, Aaron. I am Igbo, and I'm also a Messianic believer in Yeshua. I hope that doesn't create a problem for you? You see, I've been looking forward to meeting some Igbo Jews from the US. I was beginning to wonder if they only existed in Nigeria.'

'Well, there are some in America, but not as many yet as in Nigeria, where there are maybe twenty six synagogues – three in Abuja, the capital, alone. There are several thousand Igbo Jews in Nigeria.

'We have a very small group in Richmond, Virginia. We just meet together for prayers and join together to celebrate the Jewish feasts, that sort of thing. And no, we don't mind you believing in Yeshua – a lot of Igbo do. Some of our friends in Richmond might not be keen on that, but neither Yaakov nor I mind.'

'I know there are meant to be a lot of Igbo in Virginia – it's kind of Igbo Central, isn't it?' Brandon observed. 'Would you gentlemen like to get some tea, or some kind of drink and we could sit down for a minute and chat?'

'Sure,' said Yaakov, 'You two find somewhere and I'll bring the drinks over. Tea? With sugar?' he asked Brandon.

'Yes, please,' Brandon replied, heading after Aaron to a table nearby. 'I'll tell you the truth, Aaron, I'm a student of biblical prophecy. I'm interested in the end times, especially, and the role of the Ten Tribes in that. The ingathering back to Israel? Are you familiar with any of that?'

'Yes, I am,' Aaron answered, 'I find the subject quite fascinating. How long have you been interested in prophecy, Brandon?'

Yaakov arrived at this point with a tray and three cups of tea and some biscuits on a plate. He set out the cups and plate and sat down at the table with them.

'Aaron was just asking me how long I've been interested in Bible prophecy, Yaakov. I suppose since I was about eighteen, or so – so about this last seven years. I tend to read the *Tanakh* quite a bit, seeking further inspiration – you know, linking verses up that seem to say the same thing, like putting the pieces of a jigsaw puzzle together?'

'That's an interesting way to put it, Brandon,' said Yaakov.

'Well, I basically believe that *HaShem* has given us all the truth we need – it's all in there, but its kinda hidden – and He said we would find it when we search for it – and for Him – with all our heart. So, every time I read a book of the *Tanakh* I find new things coming to light, and quite often they link up with something I've read elsewhere in another book.'

'OK,' said Aaron, 'And your interest in finding Igbo Jews here in the States?'

'Well, one of those prophecies – in *Yirmeyahu* (Jeremiah) – talks about the destruction of Babylon – or mega-Babylon – and the fact that afterwards the *'sons of Judah and the sons of Israel'* will be looking for some way to get back to Zion. I have come to the conclusion that Babylon is the United States and the *'sons of Judah'* are obviously the six million regular Jews who live in America, especially in New York City. But who are the *'sons of Israel'?*

'I just learned today that there are around four million Igbo in the Americas – I'm assuming the majority of those are in the USA? So they – we – could well be the *'sons of Israel'* that *Yirmeyahu* is referring to? If so, it would be good to make the rest of the Igbo aware of such things.'

'That's quite a fascinating thought, Brandon. It's certainly worth thinking, praying and studying about. We might even invite you to come up to Richmond and share some of your ideas with us – kind of lead us in a study of some of those prophecies, eh, Yaakov? What do you think?'

'Why not, indeed?' Yaakov answered.

'Well, that's very flattering, Aaron. I'd be very interested in meeting with you guys again. Either I could come up to Richmond, or we could meet some-where around halfway?

'Tell me, do you have any contact with the aforementioned *'sons of Judah'* up there in Richmond?'

'Well, we sometimes attend one of the synagogues, but they don't really see us as 'real' Jews, you know what I mean, Brandon?'

'I certainly do. I've found the same thing in Raleigh. You're kind of a curiosity, but they don't take you seriously.'

'Exactly!' said Yaakov.

The three men talked on for some time, until Brandon glanced at his watch and said, 'Well guys, I've really enjoyed meeting you and talking about these things, but I'm driving back to Raleigh today and I don't want to arrive home in the early hours. Can I get your contact details and we can keep in touch? Are you guys on *FaceBook*, for instance?'

'Aaron is,' said Yaakov, 'I haven't gotten around to it. But we're both on email and we'll give you our cell phone numbers.'

The three men exchanged contact details and said goodbye, hugging one another. Brandon also sought out his friend, Leo, and thanked him for intro-ducing him to Aaron and Yaakov.

'All part of the *Igbo Union* ethos, Brandon. The more we Igbo interact, the better. You have a safe trip back home to Raleigh, now,' he said.

'Thanks,' said Brandon, being hugged again.

He walked out with a hand held up in farewell/thank you to the ladies and found his way out to his car. Then he drove carefully and thoughtfully back home to Raleigh. He arrived after the kids had gone to bed, but Alyssa was still waiting up for him.

In answer to her inquiry he simply replied, 'It was an interesting trip. I'll tell you all about it tomorrow. Let's go to bed.'

Alyssa didn't argue.

16 – A Day in Co. Kilkenny, Ireland

Dev, having been awake for a couple of hours during the night, finally surfaced late on the day after the wedding, thinking once again of Niamh and looking forward to spending more time with her. He had a few days still remaining of his time in Ireland and he planned, if possible, to spend most of it with Niamh, getting to know her. He realised ruefully that he was by now totally smitten with her and hoped that circumstances would be favourable to their growing relation-ship.

His aunt Mary was the only one around when he struggled downstairs after a quick shower. She greeted him and offered him breakfast, explaining that the others would probably be down before long.

'There'll be a few sore heads this morning, I reckon, after all the drink that was put away last night,' she remarked with a smile. 'How are ye feelin' yer-self, this mornin'?' she asked him.

'Not too bad, actually, Aunt Mary, I kept to the *Guinness* last night, and a few glasses of water. I kept away from the whiskey.' said Dev.

'Very wise, young man. I can't say the same for them other eedjits upstairs,' she said as a noise on the stairs heralded the arrival of his uncle Sean. 'See what I mean,' his aunt Mary remarked with a meaningful look in Sean's direction. He did indeed look the worse for wear.

'Niamh says she'll be down in a minute,' he muttered to no one in part-icular.

'I'll put something on for her breakfast then,' said Mary.

Niamh arrived looking a lot fresher and livelier than Kathy's dad. 'Mornin' all,' she chirped cheerfully.

'In tha' name a' Gawd could ye be a bit quieter, young lady,' grumbled Sean, holding his head.

'What's up there, Sean? Not got a hangover have we?'

'What on earth makes you think that?' mumbled Sean.

'What are you planning to do today, Michael? See a bit of the country?' his aunt asked.

'Well, I hope so – if Niamh is free to act as tour guide?' he said, looking in her direction.

'I might be persuaded, now,' she replied cheerfully. 'If you want I can show you around a bit?'

'Aye,' Dev pretended to deliberate, 'I don't see why not.'

'Yez're not foolin' any of us one one little bit,' Mary announced. 'I heard you two were discovered courtin' out the back of the hotel yesterday.'

Niamh went pink, but said nothing, while Micky concentrated on his breakfast.

'What's this,' Sean asked, looking surprised.

'Never you mind, old man,' said Mary, 'just love's young dream – and why not, indeed? Ye were young once yerself, if ye can remember?'

Sean wisely ignored his wife's remarks and, feeling slightly more human with half a mug of tea inside him, commented, 'I seem to remember you were pretty nifty in catching thon bouquet last night, young Niamh?'

'And what if I was?' Niamh retorted, catching Dev's eye as she spoke.

'Anyway, are you ready to go, Mr. Devlin?' she asked. 'The day's waitin'.'

'Sure thing, Niamh. Let me just grab a coat,' said Dev, swallowing the last of his coffee.

Mary watched indulgently as they headed out, 'You two enjoy yourselves, now,' she exhorted them.

'Aye, don't do anything I wouldn't do,' Sean shouted as the door closed behind them.

'Just ignore them, Michael,' Niamh urged.

'I intend to,' said Micky. 'I intend to enjoy myself today, come rain or shine.'

'Well, by the looks of it it's going to be shine,' Niamh replied.

Micky watched the green Irish countryside flash past, shimmering in the bright sunlight, as they headed out of Thomastown on a different route from yesterday – a narrow country road heading south west.

'You're very bright and cheerful, this morning, Niamh, considering the state we all were in last night,' said Dev.

'Ach sure and why shouldn't I be. What a beautiful day,' she remarked, 'It's great to be out and about to enjoy it.'

'So, where do you plan to take me, then?'

'Ah, now that's for me to know and you to find out!' she said mysteriously. 'What would you like to see?'

'I'm in your hands entirely,' said Micky. 'I'm already enjoying the beautiful countryside, not to mention the company – so anything else will be a bonus.'

'Right answer, sir.' she said, and then mystifyingly she added, 'Were you ever at the Christian Brothers?'

'I did indeed have that misfortune,' Micky replied.

'Well, the Christian Brothers, as you probably know, were founded by Edmund Rice, and they've preserved the house he grew up in. It's a two-storey thatched cottage and about three hundred years old.'

'OK, that sounds interesting – long as none of the Brothers are about, eh? I saw enough of them when I was a kid to do me a lifetime!'

As they entered the small town of Callan she turned off to the right onto the main road back to Kilkenny then, as they left the town she turned left and a few hundred yards later they turned in to the *Edmund Rice Heritage Centre*. The building was a clean white cottage with a thatched roof and a chimney in the centre.

'That's yer real English thatch, that is,' Niamh told him.

'English?'

'Yeah, they call it Norfolk Reed thatch. The old houses in Ireland used to be thatched with oat straw, which had to be repaired all the time and attracted mice and squirrels. That's why you can hardly find one now, they've nearly all fallen down – and any you *do* find were probably just built in the last dozen year for the tourist trade. This kind of thatch will last a lifetime and it doesn't attract vermin.'

'I'm learning already,' said Dev. 'You're a mine of information.'

They paid for their visit and, after a quick look at the displays at the visitor centre, went into the house itself. The centrepiece was the fireplace, with a built in oven at the side.

'Kilkenny and Carlow are the exceptional counties in Ireland – they don't have any bogland, so no peat for the peasants to burn. But there used to be a coal mine up in the hills to the west, in Coalbrook, and the poor people got the coal dust and mixed it with clay, rolled it into egg shapes, dried it and used it as fuel,' said Niamh, pointing to the examples placed on the hearth.

'Unusual,' Dev commented, admiring the antiquated furniture and fittings of the old house. 'I can see they didn't have fitted kitchens in those days.'

'Aye, and no central heating, either,' added Niamh.

As they drove away from the Rice house, Niamh turned right into Callan itself, then left into West Street and again left into Bridge Street, stopping next to a colourful red and green shop front with *Keogh's Model Bakery* in gold letters on black above. 'This is where Kathy got her wedding cake made,' Niamh explained. 'It's been going for a hundred years, or so. Thought we might pick up a snack to keep us going.'

They entered the bakery, where a heavenly aroma of newly baked bread enveloped them.

'Makes you hungry just smelling that,' Niamh remarked. 'What d'ye fancy?'

They picked out their choices, paid for them and, after also purchasing drinks in a small shop nearby, headed back to the car, which now filled with the scent of pastry.

'Where to now, driver?' Dev joked.

'Hows about an old abbey – Jerpoint Abbey, to be specific? It's pretty impressive and dates back to the twelfth century,' said Niamh. 'It's just outside Thomastown.'

'Ah, we're going in a circle,' said Dev.

'So far, yes. We can eat our buns there.'

They travelled along small country roads, at one point crossing the main Kilkenny-Waterford Road, and soon arrived at the Abbey.

'Wow!' exclaimed Micky. 'That's some place – it's huge!'

'We aim to impress,' said Niamh.

They collected their pastries and drinks and headed into the grounds of the old abbey, wandering around the extensive site.

'Look at those carvings – so much detail,' Dev remarked.

'Yeah, the monks kept themselves busy. They learned all kinds of trades, apart from copying and illustrating manuscripts – y'know like the *Book of Kells*?' said Niamh.

'I've heard of that,' said Dev. 'They were obviously very artistic.'

'They excelled in all kinds of learning and skills,' said Niamh. 'The kings of England, Scotland, Norway and other countries in Europe used to send their sons to be educated by Irish monks. That's where the whole idea of universities came from. Oxford and Cambridge were originally monasteries, too – centres of learning which developed into the universities they are today.'

'Well, I guess we owe quite a lot to the Irish, then,' said Dev. 'What do you say we find a quiet spot and eat these snacks?'

'Yeah, why not?' Niamh replied.

They found a quiet corner and sat down to eat.

'You have a lovely country, Niamh. I'm enjoying this a lot. And all the more for the beautiful company.'

'Flatterer!' replied Niamh.

'No, not at all,' Micky responded, 'I think you are really beautiful – especially in that green dress yesterday.'

'Why thank you, sir,' she replied, self-consciously.

'Seriously! It's been a revelation to me – coming to Ireland and meeting you. I just love talking to you about stuff. I feel like an explorer at the beginning of some great adventure. Everything ahead of me.'

'Ye've certainly got the Irish gift of the gab, that's for sure, Micky Devlin,' Niamh bantered.

'I might have other talents, too! Come here, Miss O'Leary,' he said, reaching for her. They kissed for a while, neither of them wanting to end the experience.

When at last they separated, Devlin remarked, 'I've been waiting for an opportunity to do that all morning.'

'Me too,' she replied, no longer playing with him.

'I didn't think that Brother Rice's house had quite the right atmosphere.'

'Mmmm,' she murmured.

After a minute he added, 'I'm really glad I met you, Niamh.'

'Yer not so bad, yerself.'

They kissed again and then began to wander around the abbey.

'You were saying yesterday that I should meet Darragh, the young pastor.'

'He's older than either of us,' replied Niamh.

'I suppose so,' said Dev, 'But he seems young to be a pastor, that's all.'

'He is very enthusiastic – about God and the Bible and stuff. He really seems to care about the young people in the church.'

'Well that's a good thing, isn't it?'

'Yes, especially in this country. The Irish people have lost their faith in the Catholic Church – after all the paedophile scandals, and so forth. The church didn't handle any of it well – tried to cover things up. So now there's a spiritual vacuum in the country. People are into all sorts of weird stuff – New Age, cults, Mormons, Hare Krishnas ...'

'Yeah, we get a lot of stuff like that in the States – especially in California,' he said.

'I think I'd like to talk to him. He sounds a bit like my friend, Brandon – and he got me interested in all this stuff in the first place. I'd like to learn a bit more about it.'

'Yeah, I know what you mean. I've learned a lot from Darragh – and also from Kathy and Damien and their friends. They're all really sincere – y'know?'

'Yep, I *do* know. So, are you thinking of joining them, then?'

'I may do – I'm still thinking about that one.'

17 – Poetry in Kabul

Ali's taxi picked up Khaista at the address she had given him, waiting only a few minutes for her to appear. Ali was disappointed that she was wearing a thick coat and had her hair covered by the traditional *hijab*. He had been looking forward to seeing that silken hair again, though it was still early in the year and the mountains were still clothed with a coating of snow.

When they arrived at the poetry venue – a large room, hidden behind a shop and up some stairs – they found seats against a wall and nodded to some of the others attending. The room was reasonably warm so – much to Ali's pleasure – Khaista removed her coat and scarf, flicking her long black hair over her shoulders. *I'd love to run my fingers through that hair*, Ali thought to himself. Instead he mumbled in Khaista's ear, 'Your hair is beautiful.'

'Thank you,' she replied modestly, smiling happily to herself.

The group seemed to be mostly women, though there were some other men – apart from Ali. They were of varied ages, also. After some minutes waiting, while more people arrived and settled into their seats, a well-dressed lady of perhaps forty, with uncovered hair, stood up and addressed the gathering.

'I am Rana Wazir. Welcome everybody. It is good to see some new faces tonight. Our little poetry group is growing.

'Poetry has become a means of expression in Afghanistan – even an illiterate farmer is likely to have memorised a line or two written by Rumi, our nation's popular poet. Poets can be male or female, and from all walks of life.

'We have examples of women poets back in history. The warrior poet Malalai famously fought the British troops in 1880 at the Battle of Maiwand, and Rabia Balkhi was one of the first poets to write in modern Persian. Seeta Habibi, from the Afghan Women's Writing Project, says, "*We talk to the paper with our pen and we fight for our rights on paper.*"

'And tonight is no exception. We have several poets who have blessed us with their offerings in the past – and perhaps some of you who are here for the first time might also be willing to share a few lines with us?' She looked around hopefully.

In Six Hours ... the world changed – *Raymond McCullough*

'First, tonight I am going to call upon a lady that those of you who have been coming here regularly will already be familiar with, Adeeba Durrani. Please come up and share with us, Adeeba.'

A young woman in a long red dress came up and stood beside Rana, who smiled at her and then sat down. Adeeba held a sheet of paper in her hand, but never appeared to look at it as she clearly enunciated her powerful words. The poem was about courage, about life in modern day Kabul, about the challenges women faced. It was a reasonably long poem, but she held everyone's attention the whole way through. At the end she dipped her head and everyone clapped enthusiastically.

Adeeba smiled shyly as Rana stood and put her arm around her. 'That was just wonderful, Adeeba. Perhaps you will share something else with us later, yes? Thank you.' Adeeba nodded and then made her way back to her seat.

Rana continued, 'We're going to hear from one of the men, now – Abdul-Karim Baddour. Would you like to come up and share, Abdul-Karim? Thank you.'

A young man in his thirties came up and cleared his throat, as Rana sat down again. He also had a sheet of paper, though in his case he often glanced at it to check his words.

He began huskily, then cleared his throat again and spoke more clearly. His poem was more about nature and mountains – majestic and colourful. It was a shorter poem, but none-the-less enjoyable. Again the audience clapped enthusiastically as he finished. He bowed to Rana and made his way back to his seat.

Ali looked across at Khaista and she caught his glance and smiled. She appeared to be enjoying herself. He thought of taking hold of her hand, but in Afghanistan any open display of affection – especially between two people who were not married – was greatly frowned upon and he didn't want to cause Khaista any embarrassment.

The poetry evening continued. One woman shared her poem about her son, who had clearly been murdered not so long ago in one of the suicide bombings which still took place in the city. The words were truly heart-breaking and the woman herself had tears streaming down her face as she finished it. At the end Rana stood up and embraced her, holding her tightly for several minutes – eventually releasing her to wipe her face and return to her seat, while the others again clapped.

Rana said, 'That was very brave of you, Tahminah – and we all really appreciated you sharing it with us. Unfortunately, life in our part of the world is still not what we would like to regard as normal. There are many tears and many heartbreaks. All of these are part of our existence and there is a great need to express our emotions through the written word. It is a very healthy thing to do.

'Now,' she continued, 'Is there anyone else with a poem to share with us?' She looked carefully around the room, 'Even just a few lines?'

Khaista swallowed and looked up at Rana, nodding, as she pulled a small piece of paper from her pocket.

'Come on up, then,' said Rana. 'Don't be shy.'

Ali watched in surprise as Khaista stood and walked to the front of the room.

'What is your name, young lady?' Rana asked.

'Khaista – Khaista Afridi.' she replied, 'My poem is in *Pashtu* – is that OK?'

'Certainly, Khaista. Most of us here understand *Pashtu*, don't we?' she said rhetorically. 'Go ahead, Khaista.'

She looked around the room, smiled slightly towards Ali and began to speak,

'I am a bird who longs to fly,
far above,
soaring and free.
I long to swoop and dive and cry out in freedom,
But I am not free.
I live on a tiny island
there is no land in sight,
anywhere around,
nowhere to fly off to.
Sometimes cries come to me on the wind –
cries from a far-off distant place,
where there is freedom,
where I could be free.
But they are only cries,
only sounds from a great distance.
I cannot hope to travel so far.
How will I escape to freedom?'

Khaista accepted the hug from Rana, who commented, 'That was excellent, Khaista. Was that your first time?'

Khaista nodded and smiled again.

'Well, you should definitely write some more. That was really enjoyable, wasn't it?' she asked the audience, who were still clapping.

Khaista returned to her seat, smiled very briefly at Ali and then looked straight ahead.

Rana wound up the evening by thanking everyone for coming – especially those who had contributed – and announced when the next gathering would be. She encouraged everyone to hang around and have some tea, which one of the women was just bringing in.

Ali turned to Khaista and asked if she would like a cup?

'OK,' she replied.

'By the way,' said Ali, 'I thought your poem was really great. Well done. You took me by surprise.'

'Thank you, Ali,' she said.

Ali nodded and got up to get the tea.

'You came with Khaista, then?' a voice said behind him and he turned to discover that it was Rana, their host.

'Yes,' replied Ali.

'She has some hidden talent, that young lady,' she added.

'Yes, I think so,' said Ali.

'Did you enjoy the evening? Did Khaista have to drag you along?' said Rana.

'Yes, I did, and not at all,' Ali replied, 'It was my idea, actually. That's why I was really surprised when Khaista got up to read.'

'So, you're a literary man, yourself, then?' she asked.

'Not really,' Ali answered truthfully. 'I'm actually a soldier. But it does give me time to think, sometimes.'

'I see,' Rana smiled at him. 'Well, please tell Khaista that we'd be happy to hear some more from her in the future. Her poem was excellent.'

'I will. Thank you,' said Ali, moving off towards Khaista with their two cups of tea.

Khaista was talking to two other young women about poetry when Ali arrived.

'Here you are,' he said.

The two girls looked at Ali and smiled, as they moved off.

'Making some new friends, then?' Ali asked.

'Mmmm, they liked my poem,' said Khaista.

'So did Rana. She's just been telling me that you have hidden talent – and I would agree, though not so hidden after tonight. She wants you to come back again and read another poem.'

'Another one? – that's the only poem I've ever written!' she exclaimed.

'Well, don't feel under pressure,' said Ali, 'But I'm sure there's more where that came from. As the Americans would say, "You're not just a pretty face."'

'I see,' she said, looking up at him demurely.

'But you certainly do have a *very* pretty face,' he added.

'Flatterer,' she retorted, but smiled, pleased by his answer.

'Are you ready to go home?' asked Ali.

'I suppose so,' Khaista answered. 'That's really what my poem was about. We're not free in this country to do what we really want to do.'

'Oh? And what do you really want to do?' asked Ali, raising his eyebrows.

'I think perhaps I'd better not tell you,' she smiled at him.

'Come on, we'd better go.'

Ali managed to find a taxi quite quickly to take them both home. He took hold of her hand surreptitiously as they drove along. He really wanted to throw his arms around her and kiss those red lips, run his hands through that silky hair – but the driver was an unknown quantity. He could be Taliban, for all they knew, or a spy for them at least. He might report them to the Religious Police. It was extremely frustrating.

'Disgusting!' Khaista said suddenly, and Ali looked up in amazement at her. She was looking at something outside. Ali looked through the taxi window and saw an elderly man with a young boy by his side. The man was holding the boy's hand.

'What is?' Ali asked, bewildered – though thankful that it wasn't him she was referring to.

'Bacha bazi,' she spat out (boy play) – the unfortunate age-old Afghan tradition, once again regaining a hold, of older men walking around with very young boy prostitutes by their side.

'Couldn't it just be a father with his son – or grandson?' he asked innocently.

'No way!' she replied. 'Oh Ali, sometimes I despair of this country.'

'Hmm, I know what you mean,' he said, taking her hand again.

Khaista sighed.

Ali thought about Khaista's poem. They really were imprisoned on a tiny island – Afghanistan – in contact with people who came from a free land, but unable to go there themselves.

Khaista thanked him for a lovely evening as he dropped her off outside her door and made the taxi driver wait until she was safely inside. Then the taxi took him back to his own apartment.

Ali spent a disturbed night thinking about Khaista and wondering how their relationship was meant to progress. In the morning he texted her, suggesting they meet at the university again for lunch.

18 – Decision Time

Devlin and Niamh arrived at a house on the outskirts of Kikenny. They looked at one another.

'OK,' Dev smiled at Niamh, 'Let's do this.'

'Right,' Niamh replied.

They got out of Niamh's car and she locked it. As they walked up the short driveway, the front door opened and Darragh waved to them.

'Hello,' he said, 'Come on in.'

'You two have hit it off then,' he observed, noticing Dev's arm around Niamh, protectively.

'Yes, you could say that,' Dev replied.

'Well, I don't know you yet – Michael, isn't it? – but I've known Niamh for a while. Mebbe you're just what she needs.'

Niamh raised her eyebrows as she looked at Dev.

Darragh brought them into a small room, lined with bookshelves, with an old desk in the centre. There was also a settee and an armchair, which Darragh seated himself in, leaving the settee for Dev and Niamh.

'You guys wanted a chat? I'm always available for that. My wife says I could talk till the bands playin'! Anything in particular you want to chat about?'

'Well, we've been doing a bit of talking recently – about spiritual things, the Bible and stuff. This is all very new to me, Darragh. I've been brought up in the traditional Catholic church. It was kinda surprising to me that my cousin's wedding wasn't in a big cathedral-type building, y'know?'

Darragh simply nodded.

'I mean, I enjoyed the music and everything – even listened to most of your sermon, actually!'

Darragh smiled.

'Well, I had this friend in the Army, Brandon. He carried his Bible around with him everywhere. We gave him a lot of stick about it, y'know? His surname's Thomas, so we called him 'Doubtin' – stuff like that.'

'But when he talked about the Bible he really seemed to come alive, y'know what I mean? He was really into Bible prophecy – about the downfall of America and this great nuclear war in the Middle East, and Israel surviving it, 'n' all that.'

'It sounds like your friend, Brandon, is quite an interesting guy?' Darragh spoke for the first time in a while.

'Yes, he is,' Dev continued. 'We were an unusual mixture. The Lieutenant, Shaul Levine, was a New York Jew, Brandon was a black Pentecostal, with Igbo background, and Ali Yusufzai was a Moslem Pashtun. All three had some Israelite origins, according to Brandon.'

'Yes, that was an unusual combination,' Darragh said.

'Well, Niamh said that you believed a lot of the same things as Brandon,' said Micky. 'She's been hearing your talks for a while, I guess? So we thought we might come and have a chat with you – about all this stuff.'

Niamh nodded.

'OK, let me get this straight. Your friend, Brandon, has been sharing about Bible prophecies which, I agree, may be coming to pass quite soon, and you and Niamh have been discussing this?'

'Yes,' said Dev.

Darragh looked across at Niamh. 'Yes,' she said.

'OK, so here's my first question. Do you believe the Bible is true?'

'Yes,' said Niamh.

'Well, I guess so,' Dev replied.

'OK,' said Darragh. 'Next question – what are you gonna do about it?

'How do you mean?' asked Micky.

'Well, it seems to me you both have a sense of God convicting you that His word is true and you both feel a need to move forward a step as a result. Is that right? Or have I got it wrong?' Darragh enquired.

'I guess you're right,' said Dev. 'We hadn't really spelled it out like that, but I guess you've got it right. What do you think, Niamh?'

'Yeah, we've been talking a lot about what Micky's friend has told him and the stuff you've been teaching about here,' said Niamh. 'I guess we do believe it, but we're not sure where we go from there.'

Chapter 18 – Decision Time

'Well, you can put it off indefinitely, but you won't have that sense of peace in knowing exactly where you stand. Niamh, I've got to know you a bit since you've been coming along to our meetings. I've watched you observing and looking as if you'd really like to be part of things, but so far you haven't taken the plunge. Is that right?'

'Yeah, that sounds pretty accurate,' she said.

'Well, it seems like both of you need to decide something – and that is whether you are at the point yet where you want to make a commitment to Jesus – Yeshua? Whether you want to continue living your life under your own control, or whether you're prepared to let him have control instead?'

'OK,' said Niamh. 'I don't know about Micky, but yes, I think I *am* willing to do that now.'

'Michael?' asked Darragh.

'You sure have a way of getting right down to the nitty gritty, Darragh. I can see what you're saying, but I was brought up an Irish Catholic, y'know? Well, an Irish American Catholic, I suppose. Do I have to leave the Catholic Church and become one of these 'born agains', or what?'

'Not at all, Michael,' Darragh answered him, 'I was a Roman Catholic myself and I know many who are still within the Catholic Church who have had the same experience as me. This is not about leaving anything, or joining anything. It's really just a matter of saying, "Yes" to God, allowing Him to have control in your life. He may lead you to continue in the Roman Catholic Church – if so, great!

'If you feel you are ready to let him have control then we can pray right now – Niamh?'

She nodded.

'Michael?'

'OK,' said Micky, making his mind up. 'Go ahead.'

'Now what we're doing is something very simple. Just use your own words – it's like making a contract with the Lord. You're letting him know that you want Him in control from now on, not yourself. There won't be any blinding lights, angels appearing, of anything spectacular at all – necessarily. But you will know in your heart that something has been sealed. OK?'

'Yep,' said Dev.

'OK, I'll pray first and then you guys can pray in turn.

'Father, we want to come into Your presence now. I pray for Michael and Niamh to be able to make that commitment to You that they seem ready to make. Please bless them Lord and lead them in Your steps.'

Darragh waited. Niamh was quietly weeping.

Dev looked across at her and then closed his eyes again, 'Father, er, I'm no expert at this, but I want You in my life. I'm willing for you to take control, OK? Er, amen.'

'Thank you, Lord,' Darragh said quietly.

Niamh blew her nose and then prayed, 'Lord I thank You for waiting patiently for me to make up my mind. I do want to do things your way, Lord. So please help me to do your will. I give my life into your hands. Amen.'

Darragh waited a minute and then prayed again, 'Lord you've heard my two friends giving their lives into your hands. I really thank you for the privilege of witnessing that. I pray that They will know your power enabling them and your love surrounding them in the days ahead. Guide them in every decision they make, Lord. Amen!'

They sat back and looked at one another. Niamh's face was red and blotchy. Dev looked kind of stunned.

'That was something,' he commented.

'Indeed!' Darragh replied.

'I'd like to add something. You may not have any experience of this, but God quite often gives us a word for someone else – a prophetic word. Sometimes it's a simple picture. I had this picture while we were praying. You two were together in a lifeboat and you were pulling people out of the sea and placing them in the boat. Then you took them to a safe place, before going back and rescuing more people from the sea.

'Now, a lot of people would put a certain evangelical interpretation on that – that you were to become missionaries, or something, bringing many people to the Lord. I don't think that that is what the Lord is saying here. I think there is a different meaning to it, but you will probably have to wait a while to find out what it is.'

'OK,' said Dev, that's kinda strange.'

'Don't fret about it, said Darragh. 'It's not up to you to make it happen, or anything like that. You can forget all about it and when the right time comes it'll come back to you and you will know then what it means. OK?'

'OK, Darragh. And thank you for meeting with us, We really appreciate it,' said Dev.

'Yes,' agreed Niamh. 'Thank you very much.'

'No problem,' said Darragh. 'After all, it's what I'm here for. It was a real privilege, actually. Now, how's about a cup of coffee, or tea?'

'OK,' said Niamh. 'Coffee, please. And could I use your bathroom first?'

Chapter 18 – Decision Time

'Sure, it's left at the top of the stairs. Michael?'

'Yes, coffee, thanks,' said Dev.

Niamh returned looking a little more composed and they chatted for quite a while with Darragh and his wife, Claire – who was invited to join them when she brought in the coffee and some cake.

A day later Devlin said goodbye to his uncle, aunt and cousins and Niamh drove him to Shannon Airport to catch his flight back to Boston. They chatted amiably on the way.

'Listen, Niamh,' said Dev. 'I've really enjoyed my time here – and especially meeting you. I don't feel like we've had enough time together. I'd really love for you to come over to Boston for a while, meet my folks, see around a bit. What do you think? Have you got any holidays coming?'

'I do, actually. I was thinking of going somewhere like Tenerife with some friends, but I'd much rather visit Boston.'

Dev had no idea what or where Tenerife was.

'That's great, Niamh,' he replied.

'I'm gonna really look forward to seeing you again. We get on really well together, don't you think?'

'Aye,' she said slowly, 'yer not too bad – for an American, like!'

Dev remembered to write out his email address and cell phone number for her and she added them to her phone when they stopped at the airport. They had time for one last prolonged kiss and embrace, before she helped him carry his luggage to the Departures area.

He waved to her as he entered the security section. 'See you in Boston – soon!'

Niamh waved until he disappeared, then returned to her car and drove home – tears flowing freely as she drove.

In Six Hours ... the world changed – *Raymond McCullough*

19 – The Lone Soldier

Shaul arrived at the base in the south of Israel not knowing what exactly to expect. He had signed all the forms to make aliyah and discovered that he would automatically be required to do only six months of army service. He had organised the various proofs of his Jewishness and received an Oleh's Certificate – he was now officially an *Oleh*, an immigrant.

On his last visit to the office in Jerusalem he had asked for his IDF service to be brought forward – citing his age and also his US Military experience. He also insisted that he wanted to join a combat brigade, which would mean two years compulsory service, instead of the six months normally required at his age.

Eventually, several months after he arrived in Israel, he received word from the IDF to present himself for training. Shaul had now been assigned to a kibbutz for the duration of his service – this would be his 'family' in Israel as a designated 'lone soldier'. From the kibbutz he took a bus up to Jerusalem, then the *Light Rail* to the recruitment office, and joined a group of new conscripts waiting to board another bus to the training base, near Tel Aviv.

An hour later they boarded the bus and headed back down Highway One to the training base. They were herded into a large warehouse, where other young soldiers stood behind what looked like stalls. As the recruits filed past the soldiers behind threw items of kit at them, until they were all fully equipped. They were then shown to an area of six-man tents where they changed quickly into their new uniforms and stowed the rest of their gear into kit bags.

Next they were led to a square where Shaul then spent many hours waiting with the others to be selected for a particular combat regiment. After some time, a sergeant came and asked if he was Shaul Levine, and if he was a lone soldier, then asked him to follow him.

The sergeant left him in an area with a large group of other soldiers, who were joining the IDF from the USA, United Kingdom, Australia and South Africa. At least there was no language problem with these guys. The military tended to speak briskly and Shaul found that his Hebrew skills were not as perfected as he had hoped, though he knew he had scored highly in all the physical and medical tests.

In Six Hours ... the world changed – *Raymond McCullough*

During the hours of waiting that followed Shaul got to know Dave, from Manchester, UK; Yoav, from Texas, USA and Shmuel, from Adelaide, Australia, very well. They were all younger than Shaul, of course, but all were very keen to join the IDF. Each of them had also opted for a combat battalion.

At five o'clock the recruits were allowed to go back to the mess hall for a meal, then back to their tents, where they chatted and read. Shaul rose early the next morning, dressed and had breakfast, then joined his new friends on the tarmac to wait some more. Eventually, Shaul's name was called and he followed a soldier into an interview room.

There he was quizzed about why he had made aliyah, why he wanted to join a combat regiment, then about his military experiences in Afghanistan. He was asked to give examples of when he had faced dangerous situations and how he had reacted to them. He was also asked to give examples of how he had used his leadership skills.

Eventually, he was offered a place in a Southern Command battalion and told to go back to his tent and collect his kit. When he returned he found that his new friends, Yoav, Shmuel and Dave were going on the same bus to the same regiment.

The training began immediately and Shaul – who imagined he'd been through all this before – found it different in many ways from boot camp in the USA. The recruits were given stretchers filled with sand bags and told to follow a sergeant, who then took them for a long hike in the hot sun. After an hour they were given some water to drink and moved on again. They were hiking through woods on a rough trail that required all their skill to keep the stretcher balanced.

By the time Shaul and the others were beginning to feel they'd had enough they climbed a rise from which they could see the Mediterranean Sea ahead. 'Fancy a swim, men?' the sergeant asked. 'Yes, sir,' one recruit replied. Shaul wisely kept quiet. 'Okay, then, I'll give you twenty minutes to take your stretcher to the sea and back up here.' He then blew his whistle.

The track down to the beach was narrow and steep in places. Shaul's team made it to the water's edge as the sergeant shouted, 'Eleven minutes left!' They turned and began to hurry back up the hill – much harder than coming down. 'Nine minutes,' the sergeant shouted. They tried to hurry, but their legs would not obey them. Finally, they made it to the point from which they had started.

'How do you think you did?' the sergeant asked. No one replied. 'Anyone think you made it in twenty?

'No,' someone eventually mumbled.

'Correct,' the sergeant replied. 'And you know what that means, don't you?'

Chapter 19 – The Lone Soldier

'We do it again, sir?' someone volunteered.

'Exactly!' the sergeant said. 'Twenty minutes,' he repeated, then blew his whistle again. Shaul and his team headed down the narrow trail again, reached the water's edge and raced back for the hill again. It didn't actually feel any more difficult this time, in fact, maybe even a little easier.

When the sergeant asked it they thought they'd done it in time this time, a couple of the recruits replied, 'Yes.'

'OK,' said the sergeant. 'Let's go back to camp. No doubt you guys could do with a good meal, eh?'

'Yes, sir!'

An hour later they trudged into the camp, thankful that training was over for the day.

'Just a minute,' the sergeant told them. 'We've a bit more to go yet – another hour at least.' He led them off again down a new path into the woods. Over an hour later they arrived back in camp and were at last allowed to have their meal and then retire to their tents. They'd been told to set a guard, and decided to change it every hour, so Dave took the first watch. An hour later he returned and Yoav took his place. Shaul had lain down on his bunk, but with his uniform and boots still on.

Ten minutes later there was a shout outside, 'Everyone dressed and out-side, now!'

They hurried out, those who'd taken off their uniforms and boots struggling to get them on again.

The sergeant had them fall in into a 'Chet' – a 'U' formation. 'Right,' the same sergeant said, 'in the Army everything we do in the day we also do at night. Let's go.'

They picked up the stretchers they had carried during the day and set off. A couple of hours later they returned to their tents and collapsed thankfully into their beds again.

Training continued like this for several weeks, sandwiched with lectures and field trips to various places. Eventually, they began weapons training. They were each given a *Tavor TAR-21* assault rifle and shown how to operate and clean it. At last Shaul was able to demonstrate a little of the skill he had acquired in the US Military. His marksmanship and handling of the weapon earned him a 'Well done, soldier,' from the officer in charge.

After several months Shaul was one of the first of the new recruits to be promoted to *Rav Turai* – Corporal. They were also now sent out on missions, accompanying other more experienced troops. The first such exercise was across the Green Line, near Hebron. They were to provide cover for a checkpoint on a road that led off the main Hebron-Be'ersheva Road.

Shaul and nine others were left off at the edge of an olive grove, from where they crawled their way to the edge of a ridge. From here they could clearly see the checkpoint down below, where the soldiers were stopping vehicles and checking papers, asking questions of the drivers and passengers. Shaul had been given temporary command of the group.

They had been in position for over an hour and the heat of the day was beginning to take its toll. They sipped frequently from their canteens. Shaul has just finished taking a drink when he saw a flicker of light out of the corner of his eye. He grabbed a pair of binoculars and began to scan the ridge ahead, just beyond the checkpoint.

Sure enough he soon spotted movement. In the olive grove he could see four men, carrying what appeared to be rifles, moving surreptitiously from tree to tree in the direction of the checkpoint. Shaul called for the radio and reported to his command what they had seen.

'OK, we'll inform the men on the checkpoint. Any chance you guys can circle around behind them, cut them off?'

'We'll do our best, sir,' Shaul replied.

He explained to the others what was required of them. 'Silence at all times. No dislodged rocks, or broken branches, OK?' 'Yes,' the others assured him.

Shaul divided the unit into two groups of five, putting another man in charge of the second group. Then he led the first group back behind the edge of their present ridge and began to circle towards the olive grove ahead. When they reached the edge of it he waited for the second group to come in sight and signalled them to go to the right of the grove, while he and his men went left.

Soon they were well hidden in the olive grove and began to move towards the checkpoint and the men they had seen earlier. They were not in sight, but Shaul assumed they were lying in wait to attack the soldiers on the checkpoint. He motioned his men to take cover and quietly radioed that they were in position. They could see the soldiers on duty below and took note when they suddenly left the vehicles they were checking and took cover behind their own APCs.

As soon as they did this shots rang out from just in front of Shaul's position. Shaul signalled his men to keep their heads down. The soldiers at the vehicles began to return fire and, after a fairly brief exchange of fire, the terrorists decided to make a run for it. Shaul shouted, '*Waqqfu, irmiu slahkum!*' in Arabic (halt, drop your weapons). The terrorists looked confused but then began to swing their rifles in the direction of Shaul's men looking for the source of the voice. Shaul opened fire immediately and his men followed his example. The four men fell to the ground among the olive trees. There was firing from Shaul's other group as well.

Chapter 19 – The Lone Soldier

Shaul shouted loudly, 'Cease fire,' and told his men to stay in their positions. He led his own group forward, crawling towards where the men had fallen. They found one man groaning, holding his side with blood-stained hands, and removed his weapon, which was lying near him. One of Shaul's men produced a cable tie and tied his hands and feet. They moved forward slowly, finding one man clearly dead and then the other two, also injured.

When they had secured all the enemy weapons Shaul called the rest of his men over, telling them to watch the three prisoners, who seemed in no position to cause any problems. He also ordered the bound man released again – he was in no state to cause trouble, or run away. He then radioed his commander again and told him the latest position.

'Well done, *Rav Turai* Levine. Wait with the prisoners and we'll send a vehicle as close as possible to you.'

'*Beseder*, sir,' Shaul replied.

He then ordered his men to do what they could for the three injured prisoners, staunching the blood flow of the man with the side injury and strapping up the shoulder of another man. The third had an injured leg, which was also attended to.

They waited while a *Namer* tracked APC drove up into the olive grove beside them. Then they helped the crew carry the prisoners to the back of it. They also took the body of the fourth man and placed it into the APC. Two soldiers climbed into the back to guard the prisoners and the APC drove back to the road and left the area.

Shaul radioed command again to report that the prisoners had been taken away.

"*Tov ma'od*, Levine (very good). Can you take your men back the way you came and we'll arrange to have you picked up at the same place you were dropped off?'

'Certainly, sir. We should be back there in about thirty minutes,' Shaul responded.

Shaul warned his men to continue to be careful as they made their way back. There was no way of knowing if the sound of shooting might have drawn other terrorists into the area. They used the shelter of the trees to gain the edge of the olive grove, then crawled across the intervening ground to the first olive grove they had spent so much time waiting in. As they approached the far side of this olive grove they could hear the sound of their transport arriving.

They boarded the two waiting APCs, whose drivers then moved slowly forward to the edge of the road, waiting until the vehicles from the original checkpoint drove past. Then they followed them back to their base.

When they arrived the commander called Shaul into his office, 'Take a seat Levine and then report on your actions today.'

Shaul related all that had happened from the time they were dropped off earlier that day.

'*Tov, Rav Turai*,' the commander said, 'You did a good job today. You probably saved the lives of one or two of the men on that checkpoint, plus we now have one dead member of Hamas and three live ones ready to be interrogated when they've recovered a bit. You showed initiative and kept a cool head. and you also brought all your men back safely. Of course we know you were a lieutenant in the US Army, but things are a bit different in the IDF, you'll appreciate? But I think we can safely say that there's a future for you in the Army, Levine.'

'*Toda raba*, sir,' Shaul replied.

'*Beseder*, go join your men and get something to eat.'

'Yes, sir.'

20 – Project Nemesis, Haifa

'Potter' sat at his desk in a secure department of *Haifa Technion,* the *Israel Institute of Science and Technology* – Israel's oldest university, founded in 1912. Usually simply referred to as *Ha Technion*, the university was one of the world's leading institutions in technology, responsible for the production of numerous Nobel Prize winners and of three quarters of the managers of modern electronic companies in Israel.

The *Technion* occupied a 1.3 square kilometre site – *Technion City* – high up on the north side of Mount Carmel. In addition to road and the normal public transport system, students and staff were now able to access the site via the new 4.4 kilometre cable car service, which connected the University – and also the *University of Haifa* at the top of the mountain – to the new *Metronit* bus system in the lower part of the city.

Potter was chewing on a pen, surrounded by three high definition screens, a keyboard vibrating beneath his ever active fingertips. Occasionally he used the touchpad to change screen, or to call up a new window of information. The main screen was filled with coded text which would have made little sense to most programmers, never mind the general public.

The leader of *Project Nemesis,* as it was known, his colleagues called him Potter, mainly because of his appearance – with his large spectacles and youthful looks for his twenty eight years – but also because of his name, Ari Petrovsky, so easy to convert to Harry Potter that no-one could remember who had first made the obvious connection.

Not that the general public stood the slightest chance of ever visiting this secure wing of the campus, with its regular complement of Shin Bet and military guards. The personnel were the elite of the elite – many of them hand-picked from the IDF's *Intelligence Unit 8200* – the largest unit within the IDF, given recruitment priority over other units (with the exception of potential pilots) and the source of many of the country's top leaders and entrepreneurs.

The room and the rest of the suite that he shared with eleven other personnel was newly built and state of the art in every way. The windows along the north-facing wall contained a collection of healthy indoor plants – of both green and flowering varieties. The opposite wall was mostly taken up with a large aquarium through which a variety of multi-coloured fish swam languidly. The end walls between these contained a number of large paintings, some restful landscapes and some colourful abstracts.

The computer equipment was the very latest technology, regularly upgraded, fully networked together, with ultra fast access to the internet, the very highest security clearances, and with extremely sophisticated fire-walls, cloaking and protection systems.

Next to the main workroom the backup facilities were second to none. If the personnel working there chose to they need never leave the suite – for food, exercise, sleep or entertainment – and often, when the pressure was on, they did not leave the building for days on end. It played havoc with their social lives, of course, but this was a team of very dedicated men – and two women – who saw their task, the defence of Israel, as one of the utmost importance. And their superiors, of course – including the Israeli government – saw it in exactly the same way.

Project Nemesis was probably the highest priority military program currently funded by the Israeli state – although the Americans also contributed generously to the programme, and benefited accordingly. Though they were not necessarily kept fully up to date with some of the developments of the unit. This team of experts in their fields possibly held the key to Israeli military superiority in the region, more than any other.

Led by Potter, the team were probably the most sophisticated group of hackers gathered in one place in the world today. Of course, they had a head start – many software advances having been initiated by Israeli companies – which is where some of them had been recruited from. Add to that the benefits of Israeli intelligence, together with shared intelligence from the USA and other friendly states, including access to the manufacturers and suppliers of the relevant technology, and you had a very formidable force.

The team were all under thirty, highly intelligent and highly motivated – the security of the State of Israel being their ultimate aim. Between them they were fluent in sixteen languages – Arabic and Farsi (Persian), of course, included. Their combined knowledge of the nuclear industry, and in particular of missile guidance systems, was arguably unequalled in the world.

Their task, though a very difficult one, was extremely simple in concept. *Step One* was to infiltrate their enemies guidance systems to the extent that they would be capable of initiating a self-destruct of an enemy missile, particularly one carrying a nuclear warhead. This they had already achieved and were in the process of refining.

Step Two would go well beyond this, the intent being to gain such complete control of a newly launched missile as to have the capability of hijacking it from its native command system and taking over control of its destination and trigger timing. In simple terms the aim was to ensure that a nuclear missile fired towards any Israeli target would turn back and attack its home base – in the process destroying the launch base along with any further missiles housed at that base.

'Yes!' he exclaimed loudly. Apparently, another obstacle had been overcome. The others looked up from their own work, bemused, wondering what the chances were of breaking for lunch soon. Potter had at times been known to continue for a full day on just coffee and snacks.

'Does this mean you're gonna be preoccupied for a while, yet?' asked Lefevre – known to the others as *Le Bean*, due to his tall extremely thin stature and also his French accent.

'Only another ten minutes, or so, I should think,' Potter replied, his eyes fixed on the screen and his fingers continuing to flick rapidly over the keys.

'In that case I should order lunch. Has everyone put their orders in?' Le Bean was responsible for collecting the lunch orders this week.

'Oh, just a second,' said one of the girls, Pet – short for Petalula, Greek for *'butterfly'*, her surname being Dimitrios – typing her order in quickly.

'Rabbit food, as usual, I presume!' LeFevre laughed.

'Not exactly,' she responded, 'Just because I don't eat the rubbish you guys seem to be happy with! There, you can send it in, now.'

'Whatever!' LeFebvre muttered, 'Then I'll put some fresh coffee on.'

'I'll give you a hand. I need a break,' she answered, standing up from her workstation and looking around for the tray to collect the empty and half-empty but cold cups.

Potter turned away from his flickering displays, 'I think we'll have another 'catch up' session after lunch, say two thirty? That suit everybody?' A 'catch up session' enabled them all to update one another on what they had been doing for the past few days, latest intelligence, etc.

There was a general murmur of assent from around the room.

Le Bean, having now emailed the order down to the restaurant, grabbed a couple of cups and he and Pet left the room for the well equipped kitchen next door.

The team did not consist only of programmers – actually, several of them had been senior systems analysts, previous to moving here – but also of researchers tracking and sifting the ever growing intelligence being fed to them – from Unit 8200 and many other sources.

In particular, they needed to closely monitor what their enemy knew of their activities. The first hint that the opposition was in any way becoming suspicious would raise an alert and the team would focus their efforts on covering their tracks and holding off on any deep penetration until the possible crisis was past.

In Six Hours ... the world changed – *Raymond McCullough*

The main task of *Project Nemesis* involved investigating the enemy software for suitable points to insert their own diverts, then writing their own – necessarily compact – code to bypass the original. The trick was to achieve all of this without ever alerting the enemy to what they were doing.

The job was made much easier by the commonly sloppy encoding they found, which they often 'tightened up', allowing themselves more room for manoeuvre. It was also helped considerably by knowing the 'back doors' left by the original software designers, some of whom were Israeli, American or from other friendly nations.

Twenty minutes later Pet came back to announce that the food had been delivered and the others quickly tripped into the kitchen/dining area, Potter eventually joining them. Mealtimes, particularly, were a time to relax, engage in mild banter and to switch off completely from the intense work they were all engaged in.

Next to the dining area was a room with a pool table, video games and other relaxation equipment. Beyond that was a fully equipped gym, where several of the staff worked out regularly, some early in the morning, some after finishing a shift. The heavy punchbag – which featured a scrawny bearded face painted on, with the legend, *Mahmoud*, printed in Hebrew – was sometimes used to vent frustrations with the work, and even with one another.

There had been times when Pet felt impelled to leave her workstation in order to release her exasperation with her male colleagues on Mahmoud for a few minutes. She usually returned to her work more relaxed and with a wry smile which the others failed to interpret. Pet liked her colleagues – most of the time. She even had a bit of a soft spot for Le Bean and wondered if that might lead somewhere in the future. But the intensity of their work environment and the typical insensitive maleness of her colleagues sometimes built up a wall of steam in her that was best let off in private.

After a prolonged and relaxing lunch the team headed back in for a brainstorming session. Potter shared his latest success in manoeuvring around Iran's software protection. Daoud Hashem – a Bedouin from near Arad, in the Negev and the only Arab member of the team – brought them up to date on what was happening in the Arab world, as did the much more swarthy Yonatan, a descendent of Moroccan Jewish immigrants back in the fifties. Yossi, son of recent immigrants from New York City's large Jewish community, brought them up-to-date with the latest from the US and other western intelligence sources.

The team discussed and debated back and forth and, eventually, new targets were identified and additional tasks assigned. This was a regular feature of their work, remaining very flexible, taking advantage of every advance in their technological war and every new snippet of useful intelligence info.

21 – Email to Comrades

Hey you guys,

I've been training for several months now with the IDF – quite different from the US Army, or the ISAF forces in Afghanistan. Physically, the training – especially for a combat regiment – is very rigorous. A lot of running up and down hills carrying a stretcher full of sandbags!

I wasn't too worried about the physical and medical side of it, though – I scored pretty high on those when they tested me, actually. The hardest bit was learning a new language and then having to think in that language. Your brain takes its time translating into English – y'know? By the time you've figured out what the order meant everyone else is already doing it!

Luckily, there are a couple of guys in my unit who speak good English – they're from the UK and Australia – so, sometimes they translate things for me so I don't make a complete fool of myself. Like one day, we were being ordered to change into fatigues from our dress uniform, then they blew a whistle and told you to change back. When they blew the whistle again, several of us were only half dressed.

Then you have to ask permission to finish dressing. I asked an officer for permission to put my pants on and he suddenly burst out laughing. He called the other officers over and asked me to repeat what I'd said. I knew by then that I'd made some kind of mistake in my Hebrew, but had no idea what. When I repeated it the other officers doubled up laughing again. Apparently, instead of asking permission to put on my pants, I'd asked if I could pee my pants!

Anyway, all that is pretty much behind me now and I've recently been promoted to Rav Turai – corporal. I know, I was a lieutenant out in Kabul, but that's how it works here.

They send us out on patrols now – in places like the West Bank – and just last week we were sent out to back up a regular check point near Hebron. I was put in charge of ten men crawling through an olive grove to cover the checkpoint. Luckily I spotted some guys in another olive grove ahead of us. They were carrying rifles, and could have had an RPG.

In Six Hours ... the world changed – *Raymond McCullough*

Anyway, I radioed the info back to our command and they asked if we could cut the terrorists off, which we did. There was some exchange of fire with the guys on the check point and then they turned to leave, at which point I challenged them in my best Arabic to halt and drop their weapons. They obviously had no intention of complying so we opened fire – killing one and wounding the other three.

I was called in to my commander afterwards and commended, so now I've just been made up to Samal – sergeant. Looks like if I stay here long enough – and get in enough scrapes like that one – I could end up back at my old rank!

Anyway, I hope you guys (Brandon and Dev) are adjusting to civilian life. Ali and I are just turning into old soldiers, I guess! How are things in Kabul these days, Ali?

Remember how we all agreed to meet up in Jerusalem if this war takes place that Brandon told us about? Wonder if that will ever happen?

Anyway, keep safe whatever you're doing.

Your old comrade,

Sol

22 – Gaza Tunnel

The months of training had hardened Shaul and he was also beginning to feel more confident of his Hebrew skills. At the end of his first year of training he was promoted to *Samal* – sergeant – and their unit, including his British friend, Dave, was despatched to protect the small communities near the Gaza border.

Most of these were small kibbutzim engaged in farming the land around them and perhaps running a small factory as well. Now and again they saw a rocket take off from the Gaza Strip nearby and land in their area. Most of these landed in the fields, or perhaps damaged one of the extensive greenhouses around the kibbutz.

On one occasion Shaul had witnessed the operation of the *Iron Dome* system, deployed nearby in an attempt to reassure the inhabitants of these communities that they were being adequately protected. When a rocket was launched the *Iron Dome* radar immediately determined where that rocket would land – if in an open area it took no action.

But if the computer expected the missile to hit an occupied area, it then launched an Israeli-made *Tamir* counter-missile, which in most cases was successful in destroying the incoming rocket. The problem, of course, was that the incoming rocket typically cost Hamas about $500 to produce, while the *Tamir* missile typically cost Israel in excess of $50,000 – not to mention the cost of the radar, computer system and personnel manning it. The *Iron Dome* system had so far been 90% effective in destroying missiles targeting populated areas.

Since the beginning of 2014 more and more missiles had been launched into the area and then, on 12th June 2014, three young Israelis were kidnapped by Hamas. The IDF went into overdrive, searching many villages in the Hebron area where the boys had disappeared. Shaul's unit were put on alert in their area. On 7th July seven Hamas terrorists were killed in an explosion in a Gaza tunnel. Hamas blamed an Israeli airstrike, though Israel claimed it was their own munitions which had exploded.

Operation Protective Edge began the next day and continued for fifty days – during which over 4,500 rockets were fired into Israel. Although some missiles reached Tel Aviv, Jerusalem and even Haifa, the most intensively targeted area was right where Shaul's unit were based. Many of the kibbutzim members were suffering from acute stress and Shaul's men escorted several convoys of those who had been offered respite in towns in the north for them and their children for the duration of the conflict.

The stress upon these communities was exacerbated when Hamas terrorists emerged from a tunnel only one kilometre from the nearby town of Sderot – opposite the north eastern corner of the Gaza Strip – killing two IDF soldiers, before they were eliminated. On another occasion approximately a dozen terrorists emerged into the middle of a field, only a short distance from the children's house of the nearby kibbutz.

Shaul radioed for the Air Force to intervene. Meanwhile, his unit began an exchange of fire with the Hamas gunmen, who after a while attempted to retreat back to the tunnel. Before they were able to do so the IAF intervened, targeting the tunnel entrance with a missile, which killed all the terrorists.

Successful as this outcome was, it only served to highlight the problem that Israel had. At any moment terrorist gunmen could appear out of a tunnel – even in the middle of a kibbutz – and murder, or kidnap, children, or a whole family. It was unthinkable to allow that situation to continue any longer.

On 17th July a ground invasion into Gaza was authorised by the Israeli government, and Shaul's unit were ordered to the edge of the Gaza border. They spent some days waiting outside the border fence, tension mounting. Shaul went around his troops, re-assuring them and reading passages from the prophets that promised protection over Israel in battle. The men were encouraged by his words.

Then came the order for their unit to enter Gaza. The area they were assigned to was one of the worst concentrations in the Gaza Strip – the eastern area of Gaza City, known as Shuja'iya. The streets were narrow and crowded with buildings. When their *Namer* and *M113* Armoured Personnel Carriers rounded a corner they could expect incoming fire from automatic weapons – and the gunmen were not averse to kidnapping a child off the street to hold in front of them as a human shield. How could his men return fire when a child's life was at stake?

Shaul's unit had recently had some of their *M113* APCs replaced by the much better armoured *Namer* – which means Leopard in Hebrew. The new APC was based on the same chassis as the *Merkavah IV* tanks, which were also operating alongside their unit, and were much better armoured than the older and lighter American-designed *M113*.

Like the *Merkavah* tank, the *Namers* had also been fitted with the *Trophy* Active Protection system (APS), which automatically responded to incoming RPG and/or machine gun fire. Many lives – including those of several commanders – were saved in Gaza by the deployment of this technology. Unfortunately, the older *M113*s didn't have this advantage.

Chapter 22 – Gaza Tunnel

A lot of the action involved detection of the 'Terror Tunnels' as they had been dubbed. On one occasion Shaul found himself on one side of a narrow alley, firing towards a group of gunmen in a house one hundred metres ahead. Another group of his men were placed across the alley from him. Shaul signalled for their APCs to advance on the gunmen, led by one of the *Namers*. As the vehicle passed, Shaul and his men moved into its shelter, firing around the side of the vehicle.

Suddenly, his friend Dave shouted, 'RPG!' and they quickly ducked behind the APC. The rocket missed the leading *Namer*, but unfortunately scored a hit on an *M113* immediately behind it. Shrapnel flew around the area, one piece catching Dave on his arm. Another struck Shaul on his flak jacket, bruising him, but causing no actual wound.

Shaul continued firing at the gunmen as he ordered his men to get Dave into the lead APC and give him medical attention – also to check on those in the damaged APC. His next round took down the RPG launcher as he was about to fire a second rocket. Shaul and others continued firing, so that the other men were unable to retrieve the RPG, instead retreating further up the alley.

Suddenly, a *Merkavah IV* tank appeared at a junction in the alley ahead and fired a round at the fleeing gunmen. When the dust cleared there was no sign of them. The leading APC had by now passed the building the men had been guarding and Shaul ordered it to stop there and watch the alley ahead. Another *Namer* forced its way past the damaged *M113* and stopped just short of Shaul. The driver reported that there were two men dead in the *M113* and two others injured, who were now being attended to by medics.

Shaul signalled for six of his men to follow him into the building and led the way into a small room, which appeared to be empty. Shaul and another soldier covered for two of his men who moved cautiously into the next, larger, room.

'Tunnel entrance,' one of the men warned. Shaul indicated that they should use grenades and the two men ran back into the smaller room as the grenades exploded inside the tunnel opening. Shaul moved carefully back into the room with the tunnel entrance. This was the most unnerving part of their present job. You never knew what to expect inside a Hamas tunnel.

He approached the edge of the vertical shaft, which seemed to reach about four metres down into the earth. He swung himself over the edge, grasping the rungs of the metal ladder fixed to the side of the shaft.

He then descended slowly with his weapon held ready. When he reached the bottom he donned a headlight stowed in his uniform and switched it on, scanning the tunnel, which led in two directions. One Palestinian, with an AK47 still in his hand, lay dead just inside the eastern part of the tunnel. There were no others that he could see at this moment. He signalled for four of the six men waiting above to climb down to where he was. The other two stayed on guard above.

There were some boxes and bags of cement and sand stored along the sides of the tunnel nearby, so Shaul got his men to organise a protective barrier, using the sandbags and cement, a few metres further down the tunnel in each direction. After removing the body of the Hamas gunman, he placed two of them behind each barricade to watch for any enemy movement.

He switched off his light to avoid making himself, or his men, a target, then shouted up to the two men above, one of whom went out to the APC and returned with two pairs of night-sight goggles. Shaul climbed up the ladder and retrieved the goggles, then climbed down into the tunnel and handed one set to each pair of men. 'Take turns using them,' he instructed. 'We'll need a demolition squad in here to check this tunnel out and then destroy it, but we need to keep it secure in the meantime.'

He climbed out of the tunnel shaft again and made his way to the alley outside, where he found Tamari, who updated him on their deployment in the alley. Shaul then scrambled into the lead APC, where he reported their findings to Captain Gefen by radio. He was instructed to hold their position until the engineers arrived, then to hand over the tunnel to them and to secure the area immediately around it.

An hour later the engineering troops arrived. Their commander, Lieutenant Ehud, sought out Shaul, 'I believe you found another rat-hole, *Samal*?'

'Yes, we found a tunnel entrance. The tunnel runs both ways, so we have four men down there guarding it.'

'*Beseder*. Well, we're in the rat-catching and exterminating business, so lead us to the rat-hole. Once we have some of our men in position you can withdraw your men from the tunnel itself. But we'd appreciate it if you can keep the area around it secure.'

'*Ken*. My Captain has already instructed us to do that, *Segen*. Just follow me, sir.'

Shaul led *Segen* Ehud into the building where they'd found the tunnel and, once the Lieutenant's men were in position, removed his own men to the surface again to guard the perimeter.

It was several hours – during which Shaul's men alternatively ate, rested or did guard duty around the building, some watching the area from the roof parapet – before *Segen* Ehud approached Shaul again: '*Samal*, I recommend you remove your men from the immediate area – in a northerly, or southerly direction. We've finished wiring the tunnel with explosives and we're ready now to blow it.'

'*Beseder, Segen*,' Shaul replied, then radioed his commander to explain the reason for the pull-out. Shaul organised his men into their vehicles and they moved out of the area to the south, where more Israeli troops were already deployed – the stricken M113 having been extricated earlier onto a tank transporter.

Segen Ehud and his force also pulled back from the area, two men unrolling a reel of cable, which they attached to a plunger. When the area was clear, *Segen* Ehud gave the order and a soldier pressed the plunger. There was a dull roar – adding to the distant sound of artillery, tank and missile fire around them – and then several buildings collapsed along the line of the tunnel, including the building they had until recently occupied.

Seren Gefen then ordered Shaul and his men to re-occupy the area and they moved their APCs back to defend the area for that night. The following days saw them move further and further north into Shuja'iya, where there was more hand-to-hand fighting and more tunnels were discovered.

It was slow and dangerous progress for, once the Hamas were aware of their presence in an area, they would concentrate their fire on them – often using undiscovered tunnels to appear suddenly in one spot, then move quickly to another.

In the end more than thirty tunnels were discovered and – after many declarations of a ceasefire, most broken immediately by Hamas – the war finally came to an end. Israeli troops were then ordered to move out of Gaza again, having done considerable damage to Hamas' and Islamic Jihad's ability to strike Israel. The war of words, and of blame, of course continued.

Shaul found himself promoted to *Segen Mishne* (Second Lieutenant) shortly after the Gaza operation, while his corporal, Musa Tamari, was promoted to *Samal* – Sergeant. There was a lot of self-analysis following their withdrawal – officers were asked to give their opinion on what failings they had noted and what could be done better in another similar situation.

The main consensus was the failure of the *M113* APC to offer adequate protection, whereas the *Merkavah IV* tanks and the *Namer* APCs that had sustained RPG and anti-tank fire had survived with their men relatively unhurt. The other conclusion was the great success of the *Trophy* Active Protection System (APS), which had performed extremely well in taking out enemy missiles – more than justifying its expense.

The Army concluded that they should order more *Namer* APCs – over and above those in production already. They also asked the two Israeli companies – both producing rival APS systems – to work together on a newer and better APS.

The result of this co-operation – between Rafael Advanced Defence Systems and Israel Military Industries – was the new *Bright Arrow* APS, which was planned to be added to all new tanks and APCs, and even to smaller military vehicles, like jeeps. The war, the failure of so-called peace talks and the subsequent murderous attacks on Jewish civilians in Jerusalem and other places, led to a total lack of faith in the internationally much-touted 'Two State Solution', on the part of most Israelis.

23 – Email After Conflict

Hey guys,

Thanks for all the thoughts and prayers for my safety during the recent war. Things are pretty quiet now – apart from our so-called 'peace partners' inciting local Arabs to go kill some Jews. There's been far too much of that happening recently.

But back to the actual war in Gaza. Unless you've been there it is really hard to describe just how bad it was. More than sixty of our guys are dead – apart from the civilians killed, thankfully only a handful.

Some of our defences worked brilliantly – like Iron Dome and our Merkavah IV tanks and Namer APCs – especially those fitted with the Trophy Active Protection System. Unfortunately, we lost two of our men because the older M113 APCs (American made!) weren't well enough armoured to protect the men inside.

The Namers and the tanks were much safer. The APS systems worked brilliantly – saved quite a few lives by taking out anti-tank missiles before they reached their targets. Apparently, we're gonna get a new, even better APS in future – Bright Arrow – and more of the Namer APCs, too.

We had our share of hand to hand fighting in the narrow streets and alleys of Shuja'iya, which is eastern Gaza city – where many of the 'terror tunnels' were found. We found a couple of tunnels ourselves, which were wired with explosives and then blown up – but we didn't have the terrible experience of some of our comrades, who were faced with Hamas terrorists inside a tunnel.

The Hamas had brought several young teenagers into the tunnel and fitted them with suicide vests, sending them towards our troops. Our men had to make the horrendous decision whether to shoot teenagers, or be blown up by them. They had no choice really, but those soldiers were really traumatised after-wards – they'll need a lot of counselling!

Anyway, after all the tension of the war it is good to get back to fairly normal duties once again.

More and more Europeans are making aliyah to Israel this year, or planning to come next year – especially from France and Ukraine. Israel may not be the safest place in the world, but at least we have the IDF here to protect the ordinary citizen and their families. No matter what the rest of the world may think, this is our home and we're not about to give it up – especially not to those who only want to destroy us!

Well, that's the situation at the moment. Life is never dull here, that's for sure. When I'm off duty I go back to the kibbutz I was assigned to when I made aliyah. It's kind of relaxing to just work in a greenhouse or drive a tractor after fighting a war! The people on the kibbutz really treat you as part of their family and you don't feel any need to 'perform' for them – you can just be yourself.

Anyway, enough about me. What are you guys up to these days? By the sound of things both Dev and Ali are well on their way to being old married men like Brandon very soon, eh? Nothing like that on the horizon here, though there sure are some beautiful girls around.

Keep me up to date, now!

Your comrade,

Sol

2015

In Six Hours ... the world changed – *Raymond McCullough*

24 – Conspiracy in the Persian Gulf

Tehillim/Psalms 83:5 With one mind they plot together; they form an alliance against you.

The blue dome of the *Emirates Palace Hotel* glowed brightly in the dark above the dazzling golden facade on the floors below. The ten Middle Eastern men gathered in a penthouse suite just below the dome, with a beautiful sea view over the private beach to the darkened Persian Gulf beyond to the north and west. The Iranian delegate was the last to enter the suite and greeted his fellow Muslim Arab contemporaries in the traditional way – with hugs and kisses on both cheeks.

When all the greetings were complete and everyone was seated around the polished exotic wood conference table he looked around at the assembled leaders. 'Let us put our cards on the table,' he began. 'In the past we have not always seen eye to eye, but we all have one goal in common – the liberation of the historic land of Palestine from the clutches of the evil and hated Zionist entity. Brothers, I urge you all now to put your differences behind you, because that goal is now within our grasp.

'The Islamic Republic of Iran is now happy to announce that Allah – praise be unto Him – has enabled us to prepare enough highly enriched uranium to produce more than a dozen nuclear missiles – enough to wipe out every major city in the Zionist state!'

There was a growl of approval from around the table, with many nodding their heads.

'These missiles will be in place – both in Iran and Syria – and ready to launch against our hated common enemy in two months time. So, gentlemen, Iran wishes to know how your respective plans are advancing for dealing with the Jewish pigs who have dared to soil the sacred land of Allah.'

The Palestinian president replied first, 'That is great news, minister. As you all know, Fatah have broken off negotiations with the Zionist dogs' – there was a snort from the Hamas representative – 'and our men have been training exhaustively for this glorious day – aided, of course, by liberal supplies of weapons and funding from the hated United States. We will be ready to move and declare a new State of Palestine as soon as the missiles have fallen. Our enemies will have no stomach left to resist us. We will surround their so-called Ben Gurion Airport and any remaining military installations and neutralise them speedily.'

Not to be outdone by his so-called ally in the *'Palestinian Unity Government'*, the Hamas leader – having travelled only the short distance from Doha, in neighbouring Qatar, where he kept watch on his muti-million dollar investments – addressed the assembled conspirators next. 'Since our last great victory against the Zionist enemy' – this time it was the Fatah leader who smirked – 'and despite our many martyrs for the cause, the Islamic Resistance Movement have been training intensively for this coming jihad.

'We have several thousand men ready to give their lives for the glorious cause of Islam and the Palestinian State. Despite the lack of help from our Egyptian brothers' – here he glared at the representative from the Egyptian government – 'we have acquired and stored in secret underground locations many thousands of rockets, missiles and mortars ready for an all-out attack on the Zionist forces.

'We have identified military and Zionist targets which we will invade and secure once the jihad begins. Be assured that Hamas will play a glorious and heroic part in the coming liberation of our beloved Palestine.'

The Lebanese leader of Hezbollah was next to address the group. 'The Party of Allah have been successful against the Zionist enemy in previous conflicts and we will be victorious once again in the coming final jihad. Our brave soldiers are battle-hardened after their recent fighting against the foreign rebels' – he glanced across meaningfully at the representative from ISIS – 'in support of the rightful government of Syria.

'We now have many thousands of long and short-range missiles and rockets aimed at the Zionist population in the Galilee and further south. We are ready to launch and our men are more than willing to mop up any remaining Zionist opposition in the State of Palestine. The Party of Allah, along with the Lebanese Armed Forces, will play its full part in the total liberation of Palestine.'

The Sheikh was next to contribute, 'The Kingdom of Saudi Arabia has been proud to finance and support the Palestinian cause for many years. Our military forces stand ready and willing to move against the Zionist dogs. Our forces will cross the border into the Negev in support of our Palestinian brethren and force the Jewish pigs into the sea, where they belong.'

The Egyptian was not to be outdone by his traditional Sunni rival from Saudi Arabia, 'Despite the troubles our great country has recently experienced, I can assure you that we in Egypt are zealous to bring this long-running sore to an end. The Egyptian Army will be ready and available when the day comes and we will not hesitate to march through the Sinai and the Negev and to occupy Al Quds once again. This will finally be the beginning of our longed-for Islamic Caliphate.'

Chapter 20 – Gaza tunnel

The minister from the new Jordanian Islamic government was eager to add his blessing. 'Since, with popular support, we have recently overthrown the outdated king and his pathetic government, my people have been thirsting to make progress against the hated Zionists. Jordan will be ready when the time comes. We will move our forces across the River and take back the Jordan Valley, the West Bank and Jerusalem, itself.'

The Iraqi minister added his support, 'Gentlemen, as you well know, we have been working closely with our Iranian friends towards this goal. We will be co-operating with them and our brothers here from Syria – especially in the logistics of transporting missiles to Syria and in supporting our brothers in this great cause.'

The military commander of the Islamic State (ISIS) cleared his throat and began. 'Gentlemen, for the sake of the greater cause of ridding the world of the hated Jewish scum, we are prepared to bury our differences with our Muslim brothers here and to join in this glorious cause of jihad.

'As you all well know, I and my fellow soldiers are known never to hesitate in battle. You have seen how we have dealt with our enemies in the recent past. We have driven the infidels from our sacred lands and we will now drive these hated Jews into the sea. We are already moving troops into the north of our new ally, Jordan, ready to attack the Galilee.

Finally, the senior government minister from Syria stood up, 'Well, gentlemen, we have come a long hard road to reach this satisfactory point. Once the missiles we have agreed upon are delivered to us and placed in their secure locations we will be ready to initiate the attack.

'Apart from these nuclear missiles, as you well know we have many thousands of conventional missiles ready to launch at our arch enemy. Our troops are well seasoned and our airforce will swiftly clear the skies of any remaining enemy planes, and will bomb their military installations and towns. The north of Palestine will be under our control within hours of the launch of the attack.'

'Well said, gentlemen', the Iranian minister began to conclude their meeting. 'We will issue a code word when the attack is to begin. Immediately, both ourselves and our Syrian allies here will launch the nuclear missiles, followed by a massive deluge of conventional missiles and rockets from every quarter.

'Immediately after the final nuclear missile launch, our airforce and those of Syria, Iraq, Egypt, Jordan and Saudi Arabia will begin to bomb any remaining enemy targets. Our paratroops will already have advanced across Iraq and Jordan and all of our combined forces will cross the enemy borders one hour after the first signal. The code-word will be, "*Al-Tathir* – The Cleansing."

25 – Nigerian Jews

The Nigerian Airways Boeing aircraft was approaching the coast of West Africa. Brandon had decided to further explore his Igbo ancestry by going back to their African homeland. He hoped to visit with some of those Igbo who believed in their Israelite identity and saw their future as very much being with Israel.

In the seat beside him was Aaron, his Igbo Jewish friend from Richmond, Virginia. Aaron's friend, Yaakov, had originally planned to accompany him on this trip, but he'd been taken ill and the opportunity was offered to Brandon instead. They managed to change the name on the tickets and now Brandon was on his way.

He had already been up to Richmond a couple of times since their meeting in Atlanta, GA. Aaron's small group of Igbo Jews seemed to appreciate Brandon's input on the prophecies about Babylon and the coming Middle East War. They had discussed and referred to the scriptures – something Brandon really enjoyed.

He loved it when someone didn't just accept, or reject, what he said, but searched the references he gave them to see for themselves what was said and in what context. These men were happy to do just that. As a result their friendship had grown and Brandon had even persuaded a couple of interested friends from his church to come along with him on the last trip. They also had really enjoyed it – plus having friends along made the trip that much shorter and easier.

He had also persuaded Alyssa to bring Hannah and Caleb with them to the *World Igbo Festival of Arts & Culture* at the Staunton, VA, site of the *Igbo Farm Village*. The kids enjoyed roaming around the thatched cottages in the village compound and also the colourful costumes worn by both men and women. When it came time for the tribal dancing the children were entranced, as the dancers whirled and leapt.

They had enjoyed the food also but, eventually, the travel and excitement became too much for them and Brandon and Alyssa had taken them to a local motel for the night. Next day they had returned for a little more culture – although, not understanding the Igbo language – some of it went right over their heads.

Once the kids had had enough they began the four-hour journey home and carried two sleeping children to their beds before falling happily into their own. It had been a memorable experience.

The aircraft landed at *Nnamdi Azikiwe International Airport* – west of Abuja, capital of Nigeria. They were welcomed to Nigeria by some Igbo Jews from Abuja and driven east into the city, where they were to stay with some members of one of the three synagogues in the city.

Aaron and Brandon enjoyed a Nigerian meal and were taken on a tour of the city centre, including *BloomsBury Mall*, just north of the city centre, where Brandon purchased a couple of colourful African shirts and some gifts for Alyssa and the kids. When they returned an even bigger meal was served – apparently the earlier one was only a snack. Brandon and Aaron struggled to do justice to the array of food.

Next morning they were taken to one of the synagogues in the city, where they found the local Igbo Jews were very excited about their visit. They obviously felt cut off from the Jewish world and wished for closer ties with Jews, both in the USA and in Israel.

One or two rabbis had paid them a visit, so far, and some Jewish congregations in the US had sent them prayer shawls, books and other items to aid them in their worship – but they needed more sense of inclusion. There were upwards of five thousand practicing Igbo Jews in Nigeria.

Of the forty million Igbos in the country the majority were Christian, but many of these also – like Brandon – felt an affinity with Israel and thought of themselves as Israelites. Brandon wondered just how many of these people had a desire to return to the land of Israel in the future.

It was strange to see the deep enthusiasm and the depth of knowledge of Hebrew and Jewish ritual that these men – and women – had. When they sang Hebrew songs together it sounded like a heavenly choir. Brandon determined to bring back some recordings of their songs to Raleigh.

On Friday evening they went to another of the Abuja synagogues for the Shabbat service. The building was not sophisticated, but the passion of their worship was unsurpassed. Aaron was asked to speak and his words were received with great enthusiasm.

On Saturday morning they visited the third synagogue in the city and Brandon was asked to share a few words. He greeted the men and women there with *'Shabbat shalom'*, but then continued in English. He reminded them that the prophets spoke of a day when the scattered people of Israel would be gathered in 'from the four corners of the earth'. There were many 'Amens'.

He also referred to the passage in Isaiah where it says:

Isaiah 43:3 For I am the Lord your God, the Holy One of Israel, your Saviour; I give Egypt for your ransom, Cush and Seba in your stead.

4 Since you are precious and honoured in my sight, and because I love you, I will give people in exchange for you, nations in exchange for your life.

5 Do not be afraid, for I am with you; I will bring your children from the east and gather you from the west.

6 I will say to the north, "Give them up!" and to the south, "Do not hold them back." Bring my sons from afar and my daughters from the ends of the earth –

7 everyone who is called by my name, whom I created for my glory, whom I formed and made.'

8 Lead out those who have eyes but are blind, who have ears but are deaf.

9 All the nations gather together and the peoples assemble. Which of their gods foretold this and proclaimed to us the former things? Let them bring in their witnesses to prove they were right, so that others may hear and say, 'It is true.'

10 'You are my witnesses,' declares the Lord, 'and my servant whom I have chosen, so that you may know and believe me and understand that I am he. Before me no god was formed, nor will there be one after me.

11 I, even I, am the Lord, and apart from me there is no saviour.

'You are special to *HaShem*,' said Brandon. 'So special that he will exchange other nations for your sake. You are His witnesses before all the nations of the earth that He is the only God. No matter how far away you are, He has promised to bring you back – from the south and from the west, *"Do not hold them back."*'

There was a loud murmur of approval and many nodding heads as Brandon sat down.

'Well done, Brandon,' said Aaron, as he resumed his place beside him.

There was another huge feast that evening – the end of Shabbat – and Aaron and Brandon did their best to do it justice. It was followed by dancing from the women of the congregation – more subdued than the kind Brandon had seen at Staunton, Virginia, but certainly just as beautiful, colourful and graceful.

The next day they had been invited to a large Pentecostal church in Abuja where, although Christian, the leaders had a great interest in re-connecting with their Jewish heritage. Aaron did the introduction and then invited Brandon to share. He read the same passage from Isaiah and expounded on it a little more than the previous day.

When he finished there was a loud chorus of 'Amen!' from the congregation and the pastor – a huge man – thanked him for his encouragement from the word. There was plenty of enthusiastic singing, in both Igbo and in English – which Aaron and Brandon were able to join in on.

They were once again well fed Nigerian style. And on Sunday evening Brandon and Aaron were invited to share with another large church in the city. Both of them shared this time and again the response was very enthusiastic. Brandon sensed such a hunger in Nigeria – from both practising Jews and from Christians – for a re-connection with their heritage. Brandon determined that he would come back to this country and travel further around it, to encourage the people of God.

All too soon their time in Nigeria was over and they were being sent off home with cheers and tears from *Nnamdi Azikiwe International Airport.* On the flight home Brandon and Aaron discussed the response they had experienced and made plans to further their connection with the Igbos in Nigeria.

Sometime in the Near Future

26 – Tabriz, Northern Iran

A few miles south of the Azerbaijani border, east of Lake Urmia, the Assyrian boy watched motionlessly from behind a rock perched high above the industrial buildings below him.

His father had been killed in 2009, in a vicious Muslim attack on the small Assyrian Pentecostal Church to which he had belonged. The church had been accused of allowing 'non-Assyrians' – in other words converts from Islam – to attend their services.

Yonathan had watched helplessly as his father had been dragged out into the street and beaten mercilessly to death to shouts of, *'Allahu akbar,'* from the hysterical Muslim crowd. Shortly after that the Assyrian Pentecostal Church in Tabriz had been officially closed by the Islamic Revolutionary Court.

He'd been just eleven then. And he had missed his kind and gentle father every day since. Now, though, at eighteen, he was happy to feel that he was doing something to fight back for his father's death and the persecution of his friends. He no longer felt impotent and the frustration within him had nearly disappeared.

The man who had recruited him had checked out his history very carefully, before approaching him one day as he wandered in the countryside near his village. He knew the dark-skinned man only as Sami, but he was aware that he was a Yemenite Israeli.

Sami had met many times now with Yonathan, patiently instructing him about the whole process of production of nuclear materials, making him aware of the critical information that Israel needed about Iran's nuclear programme.

* * *

He knew that a single nuclear bomb requires approximately 25 kilograms of Highly Enriched Uranium (HEU), that has been boosted to at least a concentration of 90 percent.

His country, Iran, currently had more than 10,000 centrifuges in operation – adding thousands of additional machines at a time. Those thousands of machines month by month were steadily increasing the supply of basic nuclear material.

Iran already had the material – low enriched uranium (LEU) – to create five or six bombs. But first that LEU material had to be boosted to weapons-grade, or 90 percent. Each day that passed, that stock of LEU material grew both in volume and potency. The government had admitted (verified by international inspectors) that they had already reached the threshold of 20 percent, with about 300 kilograms by now produced. That was enough to move to the next stage of producing weapons-grade. First they must enrich that to the next level, say 60 percent, and then to 90 percent – then they would have the material for a nuclear bomb!

When they reached the level of 20 percent, they were 90 percent of the way to having weapons-grade uranium. Now it was only a matter of time before 90 percent bomb-quality HEU was available. Depending upon how many cascades and centrifuges were acting in concert, Iran could acquire some 25 kilograms of bomb-ready 90 percent HEU in six to twelve months., At the current exponential growth rate, Iran would have enough HEU to arm several bombs within a year.

His country had constructed many redundant facilities, some under-ground, some probably operating secretly beyond the view of IAEA monitors, some in hospitals. Iran had adopted the Nuclear Non-Proliferation Treaty in 1968 and agreed to permit IAEA inspectors when, in 1974, they signed the 'Safeguards Agreement'.

These enrichment facilities — known or unknown — were crammed with cascades of tall, shiny aluminium centrifuges. Each cascade was made up of dozens of centrifuges. If one cascade went down, even if a complete multi-cascade *'production hall'* stopped operating, or if an entire plant was destroyed, others situated elsewhere in Iran could take up the slack.

Every hour, every day, those centrifuges were creating the HEU nuclear material needed to create a bomb. The centrifuges continued to spin non-stop – despite international sanctions and global pressure.

But even with all the nuclear material accumulated, that still needed to be made into a bomb – not a simple step. The next thing required was for Iran's stockpile of enriched uranium to be formed into a weaponised spheroid object – the warhead – a process that had been under development for many years.

Iran had been seeking to master the machining and engineering skills needed for more than fifteen years, in order to turn HEU into a hemispherical mass capable of being loaded into the cone of a missile to create a warhead.

Chapter 22 – Nigerian Jews

The IAEA had reported that long ago Tehran acknowledged that it had established *"contacts with intermediaries of a clandestine nuclear-supply network in 1987 and the early 1990s, and that, in 1987, it had received ... a 15-page document (the 'uranium metal document'), which outlines the conversion of uranium fluoride compounds into uranium metal and the production of hemispherical enriched uranium metallic components."*

For years Iran had been on a quest to build and detonate a nuclear spheroid payload. Iranian scientists had contacted the Pakistani expert, Khan, and had been particularly eager to learn more about *"neutron cross-section calculations ... and shock-wave inter-actions with metals,"* according to an IAEA report in November 2011.

That same IAEA report attributed to a Member State said that, later, Iranian scientists sought *"complex calculations relating to the state of criticality of a solid sphere of uranium being compressed by high explosives,"*. Those calculations were needed to test the potency of any spheroid warhead Iran would load into the nosecone of a missile. The IAEA had known about this since 2005.

* * *

As he thought about this the sun beat down on the mountainside around Yoni, the rocks shimmering in the heat. To the south west the lake glittered with reflected light. There was a lot of activity in the site down below him today.

The activity had been increasing over recent weeks and yesterday a whole convoy of large articulated trucks had arrived and manoeuvred themselves into position parallel to one another. Today a mobile crane had begun to load the trucks one by one. As soon as loading was complete and the load secured, the huge transporter would head south east, away from the lake towards the Tehran area.

Yonathan knew that things were coming to a climax. He had to get a report to his friend Sami, but once again he heard the unmistakable sound of jets from the Iranian Air Force approaching the valley. Before they screamed immediately overhead Yonathan had disappeared behind the familiar rocks.

Long after the jets had returned to the south he waited patiently in the shadows until, eventually, they began to lengthen and he could move freely out of the mountains, without fear of discovery. Even so he hid by the road-side every time a vehicle approached. Many times patrols of the Revolutionary Guard came this way.

He reached the town of Tabriz safely and melted into its streets and alleys, taking care when crossing the main streets and coming at last to the Assyrian bakery in an alley near the Armenian Cemetery. He slipped in the open back door of the bakery, nodded silently to Raman's wife, Aramina, and went into the store, where Raman joined him, wiping flour from his hands.

Yonathan handed him the tiny SD card with yesterday and today's pictures from his digital camera and reported on the greatly increased activity at the nuclear site. They appeared to be moving out completed missiles, Yonathan reported. Raman handed him a fresh SD card, blessed him and told him to be careful, as he did every time they met.

Next morning the SD card contained an extra text file containing a written summary of Yonathan's report, the card wrapped and sealed in a clean little polythene bag inside a fresh loaf of Raman's bread. An elderly woman bought the loaf early that morning and the message began its journey from Tabriz to Israel.

Neither Yonathan, who continued to watch from his perch in the hills, nor Raman and his wife, were to know that the intelligence would arrive in Israel just a few hours too late.

27 – BBC News 24: 'At Evening Terror ...'

'We interrupt our normal news broadcast to bring you an important breaking story. News is just coming in of a nuclear missile having exploded near Tel Aviv in Israel.

'Good evening. I'm David Olegyah. The BBC have just received news of a tremendous nuclear explosion in Israel. Reports are also coming in of the launch of hundreds of conventional missiles against Israel – fired from southern Lebanon, the Gaza Strip, the Sinai Peninsula, Saudi Arabia, Egypt and Syria. There are alarms sounding all over Israel at the moment. There are flashes and explosions in every part of the country. As far as we can tell, from satellite sources, the nuclear missile was fired from Syrian territory.

'As we try to bring you footage of those explosions, we go now to our Middle East expert, Dr. Rahm Ibrahim, of the British Middle East Institute, for his input on the developing situation. Dr. Ibrahim, what do you make of this news?'

'Well, David, it would appear that Arab and Iranian despair over the failure of the recent Israeli/Palestinian peace process has led to an all out attack on the Jewish state. I can see the explosions on your display as we speak. I'm afraid this situation was almost inevitable. When peace is no longer possible, then war is the only logical outcome.'

'What do you think could be the outcome here?'

'Well, we all know Israel has the most advanced army in the Middle East. They have many missile defence systems, some provided by their allies, the United States, but I can see no way that they can survive a concerted attack from such a combination of forces. This must surely be the demise of the State of Israel as we know it!'

'You really think this could be the end of Israel, Dr. Ibrahim?'

'I fear so. It is a terrible thing to contemplate, but I cannot realistically suggest any other outcome. In the past Israel has succeeded in beating off attacks from one or two countries, but never have they been surrounded by such a formidable ...'

'Sorry to interrupt you, Dr. Ibrahim, but we've just received word of an official statement from Jerusalem, from The Israeli Prime Minister:'

"Good evening. The State of Israel has just come under sustained attack – using both conventional AND nuclear missiles, mortars and rockets – from Syria, Iran, Iraq, Lebanon, Saudi Arabia, Jordan, Egypt, Sudan, the Gaza Strip and possibly other states. Israel is under full red alert, though we do not yet know how many casualties there are. But I want you to know that we will resist this unwarranted attack on our peaceful nation to the utmost. We call upon the United States, and all of our western and other allies, to come to Israel's aid in this our time of greatest need.

"I repeat, this is a totally unwarranted attack on a peaceful nation. We are in dire need of your full support, now. Please use every means possible to come to our aid. Please do not fail us! I leave you now to see to the defence of my country. May the God of Israel come to our aid. Shalom aleichem."

'Well, that was a powerful statement there from the Israeli Prime Minister. If you've just joined us, Israel has come under an all out attack from all sides. At least one nuclear missile has exploded in Israel. We have no idea yet of what casualties are involved, but it must surely be in the tens of thousands? Would you agree, Dr. Ibrahim?'

'Yes, David. It must surely be in the hundreds of thousands, if not more. I'm afraid we will not know the true extent of this terrible calamity for some time ...'

'Sorry, Dr. Ibrahim. We have received a statement from the President of Iran. He says,

'"The Islamic Republic of Iran, together with our Arab allies, have taken a stand on behalf of our Palestinian brothers. We have watched the unbearable arrogance of the Jewish occupiers come to the full, and now, on behalf of the Palestinian people, we have taken the steps necessary to deal with this unacceptable rogue regime.

'"The liberation of Palestine has finally begun. The hated and despised name of Israel will be removed from the Middle East and the land will be restored to its rightful owners, who have been patient with our failure for so long. We will not fail them this time. We will conquer in the name of Allah and of our Palestinian brothers. Allahu akhbar! Allahu akhbar!"

'Similar statements are coming in from Syria, Egypt, Saudi Arabia, etc. – and we are also getting reports of explosions in Lebanon, Saudi Arabia and even in Iraq. Israeli fighters are reported to be in action against targets in southern Lebanon, Gaza and the Sinai Peninsula.

'Back to you, Dr. Ibrahim. This is a very tense situation. Do you think Israel can fight back against such an onslaught?'

'I think what we are seeing are simply the dying struggles of a defeated foe. The Jewish State have carried on their crimes and occupation against the Palestinian people, despite the tide of world opinion against them. They have ignored every agreement aimed at restoring peace. They have continued in their aggression against the Arab nations and against the Islamic Republic of Iran. What we are seeing on your screen tonight was inevitable. I'm afraid there will shortly be no more Israel. The world may mourn, but really, they have brought this upon themselves.'

'No more Israel! Can it really be as serious as that? I know that back in 1948, when Israel fought their War of Independence, the nations who attacked them swore to 'drive the Jews into the sea.'

'Well, it did not happen then, because of western and American interference, but this irritating wound has been festering for far too long. The Palestinian people – who have suffered so much from Israeli occupation and deprivation – will finally be able to live in peace. A great wrong is being righted, at long last.'

'Hmm, that's an interesting opinion, Dr. Ibrahim. But surely, if the Syrians – or the Iranians, maybe – are using nuclear missiles, the land will not be fit to live in any more. The Palestinians will inherit only a nuclear desert? And what about Israel's nuclear missiles? Don't they have what they call 'The Sampson Option'? If Israel's very existence is being threatened, don't you think they will try to use those weapons against those who attack them?

In Six Hours ... the world changed – *Raymond McCullough*

28 – Six Hour War: Aqaba

The young corporal raced the Toyota jeep east and south from Ben Gurion airport on Israel's Highway One, turning south onto Highway 40, bypassing the former Arab towns of Lod and Ramle and merging onto the Highway 6 toll road south and east again towards Beersheva.

Shaul had only just returned from leave, after visiting his brother Reuben and his family in New York City – witnessing the first nuclear strike of the war as his plane had approached the coast of Israel. As they drove Shaul said, 'So, we're at war again? Do you know what my orders are?

'You just arrived in the nick of time, sir,' the young man replied, 'Your company, under *Seren* (Captain) Gefen, are about to head out immediately from Beersheva to Eilat. I believe your captain is expecting to receive further orders by radio before you get to Eilat.

'The Egyptians have been moving heavy armour into the Sinai since darkness fell and the IAF have engaged their F16 fighters over the Sinai and the Saudi Air Force over Midian. Saudi tank squadrons are also moving north towards Aqaba and Eilat. Hamas and their colleagues have been launching hundreds of missiles from the Sinai and the Gaza Strip. I think Israel probably has every drone we own in the air at the moment, and probably every aircraft. All Army reserves have been called up. It's a real make or break situation, sir.'

'So Eilat could be a real hot spot in a few hours, eh?' Shaul mused.

'Looks like it, sir.' the young man replied.

Highway 6 became Highway 40 again and soon they were skirting around the east of the modern desert city of Beersheva (Pop. 250,000). They arrived at the military base outside Beersheva after about an hour. The driver dropped Shaul off at the HQ building and told him Captain Gefen was expecting him. Ten minutes later Shaul – changed by now into military uniform and beginning to get into a war mindset – was seated behind the driver of one of Israel's newly acquired *CombatGuard* Armoured Personnel Carriers.

Manufactured by *Israeli Military Industries*, this all-terrain vehicle – known in Hebrew as *Bodyguard* – with its 54 inch tyres and 95 mph road speed, 75 mph off-road, was capable of going just about anywhere. Carrying eight fully armed soldiers, with its armoured V-section blast-proofed floor, riding nearly three feet above the ground, the vehicle was also capable of surviving mines and IEDs. Armed with the *IMI/General Dynamics* designed *Bright Arrow* 'weapons and active protection system' – able to detect and neutralise both small arms, RPG and missile attacks, controlled remotely from inside the vehicle – it was truly a formidable weapon of war.

Levine's immediate superior, Captain Jacob Gefen (originally born Weinstein), was in the front passenger seat, leading a convoy of similar vehicles, older *Namer* APCs – Hebrew for leopard, also now equipped with *Bright Arrow* – and trucks, south down Highway 40 and eventually onto Highway 90 to Eilat. The original *Namers* had been built from the surplus older *Merkavah I* tank chassis, but the newer ones were now specially built by *General Dynamics* in Ohio, USA, then fitted out in Israel with secret reactive armour and weapons systems.

Captain Gefen studied the map of the Eilat area on his knee, working out their best route when they would reach the small holiday city – sandwiched between Egypt's Taba to the south, the larger Jordanian town of Aqaba immediately to the east, with Saudi Arabia just beyond to the south east.

Ahead of him Shaul could see flashes in the sky to the south and west as the by now familiar *Iron Dome* – and the very latest Star-Wars-like, laser-powered *Iron Beam* – missile defence systems did their job. The radio crackled into life and the captain listened carefully to his new orders. 'OK, lads, we're heading into bandit country very soon – we've been ordered to take Aqaba, neutralise any opposition, secure the perimeter and await further orders. Hope you've all got your passports with you?' he jested.

'We'll be going straight through the Yitzhak Rabin Jordan border terminal, although I don't think they'll be that pleased to see us! When we take the left hand turn onto Route 109 I want half of our armoured vehicles to take the lead as we approach the border. If anyone opens fire on us as we drive through I want you to take them out, understood?'

'*Ken*,' said Shaul in agreement, relaying the order by radio.

The lights of Aqaba grew steadily brighter as they approached, though Eilat was shrouded in darkness. They turned left onto the road for Aqaba and raced through the border post. The Israeli barrier rose as they approached and they heard a cheer from the Israeli Customs guys as they passed.

'Give 'em hell!' one of them shouted out in Hebrew from the darkened post.

In seconds they were smashing through the lowered, but apparently abandoned, Jordanian checkpoint barrier and on into Jordan towards their Highway 65 from the north. As they approached the highway they could see a stream of traffic heading north out of Aqaba.

The convoy slowed only slightly as they swerved right onto the main road south into the city. The traffic, entirely civilian, was all on the other side. It consisted of packed vehicles, mostly overloaded, with family possessions tied to their roofs. There was no sign of any military traffic, or any opposition of any kind. The road south into the town was completely deserted ahead of them, unlike the opposite side.

As they entered the outskirts of the town they could see a similar scramble of traffic heading out of the city to the north east on Highway 15. As they approached the junction, Captain Gefen ordered the convoy to halt as they turned south onto Highway 15. He detailed a group of his men, led by *Samal* (sergeant) Rebekkah Bar-Ilan, utilising a couple of *CombatGuard* vehicles and two of the older *Namer* APCs, to set up two checkpoints – one at the west side of the main junction, with another further up the road at the most northerly junction into the city.

'You'll need at least one Arabic speaker with you at each checkpoint. Don't stop any northbound traffic leaving the town, but check out any vehicle coming south. Looks like there's only civilian traffic to be seen at the moment. We're going into the centre for a recce, but keep us informed if there's any sign of trouble. There'll be tanks arriving shortly from the Negev, so you may need to do traffic control to let the tanks cross the main road. We'll need tanks manning both highways into the city, but the main force will be heading south towards the Saudi border.

'Let's go!' he shouted, and the remainder of the convoy moved forward behind his APC into Aqaba. There was still no sign of any opposition in the town and there was an eerie silence as they entered a town of mostly empty streets. Now and again they heard a panicked cry of *'Yahood, yahood!* (Jews)' as they passed by. They reached the second and larger of the two roundabouts – traffic circles they called them in Canada. *We didn't have them at all in the USA*, Shaul mused.

Gefen ordered his driver to circle the large roundabout as he detailed another checkpoint to be set up at the entrance to the *Prince Haya Hospital*, east of the roundabout.

Let me know if you see anything unusual, especially any military activity,' he commanded. 'Keep a sharp watch on the road to the south east, towards Saudi Arabia. We'll do one quick tour around the town centre and then we'll head past you again towards the port, where we're expecting to rendezvous with the Israeli Navy. They'll be taking over the port and the marinas, and we'll set up a mini checkpoint near them.

'We also need to see what's happening at the Jordanian Army Barracks. By the look of things I suspect that most, or all, of the Army have already fled the town, but you never know, there could be some die-hards just waiting for us to turn up for a firefight.'

After circling the roundabout the rest of the convoy continued down a divided highway to another large oval roundabout opposite the marina and just beyond the prestigious eight storey *Double Tree by Hilton Hotel*. Here the convoy turned right, opposite the marina entrance, and circled the western side of the city centre in a large loop. They could see across to the still-darkened hotels on the Eilat side as they drove.

They circled through another large roundabout and turned east towards the centre and south again after they passed the Islamic hospital on their left. This brought them back to the main divided highway in the centre and they turned right again to once more circle the main city centre roundabout beside their newly established checkpoint at the Prince Haya Hospital.

Gefen checked by radio with his men at the hospital, who reported that all was quiet so far. They headed south east this time on another divided highway, which curved first south and then almost due west towards the Red Sea again. When they reached the junction with the north-south highway, passing several brightly lit international hotels, they now turned south, passing the Aqaba Museum on their right.

The divided highway led past the first entrance road to the port and the Israeli convoy turned into the entrance road and again halted. Gefen detailed another team to set up a temporary checkpoint at the junction, instructing them not to obstruct any traffic fleeing the city to the south, but to halt any inbound traffic, if any, from the south.

Before they moved off again Gefen asked Shaul to try to raise the Israeli Navy, who were meant to be entering the port any time now.

'Shouldn't take them long, sir,' Shaul said. 'They've only had to cross the bay from Eilat. Probably already waiting on us, sir.'

'Let's hope so, Levine. This has been a pretty uneventful invasion, so far, eh?'

'Yes sir, thank HaShem!' Shaul replied.

Shortly after, the Navy replied, 'Wondered what was keeping you guys, actually,' an east European accent chuckled. 'Need any help over there? The Israeli Navy is at your service!'

'No trouble so far,' Gefen replied, taking the mike. We're at the north port entrance now, so we'll proceed in your direction. Hope to eyeball you shortly.'

'Roger and out,' replied the Navy Lieutenant.

'Move out slowly,' Gefen commanded his convoy and they approached the main gates, which appeared to have been left open, though there was no sign of anyone about. Suddenly, a Daihatsu pickup truck accelerated out of a side entrance beyond the gate, its truck filled with metal barrels. As it careered dangerously onto the main road two of the barrels fell off and the truck lurched and swerved, almost out of control.

'Looters!' shouted Gefen, 'Halt, spotlight!'

As the convoy halted and the spotlight came on, blinding the fleeing driver, the truck engine screamed in third gear as it accelerated towards the convoy.

'He's not gonna stop, sir,' Moshe warned.

'Okay, take him out, Lieutenant. There'll be no looting in this city!' he said to Shaul.

Shaul operated the control for the APCs *'Bright Arrow'* Active Protection System (APS), firing the machine gun towards the pickup, piercing the radiator of the truck and bursting one of its front tyres. The truck lurched sideways to their left and mounted the kerb, turning over in the process and coming to a sliding, screeching rest against the security fence.

By the time the truck had come to a halt, Gefen had jumped out to secure the vehicle, Shaul exiting on the right hand side. Suddenly a shot erupted from the disabled vehicle, catching Captain Gefen in the right shoulder. As he slumped to the roadway beside the jeep, Shaul opened fire from the other side with his *Tavor TAR-21* assault rifle, shattering the windscreen of the vehicle.

'La, la, salaam, salaam, shalom, peace!' came a cry from the vehicle.

The shattered windscreen was kicked out and the troops were on high alert for any sign of further aggression, but the blood covered figure who emerged was in no state for any further resistance. He staggered forward, then dropped to his knees on the road, 'Not shoot, not shoot. *Bismillah*!' he cried.

Two soldiers stopped in front of him and while one pointed his rifle, the other went behind and secured his wrists with cable ties. The other soldiers approached the vehicle and watched carefully as two other men crawled slowly out of the vehicle, quickly surrendering on their knees, also. Shaul looked inside the cab for a minute, then turned towards Gefen and drew his hand across his throat.

'Driver's dead,' he shouted to his fellow troops in the APC. 'Get a medic for the captain, now!' Shaul rushed to aid his commanding officer. Pulling a handkerchief from his pocket, he folded it and applied it to the wound inside the captain's shirt. A medic rushed up with his gear and took over, applying some morphine, a dressing and an arm sling.

'Okay,' said Gefen weakly, 'Put them in a truck and secure them to it. Keep on the lookout as we go into the port. There may be other looters hanging around. Probably a lot of valuable merchandise lying around for grabs if this place is as abandoned as it looks.' His speech began to slow and sounded slurred.

The medic said, 'He's lost a lot of blood. We need to lay him down and set up a drip in the truck.' He looked meaningfully at Shaul.

'OK, Lieutenant, take over as acting commander until Command sort something else out. You're in control, now.' Gefen said faintly, then slumped against the side of the vehicle.

'OK,' said Shaul, 'You heard him – you two, give the medic a hand to get the captain into an APC.'

Another soldier arrived at this point with a stretcher and they ferried Captain Gefen to the safety of one of the larger *Namer* tracked APCs, where the medic immediately set up a drip and made him comfortable, covering him with a blanket.

There was a small sentry post beside the open gate and Shaul detailed two of the men to man it. Then he radioed to the Navy to let them know the cause of the shooting, giving his name and explaining that Captain Gefen had handed over command to him.

'OK, we'll keep a lookout from this end. We heard some noises – banging and scraping and so forth, so we could have more unauthorised company about.'

The port area proved to be extensive so, after half an hour of careful checking, and the arrest of another two men with a small flat bed Toyota truck, Shaul decided to hand over the job to the Navy for now.

'We'll leave four men on the gate, and we have a checkpoint at the end of the street. I need to get a move on and secure the road to Saudi Arabia,' he said.

'No problem, we'll take care of the port,' the Navy Lieutenant replied, 'Catch you later.'

The convoy returned to the main roadway, leaving an extra two men to man the gate. 'No one is allowed in. If there is any aggro fire over their heads. After that feel free to shoot them,' Shaul instructed.

The convoy exited the harbour area and returned to the junction with the highway south to the Saudi border, nearly 20 kilometres to the south. While Shaul checked the situation with the men in the APC they had left there, and explained the change of command, the radio crackled. It was Southern Command. Shaul reported in, again explained the change of command and that they were just on their way towards the Saudi border.

'Okay, pity about Captain Gefen, but a good job so far, otherwise. You've had plenty of combat experience in Afghanistan, Levine. We need the border manned ASAP, the centre of town secured and then the airport taken over. We have tanks on their way to support you and we'll send a *Hercules* transport plane to the airport once you let us know you have it under your command. Where do you want to rendezvous with the tanks, Levine?'

'How about at the first junction with Jordan's Highway 65,' said Shaul, 'then they'll be close to the airport to help secure it. I want to check the Jordanian Army barracks first, if that's OK? And leave *Seren* Gefen with a medic and some of the men there to start taking it over.'

'Carry on, Levine. And we'd better make that *Seren* Levine now, I think!'

'Thank you, sir.'

'You'll earn it tonight, I'm sure. Keep us informed of progress. By the way, your men might like to know that the nuclear missile hit well south of Tel Aviv – place called Gaza City! We wanted to keep that quiet for a bit, so the world might realise what we are up against. Our troops have also entered the Sinai, southern Gaza, south Lebanon, Syria and they've crossed the Allenby Bridge heading for Amman, to your north.'

'That could explain why we've encountered no military here, sir.'

'Indeed. Well, over and out, *Seren*.'

Shaul passed on the good news and a cheer erupted from his men, relieving a little of the tension that had been building up among them.

'OK, men,' Shaul interrupted, 'We've still a lot to accomplish tonight. We've had a pretty easy time of it so far, but that may not last. Let's get down to the border and see what the situation is there. Last we heard Saudi tanks were heading our way. And who knows what Jordan's Arab Legion are up to.'

'That's it, cheer us up, why don't you? – er, Captain,' one of the men heckled. There was some good natured laughter in response.

The men on the check-point had seen no traffic at all, except for a few cars from the city, which had turned abruptly and fled on spying the troops and their torches.

The convoy sped on down the divided highway southwards towards the Saudi Arabian border, passing under large conveyors that loaded the ships from the huge works of the *Arab Potash Company* on their left. They also passed the *Red Sea Dive Center and Hotel* on the way, the roundabout opposite it featuring a wooden ship. The road ran around a bend and continued past new hotels and tourist beaches on the right and a new housing development on the left. Eventually, they approached the border along the coast road some minutes later – they could see no lights.

'Funny, you'd expect to see floodlights at an international border, wouldn't you?' Shaul queried. 'Halt!'

Shaul ordered a foot patrol to approach the Jordanian border post a couple of hundred metres ahead. A few minutes later they reported that the post was deserted.

'In that case, gentlemen, it has just become the Israeli border with Saudi Arabia!' Shaul detailed a larger group of his men to remain at the border along with their APCs.

'Some of you stay with the radio and get some rest,' he instructed his sergeant, 'but I want six men on duty at the border at all times. Use your night-sight goggles to keep an eye on the Saudis. Report any activity, OK?'

'OK, Captain' *Samal* Tamari replied.

The now much smaller force turned on the main road and headed back rapidly to Aqaba. 'One more area secured,' thought Shaul as he studied the map on his knee.

'OK, turn right towards those hotels again,' he instructed the driver, referring to *Day's Hotel* and the *Coral Bay Resort*. 'We should be able to find the barracks from here. Wait till the road straightens out and you can see the main roundabout ahead at the hospital, then take the first right.' When they had made the turn he instructed, 'Just before the road bends to the left again take another right. The barracks should be down there on the left.

As they took the last right hand turn, Shaul gave orders to his men. They swung left into the barracks compound ready to return fire, but all remained ominously quiet. Two squads of men deployed to right and left of the entrance as Shaul grabbed his weapon and headed for the door.

One of his men kicked the door open and Shaul rushed in and quickly turned to the right. More men came rapidly through the door and moved to left and right – still no opposition. Shaul signalled for some of his men to check further down the corridor. The building was empty. They quickly searched the barracks, but no one was home.

Shaul left ten men to secure the building and guard the entrance, plus *Seren* Gefen and the medic, encouraging them to search for any food and get some heated up for themselves, eat and then prepare some for the rest of the force. Shaul believed firmly in the old adage that an army marches on its stomach. He hurriedly reassembled his remaining force to head back out to the airport.

'We might be just in time to meet up with the tank company,' he told them. And, sure enough, as they turned onto Highway 65, passing their own checkpoint, they could see the trail of dust heading through the border post. They waited with the men at their northerly checkpoint until the first *Merkavah IV* tanks rolled to a halt beside them. A hatch opened and the tank squadron commander looked across at Shaul.

'*Seren* Levine, I believe?

'*Ken*,' said Shaul, 'as of half an hour ago.'

Chapter 28 – Six Hour War: Aqaba

'Congratulations. I'm *Segen* (lieutenant) Alon Peled. Appropriate name for a tank commander, eh? he said (*peled* meaning steel). 'You need some *peled* in support?' he barked with a grin on his face.

'Would sure be useful,' replied Levine. 'We have an airport to secure. Then I suppose I'll be liaising with the IAF, next! How many tanks have you?'

'No problem. We have ten,' said the commander, 'Airport's just up the road to the left here – where all the lights are? Mighty nice of the Jordanians to leave them on for us, don't you think? Want us to lead you in?'

'Be my guest,' Shaul replied, 'but I don't think we'll see much opposition, going by the situation we've found so far. Maybe three or four of your tanks could head on into the town. There's a big roundabout there and we have a checkpoint operational at the *Prince Haya Hospital* on the left hand corner of it. Your tanks could pull up on the grass in the centre, there. Should be a bit intimidating for the locals, eh? Oh, yeah, we've also secured a small barracks, so there'll be somewhere for your men to recuperate later, unless they prefer their tanks, of course!'

'No problem,' said *Segen* Peled again, and he instructed his corporal, with four of his tanks, to head for the town centre.

The tanks roared to life and four headed south, while the other six turned north onto the airport road. When the last tank had exited the road from the border post Shaul's convoy pulled in behind them.

The tanks entered the precincts of the *King Hussein International Airport* and deployed 'hull down' to right and left, their barrels pointing threateningly at the buildings. Shaul gave orders for about half of his troops to dismount their vehicles and they approached the entrance carefully. There was no sign of any activity at the entrance so they proceeded, still with care, on into the main airport terminal. This was much bigger than the *Eilat Airport* just across the border, being an international airport, whereas the current *Eilat Airport* was only a local facility – at least until the new replacement international airport was completed a little to the north.

When they gained the main concourse they found trolleys, bags and belongings scattered untidily all around the area, but no passengers or crew to be found. When they had checked all of the building pretty thoroughly Shaul returned to his vehicle and radioed Southern Command.

'Airport, Saudi border and barracks all secure, sir. The place is like the *Marie Celeste* – anyone who hasn't already left is in the process of leaving, by the looks of things. I don't understand it, sir. A few hours ago Israel seemed to be on the brink of extinction.'

'Well done, Captain Levine. They must have heard the news about Gaza?'

'But how did that happen, sir? I don't understand?'

'Well, no one knew about this except the top brass and the people involved, but apparently those egg-head cyber warfare guys up in Haifa Technion have succeeded in hacking into the control systems of the Iranian and Syrian missiles. They re-directed them in flight.

'Remember that a lot of software these days is of Israeli origin in the first place – so apparently we were able to re-program the flight paths of those missiles to either overshoot and take out a lesser target, or, preferably, to turn back on themselves and attack their own launch sites.

'There have been several nuclear strikes on Iran, Iraq and Syria – Damascus is no more! Now there's poetic justice, wouldn't you say?'

'That's unbelievable, sir. Almost a miracle! So, would you say then that we're beginning to gain the upper hand yet, sir?'

'A miracle? Yes, it just might be that, Levine. And we are most assuredly gaining the upper hand. Arab morale doesn't do well when they blow themselves up, you know. Probably explains why you've found no opposition in Aqaba. We've already taken most of the remaining Gaza strip with very few losses. Some of the Hamas leaders tried to escape in boats, but the Navy scuppered them. The same sort of story in Lebanon with Hezbollah and in the Sinai, too. They were expecting us to lie down and surrender, no doubt.'

The officer cleared his throat and continued. 'We'd like you to wait there for an IAF *Hercules C-130* transport plane, which is on its way to you as we speak. They will be carrying reserve troops and some Air Traffic Control specialists to take over the airport. Once they have control we'd like you to hand over your operations in Aqaba and get ready for an assault on Saudi Arabia.

'More reserve troops will be across very soon to take over your command posts. The tanks you have with you will be under your command from here on in, and I expect you will want them to lead the attack. Our IAF fighters have been busy tonight. They've taken out a lot of Saudi tanks with their laser guided missiles, so the Saudis should be well softened up by now. Your mission now is to take control of the ancient area of Midian – north western Saudi Arabia, just across from where you are now – as far south as the city of Tabuk. Let me know when you are ready to cross the border, Levine. *B'hatzlacha!* (Good luck!)'

'*Toda raba*, Sir,' was all Shaul could manage at this amazing – almost unbelievable – news.

He quickly relayed the gist of it to his own men and to *Segen* Peled and his tank crews. The sound of cheers filled the empty airport building.

'I wonder where they've all gone, sir?' one of his men queried.

I don't know, son, but this reminds me of some words from Isaiah that I read on the plane here from New York, just after that first missile exploded:

"At evening time, sudden terror, but before the morning they are gone!"

And it also says,

"When He rebukes them they flee far away, driven before the wind like chaff on the hills, like tumbleweed before a gale ... This is the portion of those who loot us, the lot of those who plunder us."

'Well, amen to that, Sir!'

'Check with the rest of the troop if we have any Israeli flags with us, would you? There's something else I need to do before we move down to the border.'

'Yes, sir!'

29 – BBC News 24: Cyber Warfare?

'Sorry, we've got more news coming in. It's going to be an eventful night here, I think. We've just heard that there has been a huge explosion in the heart of Damascus. It could well have been a nuclear explosion, we are told. And apparently we have some footage of that first explosion in Israel. It appears NOT to be Tel Aviv itself, but somewhere further south in Israel, perhaps Ashdod, or Ashkelon.

'You can see the huge mushroom cloud forming there – after that nuclear explosion. We are witnessing a nuclear war, here – for the first time since 1945! That is a truly terrifying sight to behold – awesome and frightening. We estimate that perhaps 250-300,000 people may have died in that explosion.

'And, as we just reported, there has been a similar explosion in the city of Damascus, in Syria. We are also getting reports of fierce fighting all around Israel: in the Gaza Strip – where we believe Israeli planes have been bombing targets. Also in the Sinai Peninsula and in southern Lebanon and Syria, east of the Golan Heights.'

'Wait, we have news of yet another large explosion – this time in Iraq, or possibly even in Iran. My goodness, Dr. Ibrahim, do you think these could be a result of Israeli retaliation? We just mentioned their 'Sampson Option' – could this be it?'

'Well, just possibly. But there is no way a small country like Israel can survive an all out attack from eight or so nations. This is terrible!'

'We are getting our first report from the US now. Their satellites apparently tracked the first missile aimed at Israel. It was indeed launched from Syria, but it appears to have overshot its target and scored a direct hit on Gaza City. My God! The Syrians have destroyed Gaza City with a nuclear weapon!'

'This cannot be true.' Dr. Ibrahim replied. 'Surely the Americans have made a mistake. I think maybe this is just US propaganda at work – trying to bolster the Israeli morale in some way. I don't think this could be Gaza City – it must be Ashdod, or maybe Ashkelon.'

'Well, Dr. Ibrahim, we're getting further word that several missiles have indeed been fired towards Israel from Iran, and possibly from Iraq, as well.

In Six Hours ... the world changed – *Raymond McCullough*

The first of those missiles has apparently mysteriously reversed its course over western Jordan and returned to Iran where it has now exploded north of Tehran. And we're getting word of more explosions in Iran – near to the city of Shiraz ... and another close to the city of Tabriz, in the north.

'We have a satellite feed coming in now. Oh. my God! You can see the lights on the dark background of the earth – those are apparently nuclear explosions ... there's another one! That looks to be in the centre of Iran, possibly near Isfahan? What we are watching here is satellite footage, from an American satellite, of nuclear weapons detonating in various parts of Iran. And there is a confirmed report of another nuclear explosion in Damascus, Syria. We may have some footage of that one soon.

'Meanwhile the breaking news is that the first missile, fired from Syrian territory, and obviously aimed at Tel Aviv, has apparently over-shot its target and exploded in Gaza City. That is surely good news for Israel, but what can have gone so badly wrong. Surely there is no way the Syrians would intentionally target the Hamas stronghold!

'We'll come back to you, Dr. Ibrahim, in a few minutes. I want to bring in another expert now, Dr. Francis Eggenhamm, from the European Defence Research Establishment, based in Stuttgart. Dr. Eggenhamm, what do YOU think is happening here?'

'Hello, David. Yes, well, this seems to be a very complex situation that we are watching develop here. Firstly, it is apparent that Iran, along with Syria and Iraq, her natural allies, has joined forces with the Sunni nations – Egypt, Saudi Arabia, Jordan, etc. This is unprecedented. Granted Egypt and Syria joined forces back in 1973 to attack Israel in the Yom Kippur War, but political allegiances have changed dramatically since then – especially with the demise of the old Soviet Union in 1991. Russia, by the way, will be watching these events closely.'

'Yes, but what has happened here. A missile – apparently targeted on Tel Aviv, has instead destroyed Gaza City. What do you think could have gone wrong?'

'Well, that was my next point, in fact. There has perhaps been some fault in the targeting circuitry, or possibly in the computer control software itself. It is certainly very unusual for a missile control system to go so badly wrong – especially to score a direct hit on another city. Then there are these other explosions which are now being reported in Iran, and possibly Iraq.

'That would lead me to think that there is something more going on here. One misdirected missile could be put down to some kind of fault, or malfunction, but several missiles, originally fired from Iran and Syria, have now turned against their own forces, or their allies. Certainly, neither Iran, nor Syria, would intentionally target the Hamas stronghold of Gaza. They have been close allies for years. Iran currently supplies most of Hamas' weaponry.

Chapter 29 – BBC News 24: Cyber Warfare?

'Nor could there be this degree of malfunction. Remember how many missiles were fired during the Iran/Iraq war, back in the eighties? They surely had enough experience of missile technology from that – though I must say, given a choice between Israeli technology and Iranian technology, I know which I'd rather bet on!

'No! I think we are most likely seeing a perfect example of cyber warfare at its best. Who better than the Israelis to infiltrate and hack into control systems. We are all dependent these days on Israeli technology. Our computer systems, smartphones and much of the software we use – for instance, social media – was most likely developed in Israel. And these are also the people who developed StuxNet!

'Now, if you were an Israeli software developer – and there was even a slight chance that, eventually, your software could be used by an enemy against you – wouldn't you perhaps build in some sort of 'back door', whereby you could later hack into their systems and make changes. I think that may well be what we are seeing here. And, if that is the case, a war that was set in motion to bring about the annihilation of the State of Israel, might well result in the annihilation, or near it, of their enemies. And wouldn't that change the whole Middle Eastern picture?'

'Well, you have really given us something to think about, there, Dr. Eggenhamm,' said David. *'Cyber warfare? Could that be what we are seeing enfolding here? Well, we have yet more news coming in, but first the headlines again ...'*

* * *

'Back now to Dr. Ibrahim. What do you think of Dr. Eggenhamm's suggestion, that we may already be seeing a turnaround in this war, because Israel may have re-directed these missiles, originally aimed at their destruction?'

'Well, it is, I suppose, just remotely possible. I think we'd need to wait and see on that score.'

'OK, we have news now that large numbers of Egyptian tanks are moving east into the Sinai – obviously on their way toward Israel. Saudi Arabian tanks are also reported to be moving rapidly north, towards the Jordanian border at Aqaba, again with Israel as their destination. We also have a report that the Sudanese Air Force has just been wiped out by the Israeli Air Force. It looks like this war is not over yet, Dr. Ibrahim?'

'Well, I really don't know what to say. We'll have to see how things develop, surely?'

'Yes, but they don't seem to be developing in either Iran's or the Arabs' favour, at the moment, do they, Dr. Ibrahim?'

Dr. Ibrahim was looking increasingly more upset and looked around him wildly, raising his hands in a sort of shrug.

'Perhaps we'll come back to you in a moment – Dr. Eggenhamm, you mentioned that this was perhaps an unlikely alliance: Egypt and Saudi Arabia – Sunni Muslim countries – teaming up with Shi'ite Iran and Alawite controlled Syria?'

'Yes, indeed! This is, I think, a once in a lifetime venture. Iran have obviously been able to develop the nuclear weapons – which we in the west allowed them to do, despite repeated warnings from Israel. In fact, let me be Frank here – Dr. Francis Eggenhamm smiled fleetingly at his own often used pun – if Israel survives this night, then it will certainly be in spite of what we, the western nations have failed to do – that is, prevent a nuclear Iran.

'If, as I just said, we all come out of this intact, then we will certainly owe a debt of gratitude to the nation of Israel, who are paying the price for our failure and ineptitude. The United States in particular, will be deeply in their debt, for surely, if this had gone Iran's way, would the US and Europe not be the next targets in their sights?

'But back to my other point – about this being an unlikely coalition ..?'

'Sorry, I have to interrupt you again, Dr. Eggenhamm ... We have more reports of explosions in Iran and Iraq – and another nuclear missile has apparently destroyed the Muslim holy pilgrimage site of Mecca! Any thoughts on that, Dr. Ibrahim?'

Dr. Ibrahim sputtered, 'Mecca! They've destroyed Mecca? This is a disaster ... a disaster! Mecca, Bismillah!' He bowed his head and was clearly weeping.

'Back to you, then, Dr. Eggenhamm. You were about to tell us something further?'

'Yes, and what you've just told us emphasises the point I was about to make. A coalition of Iran and Syria with the Sunni states would only have a hope of lasting if it succeeded in its plan from the outset. The fact that it is obviously going badly wrong – probably at Israel's instigation – will greatly weaken its coherence.

'With Mecca destroyed now, the breakup may already be under way. Mecca, as we know, is in Saudi territory, destroyed by an Iranian missile – so I don't see the Saudis lasting too long in this. Either they may pull out in disgust, or they could well blame Iran for the missile and turn against them! As Dr. Ibrahim just said, for Muslims of any persuasion this is looking to become a complete disaster. Of course, I don't know what the outcome will be, but Sunni/Shi'ite/ Alawite unity doesn't feature high on my list of the probabilities.'

Chapter 29 – BBC News 24: Cyber Warfare?

The camera briefly switched to a shot of Dr. Ibrahim for possible affirmation of this, but he turned his face away and waved his hands at the camera, as if to shoo it away. Then he staggered to his feet and, muttering to himself, stumbled out of the TV studio. The camera switched back to the presenter.

'Well, it would appear that Dr. Ibrahim has left the discussion ...

He paused, briefly, 'And now the news headlines again: an all out war has erupted across the Middle East after nuclear explosions in ...'

In Six Hours ... the world changed – *Raymond McCullough*

30 – Six Hour War: The Land of Midian

Shaul handed over control of the airport to the IAF and newly arrived Army reserve troops and their Air Traffic Control and other experts, explaining to the Reserve commander where his own men were stationed, so they could relieve them shortly. They planned to have the airport operational again as soon as possible, linked in with the other Israeli airports. They were obviously planning a lengthy stay.

Shaul bid them farewell and spoke briefly to the commander of the tank unit, then headed to his own vehicle and they moved off towards the town centre, the tanks rumbling in their rear.

Shaul checked first with his two checkpoints in the north of the city. They had seen little action, apart from witnessing the mass evacuation of Aqaba on the roads north. The traffic had almost ceased now. Shaul instructed *Samal* Bar-Ilan that they were to be replaced very soon and where to rendezvous with the remainder of the unit at the Jordanian Army barracks.

'We'll try to get some food rustled up. We've got a long night ahead of us, yet,' he told her, thinking briefly that she seemed to be quite an attractive woman, even dressed in military garb.

Next they checked on the post outside the hospital. There were only a couple of doctors remaining to care for a few patients too seriously ill to be safely evacuated. Shaul took an interpreter and spoke to them, trying to reassure them that they were in no danger from the Israeli troops. They didn't seem too convinced, but nodded nervously anyway.

Shaul then sent the majority of his troops back to the barracks, instructing them to organise food for the whole unit, including the tank crews, and to rest for a short while.

Meanwhile he took a small task force and headed towards the Red Sea.

'Got that flag, then?' he asked.

'Sure,' came the reply from the rear seats.

Let's claim this as Israeli territory, then,' he proclaimed.

They halted beside the huge flagpole, which was one of the better known landmarks of Aqaba – visible from well out in the Red Sea. Two of his troopers quickly lowered the Jordanian flag, releasing it, folding it carefully and handing it over to Shaul. He placed it on the seat of the jeep and attached the Star of David flag to the rope, then hauled it aloft. His men cheered as it flew high over the town.

They turned back to their vehicles and Shaul remarked, 'That's another good job accomplished, then. Quite a night so far, eh?'

His men agreed.

By the time they arrived back at the barracks the tank crews had dismounted their tanks and were queueing for hot food in the small canteen.

'They left us some food, then?' Shaul asked.

'Plenty, sir,' they replied, 'Get yourself a plate, sir.'

Shaul filled his plate and took it to a table with his men. His northerly outposts reported in and got some food and then his city centre outpost at the hospital returned. Again he noticed the lithe movement of Rebekkah Bar-Ilan as she sauntered over to their table and began to eat. *Hmm, an interesting soldier,* he thought to himself.

He quickly assigned a group of those who had already eaten to relieve the men at the port entrance and at the border post. The tank commander also detailed some of his tank crews who had eaten to relieve the tanks on the border.

Shaul ate quickly and then stood, looking around at his own men and the tank crews.

'OK, guys, we are now a joint force. Once the other guys have arrived and eaten we move out. We are leaving Aqaba in safe hands. Our harbour and border squads should have been replaced by the time we join them, then we cross the border into Saudi Arabia.'

Twenty minutes later the combined force moved out of the barracks, by which time new troops had arrived to take their place. The convoy re-assembled and headed to the border, collecting their stray outposts as they went. The replacement border unit had reported no action on the Saudi side of the border at all. Their night-sights had shown no sign of human activity.

'Only sign of life we've seen was a porcupine scuttling down the road,' they said.

'OK, well, maybe we can supply you with some action in Saudi Arabia, then,' Shaul jested.

The men smiled at him, but their faces were set. This might not be any picnic. They had heard the reports earlier of tanks heading north for their area and watched as Israeli jets screamed overhead moving south to engage the enemy forces.

Shaul took the radio and called in to Southern Command.

'We're ready to cross the Saudi border, sir. All our men have been replaced by Reserve troops and we're fed and ready to go. No injuries so far, sir. And we've left prisoners – looters from the port area – back in the cells at the barracks. *Seren* Gefen is in charge there, sir. He seems to be recovering a bit after some food and medical attention.'

'Well done, Levine. Well, the news most relevant to you guys, is the nuclear missile that struck Mecca a short while ago! Now the Saudis are trying to figure out who their enemies really are. For your sakes we hope they decide its Iran, more than Israel. Our fighters have already engaged enemy tanks heading north, earlier on, but the last sortie reported tanks heading east and then north east towards Iraq, so maybe they've had a change of plan.

'Have you a map of Saudi Arabia, Levine?'

'Yes, sir,' Shaul replied, 'One that covers the north west area, anyway.'

'Should be all you need, as long as you can see Tabuk on it?'

'Yes, sir, Tabuk, and the whole surrounding area.'

'Good, we want you to help take Tabuk, if possible. It's a city of around half a million population. There are two roads out of Tabuk to the south and east. We need to guard those roads. Then, if all goes well, it would be a bonus to take the small town of Duba, on the Red Sea and double back up Highway 5, then 392 to the Gulf of Aqaba, a little place called Seham Bay – opposite Sharm El Sheikh, on the Egyptian side. Accomplish that and the Land of Midian is in our hands. With our tanks now in the Sinai, we'll soon control both sides of the Straits of Tiran. Make sure you've got plenty of water with you. A bit dry down there.'

'No problem. Land of Midian it is, sir! Roger and out.'

Shaul replaced the handset and relayed the latest war news to his men, who were greatly encouraged to hear about the destruction of Mecca.

'Wow! That should give the Saudis something to think about – hit by an Iranian missile, eh?' Bar-Ilan mused. 'Let's hope that starts up the old Sunni-Shia enmity once again. Get some of them out of our hair, at least.'

Shaul agreed, then returned to study the map. Just 5km across the border was the small Red Sea resort town of Haql. A short distance south of Haql Highway 5 turned inland through the mountains until it forked south again, with 394 going east to meet Highway 15, leading south to Tabuk.

Highway 5 was bounded by the Red Sea on the west and impenetrable mountains on the east. As they neared the town Shaul ordered his convoy to stop between two bends, where the road swept out towards the sea, then turned south again. According to the map they would approach the town by a long section of straight road, where they would be vulnerable to enemy fire. He sent four of his tanks to move carefully around the final bend, searching the road ahead for signs of enemy forces.

A shell exploded in the road close to the tanks. A second shell was taken out by the *Bright Arrow* weapon system firing its defensive grenade. The commanders veered their tanks east to the edge of the road, to present a lesser target, at the same time as their barrels raised and fired at a Saudi tank on the eastern edge of the road close to the town ahead. Shaul gave his tank crews free reign and the first two revved up and charged towards the enemy – which appeared to consist of only a single tank – firing as they went.

The enemy tank was at the northern edge of the entrance to a large wadi, which headed east into the interior. The flat area of the town itself had been formed by the outflow from this wadi. As the lead tank drew nearer, the Israeli tank commander saw the hatches open and the crew jump to the ground, running rapidly across the wadi towards the town.

As he drew level, he realised why the tank had not moved – the track had been damaged, probably before they had engaged it. He reported the situation to Shaul, who began moving his convoy forwards again, as the tanks closed with the town, experiencing no further resistance. They could hear traffic revving in the distance and what could have been the sound of other tanks receding from the town southwards.

The town itself was all but deserted as they arrived. A modern settlement, with a divided highway approaching and encircling it to the east, with six similar radiating roads leading to a large, roughly hexagonal, open central area, surrounding a large square mall in the centre. All the buildings looked clean and very new. To the west of this, between the town and the Red Sea, several modern hotels and apartment buildings were still brightly lit.

Shaul sent two tanks along Highway 5 to the east of Haql, while another two crossed some open ground to join the town's ring road on the seaward side. He ordered the two sets of tanks to halt short of the junction south of the town, opposite two of the radial roads, where they both had a good field of fire towards any enemy coming from the south.

Another pair followed the second pair, stopping when they gained the ring road, opposite the first of the radial roads. The remainder of Shaul's forces followed Highway 5 to the east, then turned towards the town centre – apart from a pair of tanks which travelled on to the next radial road on the east side of Haql, and halted. Five of the six radial roads were now covered, and the sixth was under view from both of Shaul's leading tank pairs.

There was no sign of any more enemy activity as Shaul's convoy, with the remaining two tanks in the lead, approached the city's hexagonal centre.

'Quite a tidy little town, eh? Nice place for a holiday, maybe?' Shaul commented. His driver mumbled, *"Like chaff in the wind, tumbleweed in a gale!"*

The column forked in two as they entered the centre ring and halted. The centre of the city was deserted.

Shaul radioed Southern Command. 'We met only one tank in Haql, sir. The crew abandoned it and ran away. No other resistance and no sign of anybody around. We have the town surrounded at the moment, sir. There was some traffic leaving the city to the south and a possibility that there were tanks heading that way, too. Permission to carry on south and east, sir?'

'That might be something to do with the fact that Mecca's been hit by a nuclear missile, Levine. I expect word has travelled by now. We have reports of tanks moving away from your area, north east towards the Iraqi border. The Saudis may well be blaming Iran on the destruction of Mecca – it was their missile after all!

'At any rate they have fired conventional missiles at Iranian targets and the Saudi and Iranian navies appear to have engaged. The Iranians also appear to have attacked ISIS positions with rockets and mortars and ISIS are returning their fire. Our own F16 fighters are having a problem choosing free targets!

'All the more reason for you to hasten south to Tabuk, Levine. Take advantage of the Saudis being distracted by Iran. We have some of the Reserve reinforcements coming behind you, so they can secure Haql. It looks as if this coalition against us is beginning to unravel fast.'

'Yes, sir. Maybe HaShem has given them into our hands, sir? *"He who watches Israel neither slumbers nor sleeps."*' Shaul volunteered.

'Well, I'm not religious, myself, but somebody has sure been on Israel's side this night – so I won't argue with you, Levine. Over and out.'

Shaul gave instructions to his forces to head out to the south and they re-formed on Highway 5. The easterly pair of tanks he instructed to turn north and then east again to follow the parallel road, joining highway 5 further south. The main force continued south, passing the small Hyatt Haql Hotel, before passing through a roundabout, where the alternative route joined again and Highway 5 began to head south east into the interior, towards Tabuk. The road continued into more mountainous territory and after half an hour they reached Aisharaf, the junction with 394, which turned due east, while Highway 5 continued to the south.

On their way through the mountains they passed eight Saudi tanks which were completely burnt-out. The convoy manoeuvred slowly around the remains and, after another half hour of travel through the mountains, the surroundings became more flat and desert-like, as they approached the village of Bir Ibn Hirmas and the junction with Highway 15, which ran north to the nearby

Jordanian border and south to Tabuk – only a few kilometres away to the south, now.

Shaul again sent four of his tanks ahead, two turning north at the junction and halting, the other pair turning to the south and also halting. Shaul's forces came to a standstill. Several more destroyed tanks and APCs were scattered along the highway to the south, still smouldering. About 30 km further south along the highway was the Saudi city of Tabuk, population around 570,000.

31 – BBC News 24: Enemies Divided?

'*The Headlines at 4 am:*
Nuclear War in the Middle East!

'*Good morning. I'm David Olegyah. The Middle East is in flames! Several nuclear missiles have been launched towards Israel – apparently from both Syria and Iran – but instead they have hit Gaza City, Damascus, Beirut, Mecca and several cities and military targets in Iraq and Iran.*

'*All the countries surrounding Israel, including Iran and Sudan, had apparently conspired together to attack Israel, using both nuclear missiles and conventional weapons. The first nuclear attack appears to have overshot its target – Tel Aviv – and instead completely destroyed the Palestinian city of Gaza. Hundreds of thousands would appear to have died in this city alone. We see footage here from an American destroyer in the eastern Mediterranean Sea, of smoke rising from what used to be Gaza City.*

'*Other missiles – mostly fired from Iran – have destroyed Damascus, Beirut, Mecca – again with great loss of life – and other missiles have mysteriously appeared to turn around and return to strike their own launch sites in Iran, resulting in great loss of life there, too.*

'*Meanwhile, Israel appears to be fighting a battle on all fronts for her very existence – though none of the intended nuclear strikes have been successful in hitting Israeli targets. Conventional missiles, however, have been launched in their hundreds – if not thousands – from Syria, southern Lebanon, Jordan, the Gaza Strip and the Sinai Peninsula.*

'*Egyptian tanks have been moving into the Sinai area and Saudi tanks have been moving towards the Jordanian and Israeli borders. Israeli tanks and aircraft have been engaging these attackers. Israeli jets have been active all over the Middle East, even as far as the Sudan, where the Sudanese Air Force is reported to have been completely destroyed.*

'*The Israeli navy have also been active in defending against this apparently unprovoked attack. There are unconfirmed reports of Egyptian and Saudi warships being attacked in the Red Sea. We'll bring you more news on that as we receive it.*

'Israel has stated that it has not yet fired ANY of its own nuclear missiles in its defence and that their air, sea and land forces are currently engaged in fierce battles on all sides for their very survival. The Israeli Prime Minister called upon the USA and other western nations to intervene on their behalf. It remains to be seen whether Israel can indeed survive this onslaught from at least ten different nations, if we include the Palestinians of the West Bank and Gaza Strip.

'Just a few minutes ago our European war expert – Dr. Francis Eggen-hamm, from the European Defence Research Establishment in Stuttgart – speculated that such a malfunction of so many missiles could only be due to cyber warfare by Israel, using their enemies weapons against them. He'll be joining us again in a few moments.

'And we are just getting a report that Saudi Arabia has now launched missile strikes against Iran and that Saudi tanks are heading towards the Iraq/Kuwait border, en route to Iran. Iranian missiles have also been fired at Saudi Arabia, hitting Riyadh and several other cities. It seems that the Sunni/Shi'ite coalition against Israel is already beginning to fall apart. Iran and Saudi Arabia are not natural allies, and it seems that the missile strike against Mecca has put paid to their united front against Israel.

'Meanwhile, we are getting reports that Israeli tanks and troops have taken Aqaba, in Jordan, and are also moving towards Amman, Jordan's capital. Jordan have also participated in this attack against Israel, but it appears to be backfiring in their case, at least. Israeli tanks are also moving deep into the Sinai and towards the Suez Canal, while other Israeli forces appear to have crossed the border into Saudi Arabia and are moving south towards the city of Tabuk.

'There is just total chaos in the whole Middle East region at the moment! So much is happening at once that it is very difficult to keep up with events as they happen.

'The American Fifth Fleet, based in the Gulf State of Bahrain have gone to full scale alert, due to the fighting now between Saudi Arabia and Iran. Many ships of the fleet have already left port and are deploying further out in the Persian Gulf. Actually, incredibly, the US have warned Israel not to approach the Gulf States, or the US will be forced to retaliate!

'This is unbelievable! The US is regarded as Israel's faithful ally, yet not only have they not come to the aid of Israel – as requested by the Israeli Prime Minister at the beginning of this war – but they have now threatened to attack Israeli forces, if they approach the Gulf States! US warships in the Mediterr-anean are also on full alert, but appear to be simply keeping a watchful eye on developments along the coast. They are also there, presumably, to keep the Russians in check. What is your opinion, Dr. Eggenhamm?'

Chapter 31 – BBC News 24: enemies divided?

'Yes,' Dr. Frank Eggenhamm replied, 'I would think they are there partly to achieve that – and to defend their Turkish NATO ally. Turkey, as far as we know, has not yet been involved in this conflict. I suppose that is something to be thankful for. But the US are also, like the rest of the world, curious to find out what is really going on here. This war has taken the whole world by surprise.

'This is not just a flare-up between Israel and Hamas, or Israel and Hezbollah – this is a full scale Middle Eastern war, bigger than any other conflict since the Second World War. And, as I said earlier, brought about by the US and Europe's failure to limit Iran's development of nuclear weapons.

'We can now see that Israel's constant warnings, ignored by the rest of the world, have proven to be prophetic. And Israel is now paying the price for the reluctance of the West to take Iran's threats seriously. If, indeed, Israel manages to survive this war and still remain a viable nation, it will have been entirely due to their own efforts, and certainly no thanks to their so-called ally, The United States, or their other western allies.'

'Dr. Eggenhamm, what do you think is happening with Israeli forces reportedly entering Jordan and Saudi Arabia?'

'Well, Israel have now got nothing left to lose. They have found themselves once again completely on their own and outnumbered and now there seem to be some cracks appearing in the forces of their enemies. Saudi Arabia are now retaliating against what they see as an Iranian nuclear strike – not only against a Saudi city, but against their most holy place, the birthplace and focus of Islam. Israel appear to be taking advantage of this split in their enemies forces to take Saudi territory ...'

'Yes, what do you think the Israelis would hope to gain from this?'

'I would expect they hope to create as large a buffer zone as they can – the same thing appears to be happening with them entering Sinai. Before they handed the Sinai Peninsula back to Egypt, as part of the peace deal back then, Israel had a large area of desert between them and Egyptian forces. Now that Egypt has broken their peace treaty, without any Israeli provocation, Israel are going to try to take back all, or as much as they can of the Sinai, again as a buffer zone.

'I wouldn't be surprised that, if Israel can gain any ground in southern Lebanon and Syria – also in Jordan – they will try to achieve a similar situation there. That, of course, remains to be seen. One problem Israel has, among many, is that they are a very small country, even with their very effective military. They could find themselves too thinly spread and, if their enemies are able to retaliate, Israeli forces could be overrun, even cut off in enemy territory. We can all too easily imagine what would happen to them if that were to occur!'

'I want to bring in an American spokesman, now – Senator Johnson, from New York. Senator, what is the US perception as to what is currently happening in the Middle East?'

'Thank you, David. We became aware of this conflict very early on as our satellites were able to track these nuclear missiles from their launch. Let me say first that these missiles were clearly fired from Syria and Iran towards targets in Israel. We believe that, somehow, the Israeli military have been able to divert these rockets to alternative targets. We have not detected any launch of Israeli-based nuclear devices.

'In the case of those missiles launched from Syria – only three, as far as we can determine – the distance flown was short and the time to re-direct would therefore have been very limited, so we have seen those missiles hit Gaza City, Beirut and, finally, Damascus. In the case of missiles launched from Iran, there was a longer time span in which to re-direct the missiles, so we have seen one hit Mecca, in Saudi Arabia, and the others return to their launch sites in Iran, destroying those sites and the further missiles which were due to be launched from them, along with several military bases and some population centers, also.'

'Senator, what about other players at this point? For instance, what do you think is the Russian position on this conflict?'

'Well, David, we have seen the Russians mobilising forces – including tanks – along the Iranian border. They also have several warships in the Mediterranean, which our forces are monitoring. So far they have not intervened, and now, with this new development of a conflict between Iran and Saudi Arabia, I think the Russians are going to wait and see what transpires.

'This has been one hell of a night but, so far, Israel seem to be more than holding their own – for instance, we have reports that their Air Force have been busy in Egypt, Syria, Jordan, Saudi Arabia and Iraq. Their tanks have entered both south Lebanon and Syria and have already bypassed the Damascus area. The port of Tyre is now in Israeli hands ...'

'Yes, senator, I'm sorry to interrupt you, but we are getting some news now from Turkey. To our knowledge, Turkey have not been involved in this conflict, but we are getting reports of a massive influx of refugees from Lebanon and Syria crossing the border. As we know, Turkey already have a huge refugee population from the recent civil war in Syria, but these numbers are now swelling greatly. The Turkish government are asking for western help in coping with these refugees.

'And we can now go live to our Jerusalem correspondent, Susan Reilly – Susan, what can you tell us of this conflict from Israel's perspective?'

'Hello, David. Well, things have been pretty hectic in Israel tonight, as I'm sure you can imagine. First, there was the news of a nuclear missile strike and sirens going off in every part of Israel. Most of the civilian population have spent the night in bomb shelters of some kind. Conventional missiles have been raining down on Israeli cities and on the countryside. There have

been so many explosions that we have completely lost count. Certainly, by now, there have been thousands of missile attacks.

'Israel's Iron Dome defence system – missile defence system – has been completely overwhelmed by the sheer number of rockets incoming. But Israel has also developed a new missile defence system, called Iron Beam, which is really a 'Star Wars' type anti-missile system – and it seems to have been very effective. We've been watching it in operation tonight and it's really quite impressive. I think you are seeing some footage of that, now?'

'Yes, Susan. We can see that footage, now.'

'One of the advantages of the new Iron Beam system is that it doesn't require expensive missiles to be launched and it therefore cannot run out of ammunition – it can keep firing as long as there are targets to aim at.'

'Tell me, what about the missiles that have managed to get through this defence shield? Have you any idea of what damage there has been?'

'David, it is very hard to estimate the amount of damage – we've certainly been hearing sirens all night long here in Jerusalem. There have also been some explosions in the city, which apparently were missiles from Lebanon which had penetrated the defence shield.

'I think the most significant were two rockets which hit the Temple Mount area and have caused major damage to the Dome of the Rock and the Al-Aqsa mosque. There has been damage in other parts of the city – for instance, one missile exploded in a park in the center of Jerusalem – but the Temple Mount is the most significant damage, which will impact Moslems in Israel and around the world – especially coming on top of that nuclear strike on Mecca!'

'Thank you, Susan. We'll come back to you shortly. I think we have a report now from the official Israeli spokesman, Michael Katz, in Jerusalem ... Michael, can you hear me?'

'Yes, David. I can hear you clearly.'

'OK. Go ahead, Michael.'

'Earlier this evening Israel suffered an unprovoked deadly assault from ALL of the nations surrounding us, plus Iran and Sudan. We were attacked with both nuclear missiles and conventional weapons.

'Thousands of rockets have been launched at Israel from the Gaza Strip, Sinai, southern Lebanon and Syria. We have been able to divert these nuclear missiles to alternative targets – where possible, we have sent them back to their own bases, but this has not been possible in every case. Our Arrow 3 missile defence system has also destroyed many incoming missiles.

'The Israeli Air Force have been very busy since this conflict began, destroying military targets in each of the enemy countries. They have also been active against tank forces moving towards our borders.

In Six Hours ... the world changed – *Raymond McCullough*

'Our ground forces are now operating effectively in the Sinai Peninsula, Jordan, Saudi Arabia, Lebanon and Syria. We have also re-taken all of the Gaza Strip, although northern Gaza is currently an exclusion zone, because of the Syrian nuclear weapon which destroyed the city. We have medical teams endeavouring to rescue any survivors we can from the surrounding area.

'Also, in Judea and Samaria our forces have taken complete control'. From tonight Israel has abolished the Palestinian Authority and arrested many of their leaders – although some have been killed and others appear to have fled, deserting their own people. We have no intent to harm any civilian in Judaea or Samaria, but any member of Hamas, Fatah, Islamic Jihad, etc. will be arrested on sight. These have proven themselves to be enemies of Israel.

'As I said at the beginning, this was a totally unprovoked attack, with the express purpose of wiping Israel off the map. Well, Israel is still here, and we will be here for a long time to come! Our enemies have totally failed in their intention to destroy us. They began this war, but we will finish it, in our own good time. They may have caused us considerable damage, but Israel remains strong, effective and determined and, God willing, we will continue to pursue our enemies with all of the ability at our disposal. Shalom!'

'Well, that was Israeli spokesman, Michael Katz, with an official bulletin from the Israeli government. Dr. Eggenhamm, that announcement would seem to confirm your suggestion of Israeli cyber warfare, wouldn't it?'

'Yes, David. I suppose there is no longer any need for Israel to conceal it, the effects speak for themselves.'

'Dr. Eggenhamm, Michael Katz, spoke of 'pursuing their enemies' – what do you think he meant by that?'

'Well, in previous conflicts between Israel and their Arab neighbours, Israel have often be hindered from a decisive victory by the intervention of inter-national pressure – from the United Nations and particularly from the United States. I think the Israelis were serving notice that they are going to end this war when it suits them. After all, the expressed intention of their Arab and Iranian enemies was the complete destruction of Israel, so I don't think Israel can really be blamed for wanting to conclude this conflict decisively in their favour.'

'And do you think Israel still have the ability to do that. Dr. Eggenhamm?'

'Well, it remains to be seen, but the indications are there already – with the numbers of refugees fleeing Lebanon and Syria into Turkey, for instance – that Israel have their enemies on the run. Israel is a very resilient nation and I believe they will use every means at their disposal to see a satisfactory outcome – for themselves – from this conflict.

Chapter 31 – BBC News 24: enemies divided?

'Their allies have noticeably held off from coming to Israel's aid, so Israel will feel no compunction to oblige a world which has sat back and waited while they were in dire need. I think Israel is probably very likely now to adapt a much more aggressive attitude to world opinion – and, I think, understandably so.'

'Thank you, Dr. Eggenhamm. You have been very informative. We're about to come up to the news headlines in a few minutes. First, here is the BBC weather.'

David Olegvah hurried from the BBC Newsroom, muttering to a colleague, 'Thank God that's over. It was a truly amazing night to be on the news desk but, if I had to say 'Dr. Egg 'n' ham' one more time with a straight face, I think my career could have taken a serious nosedive!'

32 – Six Hour War: Tabuk, Saudi Arabia

Shaul radioed Southern Command to update his position. 'We've just arrived at Highway 15, about 30 km from Tabuk. Any updates, sir?'

'Levine. as far as we can tell the Saudis have removed a lot of their tanks towards the Kuwaiti/Iraq border, but we believe there are still some forces left to guard Tabuk. You'll see the *Fahad Bin Sultan University* on your right when you approach the city. The regional airport is on the opposite side of the city. We're sending a team of paratroopers in to take the airport. Meanwhile, we want your unit to take the University. If they choose to make a run for it, that will leave them an escape route east, towards Buraydah and Riyadh – and then the Israeli Air Force can take them on the highway.'

'It should take us about 35 minutes to reach the University, sir.' Shaul replied.

'Well, take a break where you are, now. We'll time your attack and the airport attack simultaneously for one hour from now, OK?'

'Yes sir. How is the war going elsewhere, sir?'

'Well, we sent in hundreds of drones first, to take out the bulk of the missiles and Triple A fire, before our aircraft went in to mop up. We've re-taken all of the Gaza Strip – what's left of it! We're engaging the Egyptian tanks in western Sinai. Tyre and Sidon are fully in our control. I think it was a major blow to Hezbollah when Damascus and then Beirut were destroyed, damaged their morale quite a bit – plus our accurate targeting of their missile launchers with drones, laser guided artillery and tank missiles.

'Our tanks have circled north of the ruins of Damascus, and our forces have surrounded Amman and are fighting ISIS forces in eastern Jordan. The unit which took over Aqaba Airport are currently surrounding Ma'an and will, eventually, link up with you along Highway 5, once they have taken control of it. *Mazel tov*, Levine! Over and out.'

'OK, troops,' Shaul announced, 'let's get some food into us in the next few minutes. We head out for Tabuk in 20 minutes. Bar-Ilan, Tamari and Peled report to my vehicle, now.'

This was the first time Shaul had seen Rebekkah Bar-Ilan up close, and he wasn't disappointed. She also seemed a fully professional soldier, as did the older tank commander, Alon Peled. After updating them on the war situation, Shaul described the current mission to take Tabuk University.

Peled interrupted him, 'Sir, if you don't mind me suggesting it, if we're expecting opposition, maybe some of your troops should ride with us. We can carry five per tank.'

'That's a good suggestion, Peled. We'll keep our soft transports well in the rear and transfer their personnel to your tanks. Once we've neutralised any Saudi tanks, they will deploy around the University to mop up any further resistance. OK, Bar-Ilan?'

'Wouldn't be my favourite means of transport, sir, but it does make sense.' replied Bar-Ilan.'

'OK, you guys get some food into you and Bar-Ilan, Tamari, you can organise the troop distribution with Peled, here, OK.'

'*Beseder*, sir.' said Bar-Ilan.

'Will do,' Tamari replied.

Twenty minutes later Shaul's force were fed and fifty of them had deployed into the ten tanks commanded by Peled. They turned south onto Saudi Highway 15 and headed towards Tabuk across the flat land of the Saudi interior.

The sky was beginning to lighten as they began to pick out the buildings of the city ahead, the University being the nearest. A huge roundabout appeared in the divided highway ahead, in the centre of which was a large sculpture of Islamic gateways, silhouetted in the growing light.

Shaul radioed his forces, 'Just a hundred metres beyond the sculpture we take the branch road to the right, parallel to the main highway. The next buildings are the *Tabuk Stadium* on the right – be prepared for a possible ambush from there.

'Another kilometre after that is the University site on the right, which is a large rectangle with a divided road along the northern and southern sides. We need to cover both sides, three tanks to each, plus two to the main entrance in the center. The oil refinery is opposite, on our left. That may be guarded, too.

'First sign of any resistance from tank forces, we move rapidly to out-flank them, firing at will. Infantry will deploy as soon as any tanks have been dealt with, moving in on the main University buildings. Two of our tanks will travel on to the next roundabout, about 500 metres beyond, and guard the main roads south, west and east. The others will cover the front and side entrances. *B'hatzlacha!*'

Peled's ten *Merkavah IV* tanks headed down the highway towards Tabuk's *Fahad Bin Sultan University*, Shaul's APCs and trucks following. Thirty five minutes later they passed the huge roundabout with the Islamic gates sculpture in the centre.

To their left were signs of advanced agriculture – large circles of crops under irrigation. After negotiating the roundabout the convoy moved into the separate branch road, right of the main King Khalid highway, passing a new residential area on their left and what looked like another under construction to the right.

As they approached the Tabuk Stadium on the right, suddenly two tanks appeared in front of them, opening fire in their direction. Two of Peled's force peeled off to the right, turrets swivelling, firing as they went. The main force continued along the branch road, but also firing towards the enemy tanks. One shell scored a direct hit and a Saudi tank erupted in flame, swerving wildly with only one track left functional.

The two Israeli tanks which had moved towards the stadium now focussed on the remaining Saudi tank, disabling it with one missile. Peled radioed to Shaul, who had halted his APCs and trucks down-range. 'More Saudi tanks advancing from the University area, sir.'

'OK, Peled, advance and fire at will. Careful there aren't any more surprises hidden in that stadium.'

'Looks like Bar-Ilan has plans to deal with that, sir.'

The two tanks near the stadium halted briefly and ten Israeli soldiers exited rapidly from the rear doors of each tank. Joined by Rebekkah Bar-Ilan and the crew of her APC, they raced westwards towards a high wall near the north entrance to the stadium, while the tanks charged on towards the entrance. Bar-Ilan's squad rounded the end of the wall and moved behind the shelter of a small building closer to the stadium arena, which was marked out with a soccer pitch.

As they peered out from the shelter of the building they saw two Saudi tanks moving north towards the exit to back up their compatriots. As the Israeli tanks spotted them and opened fire Bar-Ilan ordered one of her troops carrying an anti-tank missile launcher to fire. The missile destroyed the left-hand track of the tank, rendering it immobile, while one of the Israeli tanks had taken out the other Saudi tank.

The Saudi tank crew opened their hatches, jumped down from their destroyed tank and began to run towards the stands. The second Saudi tank crew also leapt down and fled. Bar-Ilan encouraged them on their way with a short burst from her *Tavor TAR-21* assault rifle. The two Israeli tanks moved towards them and halted between them and the fleeing Saudis. Bar-Ilan gave the order to mount up and the APC and tanks sped on their way to join the remainder of Peled's force now further down the highway.

Rebekkah radioed to Shaul, 'All four enemy tanks destroyed, sir. Crews in the stadium fleeing towards the shelter of the stands. Didn't think we had time to spare to deal with them further, sir,' she said, catching her breath.

'Well done, Bar-Ilan. Now we have more trouble ahead. Tanks coming from the University area – about one kilometre ahead. Over and out.'

In the distance ahead, Shaul could make out the dust cloud from the approaching Saudi tanks. He radioed Peled, 'How about we divert some of your tanks around behind the oil refinery?'

'Just what I was thinking, sir. We can play peek-a-boo with them from there. There are some warehouses near the road on our left, too. I'll send the two trailing tanks around behind them.'

'OK, Peled. Take command of your force from here on.'

'Yes, sir.'

Shaul's infantry force passed the stadium as they watched the two trailing tanks cross the highway and begin to circle behind the row of large warehouses on the north east side of the road. He commanded his own APCs to follow them.

Peled's main force also crossed the King Khalid Road and headed across the desert towards the oil storage tanks of the refinery. The attacking Saudi tanks – ten of them – were now between the University and the oil refinery. When they realised the Israeli manoeuvre, several Saudi tanks swerved east along the south side of the refinery. The main Saudi force headed north east across the highway towards the Israeli tanks.

Peled had split his force into four groups of two tanks each, three pairs each taking a different route between the oil storage tanks towards the main road, the fourth heading south east and halting between the refinery buildings. As the first three pairs neared the refinery car park – between the storage tanks and the highway – they opened fire on the Saudi tanks as they came into view. Several of the Saudi tanks were caught sideways on and their tracks were quickly disabled by Israeli fire.

The three pairs had also set down their infantry passengers while in the shelter of the oil tanks, and the troops moved quickly to engage the Saudi forces from the shelter of the nearest oil containers. A stray Saudi shell hit one of the further oil containers, which exploded in a spectacular fireball. The remaining two Israeli tanks had each driven into the middle of one of the huge tanker sheds and opened fire on the separate Saudi tank force as they came towards them from the south.

Two Saudi tanks were disabled, but the others spread out and continued the attack. One Israeli tank reversed back through the tanker shed, swerving to the right to round the end of the huge building. The second Israeli tank fired a shell into the row of parked tankers ahead of it, igniting one of them, then shot forward out of the tanker shed, swerving left to gain the shelter of the burning tanker, keeping well to the left to avoid any further explosions from the tankers. The billowing smoke helped to camouflage its position as it halted opposite a gap between the tankers, waiting for a view of a Saudi tank. When one appeared an armour piercing sabot ended its part in the fight.

The tank moved quickly to the south of its former position and took up an identical position between and behind another pair of oil tankers. Again a Saudi tank came into sight and another shell put it out of action also. The Israeli tank, commanded by Peled, turned south and rounded the protective line of tankers, just in time to spot another Saudi tank racing for shelter within the tanker shed. Peled's tank fired another round, almost simultaneously with the other Israeli tank of his pair. The Saudi tank turned into a fireball at the edge of the shed.

No further targets in sight, Peled ordered his colleague to move towards the highway around the north side of a group of buildings, while he travelled along the south side, towards the main car park. As they emerged they could see three remaining Saudi tanks scrambling to get north of the killing zone that the refinery had become.

Rather than give immediate chase himself, Peled allowed his colleague to continue in pursuit, while he checked the condition of the rest of his tanks. One tank had a damaged track and he directed another crew to their aid, instructing two of the remaining four tanks to follow the retreating Saudi tanks, but to keep towards the main road, rather than follow directly behind them.

The other pair of tanks he directed to keep a lookout for further enemy forces from the refinery buildings, towards the University and the main road south into Tabuk.

As he turned to follow the other three tanks he saw fire erupt from the trees just to the north of the fleeing enemy, destroying one of the Saudi tanks. Further shells were fired from the shelter of the trees, and the remaining pair of Saudi tanks turned east along the small side road and fled towards the desert. After a number of shells had been fired after them without result, Peled ordered his tanks to cease fire and regroup.

He checked with his lookouts at the refinery, who reported some movement around the University, but no immediate threat. His disabled tank was in the throes of having new track links fitted and would take another twenty minutes to complete. The crew had suffered some slight injuries, which had now been treated. The infantry had already disembarked and taken defensive positions around the refinery buildings. Two of the infantry had been injured in the explosion when the oil storage tank had taken a hit. Tamari's APC raced to the two stricken men, suffering from shock and extensive burns. They were quickly transferred to an APC, where medics tended to their wounds, setting up IV drips to both men.

Peled radioed Shaul, whose remaining vehicles were approaching from behind the warehouses north of the refinery. He reported on the recent tank battle, 'Eight Saudi tanks disabled, or destroyed. Two on their way to Riyadh, by the look of them! Some activity at the University, but nothing more coming our way just yet. I've got two of my tanks keeping watch across the road and towards Tabuk. One tank is having a track replaced as we speak. Some minor injuries, but nothing disabling. Over.'

'OK, Peled. well done. I don't think we'll worry about the two escaped tanks for now. We've two injured men being tended to at the moment. We'll join you at the refinery shortly and take stock of the University from there. You can let our troops stay out for a breather, I'm sure they've been cooped up for long enough!'

'Already released them, sir. We'll wait for you here, then. Out.'

Peled ordered his driver to head into the main tanker shed out of the sun. The other five un-deployed tanks joined him there and shortly after the APCs, trucks and jeeps of Shaul's force arrived to join them.

Shaul greeted the tank crews with praise for their part in the recent action. He told them to get some refreshment and motioned for Bar-Ilan, Peled and Sergeant Tamari to join him.

'First of all, Peled, Tamari and Bar-Ilan, well done on the action there. You've all shown excellent leadership. We've managed to knock out twelve Saudi tanks, with two men moderately injured, some minor injuries and only slight damage to our own equipment, which is being repaired already.'

Just then the rumble of the remaining two tanks returning confirmed that the damaged tank was once again battle ready.

'Let me just get in touch with Command, to see how things are going at the other end of the city.'

Shaul took the radio handset and called Southern Command. 'Shalom, sir. We've engaged Saudi tank forces on our way to the University – at the Stadium and around the refinery. Twelve Saudi tanks out of action, sir. Two escaped to the east. Track repairs to one of our own tanks now complete. Two men with moderate injuries – burns and shock. All other personnel intact. We are grouped behind the Oil Refinery at present, sir – about to launch our assault on the University itself. Over.'

'*Beseder*, Levine. The assault on the airport was met with heavy resistance, but I believe we're getting the upper hand now. Continue with your assault on the University. Any idea what resistance you expect there?'

'No sir. We've spotted some activity, so infantry forces at least. If there are more tanks waiting for us we haven't seen any sign of them yet, sir. Over.'

'Very well, Levine. Carry on. Over and out.'

33 – BBC News 24: The Six Hour War

A new presenter had taken over on *BBC News 24*.

'This is the news on BBC News 24. All out war throughout the Middle East.

'Good morning. A major war, involving multiple nuclear missile attacks has been raging all night throughout the Middle East. Millions are feared dead and many more millions injured. They're beginning to call this the Six Hour War. Late yesterday evening an all-out nuclear attack was launched against Israel, with the express intention of wiping Israel off the map.

'Ten nations in the Middle East have conspired together to attack Israel – first with nuclear missiles launched from both Syria and Iran, then with a full scale cross-border attack from every side with conventional missiles, rockets, mortars and tanks. The first missile appeared to have struck somewhere near Tel Aviv, but later it became clear that this missile, although clearly aimed at Tel Aviv, had actually destroyed the city of Gaza.

'Further missiles then destroyed Damascus, Beirut and Mecca, with other nuclear strikes on military targets in Iran and Iraq. Many millions are feared dead, but there is just no way to assess the loss of life at this point in time.'

'What has become clear, though, is that – far from being wiped off the face of the earth – Israel has miraculously rebounded from this devastating attack and have gone on the offensive against all those who had attacked her. Egypt have also sustained heavy losses in tanks and aircraft and have called for a ceasefire, to which Israel has not yet responded.

'Israeli forces have destroyed the airforces and missile batteries of Egypt, Sudan, Syria, Lebanon, Jordan, Iran, Iraq and Saudi Arabia. Iran and parts of Iraq have been devastated by nuclear missiles – apparently launched by Iran, in the first place, although a few were launched from Syria, also. These missiles apparently returned to their home bases, wreaking complete destruction upon Iran's nuclear launch sites and dealing a devastating blow to her formidable military machine.

'The Israeli navy have also been deployed with great effect, taking out the majority of Iran's ten frigates and many of their submarines. Israel now appear to have control of much of the Middle East at this point. The Israeli

government have referred to this event as having been prophesied in the Bible, and that the outcome was never in doubt, but that their enemies would "become as dust, chaff in the wind and tumbleweed in a gale." Well, that certainly appears a pretty accurate description of the events of last night.

'*As it became apparent during the night that Israel had NOT been destroyed, or even seriously weakened, the coalition arrayed against them began to fall apart. After a nuclear missile – apparently fired from Shi'ite Iran – destroyed the Saudi Arabian city of Mecca, holy to Muslims the world over, Saudi Arabia abandoned their attack on Israel and turned against both Shi'Ite Iran and Shi'ite southern Iraq. ISIS forces in northern and western Iraq and Syria also turned to fight Iran and southern Iraq, while Kurdish forces have been supportive of Israel and have taken large areas of northern Iraq.*

'*Meanwhile, Israeli forces have taken control of all of Lebanon, most of Syria and Jordan, the Gaza Strip, the Sinai Peninsula and part of north western Saudi Arabia. Millions of survivors have become refugees and are fleeing north across the Turkish-Syrian border. Turkey, who have remained distant from the conflict, though condemning Israel, have called urgently for international help to deal with the vast numbers of incoming refugees.*

'*Azerbaijan, Turkmenistan, Afghanistan and Pakistan have also called for international help as millions of refugees begin to pour across their borders.*

'*The Israelis have reported that many thousands of Israeli people – both Jews and Arabs – have been killed or injured, in what they regard as an unprovoked attack upon their state. Because of the full complicity of the Palestinian Authority and the PLO in this attack, the Israeli government have announced that the Palestinian Authority has been revoked. And indeed, it seems that the PA/PLO leaders have either been killed in the conflict, or they have fled the area, abandoning their people.*

'*The leaders of Hamas and Islamic Jihad have likewise either been killed in the Gaza strike, in the ensuing fighting, or have fled the area. A boat containing several leaders of Hamas was intercepted by the Israeli navy and, when they refused to surrender to them, opening fire on the Israeli forces, the boat was sunk by the navy.*

'"*We have no fight with ordinary Palestinian people,*" *an Israeli spokesman said. "We would ask the people living in Judaea, Samaria and the remaining parts of the Gaza Strip, to stay in their homes and towns, to remain calm. We will take some time to work out a new proposal for the Arab residents of Judaea and Samaria.*

'"*In the meantime, we have established military rule over the areas, formerly known as the West Bank and Gaza Strip. We have declared radioactive exclusion zones around the former Gaza City, Damascus and Beirut. Israeli hospitals are endeavouring to deal with the survivors of these nuclear explosions, but we call upon the international community to help us to deal with an unprecedented humanitarian situation.*

'"We did not in any way seek for this conflict. This was a totally unwarranted and unprovoked attack, the result of the failed policies of militant Islam. We did not fire a single one of our own nuclear missiles in our defence. By our skill and endeavour we were able to deflect those missiles sent to destroy the Jewish nation to enemy locations.

'The Israeli spokesman also said, "Where possible most missiles were returned to their launch sites, thus destroying many more missiles before they also could be launched. Unfortunately, a few of these missiles were launched from Syria – only a few miles from Israel – and there was not enough time to turn all of them around, they could only be deflected, destroying Gaza City and Beirut, with the consequent loss of many lives, which we greatly regret."

'The United Nations Secretary General has also called upon member states to supply emergency aid to those stricken in these and other cities such as Mecca, Tehran and Baghdad.

'The leaders of China, Russia and also the USA have been openly hostile to Israel – the United States even threatening to attack Israeli planes if they approached the Gulf States, where the US 5th fleet is based. The US failed to respond to calls for help and military aid from Israel, nor did any other NATO, or European state agree to help Israel in any way.

'The United Kingdom government, however, has supported Israel's right to self-defence against such an outright unprovoked attack on her existence. The prime minister said this morning, "The leaders of Israel could have retaliated with their full nuclear arsenal. They, thankfully, refused to do so, showing a humanitarian concern totally lacking in those who instigated this horrendous nuclear war.

'"Militant Islam has now proved itself to be a completely immoral and bankrupt ideology. By their complete failure in their goal to destroy the State of Israel, and their destruction of their own holiest city, they have shaken the faith of fellow Muslims throughout the world. The Muslim world is now in abject mourning for this self-inflicted tragedy."

'That was the British Prime Minister speaking just a few moments ago.

'Good morning. If you've just joined us we are reporting on the news of the overnight nuclear war in the Middle East. Many reporters are now referring to this as the Six Hour War – six hours from the explosion of the first nuclear missile, fired against Israel last night, to the situation this morning were, somehow, Israel has not only survived this onslaught, but they have turned the tables completely, driving their enemies far from them.'

In Six Hours ... the world changed – *Raymond McCullough*

34 – Six Hour War: Tabuk/Duba, Saudi Arabia

'OK,' Shaul returned to his own commanders, 'I want to divide our forces into three. Peled, leave two tanks to guard the highway into Tabuk, three down the right hand road – north of the University – three down the left and two through the main University entrance – all with infantry support.

'Bar-Ilan, take your troops to the right hand entrance, north side, Tamari the left, south side. I'll take the main entrance myself. We don't want to do any more damage to the buildings than we can help, but if we meet fierce resistance, we take no unnecessary risks to our own personnel. Understood?'

'Yes, sir,' all three replied.

'We'll give Tamari's squad a little time to get into position, then Tamari and Bar-Ilan, together with the tanks, proceed smartly down each side. My squad will hold back a few minutes to give you time to get near the side entrances. Then we move in. OK?'

'Yes, sir,' they both replied again.

'Let's go then.'

The tanks rolled forward, five of them travelled down the highway towards Tabuk, three of these crossing the highway, accompanied by Sergeant Tamari and his APCs, to take the road down the south side of the University. The other two travelled on towards a roundabout – not quite so huge as the previous one, and with two strange winged sculptures this time. They pulled off the main road to either side and stationed themselves behind the row of palm trees on either side, between the main road and the branch road on either side.

Another three tanks, accompanied by Bar-Ilan and her APCs, crossed the highway to enter the road along the north side of the University. When each group had almost reached the buildings, Shaul waved his two accompanying tanks to follow, jumped into his APC and then headed down the main entrance road to the University.

The main sliding gates on either side were closed so Shaul pulled his APC to the right and motioned the tanks forward. Each drove through and over the gate on either side and Shaul and his APCs followed them through a small roundabout and on down the main avenue, leading to a hollow open V-shaped frontage with tall blue glass windows around the round central tower. On either side of the V the five-storey building overhung a covered walkway. The tanks positioned themselves on either side of the central round-about at the opening into the courtyard, to give covering fire, the APCs behind them.

Suddenly they heard the sound of gunfire from behind the buildings. Bar-Ilan, Tamari, or both, were being given a warm reception. Then shots rang out from ahead of them also, rattling off the APCs' armour. The machine gunners on both tanks and APCs opened fire, using their *Bright Arrow* APS, controlled from within the vehicles.

Looking across the central courtyard, Shaul could see enemy infantry firing from the main doorway, from behind the pillars near it, and from the windows on the floors above. His APC opened fire on the troops visible across from him and the vehicle on the right did the same.

This could become one hell of a trap, Shaul thought to himself.

He told his *CombatGuard* APC driver to charge directly into the main entrance door. The vehicle revved up, raced towards the entrance and crashed through the glass doors, with a second *Namer* tracked APC close behind – the machine gunners on each APC firing rapidly around the entrance area. After a few minutes of cacophony Shaul radioed for both APCs to cease fire.

There was an eerie silence. He instructed the driver to back the *Combat-Guard* up close to the left hand wall. Then Shaul led his troops out carefully in the shelter between the vehicle and the wall. The second APC did the same on the other side of the foyer, exiting from the rear. They carefully reconnoitred the reception area, now covered in broken glass and several broken bodies of Saudi troops.

There were corridors to either side of the entrance area and Shaul pointed the other squad to the right hand one, while he and his troops moved cautiously to the left. As they pointed their weapons into the corridor more shots rang out and Shaul fired, killing one soldier. Another threw his weapon out of a doorway and shouted, 'Not shoot. Surrender. Not shoot!'

Not wanting to be led into a trap Shaul asked one of his Arabic-speaking men – a Druze soldier named Samir Junbalat – to instruct the soldier to lie down in the hallway where he could be seen. The enemy soldier complied. 'Tell him to stay there and not to move,' Shaul instructed, noticing for the first time the stripes on the Saudi soldiers uniform.

'Ask him his rank,' Shaul commanded Samir.

'He says he is a captain and that he is the commander of these men,' Samir replied.

'Tell him we've just destroyed twelve of their tanks and the other two have run way east. Is he now willing to surrender the University to our forces?' Shaul asked.

After listening to the commander's reply, Samir nodded.

'Tell him to give the order for his men to lay down their guns, come out with their hands in the air and lie face down,' Shaul told Samir.

Samir translated and the Saudi officer barked out an order. Soon several weapons were laid in the corridors and a dozen men lay face down. Shaul instructed his troops to take control of the two corridors and collect the weapons.

'Wait, let's get him on loudspeaker.'

Shaul, with Samir in attendance, led the captured commander to his APC, whose driver he then instructed to move out back into the courtyard. Sporadic firing still came from above. The APC drove as far as the two tanks and the other APCs and stopped. Shaul handed the microphone to the commander and told Shamir what he wanted him to say. The commander carried out Shaul's instructions and the sporadic firing ceased.

Shortly after, men began to file out with hands raised and were seated with their hands tied behind them in the shade of the two arcades on either side.

Shaul asked Samir to elicit how many troops the commander had at the University, where their vehicles were hidden and what reinforcements they were able to call upon. Samir retrieved the information Shaul was looking for.

'Tell him his men will be well treated,' said Shaul. Samir told the commander, who replied, *'Shukran, shukran.* (Thank you.)'

'What is his name?' Shaul asked.

When Samir asked, the commander drew himself erect and replied, 'Captain Mohammed Ibn Ahmed Abu Hassan Al-Fulani.'

'Mohammed Al-Fulani,' Shaul repeated, extracting the essential bit.

'Captain Al-Fulani, I want you to repeat these instructions to your troops at the rear entrances to the buildings.' Shaul waited while this was translated to the officer, then asked the translator to accompany Al-Fulani and Corporal Katz in an APC to the rear entrances, while Peled organised some spare drivers to take charge of the Saudi transport and sent them in another APC to find the vehicles.

While they were waiting for these tasks to be completed, Shaul organised his men to escort the bound Saudi fighters to a lecture hall near to the entrance. The wounded were already being attended to by his medics and were made comfortable in the lecture theatre. He also detailed men to begin removing the bodies, which were taken to a waiting Saudi truck and loaded carefully. Others were detailed to begin sweeping up the glass in the foyer and making things more normal there.

When the APC returned with Fulani, the corporal, and the Druze interpreter, he asked how things had gone. 'No problems, sir,' Katz replied. Shaul turned to Samir, 'Ask Al-Fulani how many men he has under his command.' When he received his reply he radioed both Tamari and Bar-Ilan to enquire how many prisoners and how many dead bodies they had, respectively.

Shaul added those totals to the number of men in the lecture hall and the bodies in the truck. There was a discrepancy of two. He then selected several squads of four men each and sent them to check out the halls and rooms of the buildings, searching for the two remaining enemy personnel.

Meanwhile, Shaul turned to Fulani and the translator, 'Please ask him to select four of his men to help with the bodies.' Shaul explained what he wanted to Katz. Samir translated and Katz took Fulani to select the men, released the four soldiers from their bonds and accompanied them to the waiting truck, where they collected the dog tags of the dead, under Fulani's supervision.

Shaul noted their details in a notebook which Katz provided him with. He then gave Katz further instructions and he, Junbalat and Al-Fulani went off in the truck to collect the other bodies, followed by another truck for the prisoners and two of the larger *Namer* APCs, which collected the remainder of the wounded from the rear entrances.

After about a twenty minute interval there came the sound of shots fired at a distance. The search squads returned with two dejected and defiant Saudi soldiers, one of whom was wounded in the right arm. The injured man was attended to by the medics, glowering at them all the while, while another soldier held his rifle on him.

The uninjured soldier was cable tied and also held under guard. When Fulani eventually returned, Shaul explained what had occurred and Al-Fulani rebuked them both severely for disobeying his orders. The two men were led sullenly to the lecture hall to join the others.

Shaul retreated to his APC and radioed Southern Command. *'Fahad bin Sultan University* is now fully in our control. We have the Saudi commander, who is co-operating with us and 89 of his men, including two dozen injured men. We also have 12 bodies of enemy personnel, ready to be buried. Our men are all accounted for. No further injuries. There is some superficial damage to the building, mostly to the main entrance and the side entrances. My men are about to move to the dining hall for some breakfast, now, sir.'

'Well done, Levine. The paratroop attack on the airport also sustained some casualties on our side and a lot more on theirs, but all is quiet, now. We are about to fly in reinforcements via the airport. When your men are all fed and watered – say in about forty minutes – you can leave a reasonable force to hold the University area, then move on to take your other objectives.'

'Yes, sir. Understood. We have two injured men, plus a couple of the Saudis are quite seriously injured, sir. What can we do for them?'

'We'll send a helicopter over from the airport shortly, to take the worst cases. They'll let you know what capacity they have. We'll fly them back to Israel from there. The helicopter can ferry the rest of those who need further medical attention after that.

'We're pouring more troops in through the airport over the next hour or so. Then we hope to take complete control of the town. There is little sign of further resistance, there, so it looks like it will just be a mopping up operation. seems like they had most of their forces concentrated in the north – which you've taken care of – and around the airport.

'The bulk of Saudi forces are now concentrating their attack on Iran and southern Iraq. The Sunni-Shia feud is back at full strength, though Iran appears to be almost completely devastated. Their own missiles – nuclear and conventional, coming back to haunt them – have destroyed a large part of their military capability. We have reports of mass movement of Iranian refugees east towards Afghanistan and north towards Azerbaijan and Turkmenistan. The Saudis have been under major attack also, mainly from Iran, but also from southern Iraq.

'There are also large refugee convoys heading north from Lebanon, Syria and former Iraq into Turkey. The only people who aren't fleeing seem to be the Kurds, who have declared that they have no quarrel with the State of Israel. They are standing firm in their own state and in the parts of Syria, east of the Euphrates, that they now control. The Kurds have also taken the city of Mosul and a large swathe of northern Iraq.

'Egypt have declared a ceasefire. Israel now holds all the land from the Sinai peninsula to the Turkish border in the north, and the Euphrates in the east, including all of western Jordan as far as Highway 5. ISIS have collapsed in the west of Iraq, though they appear to still be fighting the remainder of the Iranian forces in the east and the Shi'ites in southern Iraq.

'Our troops are spread pretty thin on the ground, but we have complete air supremacy, and we're getting a clearer picture minute by minute of what's happening on the ground in Iraq, Iran and Saudi Arabia. Between the nuclear missiles and Muslims fighting one another, there is much less left for Israel to do – only to take control of what's left.

'The international media are starting to call this the *Six Hour War* – six hours from the first nuclear strike until Israel were on the offensive in every direction! As far as your arena goes, Saudi Arabia have not yet called a ceasefire with Israel, so we can consolidate the territory we hold there. *B'hatzlacha*, Levine.'

'*Toda*, sir,' Levine replied.

Sergeants Bar-Ilan and Tamari had by now joined them, escorting the other injured and uninjured prisoners to the lecture hall. Peled arrived back soon after, reporting on the extra vehicles captured. Shaul arranged for a squad of troops to guard the prisoners and the front of the building, leaving Bar-Ilan in charge for now. He instructed the others, including Peled and two thirds of his tank crews, to move to the university dining facilities, which Junbalat directed them towards, following the signs in Arabic in the corridor.

When they arrived, Tamari organised some of the men to rustle up breakfast for the remainder of the men. Shaul, Peled and Katz settled around a table as they waited for breakfast, coffee appearing soon after. Bar-Ilan arrived to inform him that the Israeli flag was now flying from the main building.

'Well done,' he said, 'Good thinking, Bar-Ilan.'

By the time all his men had been fed and the wounded made comfortable, the first helicopter had arrived to take their own two men and the worst of the Saudi wounded to the airport, then back to Israel for treatment. Shaul, having now been informed by radio of the arrival of fresh troops at Tabuk airport, began to divide up his forces. He left Tamari in command of his own men, with Peled commanding the bulk of his tanks remaining with them. Katz also remained with Tamari.

Shaul took only four of the tanks, led by a Corporal Gold, who'd been recommended to Shaul by Peled. He also asked Bar-Ilan and Samir Junbalat, along with the crews of six of the new *CombatGuard* APCs, to accompany him. As the sun appeared over the mountains to the east, they set off again heading first of all west, then south on Tabuk's outer ring, passing the larger *University of Tabuk* on their left – where they could see more Israeli troops surrounding the buildings. At a major intersection they turned off southwest along Highway 80 towards the Red Sea and the small town of Duba, approximately 200 kilometres away.

The road was a well paved divided highway heading across the plain before cutting through some rocky hills. It then swung southwards for some distance before entering more mountainous terrain. The road had become a single highway by then, following a narrow wadi west, then south, where the wadi widened out into a wide plain.

The road meandered through further wadis until it finally entered a narrow one heading south west again. As they progressed the sun appeared from time to time behind them as the road turned briefly north on its way west. Finally, the Red Sea appeared glittering ahead and the highway divided again for the last kilometre into the small town of Duba.

As they entered the town they passed an area of warehouses on their right, with a large number of trucks parked in front. Ahead was a large roundabout, where Shaul left two of his tanks. He instructed Bar-Ilan to take one of the tanks and a couple of APCs and follow the road to the south and to turn right towards the sea at the next major junction.

Meanwhile, he would continue straight ahead, accompanied by the other tank, following the shoreline south. As Shaul passed a main street on his right, he sent a couple of APCs down it. In a few minutes all three groups met up again and neither group had seen any sign of life.

The town appeared to be divided into two parts by the sea inlet Bar-Ilan had just followed. They returned around it and, when the road divided at a small roundabout, Shaul took the road to the left, sending Bar-Ilan's group further along the south side of the inlet towards the shore. Again, after Shaul had travelled through some of the main residential streets towards the south, then turned west to the shore, they met up outside Duba Hospital and neither reported any activity.

'Let's check out the hospital,' Shaul told Rebekkah. When they entered, cautiously, and found no-one, Shaul radioed his other tanks and instructed them to follow the highway south until they met an APC. He then sent an APC crew to meet the main highway and wait for the tanks to arrive. When they did the tanks were to take station just off the highway, while the APC would return to let Shaul know the tanks were in position.

Shaul left Bar-Ilan to organise accommodation for their men in the hospital and, if possible, to rustle up coffee and some food as well. Shaul, meanwhile, contacted Southern Command and reported their situation.

'We've had a clear run, sir. No sign of anyone left in Duba – the place seems to be deserted. We're now based at the hospital on the south side – two tanks outside and the other two up at the junction with the main Highway 5 along the coast.'

'Well done, Levine. We now have complete control of both sides of the Gulf of Aqaba. We'd like you to check one more thing today, if possible? Just north of you about 20 kilometres is the Duba Port ferry terminal to Safaga in Egypt. We'd like to know that that is secure also.'

'Will do, sir. OK if my men get some lunch first?'

'I'll leave the details up to you. You've done well up to now, Captain. We will contact the Navy and get them to send a ship along as soon as they can. The ferry terminal can take reasonably large vessels – compared to Duba itself, which can only accommodate leisure craft. The Navy will probably be in contact with you as soon as they are organised.

'As usual, when Israel is winning the whole world are screaming for us to stop. However, as the Arabs and Iran tried to wipe us out of existence this time we *do* hold the moral high ground and our government, for once, are taking a strong stance. We won't be giving any territory back to anyone in a hurry, I can tell you.

'We also hope to have a convoy of reserve troops heading your way from Aqaba down Highway Five tomorrow. Hopefully, they will reach you before the end of the day.

'You can hand over responsibility to them once they arrive. By that time the Navy should be in residence at the ferry terminal, too. After that you are free to return to the rest of your command in Tabuk. Maybe we can organise some leave for your men soon after – no promises yet. The situation is still very fluid, you understand?'

'Yes, sir. Some sleep would be good in the meantime, sir.'

'No problem, Levine. We'll be in touch.'

'Over and out, sir.'

35 – Six Hour War: Red Sea Interlude

After a quick lunch, provided from the stores of the Duba Hospital canteen, Shaul asked Bar-Ilan to accompany him, with two other APCs, leaving Corporal Gold in charge of the four tanks and remaining three APCs. They headed north along Highway 5 and were at the ferry terminal in less than twenty minutes.

The second entrance seemed to be the main one and they travelled through a small roundabout and down the side of the main building to the dock itself. The sea inlet seemed to be in the shape of a hammer, with the entrance channel the shaft, leading to a wider area shaped like the head of the hammer.

There were two main buildings, about the same size and parallel to one another – one closer to the water than the other – with a wide concrete area around them. The building further inland was surrounded by a number of articulated trucks. More trucks were parked to the north of the terminal. To the south was what appeared to be an office building. There was no sign of life anywhere.

Shaul left the other two APCs parked in the shade of the western building – instructing one crew to be on guard, while the other caught up on some sleep. After two hours the shifts would change.

Shaul drove the remaining APC out towards the entrance, then swung right parallel to the highway and on towards a road leading around the south side of the terminal area. They passed another area of containers and other goods stacked up ready for transport. The road reached the Red Sea and then turned north again towards the terminal channel entrance. Before reaching the channel, they came to a villa on the shore, which also appeared to be deserted.

Shaul pulled into the shade of the building and stopped the APC.

'Care to explore a little, Bar-Ilan?' he asked.

'Why not?' she replied.

They walked towards the sea, where a shallow beach spanned the area between two sand bars – one each to north and south of the villa. As they approached the water's edge Bar-Ilan spoke, 'Permission to paddle, sir?'

'Oh I should think so, Bar-Ilan – or may I call you Rebekkah in private?'

'Sure, be my guest.' she replied chirpily, removing her boots, followed by her uniform. Dressed only in her black underwear she ran into the water and lay down in the shallow lagoon just to the north of the villa. Her body was tanned a light olive all over. Shaul removed his boots and uniform also and joined her.

'Oh God, this is such a relief!' she cried.

'Well, I think we both deserve a little relaxation, Rebekkah. You've been doing a pretty good job so far.'

'Glad you think so, sir,' she replied.

'You can call me Shaul, after all I am out of uniform, aren't I?'

'You could say that!' she said, laughing and looking pointedly at his pale, almost naked body.

She stood up then and ran into the sea, splashing through the waves until she fell forward into the water, then beginning to swim. Shaul followed her and they swam and splashed water over one another.

'Where are you from, then, Rebekkah?'

'Way up in the north,' she said, 'a kibbutz called Kfar Giladi. It's right on the Lebanese border.'

'Or it used to be,' replied Shaul.

'Right enough, things have changed a bit in the last day, or so. Are you always known as Shaul, then?'

'No, in the US Army I was usually known as Sol, sometimes Solly,' he answered.

'That sounds a lot better – Shaul seems very formal, very biblical,' she said.

'I suppose so,' he replied, 'How long have you been in the IDF, then?'

'Almost four years, now,' she said.

'So, you stayed on after your national service. You like the army?'

'I enjoy having responsibility, getting a job done that needs to be done,' she said, 'What about you? You were in the US Army, then? Why did you join the IDF?

'It's a long story. I had some interesting buddies back in Afghanistan – one in particular, a black American who read the Bible a lot. Then my parents were killed – in a stupid car accident. My dad always talked about going to Israel, but it was always going to be 'next year.' After the funeral I thought, 'Why don't I just go and check it out? Anyway, if I'd stayed I'd only have been under pressure to join my brother in running dad's business.

'So, I came to Israel, started learning Hebrew, wandered around for a few weeks, liked it – felt I belonged here, y'know? So then I decided to go the whole way – join the IDF as soon as possible, ask for a combat position and contribute something to the place, be a part of it, you know?'

'Yes, I *do* know,' she answered, 'Being in the IDF is the best way I know of contributing to Israel and belonging to it.'

'My friend, Brandon, told me that there was going to be a *Six Hour War* between Israel and all the surrounding countries. I guess we know now he was right about that.'

'Wow, he sure was. But how did he know about it?'

'Actually, he's not even Jewish – he's a black Pentecostal Christian – but he said that this was all in the Bible, and a whole lot of other stuff besides.'

'Hey, you think we should move into the shade now? You New York American guys burn a lot easier than us sabras. You might want to take it easy in this climate?'

'Might be wise,' he answered, 'Don't want to be laid up with something as stupid as sunburn – especially after being given a new command!'

'Right.'

Gathering their boots and clothes on the way they moved into the shade of the villa, sitting down on a low wall in the shade.

'Just hope nobody's home,' said Shaul, 'We might give them a shock, eh?'

'Yeah, it's sure strange how all these guys – Aqaba, Haql and now down here – have just run away without a fight?'

'Well, that's another thing my friend Brandon told us – that the fear of God would come upon our enemies and they would flee before us *"like dust, like chaff in the wind, like tumbleweed in a gale."* It happened before in places like Safad in 1948, he said.'

'I've heard about Safad, But how come he knew about all this stuff? What else did he have to say?'

'Mainly that Israel would win this war – contrary to the expectations of the whole world – and that it would result in the great ingathering.'

'You mean all that 'Lost Tribes' stuff?'

'Yeah, the Ten Tribes would begin to return to a greatly expanded Israel – from Afghanistan, Pakistan, India, Nigeria, Zimbabwe – all these different places. That the River Euphrates would dry up – the Nile too – so it would be easier for them to cross over.'

'Well, it'll be interesting to see what happens after the dust settles on this war,' she said.

'One thing he said was that the obstacles would be removed out of the way – like Iran no longer being a problem or a barrier in the way to Pashtuns coming from Afghanistan and Pakistan, or Egypt or Sudan no longer being a barrier to Igbos coming from Nigeria, or other African tribes.'

'Hmm, well that might be on the way to happening, then. We control Sinai again, right?'

'*Ken* – and all of Jordan, Lebanon and most of Syria, plus our little bit down here – the Land of Midian.'

'It's sure going to be a different Israel after this war,' she pondered.

'Very different. I don't think we'll be able to take in how different for quite a while. But think of all the room we'd have for new immigrants – empty cities, like Tabuk back there, or Duba, or Haql. Apparently thousands of refugees have been fleeing Lebanon and Syria into Turkey. And we can see for ourselves what's been happening here in Saudi Arabia.'

'Just how many new immigrants are you suggesting,' she asked.

'Well, according to what I've learned from my friend Brandon, maybe something in the order of 90-100,000 new *olim*.'

'But Israel would become more than ten times the size it is now,' she said.

'Exactly!'

'How on earth could the country begin to cope with an aliyah of that magnitude?'

'I have no idea – but I tell you this, the only country on earth with even a hope of pulling off something like this would be Israel.

'Hey, I'm quite dry again,' said Shaul. 'We should get back to work, now, I think?'

'Whatever you say, Captain!' Rebekkah replied.

Shaul and Rebekkah dressed quickly and then drove back to Duba, where Shaul picked out four men who'd already been sleeping for a while – including Samir. 'You guys can go back to sleep in the APC,' he told them, 'we're gonna be travelling for quite a bit.'

The trip north took two and a half hours. Rebekkah fell asleep after only a few minutes and, as Shaul had suggested, the guys in the rear did likewise.

'Almost there,' Shaul shouted a while later, eliciting groans from behind.

'Almost where, then,' asked Samir, stretching, 'Where exactly are we?'

'A little place called Seham Bay,' replied Shaul.

'And the significance of that ..?' queried Bar-Ilan, waking up.

'It's right across the Straights of Tiran from Sharm el Sheik – the southern tip of Sinai. We now control both sides of the Gulf of Aqaba,' added Shaul.

'What are we doing here, then,' asked Rebekkah.

'Well, first we're looking for a flagpole,' said Shaul.

'I see,' Bar-Ilan replied.

The few buildings at Seham Bay – mostly connected with the radio transmitters there – were as deserted as they had found Duba to be. The soldiers left the APC and stretched their legs stiffly.

'What is that across the bay?' asked Samir.

'Looks like a plane – a broken one,' one of his mates replied.

'Yeah, it's an old Catalina that crashed there years ago,' said Shaul. As they stared at him in wonder he explained, 'It happens to be marked on *Google Maps!*'

'OK.'

On the shore between the transmitters behind them and the plane on the far side of the bay, were several small power boats – apparently abandoned there.

'I suppose they left in too much of a hurry to think about moving boats,' observed Samir.

'OK, I think it's going to have to be one of the transmitters – any volunteers?' said Shaul.

'I'll do it,' replied a young soldier, who looked about eighteen or nineteen.

'What's your name, soldier?' asked Shaul.

'Avi Lieberman, sir.'

Samir appeared with a pair of bolt-cutters from the rear of the APC. 'Might need a way in first,' he said, striding to the gate in the security fence and neatly snapping the padlock that held it secure. He turned then and looked in Shaul's direction.

'OK, off you go then, Avi, but be careful. We don't want any stupid accidents at this stage.'

The young man entered the small compound and nimbly climbed up the radio tower. When he was about halfway up Shaul shouted to him, 'That's far enough, Avi, put it up there.'

Avi hooked one leg around the metal upright, leaving his hands free to tie the flag in place. When it was done he waved down at them and climbed carefully down again.

'*Toda*, soldier,' Shaul said, '*Tov ma'od.*

'If you guys fancy a quick swim, you can have fifteen minutes. I'll drive around that compound with Bar-Ilan, here.' The four soldiers looked at Shaul and Rebekkah, then ran down to the water's edge, removing boots and uniforms, running into the sea, shouting and splashing like kids in a park.

Shaul and Rebekkah returned to the APC and Shaul drove out to the point facing west to Sharm el Sheikh. On their right was a fence, with a tall building in the centre of the large compound it enclosed – almost a tower. They drove slowly around the compound, stopping for a few minutes at the south western end to gaze across in the direction of Sharm el Sheikh.

The far shore was maybe 20km away, but the Sinai mountains, which backed Sharm, were now silhouetted by the sun, which was getting much lower in the sky. As they watched an Israeli helicopter appeared across the straits from their right, from the north, and landed at Sharm el Sheikh airport.

'Everything looks under control, there,' commented Shaul.

'Good to know,' replied Rebekkah.

'Your turn to drive on the way back, Bar-Ilan – it's a pretty straight road,' said Shaul.

'OK, captain,' she replied, raising an eyebrow.

They returned to the APC and Bar-Ilan jumped into the driving seat, driving around the northern side of the compound and back to the beach, where the guys were now struggling back into their uniforms.

'OK, guys, back to Duba. Wake me when we get there, unless there's a radio call. Drive on, Bar-Ilan.'

Rebekkah put the APC into gear and drove off south again. She wondered what to make of this young American captain, with all his experience of war in Afghanistan. She wondered also what the future of her country would be now, after such a devastating war. Would the country survive the aftermath? Levine seemed to think it would not only survive, but even grow and flourish.

He was an interesting person, she decided – not sore on the eyes, either, as she looked across at his sleeping form. She wondered if that brief period of him letting his hair down meant anything – if she should hope for anything more to come of it.

Rebekkah had kept herself aloof since she joined the army. Many of her female colleagues had relished the attention of their male colleagues – two friends of hers had had abortions during their army service – but Rebekkah had no intention of making that mistake.

But Levine – Shaul, Sol – intrigued her. He seemed quite a serious person, especially for an American. He seemed very focussed on Israel and its future – like herself. She wondered if there was any point in hoping that maybe something would develop between them.

The sun plunged into the Red Sea as they drove south. Shortly before they reached the ferry terminal the radio crackled to life. Rebekkah shook Shaul by the arm, 'Radio call, sir.'

He grunted and lifted the handset, rubbing his eyes and straightening up as he did so. '*Seren* Levine, here.'

'This is Israeli missile boat, *Ashdod* – Captain Rehov speaking. We are within ten minutes of arriving at the Duba Port ferry terminal. You have men there already, I understand?'

'*Ken*. We have two Armoured Personnel Carriers on guard and I should be there myself in ...' Shaul looked across to Bar-Ilan to see how close they were. She pointed to a highway sign coming up which showed, 'Duba 40 km. Duba Port 20km.' 'We should be with you in 15 or 20 mins,' he replied.

'Very well, *Ashdod* out.'

Shaul turned around to the four men in the rear, 'Wake up lads. We're gonna say *Shalom* to the Israeli Navy.' He then radioed his own APCs at the terminal to tell them what to expect.

Twenty minutes later, as Rebekkah pulled the APC up at the edge of the dock, sounding the horn to alert their own men to their presence, the missile boat was just coming up the channel ahead. As it approached a searchlight blinded them for a few seconds as it found the edge of the dock.

A few minutes later the ship was moored to the dock and the captain was making his way onto it. 'Captain Levine, I believe?' he asked Shaul.

'Yes, and you're Captain Rehov?'

'Correct. We'll be stationed here for the next few days. Apparently we might possibly be bringing some passengers over from the Egyptian side in the near future, we're told. So just call us Red Sea Ferries, from now on.'

'In that case my men won't be needed here any longer, is that right?' Shaul asked.

'That's correct. You boys have been having a holiday in the Saudi Kingdom, I believe?

'We haven't been here long, but the welcome back in Tabuk was warm enough! Quiet now, though, and under our control.' Shaul explained. 'Duba is 20 kilometres south of here and quiet as the grave – same the whole way up this coast. We've just driven back from the Straights of Tiran – no sign of life anywhere. Everyone appears to have fled south, or taken to boats for Egypt, as far as we can tell.'

'Makes our job all the easier, then,' Captain Rehov commented. 'It's been a strange kind of war, but we appear to be winning, which is the main thing. You guys look kinda bushed. I expect you want to push off now?'

'Yes,' replied Shaul, 'We'll leave this place in the capable hands of the Navy. Carry on, Captain.'

'*L'hitraot, Segen* Levine (See you),' Rehov replied, saluting. He turned and went back aboard the missile boat to organise his men.

Shaul turned to the crews of the other two APCs and told them to follow him south. 'Time we all had some food and a proper night's rest.'

'Amen to that,' Junbalat chuckled.

The three APCs returned in the dark to the front of *Duba Hospital.*, where they grabbed some food from the canteen. Shaul organised some men to take the first watch, leaving Bar-Ilan to organise the second watch from Samir and company. Eventually, Shaul tumbled into a bed and knew nothing more until sunrise next morning.

36 – The Knesset, Jerusalem

The Israeli Prime Minister addressed a crowded emergency session of the Knesset:

'Fellow MKs, we find ourselves today in an unique situation. Our enemies have joined forces with the intention of wiping out the State of Israel forever.'

He paused briefly, then continued, 'They did *not* succeed. I firmly believe that the God of Israel delivered us from destruction, just as he did in the days of Queen Esther.

'The fear of the God of Israel has caused our enemies to flee before us in every direction. Our faithful IDF forces have been victorious – in the air, on land and on sea. Israel now controls lands more than ten times its previous size. We control large cities whose populations have fled. We control natural resources and assets that we could never have dreamed of.'

There were loud cheers from all across the house.

'Our enemies are destroyed or have fled far away. Our new borders today are open desert on the south and east. In the north east we face only our allies, the Kurds, who wish to work with the newly enlarged State of Israel. In the north we have a border with the Islamic state of Turkey – no longer an ally of Israel – but with a heavy Kurdish population in the east, who will now be in a stronger position because of the existence next door of a Kurdish State.

'Fellow MKs, we must make crucial decisions in the light of this new reality. No longer do we need to be overly concerned with world opinion, or with the threats of Islamic nations on our borders, or with the threat of a nuclear attack against us. Israel has grown, Israel remains strong, while our enemies are weak and defeated. Israel can now afford to operate from a new position of strength.'

There were more cheers across the house.

'But now we must make some crucial decisions. How best can we hold onto the land we have conquered, the biblical land which was promised to us – *"from the wadi of Egypt to the great River Euphrates,"* as the Bible says. We have peace already, so we have no need to exchange any of this land for peace – a policy which never ever worked, anyway!'

More cheers.

'We are in a unique position today. The forces of radical Islam around the world have been dealt a very heavy blow. The heart of Islam – the city of Mecca – has been obliterated by an Iranian nuclear missile. I can assure you that Israel had no hand in that. Islam is reeling and many are defecting from what remains of those militant Islamic extremist groups.

'Even in countries such as Afghanistan and Pakistan there is a new movement among those people who have long regarded themselves – *not* ever as Jewish, but as Israelite – part of the people of Israel. I can now reveal that I have already been contacted by representatives of the Pashtun people in these countries and also in India, also by the Kashmiris and the Menashe – many of whom are already present in Israel, many of whom have been fighting for Israel in this recent war as soldiers in the IDF.

'We have also been contacted by representatives of the Igbo people in Nigeria, the Lemba in Zimbabwe and South Africa, and by other groups. There is a great desire now in the hearts of these people to come home to Eretz Israel.

'This is not a decision that I, as Prime Minister of Israel, can make alone, or even that the cabinet can make alone. This decision will require the input of the Chief Rabbis, the Sanhedrin and every Knesset member. We must search our souls to know what is the right decision. Is this the time of the great ingathering? The doors are open. Iran no longer stands in the way. Egypt and Sudan no longer stand in the way. When will we have such a great opportunity ever again? I believe we should strike while the iron is hot!'

The Prime Minister waited while cheering died down.

'As regards the Menashe in India, the government had previously given permission for another seven thousand to come to Israel, but we have only been allowing a few hundred to come at a time. Now I say, we have empty towns, empty cities, empty lands. I am going to direct that these seven thousand Israelites be allowed to come now, as a taste of what may be to come.'

There was some cheering, but also a lot of discussion among members. Clearly this idea was a novel one to many there and would require a lot of debate and discussion.

The Prime Minister continued:

'In the meantime, we must not make the mistake made by our American and other allies when they conquered Saddam Hussein's Iraq. We cannot afford to have a vacuum. We need a modern day Israeli-style *Marshall Plan*. Just as Europe was rebuilt after World War II, under the *Marshall Plan*, so we must rebuild the infrastructure in these conquered lands.

'Currently Israeli Military Law extends over these areas, but I propose that we move quickly to a situation very soon where Israeli Civil Law applies to all the biblical land under our control. We no longer have a 'Palestinian Authority'

– either in Judaea and Samaria, or in what remains of Gaza. The members of Hamas, Fatah and Islamic Jihad, who have bitterly opposed us for so long, have either fled – abandoning their people – or are no longer alive. To begin with I propose that Israeli Civil Law should now be extended to both areas.

'The heart of Gaza City – and also of Damascus and Beirut – has been destroyed and each of those areas will remain uninhabitable for the foreseeable future. But we wish to extend to those non-Jewish populations who have remained in the Gaza Strip, who have remained in Judaea and Samaria, the possibility of becoming full Israeli citizens. But let the rest of the world take note, there is longer any such entity as the Palestinian Authority.'

Some started to cheer again, but the Prime Minister carried on:

'We will take immediate steps to apply Israeli Law, Israeli policing, Israeli Education and Health to every part of Judaea, Samaria and the Gaza Strip, which are now an integral part of the nation of Israel. There is one land and one people – no matter what their religion or ethnic background – Israel.'

Again there were loud cheers.

'We call upon our brethren in Europe, in North America and in every part of the world to make aliyah now to Israel. Now is the time to come to our aid. We will need doctors, mechanics, civil servants – many skills and occupations. We will also welcome volunteers – from every nation – to come and help us to build the new Israel, and we plan to put steps into operation to enable this.'

'How will we execute this Israeli Marshall Plan? – I would like to call it the *New Israel Plan*. Firstly, we call upon those within Israel who are in positions of civil leadership, business leadership, etc. to volunteer their skills and their expertise. We have empty cities – such as Aleppo, in former Syria, a city of over two million people, now empty; Tabuk, in Midian, formerly of Saudi Arabia, a city of over half a million, empty! Amman in former Jordan, with only a quarter of its original population, Aqaba ... many cities like these.

'Instead of leaving a vacuum, let us build the new Israel. Let us build roads and railways and airports and holiday resorts and factories ... Let us build for the ingathering that is to come. Let us build a new and much greater Israel – an example to the whole world. We no longer need to fight terrorism within, or on our borders, so let us turn our energies – and our budget – to building a truly great nation. Let us ignore the rumbling threats of Russia and China, even – dare I say it? – those of the USA. We will welcome their help, if it is offered, but if it is not, we will do what Israelis do best and we will build anyway.

'But let me remind you of one important thing. We must decide very quickly whether we are going to welcome home our brothers from the tribes who have been lost for so long. We cannot build such a nation as I am presenting to you without the people who will be its foundation.

'And yes, that will mean a much different Israel – but, I ask you, can Israel ever be the same? We are known the world over for our ability to innovate, to invent, to solve problems, to bring productive land out of swamps and deserts. We have conquered the nations who attacked us, who wished for our destruction. Let us cement our recent victory by building something now that will last.

'I'm not going to promise you that this will be an easy road. Not one of us can envisage what that future Israel will be like. I'm talking about an Israel that may be ten times its present size. If our brethren are willing to come, I believe we should invite them to come. We should extend a hand of welcome.

'Some of these people – the Igbo and Lemba and another four million of the Menashe, for instance – have been largely Christian for generations. Some of them have been Moslem for generations, though the Pashtun have their own Pashtunwali code, mostly based on the Tanakh. I would never suggest that there will not be problems but, if they want to come and be an integral part of the new Israel, I say we should let them come!'

'My government have already taken some decisions that are necessary to prepare the way to govern this newly extended land that is now ours. Those who wish to be a part of the *New Israel Plan* – I'm thinking of town and city mayors and deputy mayors, heads of companies, top doctors and lawyers, that calibre of people – are welcome to contact us now.

'To get things under way, I have asked a good friend of mine, Dr. Samuel Goldman, a very successful entrepreneur and businessman, to be the interim head of the *New Israel Plan*. The Knesset may decide at a later date either to confirm or replace him, but he has agreed to take on the task of getting this plan under way, of recruiting staff and making initial surveys of the new territories and cities, available resources, etc.

'My government will take the initial steps by proposing bills, etc., but I think this new situation is so unique that we may need to combine all our forces. So, I call upon the opposition to consider forming a new national unity government, so that we can most effectively deal with the new situation that has been forced upon us. *Toda raba*.'

37 – Six Hour War: South to the Border

The sun was already shining when Shaul awoke and headed for the nearest shower in Duba Hospital. He made his way to the cafeteria, where Bar-Ilan, Junbalat and Gold had already organised breakfast for their troops. Shaul grabbed some food on a tray and joined them.

'*Boker tov* (good morning), sir,' they greeted him.

'*Boker tov*,' Shaul replied, 'I trust you guys have had a reasonable night's sleep?'

'We're ready for action, Sir,' Bar-Ilan responded, the others nodding in agreement.

'Well, I don't envisage anything strenuous happening the early part of the day. I suggest we divide into two groups – one to patrol this town – which seems to be completely empty. The other group can relax and swim, or rest – but in one group. Gold, your men can take two shifts also, let the others relax for a few hours, OK?'

'Yes, sir.' Gold replied.

'I imagine the reserve troops might be with us by about midday. If they are I'm going to suggest to Southern Command that we let them go ahead and get set up here while we take a little trip further south – to Al Wajh and Umluj, which are small resort towns along Highway 5. Al Wajh also has an airport to the south, while Umluj just has a couple of small marinas.

'They're both part of Tabuk province, so it makes sense to take them, if they prove to be as deserted as this place. This could become a veritable gold coast for Israel in the future, as far as tourism is concerned. I'm no expert on fishing, but I imagine they could be valuable to Israel from that perspective as well.'

'Sounds like a plan, sir,' Junbalat answered. The others murmured assent.

'Another little 300 kilometre jaunt, then?' Bar-Ilan observed.

'Yes, I think so,' Shaul replied.

'How are we for fuel at the moment – Gold? Bar-Ilan?' Shaul asked.

'The tanks need topping up, for sure,' replied Gold.

'The APCs we used yesterday are pretty near empty,' Bar-Ilan responded. 'We could go back to the ferry terminal – plenty of fuel there.'

'Great idea, Bar-Ilan. You and Gold here organise half of our vehicles to go and refuel as soon as we finish here. When you return, Junbalat here can take the other vehicles up in turn. Be sure to keep the Navy sweet – we don't want to tread on their toes.'

'Okay, sir. We'll try to keep 'em happy.'

'After that we can divide into those on patrol or guard duty and the others chilling out, OK?'

'Sir!' they replied.

The Reserve troops arrived just as Shaul and his men were relaxing at the end of a leisurely lunch. Shaul had already put his suggestion to Southern Command and received their approval – commending him for his initiative.

After a brief conversation with Bergman, the officer in charge of the Reserve force, Shaul gathered his men. 'OK, this should be a fairly routine trip but, officially, we are still at war – so keep your eyes open when we approach Al Wajh and again when we get to Umluj. We'll probably be staying over-night in both places, then we'll hand both towns over to Bergman, here, and we'll head back to join the rest of the squad at Tabuk. Al Wajh is about 150k from here, and Umluj about the same distance again'

'Any word of what's happening with our guys there, sir?' Bar-Ilan asked.

'Yes, I radioed earlier – spoke to Tamari and Peled. They've been having a fairly easy time of it. Sharing patrols into the city with the other troops now stationed there. No sign of any trouble. Unless we find some action today, I guess the war is over from our unit's point of view.'

Shaul gave the order to move out, heading for his own APC as the troops mounted up to follow him – three APCs in front, followed by the four tanks, then the other three APCs in the rear.

It took just over two hours to arrive in the sleepy town of Al Wajh. As they left the divided highway to enter the town the road was lined with mosques, apartment buildings and hotels – a lot of the construction looked new and some was obviously still in process. A large boat sculpture was set in the centre of one roundabout, while a huge jug decorated another.

Like Duba the town was a coastal strip with a beach along the Red Sea; a small port in the centre, with some warehouses; and an inlet to the south which served as a small marina, with a few small boats still moored in the inlet.

Chapter 37 – Six Hour War: South to the Border

As they approached the southern end of the town – still with no sign of habitation – they were forced to turn right to the sea front before they could swing inland along the bay with the marina. On their left were some ancient stone buildings in a precarious state of repair. It wasn't clear whether these were being preserved or simply left to fall down of their own accord.

They drove east along the north edge of this bay until they reached Highway 5 again. Almost opposite the road they were on – about two hundred metres to the north – was another road leading off into the interior, with a large hotel standing on the north east corner of the junction.

Shaul halted at the junction and waved down the other vehicles. 'OK,' he said, pointing north east to the hotel, 'that will be our temporary headquarters until we hand over to Bergman's guys tomorrow. We'll see if we can rustle up some food here – Junbalat, can you organise that? Gold, we'll leave one of your tanks here tonight, so pick a good man and get him positioned outside the hotel.

'Bar-Ilan, take a couple of APC's and do a brief recce around the town, along the shore road. Pay particular attention to the port area. I'm going to check out the airport, which is two or three kilometres south of here, on the edge of the Red Sea. We'll meet back here in half an hour.'

The men quickly dispersed to their tasks, Shaul taking two APCs and heading south along Highway 5. They were back just in time for some lunch, provided by Junbalat and some of his men.

As they got stuck in to the food Shaul asked Bar-Ilan to report.

'Still no sign of human beings, sir, but there is a fishing port in the middle of the town – a couple of fishing boats still tied up at the dock. Lots of beaches further north, hotels, shops and the odd mosque. Everything is very neat and tidy – but deserted.'

'OK, well, the airport is small,' he said, 'just a domestic service, I'd say. Also deserted. We'll put a tank on guard at the turnoff from Highway 5, I think. I'll radio Bergman now to send some reinforcements today.'

Shaul went out to his APC and radioed Bergman in Duba. He arranged for a small force of men to head to Al Wajh that afternoon, then he returned to the hotel.

'Bar-Ilan, I'm gonna leave you in charge here for now – with two APCs and Gold looking after the two tank crews. The rest of us will head south as soon as we're finished. Bergman is sending a small force to relieve you – they should be here in a couple of hours, or so. As soon as they arrive bring your men on down to Umluj. Contact me by radio when you're approaching the town, OK?'

'OK, sir,' Rebekkah replied.

The remaining two tanks and four APCs headed south again, taking another two hours and a bit more to reach Umluj. Again this town was a long strip along the coast of the Red Sea, but this time, instead of bypassing the town, Highway 5 headed at an angle towards the centre of the town – next to a half-moon shaped bay filled with small pleasure craft.

As they approached the centre they saw dust rising ahead. Shaul grabbed a pair of binoculars from the front of the APC. 'Looks like looters.' he said. They've spotted our approach and decided to exit.' He reported by radio. 'They might be Army, though – so I think we'll give them a show of strength. Let's keep going and give them something to think about.'

As they accelerated out of the town they began to catch up on the fleeing vehicles. They certainly appeared to be a couple of Saudi Army trucks, with two jeeps in front. Once they were within a few hundred yards of the trucks Shaul ordered his tanks to load up. 'Fire a couple of rounds over their heads. We don't want to kill anyone, just give them a scare, so they'll know we're here and they better not come back.'

The tank barrels elevated and puffs of smoke appeared as they both fired in unison. The rounds exploded ahead and inland of the Saudi vehicles. The tanks fired a second time and then Shaul ordered them to cease firing. 'That ought to give them something to think about,' he said over the radio link. 'Hopefully, they'll pass the message on to their superiors and they won't dare think of sending anyone back up this way.

'A good job, men,' he said. 'But to be on the safe side I want to leave a guard on this road tonight. See that sign just there announcing the boundary of Tabuk Governate – that's where we'll have our border post. We're on a hill here, overlooking that large wadi, so we can see anyone coming a good way off. And there are plenty of rocks and hills making it difficult to bypass the main road – and there's a small building just over there which we can use as a border post for now.

'If we had a bulldozer with us I would dig up the road and make a proper barrier but, so there's no doubt about it, I think we'll put an Israeli flag up at least.'

The vehicles halted briefly on the ridge while one young soldier was detailed to attach the flag high up on a nearby pole.

'We'll head back now and find somewhere as our base for tonight.' Shaul said. The tanks and APCs turned around and followed Shaul back towards Umluj again. They had travelled around twenty five kilometres in pursuit of the looters, so by the time they arrived back in Umluj, the sun was getting quite low in the sky.

As they entered the area of Anassim, south of Umluj proper, Shaul spotted an hotel on the right, just off a roundabout on the main road. He instructed his driver to slow down his vehicle for the roundabout and to turn right into the hotel grounds. The other vehicles followed. By radio Shaul instructed his men to alight armed and ready for action, if necessary. They approached the entrance carefully, but found the building empty, as in the previous towns.

'OK, set up a perimeter, Junbalat – tanks out front facing both ways, APCs lined up facing outwards near the entrance. Look-outs in both tanks at all times. I have my suspicions about this town – maybe it's just because we're so much closer to the big Saudi population centres. Medina and Jeddah are not so far from here.'

As the vehicles got themselves into position, Shaul took his own crew into the hotel. There was no one about, but they quickly found the restaurant and kitchens and soon there was some hot food available. When everyone had eaten, a soldier ran into the hotel to tell Shaul that Bar-Ilan had radioed that she and her men were at the north end of Umluj. Shaul went out to the APC and contacted her.

'Keep right down Highway 5, through the centre and out to the south. We're in a hotel in Anissim, which is south of Umluj. I'll have an APC wait for you at the roundabout on Highway 5. The hotel is on the left from the round-about. There should be enough food left for you guys to eat something.'

'Sure hope so, sir!' Bar-Ilan replied.

Shaul detailed an APC with two soldiers to wait for Bar-Ilan's contingent at the roundabout. Meanwhile, he also sent Junbalat out with a tank crew and two APCs to head south to the designated 'border post' and go on guard duty there. They were equipped with night-sight goggles and were to be relieved in four hours, but were to report any enemy contact immediately.

Bar-Ilan and her twenty men arrived a few minutes later and tucked into some hot food kept for them. Shaul brought Bar-Ilan up to date with their after-noon's activities.

'I'll take the second watch,' said Shaul, 'midnight to four am, then you can take over until eight. I've been on with Bergman and he's sending a larger force down here at first light – including a bulldozer to close the road and build a barrier either side – so they should be here by the end of your watch. Now that your tanks are here I think I'll send another tank down to the border. That will leave us two here for contingencies.

'Once your guys have finished eating I'm going to take a couple of APCs on patrol around Umluj. Meanwhile, you can take an APC and accompany the other tank down to the border. That will give you a chance to assess the situation down there. Have a chat with Samir and then head back here.'

'As I said to Junbalat, earlier, I just have a feeling about this area. We're a lot closer to the big cities of Medina and Jeddah – although the nuclear strike on Mecca will have hit them hard and I'm sure a lot of people will have fled. And we have no idea what military strength the Saudis have left – but most of it is probably concentrating on Iran at the moment.

'Even so, I think we need to be pretty vigilant while we're here. We don't want to be caught napping at this stage. We'll be finished here in the morning and I'd like it to be a quiet hand over. So, be on the lookout.'

Rebekkah gathered the crew of her APC and headed out along with the extra tank to the newly set up border post.

Shaul collected the APC crews and headed north to patrol around Umluj.

38 – Six Hour War: Final Battle?

The young private shook Shaul by the shoulder, 'Sir, sir,' he called, 'Bar-Ilan reports enemy movements in the area below the post.'

'OK, Lieberman, isn't it?'

'Yes sir.'

'Wake up everyone and tell them to be in the foyer, ready to move south in five minutes, OK?'

'Sir,' Lieberman replied.

Shaul radioed from his APC, letting Bar-Ilan know that they were on their way to reinforce the post.

'What is happening, at the moment?' he asked.

'Vehicles, including APCs and a couple of tanks, are approaching along the main road. There are infantry ahead of them in the area each side of the road. All moving towards us. I think they're hoping to take us by surprise.'

'OK, Bar-Ilan, I take it you've already deployed all your men?'

'Yes, sir.'

A few minutes later Shaul's troops congregated around him in the hotel foyer. Drivers were already revving the engines of both tanks and APCs. Shaul briefed his men on what to expect. We'll approach within a few hundred metres of the post, then slow to a crawl and get into positions either side of the road. No firing until I give the order – unless they're already attacking by the time we arrive.

The convoy headed south as fast as possible.

Thirty minutes later they crept up on the ad hoc border post. There was no sign of their own vehicles at first, but as Shaul donned his night-sight goggles he could see both tanks and APCs 'hull down' behind some rock outcrops at either side of the main road. One APC was hidden behind the small building on the right of the road. From the enemy side they would be invisible.

Shaul radioed to Bar-Ilan, 'We're here,' he said, 'Good deployment. How close are the enemy?'

'Very close now, sir. They'll start firing any minute – as soon as they can be sure where we are. I'm in the APC behind the little building on the right, sir.'

'*Beseder*. How many RPGs have you got?'

'Only two, sir – one behind the rocks on either side.'

'*Beseder*, we have two more. My men are moving up behind you right now.'

'*Beseder*, I see those on my side.'

'I'll take the other side. As soon as firing commences I'm gonna get Gold to send his tanks down either side of that road. The other two tanks will be targeting the enemy tanks first. Once we're sure those are disabled all four tanks will attack the APCs, trucks, jeeps, whatever. And we'll take our own APCs and follow them. We want to totally disable this force. They've asked for war and we're gonna give it to them, understood?'

'*Tov ma'od, Seren,*' she replied (Very good, Captain.)

They waited for a few minutes, then Shaul radioed, 'Tanks and RPGs select your targets.' A minute or so later he commanded, 'Fire!'

The tanks hull down began firing their missiles at the Saudi tanks. Two were hit straight away. As the firing began, the other two tanks began to move rapidly onto the main road, charging towards the enemy, turrets swivelling and firing as they went. An enemy APC was hit, then another. The other two tanks pulled out and followed the first pair.

Shaul radioed again, 'Mount up troops, we're going after them.'

Shaul's men ran to their own APCs and scrambled inside as the drivers took off down the highway on both sides. The enemy were in some confusion, trying to turn around and getting in each others way as Shaul's force bore down on them.

Two enemy RPGs were launched at their tanks, but the *Bright Arrow* defence system immediately responded in both cases, firing a counter missile and destroying both rockets before they reached their targets.

'Target those RPGs,' Shaul ordered.

Shortly after both enemy RPGs were silenced, although machine gun fire continued all around.

Shaul radioed again, this time to Junbalat, 'Tell them to throw down their weapons, put their hands on their heads and lie down at the edge of the road. Anyone still with a weapon will be shot.'

Samir's voice echoed around the area in Arabic. Some of the enemy troops obeyed and threw their weapons down, making their way to the roadside.

Chapter 38 – Six Hour War: South to the Border

Others continued to fire and Shaul's men fired back, controlling the *Bright Arrow* machine guns on each vehicle from safety within the armoured cars.

Soon the night grew quiet. A lone enemy vehicle was attempting to escape down the highway. Shaul ordered two of his APCs to pursue it. Shortly after an RPG fired from one of the APCs and the enemy vehicle turned into a ball of fire.

'Cease fire,' Shaul ordered. 'Patrol both sides of the road and let's get these prisoners gathered up. Tell them to stand up and walk this way in front of the APCs. Don't take any unnecessary risks, mind. Junbalat, you can tell them what we expect of them.

'Bar-Ilan, take two APCs and check out the enemy vehicles for survivors. But be very careful if you're picking anyone up.'

Both responded and three APCs patrolled the roadside slowly, urging the defeated Saudi troops to get on their feet and start walking.

Bar-Ilan radioed back and reported, 'Only two survivors with the vehicles, sir. Both wounded – one man has severe burns and the other has a broken leg. We're strapping him up now, sir.'

As the walking enemy soldiers approached the small building Bar-Ilan's APCs roared up behind them. One of the enemy soldiers appeared to collapse and one of Shaul's troops left his APC to help the man.

As Shaul shouted, 'Be careful, man,' over the loudspeaker, suddenly a shot rang out and the soldier fell onto the ground. Bar-Ilan immediately swung her APC around and began to search the rocky terrain for the sniper. With the help of her night-sight goggles, quickly donned, she spotted the enemy soldier, who, realising he'd been spotted, began firing towards them again. The APC opened fire and the man collapsed, dead.

Meanwhile, Shaul's vehicle skidded to a halt beside the wounded soldier. The young man was barely moving and Shaul ordered his crew to give cover as he went to help the soldier. 'Avi,' he said, recognising the young man who had wakened him earlier and who had climbed the transmitter at Seham Bay to put up the Israeli flag.

The young soldier's breath was laboured and as Shaul whispered a Hebrew prayer over him, he died.

'He paid dearly for his instinct to help a wounded man,' Shaul murmured, 'An unnecessary death, though.'

Standing up he ordered the ten enemy soldiers tied up and the wounded man – it turned out to be just a badly twisted ankle – attended to. As the tanks trundled back to the post Shaul delegated Bar-Ilan and Junbalat to supervise loading the captives into two of the APCs. When they were safely in he instructed the crew to keep guard on the men.

'We're not going to take any more risks here in the dark,' Shaul said to Bar-Ilan. 'When it's light – quite soon, now – we can use the tanks to tow a few of the damaged enemy vehicles up here to form a barricade. We can also collect the weapons that were abandoned, then. We'll leave the dead where they are until Bergman's force relieve us. They can have that task. After all, we've done all the hard work!'

'We have, sir. Do you want me to stay here on guard then, sir?'

'Yes, I don't imagine the Saudis will send anyone else out to attack after the fiasco these guys have made of it. We'll leave Gold and the other two tanks with you, though, just in case. Junbalat will relieve you at 8 am, if Bergman's guys don't get here first.'

'Beseder, Seren.'

'Toda, Rebekkah.'

Shaul walked back to his APC and waved to the other three to move out. When they arrived back at the empty hotel the sky was already beginning to lighten. Soon, long shadows stretched out from the mountains to the east.

They marched the prisoners inside – two soldiers helping the man with the injured ankle – and took them to a ground floor room with soft furniture, where they lay down and fell asleep.

Shaul organised for breakfast to be ready for 07:00 hours, so that Junbalat could get back to the border post for 08:00.

'Let the prisoners sleep on,' he instructed. 'They can eat once Bergman's guys get here.'

He left four men on guard and told the rest to get some rest while they could.

At seven am the men were sitting down to a quick breakfast, when a soldier came in to tell Shaul that Bergman's troops were just approaching Umluj. Shaul went out to make contact, telling them where to find them and again sending an APC out to the roundabout to guide then in.

When they arrived, Junbalat was just leaving with his men and Shaul began to brief the new commander – Perez – on the early morning attack and the present situation. He showed him where the prisoners were held and offered them some breakfast, explaining that some of his own troops would be arriving back in less than an hour for their own breakfast.

The commander first detailed some of his own men to take over guard duty, while Shaul's guards got some food. He set aside a group of thirty men and briefed them on what they should expect at the new border post. They had brought a bulldozer with them, so that would be getting to work – under guard – to improve the ad hoc defences.

Shaul left him to it and instructed his men to get ready to head for Tabuk – they had quite a long day's journey ahead of them, once Bar-Ilan and the others arrived back and were fed.

While Rebekkah and the others were eating, Shaul delegated a few men to take take two APCs at a time and find fuel to top them up. The tanks would fill up on the way north. Then he radioed Southern Command and reported the events of the night before, including the death of Avi Lieberman.

'Well, the Saudis called for a ceasefire this morning, so things should be quiet from now on. Good thing you chased those looters and decided to set up a border post, though. If they'd reached the town they could have dug in and been nearly impossible to shift overnight. Your actions – and those of your men – have kept the town in our hands. Well done, Levine.'

'Well sir, it was *Samal* (Sergeant) Bar-Ilan who saved the day, sir. She spotted the enemy creeping north and called for reinforcement immediately. When we got there she had deployed the tanks and APCs behind rocks and a building. She also took out the sniper who killed Lieberman. I'd like to recommend her for some recognition, sir.'

'Very well, Levine, we'll have a think about that. Meanwhile we've organised a few transporters to take your tanks back to Tabuk – those tanks must have taken a bit of a beating with all the ground they've covered.'

'Indeed, sir.'

'The transporter drivers have been instructed to meet up with you at Duba Port – we assume you'll be refuelling there before continuing on to Tabuk.'

'Yes, sir.'

'Well, the transporters will need to refuel anyway, so it seems the best place to meet up with you.'

'Yes. sir. Er, about Lieberman, sir, any chance we can get his body picked up and taken back to Israel?'

'Yes, that would be preferable, Levine. There's an airport south of Al Wajh, isn't there? We'll organise either a chopper, or a small plane, to meet you there and collect the body. What time do you reckon you'll be there?'

'Well, we're heading out shortly, sir – say 09:00 hours – it's 150 km, so ETA around 11:30 hours, if all goes smoothly.'

'Very well, Levine, the body will be picked up at 11:30 hours at Al Wajh. Safe journey, *Seren*. Out.'

By nine o'clock Shaul's force were ready to head north once again. The tanks went ahead, led by an APC to show them the fuel depot they had used – a transport depot with lots of abandoned trucks. Shortly afterwards, Shaul led the remainder of his force to catch them up and begin their trip back to Tabuk. The body of *Turai* (Private) Lieberman was stowed carefully in the rear of Shaul's APC.

It was nearly twelve before the convoy reached the airport at Al Wajh – due to a damaged track on one of the tanks, which had to be repaired by the roadside. A small plane was waiting behind the airport building and Shaul's men formed up in two ranks as an honour guard as four of his men carried the body bag safely to the aeroplane. Shaul repeated two short Hebrew prayers as the body was transferred onto the plane:

'*Shmai Israel, Adonai elohaynu, Adonai echad.* (Hear O Israel, The Lord our God, The Lord is One)' and '*Adonai roi, lo echsaar* (The Lord is my shepherd, I shall not want).'

As the plane taxied to the runway and took off north, Shaul addressed his men, 'We've lost a good man, who served Israel well. May God be with him.'

'Soldiers, we'll stop in a few minutes at the hotel in Al Wajh. I've radioed ahead and they should have some lunch organised for us. Then we will change drivers and move on as quickly as possible to Duba, where we'll refuel and load the tanks onto transporters, that should be waiting for us. All being well we'll be back in Tabuk by late evening. Then we'll see what Tamari and Peled have been up to – probably sunning themselves while we've been fighting a war!'

The men smiled, and cheered by Shaul's comments – though still saddened by the recent loss of their comrade – climbed aboard their vehicles for the short journey into Al Wajh.

It was approaching 16:00 hours by the time they drove into the port complex north of Duba. Their convoy had been stopped twice at new checkpoints set up by the reserve company on the outskirts of Duba, and now, at the turn-off to Duba Port, by Navy personnel. The missile boat was still moored at the dock and the Navy were in evidence around the area. The APCs were directed towards the refuelling area, beside which four tank transporters were parked, waiting.

Shaul left his driver to refuel his APC, while he went over to greet the transporter drivers, who saluted him smartly.

'Joining us for a trip to Tabuk, then, men?' he asked.

'Yes, sir, and on north to Amman day after tomorrow, we understand.'

'OK, that's news to me, guys. But I'm sure we can handle whatever the Army throws at us, eh?' he grinned.

'Yes, sir,' they smiled in return, glad to see that Shaul seemed to be a fairly relaxed commander.

'We believe you've seen a bit of action in this war, sir?'

'Indeed,' Shaul replied, 'Both in Tabuk and last night down in Umluj.' As the men looked at him questioningly, he continued, 'Some of the Saudi Army decided to make a surprise early morning attack on our outpost. Actually, they'd probably hoped to re-take Umluj, after abandoning it. It was too big a force to be just a looting party. We lost one man, shot by a sniper. His body was picked up earlier this morning by plane.'

'Bad news, sir. Sorry to hear you lost a man,' one of the drivers commented, while the others nodded their agreement.

'The fortunes of war, gentlemen. It was an unnecessary death, and right before the ceasefire, too. You guys had anything to eat, yet?'

'No sir, but I think the Navy have something for us and your men, soon as we're finished refuelling and loading up.'

'Speaking of which, here comes your first tank. I'll let you get to work, men. *Rav turai* (Corporal) Gold will supervise the loading.'

The drivers saluted nonchalantly as Shaul walked away. He headed across the compound towards the main ferry building, where he met again with Captain Rehov. They saluted one another and Rehov addressed him, 'I take it your men would like some food before they head out?'

'That's very kind of you, Rehov,' Shaul replied.

'All in the name of good inter-force relations,' Rehov smiled. 'I believe you lost a man last night?'

'Yes, bad news travels fast. A young man of only nineteen. He was a good soldier, too.'

'We've lost far too many in this war. Let's hope that was the very last one.' said Rehov.

'Yes, indeed, Captain.'

'Come with me, then. We'll eat together and your men can join us when they're ready. I'll send a man over to show them where to go.'

'Okay. *Rav Turai* Gold is the tank man and *Samal* Bar-Ilan is in charge, overall, along with *Rav Turai* Junbalat. Rebekkah Bar-Ilan was in charge of the guard this morning, when the Saudis attacked us.'

'One of our savage female warriors, eh? Come and tell me about it while we eat.'

They sat at a table in the canteen area and Rehov listened as Shaul relayed the main events of the early morning. Rebekkah Bar-Ilan, Samir Junbalat and Ari Gold joined them a few minutes later, adding their own accounts of the early morning battle.

Eventually, Captain Rehov stood, 'Well Captain Levine, lady and gentlemen, I expect you want to get on the road as soon as possible. and I should get back to my duties here. I trust you'll have a safe and pleasant journey. *L'hitraot.*'

'*Toda, l'hitraot,*' they chorused in reply.

'Not a bad chap, as far as the Navy goes,' Junbalat commented with a smile, after Rehov had left them.

'A bit stiff and proper, but then he *is* Navy,' Shaul agreed. The others smiled in response. 'Well, then, let's get back on the road. It will be dark even sooner than normal travelling through those wadis.'

Shaul organised his convoy – three APCs in the lead, followed by the four tank transporters, with the other three APCs in the rear. They headed south back to Duba, where they stopped briefly at the hotel, which was still doing duty as temporary headquarters for the reserve company. Shaul spoke briefly to the commanding officer, saluted and rejoined his force as they headed east along the divided highway leading into the mountains towards Tabuk.

They made good time, despite driving most of the journey in darkness, except for one almost tragic incident. As they drove north along the section of the road that followed a broad plain between the mountains, one of the APCs veered off the road and ran into a pile of sand, the driver having briefly fallen asleep. The vehicle was tilted at an angle so that the wheels on one side had no traction, and it was unable to reverse out of trouble.

Shaul took his own APC over, reversing up to the stricken vehicle – one of the recently supplied *CombatGuard* wheeled APCs, the same as his own. His men soon had a steel rope attached to the vehicle and towed it out to safety. The vehicle was none the worse for wear, having been designed for worse terrain than this. However, some of the crew had minor injuries, due to the sudden lurch sideways as the vehicle impacted.

One soldier had a broken finger, which was soon in a splint and bandaged; another had a bleeding head wound from hitting his head against the roof of the vehicle. The driver and the others seemed to have escaped injury.

'Right!' said Shaul to the men now gathered around him, 'any driver who has found his eyes closing needs to take a break, right now. We can't afford to continue if you don't think you can stay awake. We've all missed a lot of sleep, due to the conflict this morning.'

Shaul replaced the driver who had crashed and two others who said they were having difficulty staying awake, including his own driver. The tank transporter drivers all assured him that they were fine to continue the rest of the journey, as they'd rested for a few hours before Shaul met them.

Even so, they arrived back at the *Fahad Bin Sultan University* by 21:00 hours. *Samal* Tamari, *Segen* Peled and *Rav Turai* Katz greeted them with fresh coffee and very welcome cold beers – just flown in from Israel, via

Tabuk Airport – and showed them to their quarters in the University building, where they were more than happy to drop off into deep sleep.

In Six Hours ... the world changed – *Raymond McCullough*

39 – Six Hour War: Woman at the Well

The next morning Shaul and his returning force joined the rest of their company, refreshed after their long day travelling the day before. Tamari, Peled and Katz joined them as they sat down to breakfast.

'Well,' said Tamari, 'I believe you guys went back to war down there?'

'Yes,' agreed Bar-Ilan, 'we had a bit of a skirmish with some Saudi forces in the early hours of yesterday.'

Shaul's men continued to relate the story of the night attack.

Eventually, Shaul asked Tamari, 'So what about yourselves, then – nothing exciting here in Tabuk, I suppose? Just patrolling the city, or what?'

'Well,' Tamari began, 'I don't think anything exciting happened in Tabuk, but most of us weren't here in Tabuk yesterday.'

Eyebrows raised all around, except for Peled, who remained poker-faced.

'So where were you off to, then?' Gold took the gambit.

'The commander here – Shwartz, he's called – asked if we could supply a support force,' Tamari continued, 'He wanted to send some men down to a place called Teyma, south of here about 260 kilometres, and part of Tabuk Governate.

'It's a large oasis on the pilgrim road to Medina – the King's Highway, as they call it. The plan was to garrison the town and set up a border post further south of it – much like you did at Umluj. Of course, we had to persuade Peled here to let go of four more of his precious tanks – but in the end we persuaded him, leaving him in command here.'

'A soldier in command of ten tanks is a man of steel – a soldier left with only two tanks becomes a man of clay,' was Peled's wry contribution to the conversation.

'Anyway, the trip was pretty uneventful. The town was deserted and the commander deployed his men there without any trouble. When he had released us we decided to take a short break in the middle of the town, before heading back to Tabuk. There's an ancient well there called Bir Al Haddaj, which is several thousand years old – apparently it's mentioned in the Bible a couple of times.

'Anyway, we followed the signs off the highway to the north – the older part of the town – and eventually found the well, which was quite huge and surrounded by areas marked out in lanes divided by kerbs, where the camels used to pull a rope leading over a pulley, bringing water up from the well.

'We parked on the road that circles the well and made our way over to it. The guys were stretching their legs and taking photos around the well – which is quite an amazing place, actually – when this Arab woman approached with a teenage boy following her. She was carrying a tray with a jug of liquid and some glasses on it and calling out, *'Yahood? Yahood? Salaam alekum. Tov, tov!'* (Jews? Peace to you. Good!)

Tamari continued, 'I answered her in Arabic and told her that my friends were Jewish soldiers from Israel, but that I was actually an Aramaic Christian from Israel, and that we meant her no harm. She kept saying, *'Tov, tov,'* over and over – probably the only Hebrew word she knew.

'She came over to us and poured out a glass of iced tea, which she gave to her son to drink – I suppose in case we might be suspicious of her. Then she began pouring out glasses for each of us and we accepted them thankfully. We sat together on a wall near the well and she told us a bit of her story.

'Her name, she said, was Miriam Qurayshi, and apparently she had been married to a man for nearly ten years, who had beaten her and violently abused her. "Then," she said, "he became ill – very ill – and then he died." For the past six years she has been living on her own with her son, Yosef, and has survived by running a small corner shop, quite near to the well.

'But she said that her father – whose surname was Qurayshi, she uses his name now – had always taught her secretly that they were originally from a Jewish tribe and that Mohammed was not really the great man that everyone made him out to be, because he slaughtered many of the Jews who lived in the area of Medina – almost wiping out the whole Qurayshi clan. "He taught me that Jews were good people – *'Tov'*," she said.

'"Many, many years ago this used to be a Jewish city. And we wish to welcome you Jews back to this area – *tov, tov!* Allah has brought you back here," she said. "We want to live here in peace with you and become Jews again ourselves. My son will learn Hebrew and serve in your army and we will be free again, after fourteen hundred years of slavery."

'We were quite bemused by her outburst, assuring her again that we certainly meant her and her son no harm and wishing her *Shalom* in return. Then I asked if maybe her son would like to ride in an Israeli tank and I could see his eyes light up. Myself and one of the tank drivers took him around the square in the tank, showing him the controls and swivelling the turret around a bit.

'He really seemed delighted and kept saying, *"Shukran, shukran, tov, tov!"* We taught him to say, *"Tov ma'od –* very good," and he began to repeat it, explaining the meaning to his mother, who nodded to us with a wide smile, in turn saying, *"Tov ma'od."*

'I radioed the local commander we'd just left and explained the situation to him and he arrived shortly after in person and I introduced them. He also took a glass of iced tea from her and assured her that his men would help her and protect her and her son. She pointed out the location of her shop to him and he said his men would keep an eye on it and for her to contact them if she needed anything.

'She hugged each of us and blessed us as we left them and headed back to Tabuk. We had to stop about halfway to repair a track on one of the tanks – the link was damaged. So, we got back here only a few hours before you arrived yourselves, but I still had time to look up Teyma on the internet – apparently it was a mainly Jewish city from the first century right up to Mohammed's time – and even beyond.

'Josephus referred to Teyma and I thought you might be interested in the reference in the Bible, Shaul, so I looked that up too. It's in Yeshayahu 21, and it says, *"You caravans of Dedanites, who camp in the thickets of Arabia, bring water for the thirsty; you who live in Tema, bring food for the fugitives. They flee from the sword, from the drawn sword, from the bent bow and from the heat of battle."* (Isaiah 21:13-15) It felt like we were actually fulfilling this old prophecy. And *Yermeyahu* also prophesied against Teyma – in chapter 23.'

'That's a very interesting story, indeed, Tamari. And thank you for looking up those references in the Tanakh. You may have noticed I carry one around with me. I never totally believed it was true before, but now I know that we can rely on it. Sounds like you've had the privilege of remaking history,' Shaul mused. 'I wonder just how many Arabs will have lost their faith in Islam after this war. And not just Arabs, but other Muslims – especially those that already have an Israelite connection.'

'"Muslims with an Israelite connection" – who do you have in mind?' Peled asked, intrigued. So Shaul told him some of the conversation he and his friends in Afghanistan had had in the past – about the Pashtuns, Kashmiris, Menashe – and other tribes, like the Lemba and Igbo in Africa.

'So,' Peled said thoughtfully, 'If it turns out the way you seem to be suggesting, Israel could become a very different place over the next few years!'

'Indeed,' Shaul answered. 'And I somehow think that *we* are going to be very busy being part of it all. I don't think we'll be doing much actual fighting in the future, but I think the Army are going to be called upon to bear the brunt of the work in building this new Israel.

And, in the weeks and months to come many other Qurayshis, and others who at least claimed to have some Jewish background, turned up in Teyma and Umluj. Whole families slipped across the border through desert tracks, then made an appearance in the towns, approaching the soldiers and expressing their desire to become a part of Israel.

None of them were turned away. Many had skills and local knowledge that turned out to be very useful in rebuilding the local economy – for instance in the local Teyma industry of date production and harvesting.

'Right, guys,' Shaul began, '– I'm including you, of course, Bar-Ilan – in fact, we should really address you as *Segen Mishne* Bar-Ilan (Second Lieutenant) from now on. Congratulations, *Segen Mishne.*' The others cheered her and clapped her on the back. Bar-Ilan went bright red with embarrassment, but managed to squeak out, 'Thank you, sir.'

'I think you deserve it, Bar-Ilan,' Shaul replied.

'The transporter drivers who've joined us are all qualified mechanics, so they're going to spend today checking over the tanks and APCs, servicing and repairing them where necessary – they've had quite a bit of wear and tear with the distances we've been covering. That should keep Peled, here, happy – you can keep an eye on them, right, Lieutenant?'

Peled flashed a brief grin for Shaul's benefit and nodded in the affirmative.

'Then we'll load the rest of the tanks onto the transporters and be ready to head north for Amman in the morning. I confirmed with Southern Command this morning that they want us to take our equipment there, because we're gonna be travelling again in a few days time.

'Before that – you'll be glad to know – they're giving us three days leave. The place we're going to tomorrow is south of the city of Amman, just past *Queen Alia Airport*. It's a truck depot, so our gear will be locked up and guarded there while we're on leave. There'll be a coach to take us to the airport and the *IAF* will fly us to *Ramat David Airfield,* near Haifa tomorrow evening. We report back to *Ramat David* three days from tomorrow – I'll give you all the details before we leave the aeroplane. I should also point out that *Seren* Levine will *not* be accompanying you back from *Ramat David.*'

The others looked at him and at one another, baffled.

'You will instead be accompanied by *Rav Seren* (Major) Levine when we return.'

The others burst into applause and cries of 'Well deserved, sir' and 'Congratulations, *Rav Seren.*'

'When we come back from leave we'll pick up our vehicles – including the transporters – and our destination is east to Basrah in the south of what used to be Iraq. I'm not sure what it is now, but I'm told it's a bit of an uninhabited desert at the moment, with a lot of war damage everywhere.

'We'll also be joined by additional engineering troops with coaches, trucks, a team of doctors and nurses, medical and road-building equipment – they're being organised at the moment and should be en route to Amman shortly. When we get back there I'll brief everyone on what we can expect in Basrah, but I doubt that it will include much shooting, OK?'

His officers nodded. Bar-Ilan asked about the distance from Amman to Basrah – 'Just over 1,000 kilometres, I believe,' Shaul answered her. 'It'll be a long day's drive.'

Peled observed, 'Sounds like we're gonna be repairing some roads out there, eh?'

'That and a lot of other things. We'll be going out there almost blind, and we'll have to assess the situation pretty quickly and adapt rapidly to it. What I can tell you at this stage – and this must be kept under wraps, no telling your families, or even the men at this stage, right?'

His officers nodded.

'What I *can* tell you is that there are several hundred people at the moment, maybe even thousands – in Afghanistan and Pakistan – who have pre-empted any decision our government might make in the near future. They have loaded up trucks, buses, tractors and trailers – you name it – and they're already on their way to Israel. They'll be travelling a distance of more than 3,000 kilometres on mountain and desert roads.

'Our government have already decided they are *not* going to turn these people away. They certainly must be prepared to learn Hebrew and the basics of Judaism and commit themselves to the Jewish State – but, unlike in the past, they will *not* be required to convert to Judaism. Though I expect many of them probably will, anyway.

'I imagine there will be all kinds of breakdowns, accidents, emergencies – illnesses and babies being born, etc. When we get there we'll most likely be radioing home for all sorts of back-up – more medical supplies, probably, all types of specialist personnel and volunteers. Basically, we'll be organising and policing a new aliyah.'

'Whew,' said Peled, 'It's actually happening, then!'

'The ingathering!' Bar-Ilan said quietly.

'Exactly,' said Shaul.

'Now, it's almost 400 kilometres from here to Amman, so we'll make a stop in Ma'an tomorrow, which is just over halfway. We should reach our destination south of Amman by early afternoon. Apart from a few guards on duty here – *Segen Mishne* Bar-Ilan, will you organise that? – we're just gonna chill out today.

'If some of you want to take a look around the city while we're here, co-ordinate it with *Segen Mishne* Bar-Ilan and *Segen* Peled and you can take a patrol – no one goes walkabout, *beseder*? Otherwise, I believe there is a gym and so forth on the premises? Have a nice day, as they say where I come from.'

The officers dispersed to inform their men and plan their last day in Saudi Arabia. Shaul went to find a computer – there was one in his APC, of course, but the APC was probably being serviced, or about to be. However, in a university there ought to be a computer lab somewhere. With *Samal* Tamari's help in translating the signs, he eventually found one. Thanking Tamari, he sat down at a keyboard and began typing.

40 – Email from Tabuk

Hi, Brandon, Dev and Ali,

I'm sure you've all been watching the news from the Middle East with great interest. Thank you for your msgs – which I've just discovered – asking if I'm OK. I am, but this is the first chance I've had to communicate with anyone. As you can imagine we've all been quite busy over the past five days!

My captain was wounded in the first night of the war and I took over as unit commander – the Army bumped me up to Captain (Seren in Hebrew). Over those five days we've seen a bit of action and they've now promoted me again to Rav Seren – which is Major – and are sending me more men and equipment.

I'm sending you all this from a city called Tabuk, in the ancient land of Midian, formerly in Saudi Arabia – but now a part of the newly expanded State of Israel.

We're about to head north, travelling all day tomorrow. Then we'll fly back to Israel proper for a few days leave, before we start on the real task – you know, the big event that we talked about in Kabul a couple of years ago – that you told us about, Brandon? (I can't be any more specific, or I'd get myself in trouble!)

But remember we said that if what Brandon told us came to pass that we would all meet up in Jerusalem? Well, now I am inviting you guys to come out and meet me in Jerusalem – say in about two month's time? I can get a week's leave around then, I hope. And if anyone can't afford the airfare I'll be happy to cover it. How's that for an offer?

These are truly momentous days and, though I hate to say it, Brandon, you were pretty much on the ball with all that stuff you told us. I now know for sure that the Bible really is true – and I think many people in Israel are just beginning to realise this.

What do you say Brandon and Dev? Can you make it out here? Ali, I don't know how you're fixed with the ANA? It will be a really great reunion – plus there are some things I want to tell you all about, which I can't divulge at the moment. (In two months from now I don't think there'll be any great secret about it).

So let me know when you can come – you can probably both come together on the same flight?

Looking forward to hearing from you guys,

Your brother in arms,

Shaul (Sol)

As Shaul clicked 'Send' and sat back in the chair, he noticed a figure in the doorway behind him. He turned around to see Rebekkah Bar-Ilan watching him.

'Everything, OK, Bar-Ilan?'

'Yes, sir, the guard rota is organised and Peled is telling some of the guys when they can go on patrol and what vehicles will be available.'

'That's, great, Bar-Ilan – anything else?'

Rebekkah for once looked less than her normal confident self. 'I just wondered, Shaul, if you had anything specific planned for the three days leave?'

'Well, I suppose mebbe I should pay a visit to the kibbutz they assigned me when I joined the IDF – you know the way they pair up 'lone soldiers' who have no Israeli family with a home kibbutz?'

'Sure, but I wondered if mebbe this lone soldier would like to spend a few days in the north, instead. You'd be very welcome to come with me to Kfar Giladi for a visit?'

'Well, that sounds like an offer I really shouldn't refuse, Rebekkah. In fact, I'd be very happy to take you up on that. *Toda raba!*'

'*Be va keh shah,*' she smiled demurely (You are welcome). 'We could hire a car in Haifa, if you like – and drive up through the Galil?'

'That sounds like a really great idea, Rebekkah – on one condition?'

'What's that, sir?' Drat, she hadn't meant to call him 'sir' again in this conversation – she'd intended to keep to a personal note.

'Well, two conditions, now that I think about it – one, that you stop calling me 'sir' once we get off that plane tomorrow. Just call me Sol, *beseder?*' Shaul smiled at her. 'Two, I insist on paying for the hire car, but you're very welcome to do the driving, if you want to? After all, you know that part of the country much better than me. Deal?'

Rebekkah smiled back at him, 'It's a deal, si ... I mean, it's a deal, Sol.'

The End

Glossary

Hebrew English

Bevahkehsha	Please? You're welcome
B'hatzlacha	Good luck
Boker tov	Good morning
Heshbon	The bill
Ken	Yes
L'hitraot	See you
Lo	No
Oleh	Immigrant
Olim	Immigrants (pl.)
Shalom	Peace (greeting)
Toda	Thank you
Toda raba	Thank you very much
Tov	Good
Tov ma'od	Very good
'Vahkehsha	Please? (abbreviation)
Yefe	Nice

Arabic English

Bismillah	In the name of God!
La	No
Na'am	Yes
Salaam (alekum)	Peace (to you) (greeting)
Shukran	Thank you

IDF rank UK/US equivalent rank

Rav seren	Major, Battalion executive officer
Seren	Captain, Company commander
Segen	Lieutenant
Segen mishne	Second lieutenant, Platoon leader
Rav Samal	Sergeant First Class
Samal	Sergeant
Rav turai	Corporal
Turai	Private

<u>Israeli Armaments</u>

Arrow 2, 3 Missile defence system (200-500 km) (IAI**)

Bright Arrow Vehicle Active Protection System (APS) (IMI*)

CombatGuard 4-wheel drive Armoured Personnel Carrier (IMI*)

David's Sling Missile defence system (70-250 km) (Rafael)

Iron Beam Missile defence system (<7 km) (Rafael)

Iron Dome Missile defence system (4-70 km) (Rafael/IAI**)

Iron Fist Forerunner of *Bright Arrow* APS (IMI*)

Merkavah IV Israeli made tank (IMI/IOC)

Namer Tracked APC, based on Merkavah tank chassis (IOC)

Tavor TAR-21 Modern Israeli assault rifle (IWI+)

Trophy Active Protection system (APS) (Rafael/IAI**)

*Israel Military Industries

**Israel Aerospace Industries

Israeli Ordnance Corp

+Israel Weapons Industries

Rafael Advanced Defence Systems

In Six Hours ... the world changed – *Raymond McCullough*

Bibliography

A Rabbi Looks at the Last Days
Jonathan Bernis

As America Has Done to Israel*
John P. McTernan

Blood Brothers
Elias Chacour

Britain and Zion
Frank Hardie and Irwin Herrman

Brother Shall Not Lift Sword Against Brother:*
The Roots and Solution to the Problem in the Holy Land
Tzvi Misinai

DNA and Tradition:
The Genetic Link to the Ancient Hebrews*
Rabbi Yaakov Kleiman

Fighting Hamas, BDS and Anti-Semitism
Barry Shaw

Guards Without Frontiers:
Israel's War Against Terrorism
Samuel M. Katz

Israel: Reclaiming the Narrative*
Barry Shaw

Israel's Lebanon War
Ze'ev Schiff and Ehud Ya'ari

Jews In Places You Never Thought Of *
Karen Primack

Like Dreamers*
Yossi Klein Halevi

O Jerusalem!

Larry Collins and Dominique Lapierre

Operation Babylon
Shlomo Hillel

The Lonely Soldier*
Adam Harmon

The Israel Solution:*
A One-State Plan for Peace in the Middle East
Caroline B. Glick

The Biblical Hebrew Origins of the Japanese People
Joseph Eidelberg

Phantom Nation:*
Inventing the "Palestinians" as the Obstacle to Peace – Volume 1
Sha'i ben-Tekoa

Story of My Life
Moshe Dayan

The God of the Mountain*
Penny Cox Caldwell

The Igbos: Jews in Africa
Remy Ilona

We Belong to the Land
Elias Chacour

* Recommended

About the author:

Raymond McCullough, from Co. Down, near Belfast, Northern Ireland, has been a professional writer for over twenty years, originally writing a regular series – plus other articles, reviews and reports – for several UK technical magazines.

From 1990-96 he edited and published the Irish magazine, *'Bread'* – releasing his first book, *'Ireland – now the good news!'* from this in 1995; co-edited by his wife, well-known fiction author Gerry McCullough. His articles have also been published in the *Irish Times*, Dublin, and the *Presbyterian Herald*, Belfast.

In 1993 he hosted a radio show, *'In tha Name a' Gawd!'* on *96.7 BCR*, in Belfast, which later developed into his current satellite radio show of music, news and faith-based interviews – broadcasting around the world on several satellite networks. From 1996, for seven years, he and Gerry led a cell-based Christian fellowship in the Belfast area.

Since then he's been involved in media of all kinds – from web design to podcasting, satellite and internet radio, plus documentary TV production – producing an album of Celtic and Hebrew worship music, *'Into Jerusalem,'* in 2005 and a Celtic pop-folk album, *'Different,'* in 2008.

Since 2008, Raymond has produced and hosted *'Celtic Roots Radio'* – an *iTunes* podcast and also a web station (on *Live365*) – with around 10,000 downloads per month in well over 100 countries. He published the *craic* from his *Celtic Roots Radio* shows as, *'A Wee Taste a' Craic,'* in 2011 and is working on a TV documentary, filmed mainly in Canada, entitled, *'Broken Treaties.'*

He has also produced and hosted the *'In tha Name a' Gawd!'* international series of personal testimonies and, more recently, *'Fresh Bread: Your Kingdom Come (WHM)'* – broadcasting each week on several satellite radio networks heard in most countries of the world. His *'Kingdom Come Trust'* website has hundreds of enthusiastic emails from satellite radio listeners in US, Canada, Australia and the Caribbean.

In 2011, Raymond published *'The Whore and her Mother: 9/11, Babylon and the Return of the King.'* He researched the subjects in this book for about forty years, off and on, but the events of 9/11 brought a new focus to his research and a real sense of increasing urgency encouraged him to complete the book in just four months! He felt the subject was too interesting and dramatic to simply be confined to the fairly narrow, evangelical Christian world.

Wanting to make the prophecies dealt with in that book available to a much wider audience, Raymond decided to turn the material into a fictional thriller series. The first book of the *'Six Hours thrillers series'* is: *In Six Hours ... the world changed.* The second book – *In One Hour*, covering the aftermath of the Six Hour War and the Fall of Babylon – is also available.

'What Kind of People?' will be a follow-up to *'The Whore and her Mother'* – expanding the contents of the last two chapters on how we should respond to these prophecies soon being fulfilled.

More info at:

http://raymondmccullough.com

http://kingdomcome.org.uk

http://www.preciousoil.com/publications

http://twitter.com/BreadNEWS

In One Hour

... Babylon will fall

Book #2 of the Six Hours thriller series

The debt will be called in and in one hour her destruction will come!

After a short, but devastating, nuclear war the face of the Middle East has changed forever! The 'Ingathering' – the world's greatest population transfer, involving tens of millions – has begun. Huge people groups – from India and Myanmar, Pakistan and Afghanistan; from Nigeria, Zimbabwe and South Africa, and many other parts of the world – are on the move, all travelling towards one destination.

Four young men, who met first in Afghanistan, are re-united in the heat of the impossible logistics of such a mammoth operation:

Shaul 'Solly' Levine , an Orthodox Jew from New York;

Micky 'Dev' Devlin, an Irish Catholic from Boston;

Brandon 'Doubtin'' Thomas, a black Pentecostal from North Carolina;

Khan Ali 'Zai' Yousefzai, a Muslim Pashtun from Kabul, Afghanistan.

Can a small nation survive a nuclear war and immediately after absorb an influx of ten times its population? across thousands of miles of nuclear war-devastated desert? Can Shaul and his comrades overcome such odds?

Meanwhile, America is no longer a safe haven – for Jews or for others there. Persecution is mounting and desperate measures are needed in order to avoid the coming destruction. Will Shaul's friends and family be able to reach safety before Babylon falls?

In One Hour
... Babylon will fall

Raymond McCullough

1 – The 2nd Exodus

BBC News - Sudan-Egypt border

'I'm standing near the southern Egyptian border with Sudan. As far as the eye can see they keep coming – cars, pickup trucks, buses, tractors ... The vehicles are piled high with household belongings, children clinging precariously to the tops of many. A biblical exodus appears to be well under way.

'In the wake of the recent war in the Middle East, and the overwhelming victory of Israel in that war, millions upon millions of the Nigerian Igbo people are heading 'home' – as they see it – to their promised land. Israel has just recently given them permission to come, as they have also to the Pashtuns, Kashmiris and Menashe from Afghanistan, Pakistan and India.

'The Jewish prophet, Jeremiah, referred to a highway stretching all the way from Egypt to ancient Assyria – roughly the area of modern-day Afghanistan – and that that highway will pass through Israel. It seems that this prediction may now be coming to pass.

'One convoy begins in Nigeria, west Africa, travelling east into Cameroon, Central African Republic and South Sudan, then north into Sudan and Egypt. Another convoy, of the Lemba tribe, in Zimbabwe and South Africa, is travelling north through Zambia, Tanzania, Kenya and Ethiopia, to join up with the western convoy from Sudan into Egypt. It seems likely that many of the Tutsi tribe, from Rwanda and Burundi, are also ready to join this exodus.

'Just a few weeks ago, Karen, it would have been impossible for these people to travel through Sudan or Egypt to Israel, but those countries joined forces with Iran and other Middle East nations in the recent failed attempt to wipe out Israel – and now they are a defeated and subdued enemy, currently dependent upon Israel.

'Amazingly, the great Nile River seems conveniently to have dried up to a fraction of its normal size, enabling this huge convoy to bypass the congested bridges on new crossings engineered by the Israeli Army.

'These people travelling across Africa seem to be exuberantly happy. They sing hymns and cheer as they travel. If a vehicle breaks down – as many of them do – there is always plenty of help to get them going again.

'Israeli military vehicles are patrolling along the column of refugees, while helicopters pass over the vehicles periodically. The Israelis are not taking any chances on this massive exodus being attacked en route – especially with members of the extreme Islamist group, Boko Haram, still in the area. Transit camps are being set up all along the route, with Israeli field kitchens and medical teams ready to deal with heat exhaustion, child-birth, or any other emergency.

'Israel has put a call out worldwide for volunteer engineers and mechanics to help repair vehicles and roads. Earlier today we watched as huge Caterpillar bulldozers were air-lifted to help build those extra Nile crossings. The same thing, I believe, is happening all along the convoy routes.

'This is an absolutely incredible scene! Some experts reckon that there are perhaps thirty million people on the move here from western Africa alone – with more from the south, plus some Tutsi from Rwanda and Burundi, joining them. Karen, this must be the largest people movement the modern world has ever seen.

'This is David Hawthorne, BBC news, on the Sudan-Egypt border.'

* * *

'That was David Hawthorne reporting from Africa. I'm Karen Wignall and, in case you missed our headlines, the story of the day is of the continuing massive people movement of the huge Igbo tribe, from Nigeria, and other African tribes who regard themselves as of Israelite origin, heading for the newly expanded State of Israel.

'On their way these travellers will actually be covering more or less the same ground as the many millions who recently fled from the Middle East in the other direction during the recent 'Six Hour War'.

'Another similar mass movement is taking place in Asia, also travelling towards Israel. We're going to go now to our correspondent in southern Iraq, Susan Reilly ...'

* * *

Basra, near the Iran-Iraq border

'Thank you, Karen. I'm standing by the main road east of Basra, near the border between what used to be Iran and Iraq. Both those countries have been totally devastated by the recent war and are now almost completely empty of their original inhabitants. Their populations fled originally in fear of Israeli retaliation for Iran and Syria's failed nuclear attack, just a few weeks ago and then later because of the missile and land attack from Saudi Arabia. Apart from Israeli soldiers and relief organisations, Basra is deserted.

'That attack on Israel was accompanied by massive rocket and mortar attacks across the borders from Gaza, Lebanon, Jordan, Saudi Arabia and Egypt. Unbelievably, instead of Israel being wiped out, as everyone fully expected, their attackers fled in advance of the unexpected Israeli counter-attack.

'In that short time the Middle East has changed forever. All of Iran's military facilities and most of their cities, too, are now a smoking ruin. It seems that Iran – together with Saudi Arabia and Egypt – badly miscalculated the affect of their attempt to wipe out Israel and the result is the total destruction of a former major power in the Middle East.

'This convoy of immigrants stretches as far as I can see. There must be many millions of Pashtuns, from eastern Afghanistan, and the Swat and North West Frontier Provinces of Pakistan. Karen, many of these people were linked to the Taliban that US and UK coalition forces have been fighting against for many years.

'Former members of the Taliban – an extreme Islamist force before the war – are apparently now willing to join with the State of Israel! The forces of militant Islam have indeed been dealt a great blow and many have lost their faith in the Islamic religion.

'What is happening here is something quite unbelievable. I wouldn't believe it myself if I wasn't witnessing it with my own eyes. Even at the end of the Second World War when the Indian subcontinent was partitioned into modern India and Pakistan, there were nowhere near as many people involved.

'These people are not Jews, but they regard themselves as belonging to the 'people of Israel' – just as the Jews do. And this convoy doesn't just come from Afghanistan and Pakistan – I am told that there are potentially six million Kashmiri's also on the move from northern India and another four million of the Menashe tribe from eastern India. All of these tribes apparently regard themselves as 'Israelite', also.

'In the past, Israel had permitted several thousand of the Menashe – regarded as part of the biblical tribe of Manasseh – to emigrate, or 'make aliyah' to Israel, though many more thousands had applied to emigrate. Until Israel recently dramatically changed their immigration policy, it would have taken a couple of hundred years at the previous rate to allow in those who had applied. Now, even those who are professedly Christian – the majority of the Menashe – want to make 'aliyah', and Israel have said, 'Yes, they can come!'

'There are Israeli military vehicles in evidence everywhere here, with helicopters flying overhead periodically and a pair of Israeli jets every now and then, also. The convoy is accompanied by well armed Israeli patrols, aided by transport planes who set them down all along the route of this migration. You can see that the mighty Euphrates River – normally full at this time of year – is now almost completely dried up, enabling Israeli engineers to create several new vehicle crossings here quite easily.

'Israel are keeping a watchful eye on this transfer of humanity, but they are going to have their work cut out for them when they reach their destination – rehousing of so many millions of new immigrants will be an almost superhuman task.

'This is Susan Reilly, BBC news, on the former Iran-Iraq border.'

* * *

'Well, recent events in the Middle East have caused a great deal of response around the globe. Russia and China have both condemned Israel for their sharp response to an all-out attack from all the surrounding Arab countries, along with Iran.

'The United States, who in recent years have distanced themselves more and more from their former ally, Israel, have also spoken out strongly against the Israeli occupation of the former territories of Syria, Lebanon, Jordan and parts of Saudi Arabia, Iraq and Egypt.

'We go now to our Jerusalem correspondent, Michael Farr, who is currently in south Lebanon. Michael, how are the Israelis coping with such a massive influx of refugees?'

* * *

South Lebanon

'Well, first of all, Karen, these are not really what we would normally refer to as refugees. They are not fleeing from any threat such as famine, *or war. This is a massive ideological people movement of totally biblical proportions. These people have simply decided that, after two thousand seven hundred years of separation, now is the right time to return to their original homeland.*

'And by the way, it was pointed out to me just recently that where I'm standing now – just outside the town of Sour, or Tyre, in former south Lebanon – was originally part of the British Mandate territory of Palestine in 1920, originally destined by the League of Nations to become part of the Jewish State. That was until Britain and France began a bit of wheeler-dealing, which resulted in Britain gaining control of the oilfields in what we now call the Kurdish area of Iraq, while the French added this area south of the Litani River to their newly created country, named after Mount Lebanon.'

'Michael, how are the Israelis coping with the situation?'

'Well, it is unbelievable that a nation that two weeks ago we believed was about to disappear from the map is now taking on an influx of people that will increase its population by around ten times! This has never been done before – unless you count the original biblical Exodus of two and a half million people from Egypt all those centuries ago!

'Don't forget, I'm standing here in what used to be Lebanon – where the vast majority of the population has fled from what they obviously believed would become a holocaust in retaliation for their attempt to wipe out Israel.

'As much as possible the new immigrants are being organised on the basis of their town or village of origin, with empty towns and villages here being matched with those now being emptied in Asia and Africa.

'Back in those towns and villages, Israeli officials are carefully co-ordinating the exodus so that the new immigrants know in advance where they are going. Other Israeli officials, along with the military, are organising the clearing of streets and repairing and securing empty homes for their new tenants – here in Lebanon, and in Syria, Jordan, the Sinai and north-eastern Saudi Arabia.

'An interesting development, overshadowed by this absolutely huge people movement, is that many of the Palestinian refugees, who for decades have lived in Lebanon refugee camps, by and large have NOT fled along with their Lebanese countrymen. The same is true of many of the Palestinians in the west bank and Gaza Strip. They at least appear to have learned a lesson from their previous flights, which have only resulted in their own misery. Their former leaders in Hamas and the Palestinian Authority, of course, have either fled or been destroyed by Israeli forces, after their attempt to destroy Israel. and,

of course, their former supporters in Saudi Arabia, Egypt, etc. are no longer in any position to help them.

'It has been voiced in recent years that many, perhaps even the majority, of those we refer to as 'Palestinians' actually have Jewish roots – just like those who are now coming from Afghanistan and other countries. DNA and historical evidence has tended to confirm this. So, in the changed regional situation, the Israelis have extended an open welcome to those Palestinians who sincerely want to remain as part of the new Israel. They are welcome to stay and become full Israeli citizens. No-one yet knows just how that might work out in practice, but some potential new leaders among them have cautiously welcomed the Israeli government's offer.

'Certainly, there can be no conceivable going back to the pre-war days of conflict, with outside backing in terms of missiles and monetary support – those backers have gone! And so a separate Pales-tinian State is no longer a realistic option! The Israeli government have officially dissolved the Palestinian authority – although in prac-tice it had mostly dissolved itself! Their own terrorist leaders have either fled or been annihilated and the Arab world's exploitation of the Palestinians for their own ends has seemingly come to an end – especially with Iran, Syria, Qatar and Hezbollah now out of the picture.

'It remains to be seen, Karen, just how big a task Israel has taken on in allowing so many millions to return. The population of the new Israel could become seventy, eighty – even a hundred million – probably greater than that of former Iran! This truly is a biblical exodus. And it will completely transform the make-up of the new Israel.

'No-one knows yet how this will affect the political climate in Israel – most of these immigrants are not even Jewish in terms of religion. The majority are either Christian or some variety of Muslim – the Pashtuns have their own Pashtunwali code – so at least they might feel at home in former Muslim, or Christian, towns and villages here in Lebanon, or Syria.

'How the Israelis will house and find employment for all these people is anybody's guess. Not to mention that they will presumably need to learn Hebrew to integrate fully into Israeli society. How will the present day Israelis cope with such an influx of immigrants? Could Israel even be reduced to a third world country by accepting so many poverty-stricken people?

'The current Israeli government is really an interim government. When things settle down a bit there will have to be new elections representing the changed political reality. There will probably be new political parties – a Pashtun party, perhaps? an Igbo party? No-one can really imagine how these new realities will affect the post-war Israel – but affect it they certainly will!

'Zionism has certainly been given a whole new lease of life. Israel no longer needs to apologise or bend to any outside powers. The UN have been remarkably silent in the wake of the attempt to completely destroy Israel by several of their former members.

'But the new Israel will no longer be an exclusively Jewish state. It remains to be seen how that will be received by the present population of Israel. The new immigrants will possibly outnumber the indigenous population by a factor of ten to one.

'On the other hand, Israel almost ceased to exist forever – and the collective thankfulness for what is being received as miraculous divine intervention on their behalf, has led the Israeli leadership to take this unprecedented step. One cannot conceive of another nation making such a bold move.

'From Israel's point of view it also solves the question of occupation of these former Arab lands, by immediately peopling them with out-side immigrants. Those new immigrants will be a security buffer in the future. Even the Kurds are happy – as Israel have agreed to support them in setting up their own government in the parts of Syria north east of the Euphrates River. That, combined with their present autonomous area of former northern Iraq, and the surviving Iranian Kurds, would give them their longed for new state of Kurdistan. Turkey, of course, will not be at all happy with that development!

'This is Michael Farr, BBC News, Tyre, in former south Lebanon.'

* * *

'Thank you, Michael.

'Well, the recent developments in the Middle East and Africa have taken the world by storm. The unexpected survival of Israel after an all-out nuclear and conventional attack from all the surrounding nations has left the world community reeling. Stock markets still really don't know how to gauge the current economic climate.

'Oil prices have risen due to the expected reduction in supply – though Israel have assured the world that any damage to oil production equipment in the Persian Gulf will soon be repaired and back in operation as soon as possible.

'Israel have announced that their own Leviathan oil and gas field in the eastern Mediterranean will soon be producing commercial quantities of oil. Leviathan gas is already supplying a large part of

Europe and the Middle East with energy. The government have also confirmed that the newly discovered oilfield in the Golan Heights will also be producing oil in the very near future.

'Israel are working with the fledgeling Kurdish State to provide oil supplies direct to the Mediterranean by creating a new pipeline through former Syria, connecting the existing oil terminal at Baniyas to the existing pipeline from Kirkuk. Obviously, it is in Israeli economic interest to get this pipeline up and running in record time and the Israeli company in charge of the project are currently recruiting expert engineers to facilitate this.

'In other news ...'

The Whore and her Mother:

9/11, Babylon and the Return of the King

Raymond McCullough

Could the writings of the ancient Hebrew prophets be relevant to events taking place in the world today?

These Hebrew prophets – Isaiah, Jeremiah, Habbakuk and the apostle John, in The Revelation – wrote extensively about a latter day city and empire which would dominate, exploit and corrupt all the nations of the world. They referred to it as Babylon the Great, or Mega-Babylon, and they foretold that its fall – 'in one day' – would devastate the economies of the whole world. Have these prophecies been fulfilled already?

Is Mega-Babylon:

> **the Roman Catholic Church?**
>
> **A world super-church?**
>
> **Rebuilt ancient Babylon?**
>
> **Brussels, Jerusalem, or somewhere entirely different?**
>
> **Should this city/nation have a large Jewish population?**
>
> **Why all the talk about merchants, cargoes, commodities, trade?**

Can we rely on the words of these ancient prophets?

If so, what else did they foretell that is still to be fulfilled?

Do they refer to other major nations – USA, Russia, China, Europe?

What about militant Islam?

"AMAZED when I read this book ... in awe of your extensive knowledge on so many levels: Christian, Jewish, and Muslim culture; the Jewish diaspora ... Greek & Hebrew; ... thought-provoking and troublesome ... many will be offended, but you consistently build your case instead of being sensationalistic."
James Revoir, author of *Priceless Stones*

Oh What Rapture!

Is a *'Secret Rapture'* going to spare believers from the tribulation to come?

Raymond McCullough

Many are convinced that very soon an event known as 'The Rapture' will take place, where Bible believers all over the world will suddenly dis-appear, leaving society at a loss to explain the disappearance of so many. Many non-fiction books, fiction thrillers and movies have capitalised on this theme, earning a fat revenue for their authors/producers.

But is this really what the Bible teaches?

Is 'The Rapture' genuine, or a false hope?

Are those who trust in it being duped, so that they do not get ready for what is coming?

And are they being disobedient to the clear command of the Lord?

Written by the author of Amazon best-selling book, *The Whore and her Mother*, also on the topic of Bible prophecy, this volume focusses on the false teaching of a *'secret and separate Rapture'* – an event which is NOT supported by scripture!

This book investigates the scriptures used to back up the *'secret Rapture'* theory and clearly compares them to the other scriptures concerning the return of the Messiah, Jesus (Yeshua). The evident truth is revealed and the origins of the false *'secret rapture'* doctrine are exposed.

Believers around the world are taught to expect persecution, sometimes even death, for their faith. More have been killed in the past century than in previous centuries combined – in Syria, Iraq, China, Cambodia, Nigeria, Iran, Egypt, Indonesia, Vietnam, etc. Yet many believers in the west confidently expect to avoid any persecution and be *'beamed up'* out of any coming tribulation!

If you thought believers were soon going to be lifted out of a worsening world situation, be prepared to meet the exciting challenge of scripture head on!

Other (non-fiction) books from

A Wee Taste a' Craic:

All the Irish craic from the popular
Celtic Roots Radio *shows, 2-25*

Raymond McCullough

I absolutely loved this! I found it to be very informative
about Irish life culture, language and traditions.
Elinor Carlisle (author, Reading, UK)

a unique insight into the Northern Irish people
& their self deprecating sense of humour
Strawberry

Ireland – now the good news!

The best of *'Bread'* Vols. 1 & 2 –

personal testimonies and church/fellowship
profiles from around Ireland

Edited by: Raymond & Gerry McCullough

"... fresh Bread – deals with the real issues facing the
church in Ireland today"
Ken Newell, minister of Fitzroy Presbyterian Church, Belfast

Belfast Girls

The story of three girls – Sheila, Phil and Mary – growing up into the new emerging post-conflict Belfast of money, drugs, high fashion and crime; and of their lives and loves.

Sheila, a supermodel, is kidnapped.

Phil is sent to prison.

Mary, surviving a drug overdose, has a spiritual awakening.

It is also the story of the men who matter to them –

John Branagh, former candidate for the priesthood, a modern Darcy, someone to love or hate. Will he and Sheila ever get together?

Davy Hagan, drug dealer, 'mad, bad and dangerous to know'. Is Phil also mad to have anything to do with him?

Although from different religious backgrounds, starting off as childhood friends, the girls manage to hold on to that friendship in spite of everything.

A book about contemporary Ireland and modern life. A book which both men and women can enjoy – thriller, romance, comedy, drama – and much more …

"fascinating ... original ... multilayered ... expertly travels from one genre to the next"

Kellie Chambers, Ulster Tatler (*Book of the Month*)

"romance at the core ... enriched with breathtaking action, mystery, suspense and some tear-jerking moments of tragedy.

Sheila M. Belshaw, author

"What starts out as a crime thriller quickly evolves into a literary festival beyond the boundary of genres"

PD Allen, author

"a masterclass, and a vivid dissection of the human condition in all of its inglorious foibles"

WeeScottishLassie

Danger Danger

Gerry McCullough

Two lives in parallel – twin sisters separated at birth, but their lives take strangely similar and dangerous roads until the final collision which hurls each of them to the edge of disaster.

Katie and her gambling boyfriend Dec find themselves threatened with peril from the people Dec has cheated.

Jo-Anne (Annie) through her boyfriend Steven finds herself in the hands of much more dangerous crooks.

Can they survive and achieve safety and happiness?

"starts with a bang and never quite lets up on the tension ... it will hook you from the beginning and keep you spell bound until the very last sentence."

Ellen Fritz, Books 4 Tomorrow

"The emotional intensity of the characters is beautifully drawn ... You care for these people."
Stacey Danson, author

an amazing, page turning, stunning novel ... equal to Belfast Girls in every respect. I can't wait for her next novel to be published.

Teresa Geering, author

an attention-grabbing plot, strong writing, and vivid characterization, ... fast-paced and highly addictive

L. Anne Carrington, author

Angel in Flight:

the first Angel Murphy thriller

Gerry McCullough

Is it a bird? Is it a plane? No, it's a low-flying Angel!

You've heard of Lara Croft. You've heard of Modesty Blaise. Well, here comes Angel Murphy!

Angel, a *'feisty wee Belfast girl'* on holiday in Greece, sorts out a villain who wants to make millions for his pharmaceutical company by preventing the use of a newly discovered malaria vaccine.

Angel has a broken marriage behind her and is wary of men, but perhaps her meeting with Josh Smith, who tells her he's with Interpol, may change her mind?

Fun, action, thrills, romance in a beautiful setting – so much to enjoy!

> *"it's a fast-paced read, ... exciting, and you can not put this book down"*
>
> **Thomas Baker**, Santiago, Chile

> *"I could not stop reading! ... a gripping thriller from beginning to the end"*
> **SanMarie Lamprecht**

> *"a fast-paced, exciting read. From the moment I read the first line, I was hooked"*
>
> **Cheryl Bradshaw**, author, Wyoming, USA

> *"a sassy bigger then life heroine in an action packed adventure thriller in Greece"* **Book Review Buzz**

Angel in Belfast:

the 2nd Angel Murphy thriller

Gerry McCullough

Angel Murphy is back, in true kick boxing form!

Alone in his cottage near a remote Irish village, Fitz, lead singer of the popular band *Raving*, hears the cries of the paparazzi outside and likens them in his own mind to wolves in a feeding frenzy. Next morning Fitz is found unconscious, seeming unlikely to survive, and is rushed to hospital. Has he been driven to OD? Or is someone else behind this?

His friends call in Angeline Murphy, 'Angel to her friends, devil to her enemies,' to find out the truth. But it takes all Angel's courage and skills to survive the many dangers she faces and to discover the real villain and deal with him.

Johnny McClintock's War:
One man's struggle against the hammer blows of life

The story of one man's struggle to maintain his faith in spite of everything life throws at him.

As the outbreak of the First World War looms closer, John Henry McClintock, a Northern Irish Protestant by upbringing, meets Rose Flanagan, a Catholic, at a gospel tent mission – and falls in love with her.

When Johnny enlists and sets off to fight in the War he finds himself surrounded by death and tragedy, which pushes his trust in God to the limit.

After more than five years absence he returns home to a bitter, war torn Ireland, where both he and Rose are seen as traitors to their own sides.

John Henry and Rose overcome all opposition and, finally, marry. But a few years later comes the hardest blow of all. Can John Henry still hang on to his faith in God?

"brilliant .. this book had me captured from the start"

Tom Elder, *Amazon.com*

"displays her insightful vision into the human condition ..
a gut-wrenching emotional ride .. a must read"
Tom Winton, *author, USA*

"Gerry McCullough's best book yet ..
a powerful tribute to those who died for their countries and what they believed"
Juliet B Madison, *author, UK*

"an emotional roller coaster ride .. an epiphany .. highly recommended
.. a book that will make you think about how wonderful life truly is"
Thomas Baker, *Amazon.com, Santiago, Chile*

"will hold you spellbound until the very last sentence ..
I breathed every heart-beat with the characters .. I love this book"
Sheila Mary Belshaw, *author, UK, Menorca, Cape Town*

The Seanachie series: *Tales of Old Seamus*

Gerry McCullough

A humorous series of Irish stories, set in the fictional Donegal village of Ardnakil and featuring that lovable rogue, *'Old Seamus'* – the Séanachie.

All of these stories have previously been published in the popular Irish weekly magazine, Ireland's Own, based in Wexford, Ireland.

"heart warming tales ... beautifully told with subtle Irish humour"

Babs Morton (author)

"an irresistible old rogue, but he's the kind people love to sit and listen to for hours on end whenever the opportunity presents itself"

G. Polley (author and blogger – Sapporo, Japan)

"This magnificent storyteller has done it again. Each individual story has it's own Gaelic charm"

Teresa Geering (author – UK)

"evocative characterisation brings these stories to life in a delightful, absorbing way"

Elinor Carlisle (author – Reading, UK)

Lady Molly & The Snapper

A young adult time travel adventure, set in Ireland and on the high seas

Gerry McCullough

Brother and sister Jik and Nora are bored and angry. Why does their Dad spend so much time since their mother's death drinking and ignoring them? Why must he come home at all hours and fall downstairs like a fool?

Nora goes to church and lights a candle. The cross-looking sailor saint she particularly likes seems to grow enormous and come to life. Nora is too frightened to stay.

Nora and Jik go down secretly to their father's boat, the *Lady Molly*, at Howth Marina. There they meet The Snapper, the same cross-looking saint in a sailor's cap, who takes them back in time on the yacht, *Lady Molly,* to meet Cuchulain, the legendary Irish warrior, and others.

Jik and Nora plan to use their travels to find some way of stopping their father from drinking – but it's fun, too! Or is it? When they meet the Druid priest who follows them into modern times, teams up with school bully Marty Flanagan, and threatens them, things start getting out of hand.

Meanwhile, Nora is more than interested in Sean, the boy they keep bumping into in the past ...